S R Sutton
LEGEND OF THE
Time Witches
T W
HISTORY OF THE WITCHES

WORKBOOK PRESS LLC
187 E Warm Springs Rd,
Suite B285, Las Vegas, NV 89119, USA

Website: https://workbookpress.com/
Hotline: 1-888-818-4856
Email: admin@workbookpress.com

Ordering Information:
Quantity sales. Special discounts are available on quantity purchases by corporations, associations, and others.
For details, contact the publisher at the address above.

Library of Congress Control Number:

ISBN-13:   978-1-958176-36-8 (Paperback Version)
               978-1-958176-37-5 (Digital Version

REV. DATE: 16/05/2022

LEGEND OF THE TIME WITCHES

HISTORY OF THE WITCHES

S R SUTTON

HISTORY OF WITCHES

In history, the witches have often had the reputation to be wicked old ugly women who cast spells on people and generally cause harm or death to poor unfortunate souls. Fairy tales describe them as flying on broomsticks at night and link them to Halloween, but this would be unfair to label them in this way. This is why I am writing about two categories of witches the dark witches as described and white witches who serve for the good of the people, using herbs and other natural products for healing. Witches are renowned all over the world in many countries and are involved with many traditions based on religious beliefs of their own, black magic is known in Africa and Jamaica, it is well worth reading these facts and drawing your own conclusions.

During my research for the first book called 'Eight skulls of Teversham' and this sequel 'The adventures of the time witches' I discovered many revelations from history which I include in the stories, hopefully it will provide you with a balanced view on witchcraft.

Please remember that these stories are fictitious and are designed to entertain its readers by offering a look into many adventures in time and space from the prospective of the witches who travel in space and enter the time portals in space using a time craft.

INTRODUCTION

The legend of the time witches is a sequel to the eight skulls of Teversham, after following the family line of witches through the ages to the modern times in the twentieth century, three time travelling witches' journey through time and space seeking answers to many unanswered questions about their origin and about the many secrets kept by the cave dwellers of northern Scotland then known as Alba. Natasha and Crystal meet up with witches, vampires and many strange aliens as they pursue their quest with them at the start of the journey is an android called Foster, a goblin called Shimick and Shanice a teenage witch. They travel back where the witches began, at their origins in Scotland. They were said to have obtained their powers as a result of super nova in space, this caused meteors to hail from the skies containing high levels of gamma radiation, which as a rule would be harmful to anybody. The energy omitted from the rock gave them great powers that they were unable to understand or appreciate in some cases, this caused a division in the tribe of cave dwellers resulting in the introduction of two kinds of witches, the white witches who were peace lovers who used their powers for good and the dark witches who were evil and used their powers to destroy and dominate other species.

ACKNOWLEDGEMENT

Thanks to all those who played a part in this venture to the time witches Natalie Sartora as Natasha, Michelle Bridgart as Crystal, and Shara Alexander as Shanice.

The front cover costume designs were done by Sandra Harker under my strict instruction. She did a wonderful job. I understand the pressure that she was under at the time, but she worked hard to achieve this task.

Thanks to my family and friends for their support, children Gemma, Jeni, Mike, and Dan, and anyone else I haven't mentioned, I am sure you know who you are.

Thank you, Bernadette McLoughlin for being my main literature critic your support was vital in my work.

Special thanks to my friends Anja and Ulf in Sweden or your support and friendship.

And to my parents Rita and Leonard Sutton for being there for me.

ORIGIN OF THE WITCHES

It was over 2000 years ago in the highlands of Scotland, just off the Northern Coast near Inverness that the Celts were celebrating Samhain. This was a Gaelic festival which took place in the month of October usually the 31st during the evening now known as Halloween. It was the end of the harvest, and the pagans were massed together around a circle of stones. Bonfires were burning and people were dressed for the cold night air. They danced and sang beneath the full moon. It was their belief that spirits merged on this night, and the energies of the universe were active, and the boundaries between worlds could be crossed; this is when the spirits entered the earth. Offerings were made to the gods such as food and drink which were left outside homes. People known as cave dwellers were keen to please their gods. Some felt it was not enough to leave food and drinks; they wanted to offer human sacrifices which they felt would satisfy their gods.

The cave dwellers were led by a kind of chieftain of the tribe called Gabbran, with support from Barra and his wife Alana. No one seemed to question their authority and harmony existed within the camp, but one person who did oppose them seemed to be quite powerful and influential.

Murdina was the main instigator who wanted to influence the cave dwellers into thinking like her. Both her and a friend, Fenella, already had a rebel following who were happy to sacrifice humans in order to please their gods. She was caught trying to sacrifice a young girl during the festival and was stopped by Gabbran.

"You will anger the god's Gabbran with your selfishness. Let them see we love them. Let this girl be put to death for them," she said, gripping the girl's arm. The girl trembled with fear while Murdina and Gabbran quarreled.

"The gods will be angrier if you harm her," Gabbran said, reaching out to the girl.

They were standing on the edge of a cliff, and Gabbran was concerned about them falling. The girl fought Murdina to break free from her grip, and suddenly lost her footing. She plunged to her death, her body fell a considerable way down until she reached the rocks near the sea, breaking bones and gashing herself. The blood poured from her broken body, and she lay dead.

"I have my sacrifice not quite as I planned it, but she is gone," Murdina gloated.

Meanwhile in space, the universe consisting of planets, stars, and galaxies with all other forms of matter and energy. They immersed a strange event was taking place. It was two energies that suddenly merged into one and fused together. This was followed by a massive explosion across the universe. The energies dispersed and fragments of rock flew in all directions at great velocity. They travelled like meteorites in a vast array of colours set to impress the dullest of minds; some of the meteors headed towards the earth.

The cave dwellers continued to argue about the human sacrifice unaware of the pending danger that was heading towards them. One of them noticed a change in the sky and shouted.

"Look to the heavens. See what the gods are sending us," he said.

"Fire from heaven! Run for cover," another shouted. Everybody scattered and ran as quickly as they could back to the caves.

Some fell and others were pushed out of the way; everybody was frightened. Hundreds of them were heading for shelter. Most of them managed to get to the caves in order to hide away from whatever it was that was pursuing them. Once they were inside, they hid beneath blankets and items of clothes. The meteors rained on the land and beach; exploding into the ground burning trees and plants. Everybody kept still and became overcome by an incredible energy which lit up the walls of the caves. This immense energy made their bodies glow like a form of radiation. Waves of light shone into the caves coming from outside, bodies were glowing in various colours from orange to pink and blue. Each person was as still as the night without a sound in the air.

After a while, the energy began to settle down all the bright lights seemed to vanish, and the cave dwellers began to move, slowly at first, and then back to normal or so it seemed. Gradually, they moved towards the cave entrance, and into the darkness outside. Not one soul was about near the caves or on the beach. It was as if nothing had happened. But what was amazing was that each of the cave dwellers complained of feeling odd. They could tell that they were different inside. It was like a new life was bursting to get out, a power so great that it possessed their bodies. The rocks were outside at this point, so the cave dwellers collected them together, and took them to the caves. It was just as if they knew that they possessed a very powerful energy.

After a few days passed, the pagans realised just what had happened to them; they were different. The meteors had given them powers beyond their comprehension. Some of them were levitating while others began to float on their brooms, and eventually fly. Others began sending lightning bolts across the cave using sticks they called wands. Some of the cave dwellers were making magic potions from with instructions from recently discovered parchments. They discovered the power of healing, making obstacles come to life, and even transforming their own body into animals. They felt different, and even possessed extraordinary powers which they used in their favor; powers such as premonition, levitation, divination, and much more.

Murdina was able to cast spells with a stick she called a wand. Fenella found that she could fly on a broomstick and transform her body into other creatures. They were becoming very powerful, so much so that it was time for Gabhran to step in and control the situation. He wanted the people to use such powers for good, but Murdina had her own ideas concerning conquering nations, and forming an elegance with the devil.

Before long the tribe became divided, and Murdina was leading her own army, that she referred to as 'dark witches', she called Gabhran's cave dwellers 'white witches', and cursed them for remaining with him.

"You are weak and feeble. You think with your heart not your soul," Murdina cursed Gabhran in their Gaelic tongue.

"I am the leader, and I say that we use our powers for good not evil," he said.

"You have to strike fear into people in order to rule. We are the dark witches, and we rule supreme," she replied.

"You will be defeated due to your evil ways," he said, shaking his wand.

"Do not threaten me with your religious gods. They won't defend you," she mocked him.

"See reason, and stop your wickedness. Join us," he begged her.

"Never, Gabhran. I would rather die," she said, turning her back to him.

Soon, the witches were at war, and the dark witches virtually wiped the white witches out. Eventually, the surviving white witches scattered across Scotland. Gabhran was defeated and killed by Murdina, who remained in the caves, but sent out a large army of witches to England and Europe to invade them. She claimed to possess the power to resurrect people from the dead, but this was never proven. This part of the legend remains a mystery as does the number eight spoken about in the bible, showing signs of the resurrection. Over the centuries, the dark witches became very powerful and were known throughout the world for their wickedness. White witches faded into insignificant, most of them destroyed by the dark witches, and by the seventeenth century, they were hunted down along with the dark witches by governments and other influential bodies who considered them as a threat to the world. Scotland in particular began witch hunting sanctioned by King James the First of England, and who was also known as James the Sixth of Scotland. A witch called Albelenda was aware of the kings' desire to rid Scotland of witches and wanted to avenge the witches that had already fallen victim to the witch hunters' sword.

SHANICE

Throughout history legends are born, they develop and are passed down through the ages, the eight skulls of Teversham is no exception to this. The legend talks about a coven of dark witches, who were renowned for their magic and treachery. They would terrorise villages and its occupants, even killing them. They claimed it was in revenge due to the witch hunting that was going on throughout Scotland and beyond the border into England. Eric Butterworth was a young man who had lost his family to such witches. Eight witches had entered the village at night, and stormed into Eric's parents home killing all but him.

Years later, Eric became part of a witch hunt to find these witches and avenge his family. This was backed by the local Mayor who wanted to get rid of them for his own reason. He was after the secret of the resurrection which only the witches possessed. Eric met the daughter of one of the witches who called herself Annabella. Unaware who she was, he befriended her. They fell in love and she had a child called Rosa who possessed magical powers, and became a white witch. According to legend, she went missing and took the secrets with her. No one knew where she had gone; but she reappeared in the twenty-first century. However, she was not alone as the spirits of the witches, and the mayor were with her possessing the bodies of her friends causing her harm. Eventually, she battled with them and sent them back to the spirit realm. Her only concern was her existence in this time, and if she had children would they be in danger. Therefore, she made a vow that she would not discuss her past life and family history with them.

DISCOVERY

It was a warm afternoon and school term time, when Shanice and her two friends decided to take the afternoon off school, and join her in her home. She was used to dodging her parents and spending time looking through books about history and other subjects, such as witchcraft. Although Shanice new nothing about her family history, she was curious to know where they came from. Her mother Rosa would never speak of the past as if it was some kind of sin to bring up such things. She was so curious she took her friends into the attic searching through boxes. They found nothing but old books which were not very interesting not until they discovered a book called, "The eight skulls of Teversham'. Shanice opened the book and began to read it out loud. Her friends were fascinated and remained quiet as she read about the slaughter of a family in a village. She read on and found that she could not put the book down. Hours passed until she finally reached the end speaking about Annabella and Eric, describing their love, and the revelation that she was a witch. She read of the evil of the witches and the mayor who revelation that she was a witch. She read of the evil of the witches and the mayor who had them hunted down, but the story ended with no mention of Rosa or the time link.

"This is so good. Why has my mother kept this in a box in

the attic?" Shanice said, pondering.

"Perhaps she wanted to keep it safe," one of the girls replied.

"Kayleigh, that's silly," Shanice said dismissively. "It could be a book that she didn't want you to find," the other girl said.

"Jessie, I hardly think my mother would keep anything from me."

Kayleigh was a slim blonde girl with wavy hair and blue eyes, while Jessie had dark hair like Shanice and brown eyes. She was slightly bigger than both of them; both heavier with larger bones. Shanice was so much like her grandmother, Annabella, but she had her mother's personality, her determination,   and forcefulness.

Shanice was curious about what was in the treasure chest. It looked very old and covered in dust. She looked at it for a while, and then opened it. The lid was heavy and the hinges creaked as she began to lift it up. Kayleigh helped her while Jessie stood back and seemed reluctant to join in.

"Come on, Jessica. Help us!" Kayleigh shouted. Inside the chest were a few items including bottles and letters, but what really caught their eye was a large book. They lifted it up and lowered it onto the floor. Shanice sat in front of it, and Kayleigh sat beside her. Jessica remained standing.

"Jessica, it's only a book. Come and sit beside me," Shanice said while tapping the floor.

"Come on, Jessie," Kayleigh said, "It's only a book." Jessica sat next to Shanice, but she was apprehensive and nervous. She listened while Shanice read the book out loud. Shanice was interrupted by lightning and the sound of thunder. The whole attic lit up, and what looked like a woman appeared in the room. She was pale faced and had long dark hair. Jessica screamed and the image disappeared.

"Can we go now?" she asked nervously.

"Did you see that?" Kayleigh asked Jessica.

"Who was it?" Jessica asked, shaking.

"It was what's known as a mass hallucination. We all saw it, but it wasn't real."

"It looked bloody, well, real to me!" Jessica continued, "She looked like a witch."

"Nonsense! It's because we found that other book, and it's playing on your mind. There is no such thing as witches."
At that moment, the book began to glow and then floated up. They all stood to their feet, and Shanice went into a trance. The other girls shouted to her but she could not hear them. She began chanting and reading spells. The woman reappeared but this time seemed to enter Shanice's body and then disappeared.

Shanice gasped and gazed around as if she had been asleep and just woken startled. She seemed to experience a panic attack. She became breathless, and started shaking. Kayleigh knew what to do as her mother suffered from panic attacks regularly. She began talking to her and helping her relax, trying to calm her down before her mother arrived home. She was aware that Rosa would not agree with what they were doing. She soon managed to comfort her and watched as she began to relax. All the stress disappeared from her face. Jessica just watched anxiously, and hoped that whatever had happened would not reoccur for all their sakes. She was not a lover of the unknown, and only followed the other two because they were friends.

Rosa returned home and called upstairs to Shanice. She was sure she was in the house, and was eager to see her. She called a few times but got no answer. Suddenly, Kayleigh dropped a book on the floor. She surprised herself and jumped up quickly, hoping that Rosa had not heard her.

"Shanice, I know that's you. Please, answer me," she said furiously.

"Okay, I am coming," Shanice answered, opening the hatch and letting down the ladders.

"What are you doing up there?" Rosa asked.

"Just looking around," Shanice said innocently.

"You know you're not allowed up there," Rosa was very annoyed.

"There are old books up there. Nothing special," she replied defiantly.

"What have you found?" Rosa asked.

"A book called the 'Eight skulls of Teversham.'"

Shanice said goodbye to her friends, and made sure they were out of the house before speaking further to her mother. She followed her into the kitchen and watched her put away the shopping.

"Why are you so upset?" she asked her.

"I don't like you going through my things," Rosa said, slamming down her bread and other items.

"They are books, old and dusty," Shanice replied.

"*My* books."

"About witches from the past; nothing of importance, and certainly not real," she said trying to defend her actions.

"It's a good book," Rosa said, looking at her with wild eyes.

"But you always said witches are a myth and not to take any notice of such nonsense," she said holding the book up.

"Right here, as you say, harmless."

The book shot out of her hand and began floating around the room. Eventually, it fell to the floor. Shanice was shocked. She noticed it had fallen open on a page which was about spells.

"What just happened?" Shanice asked.

"I don't know," her mother replied.

"You saw it as well as me. It floated, and then fell."

"Nonsense. You imagined it."

"Mother, I know what I saw; it floated on air."

Shanice never mentioned the book of magic in the attic, or the events that took place for fear of her mother's wrath. Rosa had a wild temper at times, and would never agree to let her share her experiences or past events.

She had seen the book float but thought it may had been her imagination due to the things that went on in the attic, her mother played it down although she knew for well that she had caused the book to float with her magic. But she had already made up her mind years ago that she would not perform magic in front of her family. She had to consider they're safety little knowing that Shanice was already in danger by enticing the spirit of one of the most powerful witches ever to live, for Nabara was inside her dormant ready to come to life at the right time.

SCHOOL ROMANCE

The next morning, Shanice went to school seemingly unaffected by the events of the previous day. She got up, washed and dressed, and headed downstairs for breakfast. Rosa had concentrated on getting her brother sorted out. Tom her nine-year-old brother sat eating his cereal and making loud crunching noises.

"Tom, close your mouth when you're eating," Rosa said sternly.

"Yes, Tom. It sounds like someone's walking on gravel," Shanice commented.

"Shanice, get your breakfast. You're late for school," Rosa remarked.

Shanice poured some milk into a bowl of cereal and some buttered toast. She took a sip of coffee, and then proceeded to eat her cereal. Suddenly, she began to cough and splutter. She had another sip of her coffee and held her throat with her hand.

"Are you alright, Shanice?" her mother asked, concerned.

"What is this cereal? It's horrid," Shanice replied.

"It's the one you usually have," Rosa said with surprise.

"It's grainy and tastes like shit!" she exclaimed.

"Mind your language, girl," Rosa said sternly. "I really don't know what's got into you lately."

"What do you mean?" Shanice said, thinking her mother had discovered something about yesterday.

"You are like a girl possessed by demons," Rosa said, banging everything about.

Shanice stood to her feet and grabbed her school bag. She picked up a piece of toast, and began walking to the door.

"Goodbye, mother," she said, opening the door. "Goodbye, and you better come home in a better mood," Rosa said, frowning at her.

Shanice thought for a minute, and decided to kiss her mother on the cheek. "Sorry," she said, hugging her and patting Tom on the head. "Goodbye, mate."

She walked to school which was only two streets away. Her brother Tom's school was a little further. Her mother walked him to school each morning on the way to work. Rosa worked at a local shop, while her husband Andrew, was a lecturer at Manchester University.

Shanice arrived at the school on time, and began to search for her friends. She found them in the classroom. They had just arrived and sorting out their books.

"Shan!" Kayleigh shouted. "Have you just got up?"

"No," she answered abruptly. "Why do you say that"

"You have toothpaste all around your mouth," Jessica said.

"Slight exaggeration, Jess," Kayleigh remarked. "You just have a bit here and there," Kayleigh said, wiping it off with a tissue that she had wet with her tongue.

"And your hair is a mess," Jessica continued.
"Anything else, Jess?" Shanice said sarcastically. "I mean is my head on the wrong way, or have my ears fell off?"

"Okay, Shan, chill," Jessica said holding her hands up. "Only trying to help."

"Jess, it's cool, okay?" Kayleigh said putting her hand up in front of her face.

"Thank you, Kay," Shanice said.
Suddenly the door slammed shut, and Jessica jumped, dropping her books on the floor. She collected them up, and began sorting some papers.

"Jess, what's wrong?" Shanice asked.
"Oh, ignore her. She has been jumpy since yesterday. She's nervous anyway," Kayleigh remarked.

"Did it affect you that much, Jess?" Shanice asked her.

"I have an overactive mind, and a strong imagination." Jessica explained.

"I would never have guessed," Kayleigh said laughing.

"Kay, don't be tight. She can't help being nervous," Shanice said, patting Jessica on the back gently.

"Something did happen in your attic, Shan," Jessica said, feeling uneasy. "Who was that freaky lady? Did someone die in your house?"

"No, I don't know who she was," Shanice replied. "But she was freaky."

"She scared the crap out of me," Jessica admitted.

"Forget it now or you will defo have nightmares," Kayleigh said.

"Let's change the subject, and think about something else."

"Like what?" Jessica asked.

"Boys," Shanice said, watching four boys enter the classroom.

"Nice," Kayleigh said, looking them up and down.

"Fit," Shanice agreed.

"Isn't that Arnold Roberts?"

"Who's that?" Kayleigh asked.

Jessica nudged Kayleigh in the ribs, "You know Arnie the rugby player, the fittest boy in the school, and I know who fancies him here."

"Who does?" Kayleigh asked.

Jessica looked at Shanice, and smiled, "Don't you?" Shanice blushed and turned away from them. She began to sort her books out.

"Well, tell us all about it, Shan," Kayleigh said, trying to get her to look at her.

"He fancies you," Jessica said, nudging Kayleigh again.

"Really?" Shanice said, turning her head towards them. "Are you joking?"

"Honestly, Shan, cross my heart and hope to die," Jessica said, crossing herself.

"How do you know?" Shanice asked curiously.

"I overheard them talking," Jessica continued near the lockers.

"He said that he thought you were hot and sexy," Jessica explained.

"Just the girl for him. He especially likes your hair, and the toothpaste around your mouth," she laughed.

"I knew you were joking. You're a witch," she said, pretending to claw her.

"It's true, Shan. Not the toothpaste bit, but all the rest," Kayleigh said.

"How do you know?" Shanice asked suspiciously.

"I was with Jess, and we both heard it this morning," Kayleigh looked at Jessie for support, and then back at Shanice.

"It's true, Shan; he likes you," Jessica watched Shanice waiting for a response.

"So, what do I do?" Shanice asked bewildered.

"Make a move; create the moment," Kayleigh said. "I will direct you and guide you. Wait behind after class, and talk to him."

"But what if he doesn't talk to me?" Shanice asked "He may be shy."

"Leave it to us, Shan," Jessica reassured her. "He will talk to you."

The lesson eventually begun, and all the pupils were attentive. Apart from Shanice, who was distracted by Arnie who sat near her. Knowing how he felt about her made her feel uneasy as he was sat so close to her. She imagined them on a date, walking down a quiet beach, admiring the coastline and enjoying each other's company. They were holding hands feeling the sea breeze on their faces, cool and refreshing. They stopped to share a kiss, a tender moment, and then walked on. This was a beautiful daydream and seemed to last forever until the teacher noticed that she was clearly not paying attention to her classroom subject. It was English literature, Shakespeare's Romeo and Juliet.

"Okay, Shanice. Please enlighten us about the balcony scene," the teacher asked her.

"Romeo, Romeo, where for art thou, Romeo," Jessica said, hoping to save Shanice the embarrassment.

"Wait, isn't that supposed to read Arnie?" Kayleigh whispered.

"I am quite sure Shanice would have quoted that herself had she been paying attention," the teacher shouted.

After the lesson, Kayleigh whispered in Shanice's ear. She nudged Jessica, and they both stood to their feet and gathered up their books. Shanice gathered her books but walked past Arnold, and stumbled forward dropping them in front of Arnold. By this time, her friends had left the room. They peaked at her from the door, and both grinned as she had deliberately dropped the books, so that Arnold would help her to pick them up. It was a trick that her friends had just taught her in order to grab Arnold's attention. It had worked judging by Arnold's quick response as he began to help her pick each book up.

"Are you okay?" he asked her.

"I am fine; just clumsy," she replied as they bumped heads.

"My name is Arnold, but people call me Arnie," he said

introducing himself.

"I am Shanice, but my friends call me Shan," she said looking into his blue eyes.

"Do you like the cinema?" he asked nervously.

"I like fantasy movies, such as vampire films like Blood Trail," she explained. "I like some romance and mystery movies, too."

"Do you want to go Friday night?" he asked apprehensively.

"Yes, that would be nice. What's on?

"A comedy called bewitched," he said. "It's supposed to be good."

"Okay," she agreed.

After their discussion Arnold left the room, and left Shanice thinking about the moment they shared together. She was thinking about their night out.

Later, she met her friends by the lockers. She appeared to be very happy as she greeted them.

"So, what is happening about Arnold? Kayleigh asked.

"We have a date on Friday. He's taking me to the cinema," Shanice replied.

"It worked then?" Jessica asked.

"Like a dream," Shanice said smiling.

Later that evening, Shanice went to bed early. She studied for a while for the next day's lesson, and spent an hour on the internet before retiring to bed. That night, she was experiencing a nightmare. She dreamt that she was back in the time of the cave dwellers in Scotland or 'Alba' as it was known then. She was being offered as a sacrifice by a woman with long dark hair who was known as Murdina, who became leader of the dark witches. She was being dragged to a place where they worshiped pagan gods, and she was placed on a large stone surrounded by many people. They all spoke in a language that she found difficult to understand; it was a Celtic tongue called Gaelic. Despite not being able to comprehend what they were saying, she somehow knew what was going on.

Murdina looked into the young girl's brown large eyes, and squeezed her cheeks with her hand speaking to her, but Shanice never said a word. She lay on the stone with her hands and feet bound, waiting for whatever fate awaited her. The cold air made her shiver and she was powerless to resist her enemies. Suddenly, at that moment, the dark sky lit up and meteors came hurling down, scattering the crowd. The rocks hit the ground all around her. Eventually, it was all over, and she remained lying down looking up at the moon and stars in the sky; and then all at once, she felt her body tingling. She noticed her hands and arms change colour. She became orange, pink, and then blue. The ropes that tied her had gone, and she was free. She tried to get up but felt too weak; but then a strange thing happened to her. She began to levitate rising a good six feet in the air. She was scared not knowing what was happening to her body. No one was there to explain anything, and all she could do was scream. She cried out loud and felt her body drop slowly to the ground.

At that moment, she awoke and found herself lying on top of the bed. Her mother Rosa was standing over her concerned; her father was close by bewildered by her actions. Rosa comforted her and notice burns on her hands and feet. She didn't seem surprised at Shanice's behaviour. It was as if she knew what to expect.

"Did you have a nightmare?" Rosa asked.

"Yes, a strange one. It was about Pagans and women like witches," Shanice replied, still shaking.

"I was afraid of this," Rosa said, trying to warm her up by rubbing her arms.

"I was about to be sacrificed to their gods," Shanice continued, "but then, a meteor storm occurred and saved me."

"Did you recognise anyone in the dream?" Rosa asked looking at Andrew.

"No one, but the woman who was dragging me was evil, like the witches in that book from the attic" Shanice remembered the woman in the attic. "I did see a woman in the attic, but I think I was hallucinating. She was like her that witch."

"How did you feel at the time?" Andrew asked.

"I felt strange when my body kept changing colours. My body tingled."

"Was there anything else unusual?" Rosa asked.

"Yes. All of a sudden, I rose up in the air. I was lying down and just floated."

Andrew left the room and returned with a bowl of water and towels. He sat on the bed, and began to sprinkle water over her wrists and ankles, bathing the burns. Rosa dabbed them with ointment and watched as Shanice drifted back to sleep. Both Rosa and Andrew stayed in the room for a while watching their daughter.

"She saw our ancestors, the dark witches," Rosa said.

"She must be told about them and about you," Andrew advised.

"No, not yet. She isn't ready," Rosa insisted.

"But she has powers. You saw her levitate, the same as I did. She also sent a bolt of lightning across the room," Andrew explained.

"I still say she isn't ready to be subjected to the type of things that I have witnessed and experienced. She is a child," Rosa said sobbing.

"What exactly are you afraid of?" he asked, trying to comfort her.

"The dark witches. They are dangerous and have the power to destroy us," Rosa looked at Shanice sleeping. "She is an innocent child and not ready for the type of magic that the dark witches possess. They could easily destroy her."

"I think she should know in order to protect herself. Didn't you know from an early age?" Andrew said, trying to persuade to tell her.

"That was different. I discovered my powers from an early age.

They had to tell me," Rosa explained.

"And now, she is displaying powers, and will use them wrongly just like the dark witches," he added.

"I must think about it," Rosa said ending the conversation.

The next day, Shanice was reluctant to discuss the nightmare, and wanted to move on with her life. She was looking forward to going on her date with Arnold, and just wanted to be happy. But deep inside her was a spirit that was not prepared to allow her to do this – Nabara, the worst witch ever to walk the earth – stayed inside her, ready to cause her harm.

When she entered the girls' toilet, she looked in the mirror and Nabara looked back at her. She reacted by shouting in a loud voice causing the mirror to break, shattering into many pieces that shot across the room.

"Who are you?" she shouted.

At that moment, a girl entered the toilet and was injured by some of the glass as it flew right at her scratching her face. She knelt down to help her, but the girl was hysterical and began screaming while lying on the floor holding her face which was covered with blood. One of the female lecturers came in the room to assist her followed by others. Shanice explained about the mirror breaking but never mentioned anything else. She was questioned a few times about the incident, and kept to the same story as she felt that no one would believe her, and label her as a troublemaker. She met her friends in class, and told them the true account of incident. They looked at her strangely at first, and then remembered the woman in the attic.

"Was it that woman in the attic?" Kayleigh asked.

"No, not her, but someone like her," Shanice said.

"That's freaky, Shan," Jessica said concerned.

"I know a clairvoyant who may be able to help you," Kayleigh offered.

"Really?" Shanice replied, sounding relieved.

"Yes. She is taking part in a psychic fayre next week," Kayleigh explained.

"We need to go to that," Shanice said relieved.

"It could be scary, you know, and maybe dangerous," Jessica said nervously.

"You don't have to go," Kayleigh said firmly. "I want to go," Jessica said. "It sounds like fun."

It was Friday, and the school ended for the weekend. Shanice met Arnold as planned outside the cinema. She was wearing a black dress, and her hair was long and touched her shoulders. She had a fringe which was neatly cut just above her eyebrows. She was wearing red lip stick and eye shadow with mascara. She had foundation on her face which made her face look tanned. The dress looked tight showing off her shapely figure. She appeared older than she was, and felt confident that Arnold would be impressed with her.

Arnold was waiting for her wearing a blue shirt and casual trousers to match. He looked very smart and complemented Shanice's attire. They entered the cinema, and queued for tickets. Arnold could hardly take his eyes off her. She looked so beautiful standing before him. She acted similar to him, and it seemed as if they were attracted to each other. They watched the movie with great interest, although Shanice was a little distracted by her thoughts of the nightmare and incident in the girl's toilet.

They left the cinema, and Arnold walked her home. It was then that Arnold couldn't resist kissing her on those generous lips. It was a warm passionate kiss that was returned in an equally generous manner by Shanice. It lasted for a good ten minutes as they fondly embraced each other. It was as if they had been going out for some time sharing a special moment. They were interrupted by Rosa who had just opened the front door. She gave a smile of admiration and approval.

"Good evening," she said politely.

"Good evening, mother," Shanice said. "This is Arnold," she continued introducing her new boyfriend.

"Good evening, Mrs. Stokes," he said offering his hand to her.

Rosa shook him by the hand. "Call me, Rosa," she insisted.

Shanice stood baffled by her mother's response to Arnold. She expected a remark or two, even a stone-cold glare that she seemed good at in moments like these. But Rosa surprised her as usual, and the evening went remarkably well. Andrew also welcomed him like a long-lost friend. This gave rise to Shanice suspecting something of a conspiracy of parenthood.

PSYCHIC FAYRE

It was a pleasant morning. The sun was out, and the birds singing in the trees near Shanice's house. She woke up in a bright mood, despite her usual confusing dream of witches and strange places such as caves. She was determined to find out more about the witch that was pestering her, if only she knew her name and why she wanted her. Her head seemed to be filled with so much nonsense. Perhaps the psychic fayre had the answers to many questions.

It was Saturday morning, and the fayre was to take place at two o'clock. Neither Rosa nor Andrew knew anything about it, or they would shortly have stopped her. But what Shanice didn't know was that the more she delved into the darkness of the witches, the more danger she was putting herself in. The spirits of the dark witches had already been awakened and inside her head. Shanice had a shower. She was washing herself down when a voice whispered in her ear as clear as the day.

"Shanice, discover the secrets of the resurrection," it said. She turned around and tried to cover her body with her hands and arms; covering her modesty and searching around the bathroom with her eyes.

"Is somebody there?" she asked.

"Don't cover your shame, girl." The woman continued, "You belong to us."

Shanice stepped outside the shower still looking around quickly. She wrapped a towel around her body.

"Leave me alone!" she shouted.

She was startled by a sudden knock at the door. She paused for a moment until the knock came again.

"Shanice, are you alright?" Rosa shouted.

"Yes. I am fine, mother," she replied.

Shanice got dressed in a hurry and put on some make-up. She dressed in dark clothing almost as if she were attending a funeral. She hardly looked in the mirror in case she saw the witch's image. Fortunately, she knew the type of make-up she wanted and applied it liberally, so that she didn't look too overdressed.

Her friends called round who were dressed a little brighter and casual, but looking mature. They were aware not to say anything to Rosa about the psychic fayre having had a discussion with Shanice the day before. Shanice appeared in the lounge and greeted her friends. She seemed nervous and seemed quite abrupt in her conversation with them.

"Shanice, are you okay?" Rosa asked.

"Yes, of course," she replied, giving no eye contact.

"What was all the shouting going on in the bathroom?" she asked.

"Nothing. I was being silly," Shanice replied.

"So, where are you going today?" she asked enquiringly.

"Around town, nowhere special," Shanice replied, glancing at her friends hoping they would keep silent.

"You are dressed. Nice ladies," Andrew commented.

"Thanks, Dad," Shanice replied apprehensively expecting him to read her thoughts.

"They are off to town, Andrew," Rosa said winking at him.

"Oh, I see. Attracting the boys, hey," he said laughing.

"Dad, really. You don't think we are like that, do you?"

"Just enjoy yourselves," he said winking back at Rosa.

Shanice and her friends started their day out in a local café discussing the forth coming event at the psychic fayre. Each one of them were eager to find out exactly what it was all about, having only ever reading about it online.

"So, what do you think Shanice?" Kayleigh asked her.

"I don't know. I just want answers I suppose," she replied.

"I feel nervous," Jessica said, "I suppose I am apprehensive."

"You usually are, Jessie," Kayleigh said critically.

"Yes, Jessie. Why have you decided to come?" Shanice asked.

"I wanted to see what the fuss was all about," Jessica replied smiling.

"Curiosity," Kayleigh remarked.

"You know what, they say curiosity killed the cat," Shanice said jokingly.

Jessica glanced at Shanice, and then Kayleigh, she seemed to be afraid but tried to mask her feelings by joking with them.

"I am no cat," she exclaimed.

"We will see," Kayleigh joked back.

They finished their drinks and cakes before leaving the café, and heading for the hall that accommodated the fayre. When they arrived, they were greeted on the door by a young but eccentric middle-aged lady adorned with colorful clothes and jewelry. She was very polite and gave the directions to the main function room who hired the clairvoyants and spiritualists. The room consisted of many stalls. Some selling charms, tarot cards, and other items for clairvoyants, and those interested in purchasing such things.

In between these stalls were clairvoyants who read fortunes from tarot cards, crystal balls, and psychometric which is a form of extra sensory perception where a person makes relevant associations from the use of objects to discover the history of its source, such as metal rings, watches or necklaces, a form of psychokinesis; while telekinesis is the movement of object by a type of energy also demonstrated at the fayre.

The girls were fascinated, especially Shanice, who demonstrated her own ability to do this to her friend's astonishment. She caused small books to heavy books to float, and coins to fly into a box without touching them. She merely raised her hands in the air.

"You have the gift," a clairvoyant said encouraging her. "Use it."

Shanice approached another clairvoyant called Ruby, and became surprised by her response to her. She sat for a reading, feeling calm and confident that she would be able to offer her answers to her troubled life. But the woman seemed to be concerned about someone who was standing beside her. She began to stammer and sweat poured from her forehead. She read the tarot cards to her telling her about travel and prosperity, but warned her of danger and a dark-haired woman who was a threat to her.

"I can see a woman looking over your left shoulder, a middle-aged woman who is looking quite turn, and has long straggly hair. She means you harm, and is a witch from long ago." Ruby said watching her reaction.

"A witch?" Shanice asked concerned.

"Yes. She is threatening me to be quiet and not interfere." She continued, "You have powers like a witch, and need to control such power to survive."

"I don't understand. How can I be a witch?" Shanice said, feeling as if she was going to be ill. She was hot and felt sick.

"Perhaps your mother is a witch," Ruby explained, "or your father maybe a Warlock."

"What is a Warlock?" Shanice asked.

"A male witch, or is he a Wizard?" she asked.

"No, neither of them. They have history books about witches that's all," she replied bewildered.

"The witch tells me you are from a long line of witches," Ruby said, looking over Shanice's shoulder.

"No, it's not true. It's a lie," Shanice shouted becoming angry. Suddenly the tarot cards flew into the air followed by other objects. They landed on the table in a heap, all but one card which landed in front of Shanice. It was the death card which appeared right before her with a picture of a skeleton dressed in black armour riding a white horse.

"What is this?" Shanice asked frightened. "It says death on it."

"It need not be death. It depends what is with this card. It can mean loss, failure, or destruction, but Shanice, please calm down, your powers are controlling you," Ruby said, dodging more missiles.

By this time her friend was getting anxious and wanted to take her away from the stall. Other clairvoyants were also concerned and they also went to Ruby's aid. Nabara, the witch that Ruby saw, began to cause a tornado close to the stall causing charms to fly into the air sending them towards Ruby causing her to topple over onto the ground. She turned to Shanice, and caused her to float high into the air and spin inside the tornado. Shanice was unable to control her body but managed to drift away from the tornado, and hit the wall with a force. She managed to break free and pushed her arms forward sending Nabara away with a jolt or an electrical charge of energy emitted from her hands. It was at this point that she could actually see her as she faded away. She could not believe what was happening and turned to her friends for help. Ruby recovered and noticed her defeat Nabara. She was free from her spirit and able to relax. Kayleigh and Jessica ran to her aid; Ruby also went towards her.

"Shanice, are you okay?" Kayleigh asked.

"Yes, I think so," she replied.

"The witch has gone," Ruby said relieved.

"Who was she?" Shanice asked.

"Someone from your family's past; an evil witch," Ruby replied. "She knew someone called Annabella."

"I don't like this," Jessica said.

"Shanice, you need help to control your powers and face your enemies," Ruby explained. "Ask your mother or someone who knows more about this."

"I will," Shanice said smiling a nervously. "We need to go." Shanice led her friends out of the hall, but before they left the building, Shanice and her friends were drawn towards a poster about a night with a Ouija board. Kayleigh put the details into her phone so that they could find out about attending it. Curiosity had gripped them once again, but did they realise the danger they were in by meddling with such things.

"This could help you to answer the questions about your past if you don't want to ask your mother," Kayleigh said.

"Those things are dangerous," Jessica said, concerned.

"Not if we follow the rules properly," Shanice said enthusiastically.

"Yes, Jessica, don't mention anything to anyone about what happened at the psychic fayre. It was too freaky to repeat," Kayleigh warned Jessica.

"Trust me. I won't say anything I am not stupid," she replied.

"That's a matter of opinion," Shanice said laughing.

THE SPIRIT OF MURDINA

Shanice was still dreaming of Murdina, the dark witch from the caves of Scotland or Alba, even though she didn't know her name, or who she was. She could see her face clearly, and knew that she was from another time, centuries in the past. She also dreamt of the girl that she wanted to sacrifice, who plunged to her death prior to the meteor storm. She saw the power of the witches in graphic detail as they performed them all those years ago.

Although it was a dream, she was bewildered by the way she had these thoughts in her head. She had read very little on the subject in history and certainly would not be able to visualise it like this. So, was this a premonition or a warning of some kind? Murdina had appeared in the attic at one point and again in dreams often as the powerful witch who processed many powers, and demonstrated them by destroying white witches and people who challenged her witchcraft.

Shanice was on her way to school on the Monday morning carrying her school bag. She was thinking about the strange events in the attic, at school in the toilets, and at the psychic fayre. She remembered what Ruth, the clairvoyant, had said to her about being a witch, and having certain powers such as telekinesis. She also had a conversation with another clairvoyant who said that she was a white witch, explaining the difference between white and dark witches, so that Shanice knew that she would have to use her powers for good and help people whenever possible. But what could she say to her mother about all this? Would she understand? Maybe she was a witch. Her mind drifted back to a row they had when the book shot across the room. Maybe that was her or was it her mother.

According to the legend, the witches got their powers from space, through energies colliding, and causing meteors to land on earth, but where did the energy originate, no one even questioned that. Could it be from an alien source? Maybe superior beings who had trouble controlling such energy of that magnitude? It was all very strange to Shanice who was still very young and was just experiencing adolescence, and all the problems that go on with teenage girls. The hormones and puberty were enough without having extra ordinary powers from space. Shanice was very confused and could only confide in her friend for support and understanding, but even they found all this witchcraft stuff a little strange and hard to accept, so to a degree. She was on her own struggling with her own thoughts and powers.

She reached the school gates where Kayleigh and Jessica greeted her. They seemed calm and relaxed which helped her to walk into school confidently. They sat in class, and Arnold greeted Shanice with a smile. She was reluctant to discuss recent events with him as she felt it would put him off her, instead, she discussed other things with him.

One girl caused her problems. She was a gang leader and bully called Sharon. She had a few faithful followers called Fiona and Kim. Fiona was a slim blonde girl, and Kim was dark-haired like herself and a little bit weightier. Sharon was in class making remarks about Shanice to her gang. She was jealous of Arnold, and had hoped that he would date her instead, but Arnold showed no interest in Sharon. He favored Shanice for her personality and good looks. But Sharon wanted to split them up and made every effort to discredit Shanice trying to tease her and cause her to fight. She tried a number of tactics that failed.

This time, she tried to humiliate her in the classroom. She tripped her up when she was heading for her seat, and then called her horrible names. The teacher never heard her but eventually Shanice lost her temper and began to cause the books and other items to fly around the room, narrowly missing the other pupils. Of course, no one realized it was her that was causing such chaos. They were all bewildered, all but Kayleigh and Jessica, of course, who had seen her performance at the psychic fayre. They looked at Shanice and the expression on her face. She was angry and wanted to punish Sharon. She had raised her arms to use her powers in an aggressive manner. They knew she needed help to control her powers and use them for good and not in this way. She was calming down but the damage was done. Windows were smashed and the classroom was a mess. She left the classroom at break time.

"Saved by the bell," Kayleigh remarked with a sigh, listening to the school bell.

"Good job, too," Jessica said, looking at Shanice.

Shanice left the classroom with her friends. She was with them physically but not in mind as her thoughts were many miles away. They walked towards the lockers which stretched almost the length of a corridor rows and rows of them. When they arrived at Shanice's locker, Sharon stood there with her gang. She was after Shanice and continued her bullying from the classroom. Shanice open her locker, and Sharon slammed it shut hitting her on the back of the head, and then, pulled her by the hair away from the locker.

"So, you think your smart, Shanice? You're the slut who took Arnie from me, and act all clever in class," she grabbed her by her blouse and pulled at her tie. "You are not so smart."

"Leave her alone," Kayleigh insisted.

"Or what? Are you going to fight me?" Sharon said, staring her in her blue eyes.

"Leave her out of this," Shanice said, feeling her blood boil. "Your fight is with me."

"I will show you," Sharon said, throwing her things out of her locker.

"Are you going to cry now like a baby?"

"Leave her," Jessica shouted.

Sharon pushed her to one side, and slapped her across the face. Jessica fell to the ground and Kim kicked her in the stomach.

"That's what you get for defending her," Sharon said, tightening her grip on Shanice's tie.

Shanice pushed her away. "Leave us alone, and that's your last warning."

"Oh, big tough Shanice," she said, punching her in the face and making her nose bleed.

By this time a crowd had gathered eager to see Sharon get beaten, but Shanice was too busy holding her nose and grabbing tissues from her locker. Kayleigh was picking up Shanice's things off the floor, and Jessie was recovering from her injuries. It was then that Sharon rushed towards Shanice in order to harm her further, but this time she was ready for Sharon, and lifted up her arms and a storm just like the one at the psychic fayre came rushing towards Sharon like a strong wind. It blew her down the full length of the corridor followed by a strange tornado that managed to slam all the lockers shut and scattered the crowd. No one could quite believe what they were seeing. They were witnessing a strange phenomenon caused by Shanice and her new found powers. She had become very powerful and sent fear into everyone with her actions.

Once the storm was over, the teachers raced down the corridor. They began to gather information about Sharon and Shanice, and they were both told to attend the headmaster's office. Both the girls remained silent. Sharon was in shock and Shanice did not know what to say about her actions. One of the teachers had phoned both their parents, and they were asked to wait in the office

"I knew you were weird, Shanice," Sharon said.

Shanice stretched her arms in the air and yarned making Sharon jump, and then smiled. "You don't really know me, or what I am capable of."

"I do now. You're dangerous." Sharon continued, "They should expel you."

Shanice failed to reply feeling it would make matters worse. She was more afraid of her own temper influencing her powers causing harm due to the lack of control or understanding of her own abilities. It wasn't long before that their parents turned up, and the teachers moved in fast to explain about the disruption they had caused. Some things, of course, couldn't be explained like the storm effect. These were regarded as freak events put down to nature. They all agreed including Rosa at this time. The last thing that she wanted to do was expose herself as a witch and reveal her powers. She sat quietly most of the time, and agreed to punish Shanice for her part in the disruption.

However, when she took Shanice home, she acted differently. She was very upset, partly with Shanice and also with herself for not telling her about the past, or that Shanice may process powers like hers and be a witch. She had battled with herself about telling her for fear of the past, but she was aware that Shanice may grow to become a witch. Now, the moment has come and she must explain everything.

"Where are you going?" Rosa asked Shanice abruptly.

"Upstairs, to my room," Shanice replied with attitude.

"No, you are not," she replied angrily. "You have some explaining to do."

Shanice threw down her school bag and jacket, and walked into the lounge, followed by her mother and father. She turned around and faced her mother.

"Well, what is it?" she spoke.

"Change your attitude for a start," Rosa said.

"Listen to your mother," her father said.

"Would you like to tell me what happened?" Rosa said.

"Sharon was bullying me with her gang. I merely defended myself. She has bullied me for years, so I finally gave it back," she explained.

"I see," Rosa said for a moment. She felt sorry for her and wanted to hug her.

"Should I have let her hit me and humiliate me in front of the entire school?" Shanice began to weep.

Her father moved forward to console her, but Rosa caught his arm and pulled him back.

"Andrew, leave this to me," she said, discouraging him.

"What are you doing, stopping my dad from coming to me?" Shanice said with her fists clenched.

"Stop acting like a spoilt brat and learn to take responsibilities for your actions," Rosa said as if she was deliberately provoking her.

"I am not a spoilt brat, and stop treating me like a child," Shanice replied.

"You are a child. Go and play with your dolls," she said mockingly.

Andrew was confused by Rosa's behaviour, but remained silent. Shanice began shouting and screaming like a banshee. She felt herself going the same way she did at school and wondered why her mother was being so mean to her. Suddenly, she had created a storm. Books came out of the book shelves and ornaments began flying around the room. Shanice's eyes turned irises turned white and she began to glow, and then, windows smashed. Andrew dodged a few books and fell to the ground. Rosa began to reverse the storm and calm it down, followed by replacing the books on the shelf and the ornaments back where they belonged.

Shanice ran to her father and hugged him. She lifted her right arm and opened her hand, so that the palm was pointed at her mother. A bolt of lightning went racing from her hand towards her mother. Rosa reflected it and sent a small charge of electricity back towards Shanice, and caused her to drop to the ground.

"Was that necessary?" Andrew asked her.

"Yes," Rosa said tearfully. "She needs to experience danger in case the dark witches pursue her. She would get worse than that and you know it."

She helped Shanice stand up and hugged her. She felt Shanice gripping her tightly, and whispered in her ear.

"I love you," she said.

"So, why be mean?" Shanice asked.

"In order to see what you could do, and where your strengths and weaknesses are," Rosa explained. "It is time for you to learn how to use your powers correctly."

"Are you going to teach me?" she asked.

"I will try, but you must be honest with me. Tell me everything you know and what is bothering you. We can work together, and I will tell you about the past right from the origin of the witches, about my parents, Annabella and Eric, and how I came to live in this century from the 17th century," Rosa seemed so keen to tell her everything.

"Wait, you mean you're not from the 21st century?" Shanice asked confused.

"No, I came from the 17th century, but that's a small part of what you need to know. I was resurrected in Scotland where you ancestors come from," Rosa sat Shanice down.

"It really is a long story, Shanice," Andrew said, also sitting down.

"Are you from the 17th century too?" She asked her father.

"No, I met your mother in Scotland, and witnessed her resurrection form sleep," he replied.

The family spoke for hours about the past including Murdina, the cave dweller, dark witch, and her evil work; how she killed a lot of white witches and destroyed lives. Her treachery had been highlighted in history books about Scotland. Her descendants travelled across the world causing destruction in their paths; living in Africa, Mexico, and many other places.

"I have been dreaming of her and her wickedness. She was in the attic too," Shanice said concerned.

"Who else have you seen, I wonder? Perhaps Alberlenda, my grandmother, who was a leader of the dark witches. She would show herself to you, although she may not reveal her name or Nabara, the evilest witch of them all," Rosa recalled of many names and described them.

They had been talking for hours about the dark witches and their wickedness, about the white witches such as Annabella and Rosa. Shanice told her mother everything she knew including the psychic fayre, but deliberately left out going to a house where they had a Ouija board.

Shanice attended school as usual. Sharon didn't speak to her or bully her, so she remained quiet.

Saturday arrived trouble free, and it was time to go to the house as planned in order to get answers from the Ouija board. They had made arrangements over the phone to attend the household of a Derek Russell, who was a clairvoyant, along with his wife, Dora, who was a spiritualist both were in their fifties, and had been involved in various aspects of the occult. Kayleigh and Jessica saw this opportunity as an educational experience and a strange type of pleasure, while Shanice wanted answers to who was around her from the spirit world.

They arrived at a large house in a lucrative area of the town. They walked up some steps to the house and they were greeting at the door by Dora. She looked older than her age with grey hair, slim, wore a small pair of glasses at the end of her nose, and a long dark dress with a white apron. She showed them into a room where Derek was standing next to a fire. He was also in dark clothes wearing a suit. He was grey with a goatee beard looking younger than Dora.

The girls were asked to join them around a table with the Ouija board in the center set up ready for them. They offered the girls refreshments and cake. They all chose orange cordial and accepted the fruit cake. Derek waited until dark before asking them to sit at the table. Each of the girls were hesitant to sat down. Jessica was the last one to sit down, they were all asked to relax, and then put one finger on a glass that was upside down.

Derek lit a few candles and placed the strategically around the room. He lit each one, and then put the lights out. Dora asked the first question.

"Is anybody there?" she asked in a clear and confident manner. The glass moved to various letters spelling out the word *'Yes.'*

"What is your name?" she continued. The glass moved again spelling *'Claire.'*

"Why are you here?" It spelt out *'To see my mother.'*

"Where does she live?" The answer came *'Here.'*

"So, did you live here?" Dora asked. *'I live here now. I died of an illness many years ago.'*

Dora commented after realizing who she was. She happened to be her great grandmother who lived in the 19th century. She died of small pox.

Shanice looked very suspiciously at Dora, believing that they were frauds with wild imaginations. She continued playing the game watching the performance of Dora and Derek, but not convinced of their authenticity as spiritualists or clairvoyants. She felt quite safe in their presence. They were just harmless head-cases living sad lives according to Shanice. But Derek noticed her fighting and asked her if she was alright. She just shrugged her shoulders like a typical teenager would do in a way of saying 'well I am here, am I not?' At that, moment the candles flickered.

"Is someone else there?" Dora asked. The glass moved again

this time it spelt *'Yes.'*

"Who are you?" she asked. The glass moved slowly and spelt out a name this time. The girl read out loud each letter in turn, beginning with *'N'* and then *'A'* and so on. Shanice was shocked, and shouted out Nabara. Each one looked at her for answers.

"She is a dark witch. A dangerous psychopath from the 17th century," she explained.

"Who are you?" Dora asked. The glass moved again and spelt *'I am your worst nightmare.'*

"What do you want?" Shanice asked. 'I want you' came the reply.

"I am not afraid of you, Nabara. You are nobody important," she replied provoking her.

With that the glass began to get very hot and burnt their fingers. It then spun across the room, and hit Jessica on the forehead, after which it shattered into thousands of pieces, and then the room shuck like the presence of an earthquake. The candle flames rose and set fire to objects around them. Jessica was lying with her forehead bleeding. Dora caught fire and was screaming. Derek was pinned to the door by a knife.

Shanice headed for Jessica with Kayleigh battling a wind blowing in their direction. Shanice saw Nabara in the distance controlling the wind and laughing. Derek was struggling still pinned to the door. Dora was no longer on fire, and Jessica was still bleeding. Shanice raised her arms in the direction of Nabara being careful to avoid causing harm to anyone else. She sent the wind back to Nabara, and added thunderbolts. Even if Dora and Derek were frauds, they would be shocked by the actions of Nabara and Shanice as they battled for supremacy.

Shanice finally beat Nabara, at least long enough to escape from the house with her friends. They went straight to the hospital with Jessica, spending time in casualty making up a cover story. After all, they didn't want to tell people the truth. It was too bizarre to mention.

Shanice knew Dora and Derek would be alright and they too would probably attend casualty at some point. Shanice knew also that she would have to tell her mother, and no doubt, she would be angry with her again. She also considered that Nabara would be back to fight again and that she would be more powerful and may defeat her. So, she needed her mother's protection.

Jessica suffered minor injuries which she said was caused by somebody throwing a glass at her on the street. Shanice had been told the story of the Eight Skulls of Teversham, and the significance of the number eight in history written in many cultures concerning the resurrection. The fact that her mother was resurrected proves the theory and enables her to pursue the story further, and understand it more fully. Also, she was born on the 8th August, which is the eighth month 2008, a strange coincidence.

When Shanice arrived home, she went straight to her mother and told her the events of the evening explaining about Nabara. Her mother was upset but surprisingly calm, as if she expected her to discuss such things and tell the truth. Rosa said that she was wrong doing it but she understood why she did it. She explained that Dora and Derek were just entering casualty as they were leaving. They looked shaken but not too bad considering the injuries they sustained. Rosa explained more about the past and taught her how to control her powers.

THE MYSTERY OF EIGHT

It was a bright sunny morning. The streets were busy with traffic and children making their way to school. Shanice made the most of her journey deep in thought. Her mind drifted back to a dream she had experience the night before, as she was thinking about the resurrection and the origin of the witches. She had been thinking about the secrets that had been with her family for generations, and of the significance of the number eight. This must have fitted into the secrets in some way as it was mentioned in the book of shadows, that her mother had in the attic for many years. In fact, her mother had taught her spells and potions from it recently.

Her dream was set in space. She stood at a mountain gazing at the stars when a figure dressed in a white satin dress approached her. She was blonde with blue eyes, and a radiant complexion. All around her was a glowing light. She was omitting a strange energy so powerful Shanice could hardly stand the power of this woman.

"Who are you?" she asked.

"I am the source of the energy inside you. You have inherited my power. Do good with it, and share my love for the universe," she replied. "Let my light shine in you and all around your

world for eternity. Eight represents infinity, infinite love, infinite energy, and infinite time."
With the words she vanished leaving Shanice bewildered, but feeling happy and contented in a state of ecstasy.

She awoke with the same feeling which continued to this moment as she was heading to school. She arrived determined that nothing was going to ruin her day. She met her friends as usual, and told them her dream. She then spent some time with her boyfriend Arnold. She met her friends later in the library, and explained about her research into the number eight trying to find the symbolic to find the symbolic meaning of the number. She explained about the woman and how she spoke about infinity. She couldn't fathom out whether she was meant to be an angel or some sort of alien being, but she was powerful and appeared to have much wisdom.

Shanice and her friends surfed the internet for answers hoping to find some kind of clue to the mysteries of the universe. It took a long time to do a complete search. Kayleigh found the first clue through Egyptian culture, looking through the dynasty's numerical equations and definitions explaining the Egyptian nation and their gods. Jessica found the information regarding the Chinese culture. How the number eight is the luckiest number in Chinese culture meaning wealth, fortune, and prosperity; the number brings good luck. Other searches resulted in a life pathway number or destiny number this offers insight into your personality, and an insight into the pathway of success.

In religious terms, 888 represents Jesus, specifically Christ the Redeemer. The Greeks counted the number down according to his name; the opposite being 666, the number of the beast. Shanice considered that her date of birth was significant by number, and that she was surviving a purpose on the earth as that woman had said. But this still didn't link the number eight to the resurrection, not until Kayleigh came up with a possible answer that seemed to make sense.

"The number eight is very significant as it is used seventy-three times in the bible," she explained reading an article out to them. "It is the symbol of resurrection and regeneration in Bible numerology, represents a new beginning, a new order of creation, man being resurrected into eternal life."

"That's why, so many are keen on knowing the secret. They think the witches found the answer and my mother was resurrected, that makes sense now," Shanice said, clapping her hands together and making Jessica jump out of her chair. "Sorry, Jessie."

"Jesus was said to have raised the dead, and He too was resurrected in a way," Kayleigh said, "if you believe in the Bible and God."

"Here it is," Shanice shouted, causing people to react with frowning faces saying 'shhh'.

"Infinity," she whispered. "The number eight represents infinity and everything in the universe, which of course, is infinity. The infinity of love, infinity of energy, infinity of time. Everything is complete and endless abundance without any disadvantages, it says here."

"A balance between physical, mental, and spiritual being," Jessica read on.

"The secret influence of angel number eight means the resonation with the power and vibrations of self-confidence, inner strength, and personal power. It is said to be associated with authority, professionalism, and wealth," Kayleigh said, reading more from a wealth of information.

"So, what we have is documentation that the number eight is part of the resurrection, a key fact in the scheme of things, and by definition, part of the infinite universe. So, how did my mother survive, and apparently Annabella and Eric my grandparents? The answer must lie in the caves of Scotland where the cave dwellers lived," Shanice said pondering.

"And in the town and village of Teversham," Kayleigh agreed.

"We need to visit Teversham," Shanice said. "See exactly what happened."

"But, what if the witches pursue us?" Jessica said.

"Oh, Jessie, where is your sense of adventure?" Kayleigh asked.

"I seemed to recollect that I was the one who got injured by a witch at the home of those wierdos," Jessica objected.

"That's true. She did get injured," Shanice said. "So, it's your choice, Jessie."

"Of course, I am going. I wouldn't miss it for the world," she replied.

At that point a teacher approach them. She stopped in front of Shanice.

"Girls, if you insist on disturbing people in here with your chatter and noisiness, I must ask you to leave," she said abruptly.

"We were just going. We have better things to do," Shanice replied insolently.

They all left the library led by Shanice taking their information and school bags with them. Walking out noisily and entering the corridor. They headed for the lockers. Each of them opened their lockers, and sorted out books for their next lesson.

"So, what now?" Kayleigh asked.

"Science or physics?" Jessica said, "Chemistry class?"

"Make your mind up," Shanice said laughing.

"So, are we going to Teversham?" Kayleigh asked.

"The town doesn't really exist, Kay. It disappeared as far as we know after being cursed by witches when my grandfather took back the eight skulls of the witches back in history," Shanice said sadly.

"But we should find something," Kayleigh replied.

"You are right, of course," Shanice agreed. "We will go."

"Okay. I will go with you," Kayleigh said.

"Count me in," Jessica said.

"But for now, let's have some fun," Shanice said, leading them to the gymnasium.

"What are we going to do?" Jessica asked.

"Do you want to see some magic?" Shanice said, producing a wand.

Both girls looked at each other, and then at Shanice. They were speechless and followed her in anticipation of events to come.

"I predict Sharon and her friend are about to be embarrassed," Shanice said laughing.

They walked into the gym and sat against a wall watching the girls' session of sports, namely gymnastics. Sharon's gang were there practicing their skills using various pieces of the equipment. Shanice had pushed her wand up her sleeve. She whispered incantations, and watched as Sharon leapt onto the air off the horse. She spun her around and dropped her onto the floor. She then turned to Kim who was climbing a rope, and caused the rope to entwine, then spun her around wildly until she too fell to the floor. Fiona ran up to the horse, and Shanice made it disappear, so she fell flat on her face. She recovered and limped to the others. Finally, Shanice got bored with using such spells, and just to finish, she made their leotards split open as a few boys were passing. Fortunately, the boys didn't see anything.

"That was mean, Shanice" Kayleigh said smiling.

"Yes. You should not use your magic for that sort of thing," Jessica agreed.

"I wish you to had these powers, too," Shanice said. "I feel like a misfit".

THE RESURRECTION OF TEVERSHAM

It was a pleasant day for travelling as Shanice and her friends, Kayleigh and Jessica, ventured on the train heading north to the border of Scotland seeking Teversham. They knew it had been renamed, and believed it was in the location of Ednam, near Kelso in the county of Roxburghshire. Janice had told her mother that they were headed for Blackpool. However, Rosa suspected that she was still seeking the family history. Rosa discussed this with Andrew, and so they contacted his uncle professor Graham Stokes for advice. Graham immediately responded by organizing some of his colleagues to get together and plan a journey to Scotland.

"I should have realized Shanice would do this Andrew," Rosa said.

"You were not to know. Besides, my uncle will help us," Andrew reassured her.

Shanice sat at a table on the train with her friend looking outside the window admiring the view, when her phone rang. It was her mother trying to reach her. She was hesitant and tried to avoid the call, however, her mother was persistent, and rang several times before Shanice answered it.

"Hello, mother," she said abruptly.

"Where are you now?" Rosa asked.

"Nearly in Blackpool," she said hesitantly.

"Really," Rosa said sarcastically. "Since when was Blackpool in Scotland?"

"What do you mean?" she said innocently.

"You are heading for Teversham, aren't you?" Rosa said knowing that she would have to admit where she was going.

"Yes," she admitted. "Sorry, mother."

"Well, all I can say is be careful, and wait for us to come up before you do anything else. While you're at the village, you will be in danger," she warned.

"We will wait for you to arrive," she nodded to her friends, so that they knew and would agree to do the same.

Hours later, they reached their destination at Ednam which was a bus journey away from Kelso. They discovered a place to stay at the King's Head Tavern. They booked a room with a king size bed for the three of them. It was cheaper and safer to stay together as a group. They unpacked and made themselves comfortable. Each found a draw for their clothes and spent about an hour indoors before venturing out into the street. Shanice led them to the local church which was in view on the other end of the street. They found the village to be very quiet with few people about.

On entering the gates to the church, they found themselves in a graveyard surrounded by Yew trees, which were supposed to ward away evil spirits back in history. Shanice searched the graveyard for the Butterworth tomb stones. They walked for a while until she finally found them. The stoned was weather beaten, and the names showed faintly through the mould and decay. All the family, except for her grandfather Eric Butterworth, who survived the massacre from the eight witches who brutally murdered them.

"This is it," Shanice said tearfully. "This is Teversham."

"Oh my god, Shanice," Kayleigh said. "So, this was your family."

"What now?" Jessica asked. "This place is creepy."

"We wait for something to happen," Shanice said. "Nabara knows I am here."

"Really? How?" Kayleigh asked nervously.

"I can feel her presence. She is watching me," Shanice said, looking around her.

"Are you kidding, Shan?" Jessica asked.

"No, but don't worry. She won't appear in the day time, and we are protected by these Yew trees. She is just curious at present," Shanice reassured her friends.

They stayed by the graveside for a while, and then entered the church and looked around. It was as if time had not altered anything in the church. It was as it was centuries ago when Eric's family used to attend church on a Sunday. In fact, the entire village was stuck in the middle of a time warp. The tavern was renamed as was the village, and they even located the cottage where the Butterworth's once lived opposite the tavern. The villagers were walking about and looking at the girls strangely as if they knew why they were there. By this time, the girls had covered the entire village of just a few streets. There was a bus to the nearest town which would have been Teversham town, now renamed, in order to protect the local people from harm as the witches had caused so much devastation, and cursed the towns folk. The area where the eight skulls were displayed was now a park area with a war monument in the centre of it. People were walking across the grass to the local shops.

They entered a butcher's shop, and looked at the large display of meats available. Each bought a pork pie, and left the shop for another next door, the local news agency. While they were in there, Shanice, without a thought, mentioned to her friends about Teversham. She was referring to the fact that it had hardly changed according to her mother's describing of it.

"There is no such place as Teversham, girl," an old woman remarked.

"No. So, don't speak of it," another woman said angrily.

"Sorry. I was only comparing this place to Teversham," Shanice explained.

"Don't even utter the name," she continued. "Less you be cursed."

"Like she said, she is sorry," Kayleigh said defending her.

"You are strangers here. You have no right to critic our place," she continued.

"Come on, girls. Let's go. We don't need to hear this. We have apologized and that's it," Shanice said, leading her friends out of the shop.

"Well, I never," the woman said, looking at the other customers with a discussed look on her face.

The girls headed back to the tavern and went straight to their room. Shanice was still annoyed by the woman's behaviour, and slumped herself on the bed.

"Was I rude?" she asked them.

"No," they both said.

"She was rude," Kayleigh remarked. "Very rude," Jessica agreed.

They joined her on the bed.

"This is so comfortable," Kayleigh said, bouncing on it.

"We will sleep tonight," Shanice said, also bouncing.

"What if Nabara comes?" Jessica said, worried.

"I will be waiting for her," Shanice said. "I am not afraid of her."

Meanwhile, in the caves of Inverness, the witches sat in a circle. Alberenda was reading from a large book. They could all see Shanice in a fire in the middle of them. Within the flames, it was a vision of her and her friends on the bed.

"Foolish child," Alberenda remarked. "She thinks she is safe there and only you, Nabara, to worry about, but we are eight witches and she is one."

"I could destroy her on my own," Nabara said.

"No, Nabara. You must work with us to avenge all of us. Florina, Babeth, Renilda, Rosulinda, Jeliana, and Pasara, we all play a part." Alberenda said acknowledging each of them.

"We will once again destroy Teversham as we did before, and reinforce our curse. Everyone will fear us, and we will be the most famous dark witches to live on earth".

"You are so dramatic, Alberenda," Florina said cackling along with the others.

"She always has been," Babeth agreed.

"So, when do we strike?" Renilda asked. "I want to see them squirm."

"Patience, ladies. All in good time. We want to leave our mark and let people know we may be spirits, but we are alive and mighty in power and strength."

"Curse be upon the people of Teversham, and all those who oppose the dark witches of Scotland," Nabara said using her wand to fire a thunderbolt towards the outside of the cave causing an explosion.

That night, Rosa and Andrew were visited by Professor Graham Stokes and friends. He had grown a goat's beard, and wore small glasses on the end of his nose. He was renowned for dressing eccentrically with a Burgundy jacket, black trousers, and a mustard waste coat. He was with other people from the university, including Professor Linus Svenssen, and two graduates,

Paula Matterson and John Astle, each eager to see what what was happening in Teversham.

"My dear nephew Andrew," the Professor said, shaking his nephew by the hand.

"Uncle Graham," Andrew said excitedly, "so glad to see you."

"Likewise," Graham said, smiling and introducing his party of friends.

"You are all welcome," Rosa said.

"Rosa, my dear lady," Graham said, hugging her. "May I say you are as beautiful as ever."

"Flattery will get you everywhere," she said blushing.

"My dear, you were resurrected or reborn, and you are glowing even now," he replied. "I remember the day I found you in those caves. My friend has been brought up to speed, and were astonished by your story."

"Yes, I was there too," Linus commented, reflecting on the time she was found in the cave and resurrected. "A most remarkable event and experience I will never forget."

"Now, what of your daughter Shanice?" Graham asked.

"Come in to our lounge area. We can drink and discuss the situation further," Andrew said, leading them into the room.

Shanice had fallen asleep on the bed, and began to dream about the dark witches in the caves of Scotland. She dreamt that she was held captive with her arms and legs bound sat inside the cave. The eight witches were close by discussing how they planned to kill her parents.

"I vote we boil them in the pot, and make stew of them," Florina said.

"Yes, mixed them with herbs, and cast spells on the villagers," Babeth agreed.

"Make those villagers suffer for our deaths," Florina continued.

"And the humiliation of putting our skulls on display around the village," Babeth went on.

"They think they have lifted the curse by renaming the village, but we have found them, thanks to Shanice," Jeliana said pointing to Shanice.

"Oh, yes! I had forgotten her," Nabara said, standing to her feet and walking towards her.

Shanice was cowering in the corner too afraid to speak. Nabara took her wand, and burnt her leg with sparks from it.

"You, despicable child. So you thought you could defeat me," she teased and torched her.

Shanice screamed out loud. Her friend who was close by awoke and comforted her. She was sobbing with tears trickling down her face.

"Shan, it's Kayleigh. Are you okay?" she asked.

"My god, look at her legs," Jessica said in horror.

"Oh my god! They are burnt," Kayleigh said. "But how did that happen?"

"Fetch me my wand. Quick." Shanice instructed.

"What happened?" Jessica asked.

"It was Nabara," She replied.

"She was here?" Jessica asked, looking around the room.

"Yes, in a way. They are all in the caves of Scotland, but I can't fight them alone," she admitted. "All eight of them."

"But your mother is coming. She will help, won't she?" Jessica asked concerned.

"Probably if she gets here in time," Shanice said holding her leg up.

Kayleigh returned with her wand, and placed it in her hand. Shanice used it to heal her leg, and then grabbed Kayleigh by the arm.

"You two should leave. You are in danger," she insisted.

"No way. We are staying with you," Kayleigh said. "We are friends to the end."

"Yes, we are." Jessica said. "Wait, are we going to die?"

"Probably if you are with me. They are vicious, evil dark witches who will do anything. Look what they did to the Butterworth's," Shanice said concerned.

Rosa had told the entire story of Shanice, and watched the reaction on the faces of her friends, each one was ready to help her in any way they could.

"So, shall we start out now?" Graham asked. "I have got everything aboard."

"Yes, of course," Rosa said eagerly. "We will follow in our car. We are packed and ready to go."

"Yes. All bags are in the boot."

They all went outside. Graham's friends went into the minibus, while Rosa and Andrew went into the car. They all set off bound for the border of Scotland and England. Knowing it would take hours to get there. They packed refreshments.

Back in Teversham, Shanice and her friends sat in the tavern lounge area enjoying soft drinks and pub food. They are in a corner that is out of the way of the local villagers. But rumors have gone round about their visit, and what occurred in the local shop. Small places like these have people who gossip and everything gets known; nobody's business is their own, and people are concerned about them enquiring about Teversham and its dark and dismal history. People are afraid of the past, about the witch's curse and local superstitions. They are strong believers in the supernatural and of the witchcraft practiced in the history of Teversham. The girls could feel the eyes looking at them and the tongues were wagging uncontrollably. They began to feel uncomfortable, and soon retired to their room for the night.

They all got into bed and cuddled up close, hoping for a peaceful night. However, the witches had other plans for their night which didn't involve peace and quiet.

The spirits of the witches assembled outside the village at the location where they stood centuries ago when they murdered the Butterworth's. Alberenda and Nabara were discussing their plans to scare the villagers and kill Shanice. They were both pacing around the other witches.

"So, here we are again in Teversham," Alberenda announced. "Yes, and this time, we are after your great granddaughter and her proxy friends," Nabara agreed. "Shanice will regret coming here."

"And so will these villagers, thinking they could change the name of the village and hide it from us," Alberenda said laughing. "Foolish people, just like their ancestors."

"We shall destroy all of them," Nabara said spitting while she spoke.

"Not all, Nabara. Just a few. The others can bear witness to this event as will Shanice's friends," Alberenda said, looking to the other witches.

"Passara and Jeliana, go to the far side of the village, and wait for my signal to attack. Renilda and Rosalinda, go near to the tavern, and wait for my signal there. I will keep Florina, Babeth, and Nabara with me," she ordered.

Albelenda had arranged to shine a symbol in the night sky which resembled a charging bull meaning attack. This could be seen from each direction of the village, so that the witches knew when to attack. She was waiting for the right moment according to a time piece that she carried with her which once belonged to the Mayor Mallet of Teversham. She was waiting for midnight and for the full moon to appear clearly in the sky. The power of the lunar to be present which would aid them in their attack of the village.

Shanice was restless, but tried not to disturb her friends. She could sense the presence of the witches and felt afraid. She knew just how powerful they could be judging by their history. It was like waiting for death to deal its fatal blow, or being sentenced to death by execution. Never before did she feel more alone than now. She could feel her heart beating fast. She began to sweat and she was so tense. She tried to calm herself down but found it hard to concentrate or function effectively. She thought about her mother and father, and all those who were fond of her. Memories came flooding back to her about all the changes in her life, and the things that her mother had taught her about her powers and how to use them effectively within her realm of understanding, the importance of being in control of her emotions, and to use her powers for good.

Defending others was paramount to Shanice no matter what she felt, and how vulnerable she was; creating the element of surprise and using this to her advantage. The angel-like figure who visited her in her sleep had pointed out the correct use of her powers, in accordance with the alien energy of its origin.

Albelenda looked at the time piece. It had struck midnight, and so she raised her wand to the sky and made the bull appear in the sky. This was followed by the witches riding their brooms, and ascending to the clouds above each location of the village, and aiming their wands down towards the village. Loud thunderous sounds were heard like cannon fire and beams of light as their wands omitted bolts of lightning onto buildings knocking off tiles and burning thatch cottages and barns. It sounded like bonfire night with bangs, and the whoosh of the witches swooping down on a defenseless village. Some likened it to the blitz from the Second World War as the German planes bombed English cities or vise versa. No one was safe from the evil dark witches' vicious attack as they struggled to understand why they were being targeted. Some trying to doubt the fires; others hiding away in fear of their lives.

"Those girls have caused this," one villager shouted.

"Where are they now?" another shouted.

"In the tavern," one shouted.

Shanice heard the commotion and raced to the window waking her friend up as she got up. They were startled and responded quickly following her to the window.

"This is it, girls," she said, getting dressed.

"Wait for us, Shan," Kayleigh said, putting on her clothes.

"I am scared," Jessica admitted. "They are here to kill us."

"You two, stay here. I must face them alone," Shanice said, grabbing her wand.

"No, Shan, we are coming," Kayleigh said bravely.

"I can't come," Jessica said shaking.

"Then die here alone, Jess" Kayleigh said angrily. "We owe it to Shan."

"In that case, you two can be a diversion for me, and head towards the graveyard. Take this mat. It has a pentagram on it for added protection, then stand on this," she said, offering them the mat. "Go now. Quickly!"

Her friends hugged her and left the room, while Shanice got herself prepared for battle. She sensed that Renilda and Rosalinda were close by and moved in on them first, striking them with lightning bolts. Fortunately, she was fast enough to disable them, and followed her friends making sure they were safe. Renilda had hit a yew tree and collapsed, while Rosalinda managed to reach the girls and attacked them. Kayleigh was wounded in the arm, and Jessica in the foot before they placed down the mat and stood on it safely. Shanice struck Rosalinda and immobilized her. Meanwhile, Nabara was sending lightning bolts down towards Shanice. She tried to fend her off but Nabara was too powerful, and so she fell down. Nabara struck her again with a fatal blow.

"Shan," Kayleigh shouted attempting to leave the mat, but she was pulled back by Jessica.

"No, Kay. Stay here where you are safe," Jessica had tears in her eyes.

"Shan, you can't die," Kayleigh shouted. "Please get up." At that moment, another bolt of lightning struck Nabara, and Rosa stood looking at her daughter's limp body. She then turned to attack Albelenda. The other witches fled leaving Rosa to comfort her daughter.

"She is dying, girls," she announced. "I need to get her to safety."

"But you can resurrect her, can't you?" Kayleigh asked. "I don't know," Rosa said.

"But you were resurrected. She told me and so was Annabella," Kayleigh said anxiously. "You must help her. Please!"

"Let us take her to the caves in Scotland," Rosa said, instructing Andrew to help lift her up.

They all headed into the mini bus. Andrew followed in the car with his uncle Graham and Linus. Kayleigh was holding Shanice and crying. Jessica sat nearby, also crying, being consoled by Rosa. The graduates Paula and John took it in turns driving through the Scottish glen with mountains all around them. It took hours to get to Inverness and longer to reach the cave area where the cave dwellers once lived. Once they had arrived, Rosa had prepared everyone for another attack of the dark witches showing them strategies to counteract any attacks by them. She instructed Andrew and Graham to carry Shanice into the cave.

RISE OF THE DARK WITCHES

The inside of the cave was a dark and dreary place; a vast place with pockets like small rooms, and a big pit where Rosa was once discovered by Professors Stokes and Svensson. She had been preserved in a powerful substance which had kept her body intact as it also worked on Eric centuries before. But she needed the secret formula that would help Shanice recover and prove the resurrection was possible. The figure of eight was marked on the cave wall along with other symbols. Andrew and Graham placed Shanice on a stone slab and stood back while Rosa searched around the cave for the formula. The only thing she found was evidence that the dark witches had risen, but what she wasn't aware of was that their siblings had also risen namely Mirabell, Flora, Darnetta, Bittora, Zabal, Grisel, and Ricolda. This left Albelenda's daughter who she named Lamia better known as Annabella.

The dark witches watched the activities of Rosa and company hoping to find out the secret of eight and the resurrection. Rosa needed her mother Annabella to be present, and so she summoned her presence by using spells from her Book of Shadows. This took some time to do, and so everybody else rested.

"It is so strange being back here, Rosa," Andrew said.

"Brings back memories," Graham said, looking around.

"What are we looking for, Rosa?" Kayleigh asked.

"A trunk or box of some description," Rosa said.

"We will look," Jessica offered. "Paula and John, please help us."

They looked around until Kayleigh finally shouted in excitement.

"I have found it," she said, beckoning Jessica to join her with the others.

"This is like the one in your attic, Rosa," Jessica said, opening it up.

"Wow! It has bottles and boxes in it," Kayleigh explained.

"Something brushed past me," Jessica said, jumping. "I felt cold, then."

"I felt it, too," Kayleigh admitted. "That was creepy." They had felt the spirits of the witches pass by as they wanted to see what was in the trunk. It appeared to be full of potions once used in the caves by white witches who lived in there and nearby cottages.

When the dark witches were busy causing havoc across Scotland and England, others had gone to Jamaica and other far-off places in an attempt to take over the earth, but their futile attempt proved that they were not as powerful as they claimed. They had powers and abilities but failed to know how to use them effectively, while the white witches mastered their art and used it purely for good. Also, the white witches survived by using their wits and genius in ways no one else could as if they had been guided by the origins of the energy that had driven them in order to survive.

"Bring the trunk here to me," Rosa instructed. "It might take you all to lift it."

"It's gone!" Kayleigh shouted.

"No, it hasn't. It's here," Rosa said smiling. "Mother, where are you?"

"Honestly, Rosa, you do make a hard job of a small task," Annabella said materializing in front of her.

"I forget about my magic as I never use it, mother," Rosa said, hugging her mother. "It's good to see you."

"You, too," she said, forming a circle around them all, and creating a pentagram. "All of you, stay within this circle, please," she said, adding in the details with her wand.

"Now, Rosa, help me with these potions, and prepare Shanice for her resurrection." Annabella instructed.

The dark witches attempted to enter the circle but were driven back by a wall of fire. They began cursing the white witches trying to use their wands but each spell bounced back at them with more velocity. The other witches tried to return but were driven back by a force field like a giant web across the cave entrance. Nabara's face appeared showing anger, while Albelenda was curious to know why Annabella, her own daughter was there, even though she still insisted on calling her Lamia, daughter of the devil. They could also make out Rosa and Shanice in the background using their powers but still not gaining entry to the cave.

Rosa lifted Shanice's head, and Annabella pored liquid into her mouth. She chanted as she did this, and then used a gel from the wall of the cave and rubbed it into her body, continuing to chant repeating certain words in Gaelic. Within half an hour, Shanice began to blink. She eventually opened her eyes focusing on the cave walls, and the first thing she saw was the figure eight in front of her. After which she saw her mother, and Annabella standing before her smiling. She was very weak but alive, and relieved to be so, as were everybody else around her. Everybody seemed happy all but the dark witches of course.

"Mother, what happened?" Shanice asked.

"You have been asleep," Rosa explained.

"You mean dead," Shanice said. "Trying to get up."

"Hey child, rest for a while," Annabella said.

"Your grandmother is right," Andrew said. "Just rest."

"We can't keep these dark witches away forever. Let's form a strategy to get away," Annabella said. "Think of what our ancestors would have done at this point."

It wasn't long before Albelenda broke the spell binding the entrance and came into the cave with the others. They headed towards the circle and stopped.

"A pentagram. Very affective," Albelenda said, flying around on her broomstick.

"Good protection, but you have to come out some time," Nabara said. "And when you do, I will kill you all."

"Lamia, you have always been a strange and ugly child." Albelenda remarked.

"Don't call me that. I am Annabella," she replied.

"I should have drowned you in the river at birth," Albelenda said with venom.

"Rather than to live with you and your horrible friends. The witch's coven that gives witches a bad name, full of wickedness and deceit. I hate all of you," Annabella said shaking her finger.

"Why don't you come out and fight me, Lamia?" Nabara shouted. "I will take you and Rosa on. That daughter of yours who is mother to that dead girl, Shanice."

Annabella stepped out of the circle at one side, and Rosa stepped out the other side. Nabara was surprised by their reaction and watched them as they both stood there. Suddenly, Albelenda raced forward in the air and swooped past them. She turned and watched Nabara do the same. Seconds later, Florina and Babeth moved forward and did the same. It was as if they were playing with the white witches flying around them, like they were taunting them. But then, one of them brought out their wand and made an attack on Annabella. She made a counter attack, and the battle commenced. Wands were waving and thunderbolts going in all directions. The first casualty was Babeth who hit the cave walls and came down with a crash, followed by Passara and Renilda.

Graham ran across the room with Andrew and poured a substance on the ground. It exploded and formed a net which captured Rosalinda and Jeliana. Kayleigh and Jessica did the same with the other dark witches leaving just Albelenda and Nabara to fight, or so they thought. While they were occupied with these two, Murdina appeared, the original cave dweller and leader of the dark witches. She surprised Rosa and send her to the ground with her lightning bolt. She was ready to finish her off when she was hit in the chest by a lightning bolt and went spinning to the ground.

"Mother, you should learn to duck," Shanice shouted. "Honestly, you must know about the element of surprise."

"I will try and remember this, Shan," Rosa said smiling. It was now a case of three against three as Murdina got to her feet. The battle continued with attacks in both directions, meanwhile the others were creating another trap this time for the rest of the dark witches. Albelenda was the first to be caught followed by Murdina, and finally Nabara, as she got struck by all three of the white witches. Their spirits were captured in the trunk after everyone had emptied the contents of it and packed it to take home. The trunk was secured with the pentagram mat and sealed with a magic spell.

"Good job, everyone," Annabella said.

"Teamwork," Rosa agreed.

"White witch magic, I think," Shanice said. "And I feel refreshed."

"Well, no doubt. We have seen the last of those witches," Rosa said confidently.

"For now, anyway," Annabella said. "I mean nothing is forever."

"I think we did well, though," Shanice boasted. "Good over

evil and all that."

"You have a lot to learn," Rosa said hugging her. "But you are like your grandmother, so you will do."

"She is a little like me, isn't she?" Annabella remarked. "Forceful and determined."

"I think it is time you went back, mother," Rosa said. "Before you two gang up on me."

Annabella said farewell and vanished while everyone else got into the vehicles and returned home.

It was six in the morning and just getting light. They were able to sit quietly and take in the scenery through the glen and mountain regions of Scotland. They hardly uttered a word until they returned home. They had that much excitement that they needed a rest, but Shanice wanted to see Arnold and arranged to meet him that evening. She never mentioned the witches or any of the strange things that occurred, and just enjoyed his company, but Arnold did wonder about Shanice and the odd powers that she seemed to possess. He did ask her some unusual questions about the figure eight and the resurrection, and was disappointed by her reply when she said she doesn't know. He expected her to know. He also enquired about Teversham and the Mayor William Mallet. It was as if he knew him personally. He was certainly well versed, and knew him better than William Mallet himself.

However, the strangest thing happened later that evening as Arnold was staying with Shanice. He looked in the mirror looking at his reflection and combing his hair, but what Shanice saw was not his reflection, but an older man that resembled the description Rosa gave her of Mayor William Malet.

FINDING SHANICE

It was in the years 1630 to 1645, when Scotland was hunting down people claiming that they were witches, and therefore enemies of the crown. England was in the middle of a civil war between the parliamentarians and the royalists. Most old ladies or poor defenseless women were hunted down and went on trial. Some were torture and executed as witches. There was an element of politics involved which continued through the sixteenth century. James the First was particularly keen on getting rid of such people. But at the present time, Charles the first was king and he was concerned about his crown. No one was really safe at this time. It was a dangerous age for most people.

It was late evening when the witch hunters were searching for witches in the highlands. A group of horsemen holding up flaming torches, and armed with swords and pistols, riding and keeping a look out for the witches who were running through the heather frightened for their lives. One such woman was dressed in dark clothes with long hair waving about in the wind, clinging hold of her cape desperately trying to reach the river ahead. One of the soldiers spotted her and alerted everyone else. The horses began to gallop towards her, she heard them turned around, and then ran for her life. When she reached the river, she brought out her wand and swirled it in a circular motion saying these words *'Sniomh or spin'*, and a blue circular light appeared, and then she said, *'Forgail am portal uine'* or open the time portal. The blue light glowed brightly and began to rotate. It appeared like a giant tunnel, so she jumped inside and vanished. The soldiers were astonished and stopped close by trying to fathom out what was happening. They had seen a real witch and not a crazy old hag. The woman spun and drifted down the tunnel until she reached the other side where she fell to the ground.

"Tighim air tir garsh arthist," she said dusting herself off, meaning another rough landing.

"There must be a better way to travel through time," or in her tongue it sounded like, 'Feumaidh doigh nas thearr a bhith ann airson suibhal tro thim.'"

At that moment, she was faced by Rosa who was standing in front of her.

"Tha bearla agad?" Rosa asked her.

"Yes, of course. I only speak Gaelic in the early centuries."

"I see. Me, too," she looked at the woman with mistrust in her eyes.

"I am Natasha. I am a time witch," Natasha said introducing herself politely.

"A time witch? I have never heard of a time witch," she said frowning.

"Oh, yes. I have been travelling through time portals for many years. It's hazardous. I risk my life travelling through the time portals but it can be fun," she said, continuing to dust herself off.

"My name is Rosa. I am from generations of witches," she explained.

"I have met a few real witches and some wizards," Natasha said, looking around the room. "Nice place."

"Thank you."

"I must apologise for my entrance but I have little control where the time portals appear," Natasha felt awkward entering Rosa's home in such a manner.

"It is a bit odd and quite invasive," Rosa admitted.

At that moment the door opened, and Shanice walked in. She threw her coat down and school bag, and walked straight past her mother and Natasha just saying 'Hello, mother', followed by 'I am starving.' She headed into the kitchen, opened the cupboard and took out a packet of crisps.

"Shanice, you may want to meet this lady," Rosa shouted.

"Oh, why?" Shanice said curiously.

"Natasha is a time travelling white witch," Rosa explained.

"Is there actually such thing as time travel?" Shanice asked skeptically.

"Is there actually such thing as time travel?" Shanice asked skeptically.

"What on earth is that?" Shanice looked at Natasha oddly.

"It is a kind of tunnel through space that allows me to travel to and fro across the universe, and visiting various locations in history like aspects of 17th Century Scotland or Alba or Egypt during the reign of Cleopatra."

"Can you go back to the cave dwellers of Inverness?"

"Yes, it's possible," she said smiling. "Do you know about such people?"

"Yes, my ancestors lived in the caves," Shanice said proudly.

"So, did mine," Natasha said excitedly.

"I would love to meet them," Shanice said. "My mother taught me Gaelic."

"A bheil thu a bruidhinn gaelic?" Natasha asked if Shanice spoke gaelic.

"Tha mi a bruidhinn gaelic," Shanice replied. "Yes, I speak Gaelic."

"Have you got somewhere to stay?" Rosa asked.

"No, I made no plans," she replied. "I never do."

"You are welcome to stay," Rosa said

"Thank you. I will if it is okay, and catch up with family history," Natasha agreed.

"Of course," Rosa agreed.

Natasha stayed for a few nights. Shanice was fascinated with her. She was taught how to use her skills in many ways. One night, Shanice took Natasha to the park near the house. She led her to a group of trees and Natasha explained about controlling her powers in order to make them work effectively.

"Take out your wand, Shanice," she instructed.

Shanice produced her wand and watched Natasha as she used hers.

"You must concentrate. Think of someone you hate and use your mind to defeat them."

She pointed her wand towards a tree and spoke one word 'Obliterate!' A bolt of lightning appeared from the wand and one of the branches were blasted off.

"Now, you try it," she said.

Shanice aimed the wand and shouted the words but alas, nothing happened.

"Shanice, you must concentrate and try again," she said tutting.

"I was concentrating," Shanice replied, annoyed with herself.

"Try again and again until you get it right, because one day, it will save your life," Natasha explained.

Shanice took ten attempts before she made herself that mad and thought about the school bully Sharon and Murdina, letting out

out a shout *'obliterate!'* The power from her wand managed to destroy the entire tree leaving just the roots. At that point, Rosa came out the house hearing the bang from her kitchen.

"What was that?" she asked.

"Sorry, Rosa. I thought I saw a goblin in the tree and tried to get it," Natasha said.

Later that night, Shanice sat admiring Natasha's bracelet as the emeralds shone in the light.

"Can I look at your bracelet" she asked.

"Yes, of course. It was a gift from the wizards. When it glows, it is their way of contacting me and inviting me over to their homes. They are very hospitable and take good care of me. I have known them for years."

"Do you visit them often?" Rosa asked.

"Whenever I can, when I am not time travelling," she replied.

Shanice put the bracelet on her wrist and wore Natasha's cape. She paraded round.

"I would like to time travel and see places in history like the Egyptians."

"It is fun at times, but also dangerous," Natasha admitted.

"What are the names of the wizards?"

"Merek is the eldest, and then Saden, Arthalos, and finally, the youngest is Doran," she said, trying to visualise them. "All have beard except Doran who is much younger and the politest. Merek can be mean and grumpy."

"It all sounds very nice. I would love to meet them," Shanice said, watching her mother's reaction.

"Ignore Shanice. She is merely curious and mischievous at times," Rosa said jokingly.

"Can I keep these just for tonight, Natasha?" Shanice asked. "I will give them back tomorrow."

"Yes, that's okay." Natasha agreed.

Natasha stayed for the week, and all this time, Shanice kept her belongings. Rosa got to know Natasha and shared stories of how she came to live in the twentieth century. Natasha also shared stories but neglected to tell Rosa that she had purposely come to find Shanice, and learn about the ancient witches of Scotland.

After the week was up, Shanice had related her story to Natasha discussing the story of how the dark witches pursued her. After this Shanice was getting tired.

Natasha had described the time portal as being like a toilet. It flushes you down a tunnel and out the other side at speed or like a vacuum cleaner, sucking you up and depositing you into a bag. The journey is hazardous, and people have been trapped inside of it; some have died. Temperal displacement can occur. This can be the major cause of concern in such journeys such as losing things in time or even becoming ill due to the pressure that you can be under within the tunnel. It is a cosmic vacuum experience. This is why some time travellers travel in a vessel which protects them from harm forming a protective shield around you. Shanice seemed fascinated by what she had said, but she was getting tired and could hardly stay awake listening to her.

Shanice said goodnight and went upstairs to bed. When she got to her room, she contacted Kayleigh and Jessica telling them all about Natasha and time witches, fascinated with the stories she had heard.

"It sounds good, Shan," Jessica said. "But a bit dangerous. What about temporal displacement that is said to be harmful?"

"Yes, it can be if you are caught in the time loop or misdirected into another dimension."

"I have heard it said that people have lost something in a time zone or become sick," Kayleigh warned her.

"That is merely conjecture and an unfounded theory," Shanice said, convincing herself.

"So is time travel," Jessica said. "I wouldn't try it."

"You're just a scared cat, Jess," Kayleigh said laughing.

"So, you would try it Kay?" Jessica said.

"I didn't say that," Kayleigh said sharply.

"I would," Shanice admitted. "Time travel going back in history sounds fun."

After an hour's conversation, Shanice stopped talking and switched off her computer. They had been face timing. Shanice had shown them the cape and bracelet before switching off. She heard Natasha go to the spare room, and then lay on the bed thinking. She drifted off to sleep and was awoken by the vibration of the bracelet and bright light. By this time, it was the early hours of morning. She rose to her feet and shouted out to Natasha, but Natasha was fast asleep. Suddenly, a blue circle lit up the room at first. Shanice was apprehensive, and then she entered the ring and vanished.

The next morning, Natasha knocked on her door. She waited for a reply but there was no answer, so she knocked again. Rosa came out of her room.

"She is a heavy sleeper," Rosa said.

"She must be," Natasha replied.

Rosa opened the door and crept inside. She looked around the room and then checked the bed.

"She has gone," Rosa said.

"She has left a message on her desk," Natasha said.

"Gone to seek the wizards. I will be straight back," Rosa read the letter aloud.

"It's my fault she has gone," Natasha said. "I should never have mentioned the wizards."

"No, this is typical of Shanice. She does things without thinking. She is so impulsive and curious about everything," Rosa said. "I hope she is okay."

"Don't worry, the wizards will take care of her. They are good and wise, and they will think it is me going there," Natasha felt confident that Shanice would be safe.

"I will travel through the time portal after her."

Natasha was travelling through the time portal hoping to arrive on Zena. She fell to the ground and grumbled as usual in Gaelic as she landed. This time she was greeted by a hostile woman who was holding up a wand and chanting spells at her. Suddenly, a bolt of lightning narrowly missed her, and so she returned the attack with a bolt of lightning from her wand. The pair were engaged in battle for a while until they were interrupted by an old man.

"Stop!" he shouted loudly.

Both parties stopped and just pointed their wands at each other.

"Now, let's find out what is going on," he said.

"I am Natasha, a time witch who is seeking Shanice."

"Well, did you have to come intruding in this way?" the woman said.

"For your information, blondie, I was misdirected by the time portal," Natasha said. "I was supposed to be going to the wizards of Zena."

"What a crude way to travel. Time portal," she said mocking her.

"I suppose you know a better way?" Natasha said with her hands on her hips.

"Yes, I am Crystal, a time traveler with my own time machine," Crystal said. "This is my father who is the inventor of the time craft."

"I am Zenith, Crystal's father. I am a sorcerer and scientist," he shook hands with Natasha. "I no longer travel in time. I leave that to Crystal."

"Your friend Shanice is in danger. The wizard Merek killed his brothers and my sister, and is planning to invade other planets. He wants to rule the universe. He is suffering from a personality disorder," Crystal said.

"He must be stopped, but his magic is strong and he has an army behind him of fierce fighting creatures known as the Gizalians."

"They were evil creatures, green and slimey, and enemies of the wizards," Natasha said with anguish. "So, Merek has Dissociative Identity Disorder or D.I.D. It used to be known as multiple personality disorder."

"Yes, he has many personalities; some good but mainly bad," Crystal explained.

"He is evil, and so are his army of green slimey creatures," Zenith said. "A force to be reckoned with."

"But I must save Shanice," Natasha said anxiously. "She will die."

"The portal was blocked deliberately to stop people entering Zena."

"The wizards were expecting me to be there," Natasha said, watching Crystal and her father's reaction.

"Yes, to destroy you," Crystal said, her father nodded in agreement.

"I don't know what to do," Natasha said in despair.

"I can help," Crystal said. "Come and join me in my time craft."

"You will be safer in that," Zenith said.

She entered the craft going into the front of the ship where the cockpit was. Two chairs were at the front where the pilot and copilot sat, then two seats behind, and two seats on either side with many instruments including a computer and navigational equipment.

Sat at the computer was an android called Foster, who looked very human right down to his synthetic skin and artificial hair.

"This is Foster, my android scientist and translator of many languages," Crystal explained.

"Hello, how are you?" he asked.

"I am fine," she replied.

"Foster, plot a course from here, Aspera to Zena, and make sure we are cloaked."

"Very well, madam," Foster replied. "Cloaked and hidden from view."

Shanice was travelling through the time portal when she suddenly landed on a hard floor in the middle of a large room decorated in many colours. Before she had fully recovered, her hands were bound with some kind of handcuffs and she felt ill. She looked around the room and noticed a number of creatures surrounding her. They had green skin and wore armour. She tried to exercise her powers but felt weak, and unable to move properly.

"What has happened to me?" she cried.

A man appeared dressed in a dark blue robe. He had a long black beard and began looking her up and down.

"You are not Natasha," he looked at the bracelet. "But you are wearing her bracelet. Who are you? Speak girl!"

"I am Shanice," she replied.

"Are you a time witch?" he asked.

"No, I am from the twenty first century."

"Where is Natasha?" he asked.

"She is at my home. I wanted to come and see the wizards of Zena," Natasha explained.

"I am Merek, one of the wizards," he said. "My brothers are here too."

"I was told of your kindness and hospitality," she replied.

"My kindness? Child, you have been misinformed," Merek said laughing wickedly.

"Why be so cruel, Merek?" came a voice.

"Silence, Saden! You fool!" Merek shouted.

"She is so young," came another voice.

"Arthalos, you are too soft. Be gone," Merek commanded.

Shanice could see faint images in the background. These could have been his brothers, she thought.

"Take her to a cell, and I will deal with her later," he ordered.

"Wait! Did you say a cell? Am I a prisoner?" she asked.

"You are to be kept alive until Natasha arrives, then I will dispose of you both."

"She will be coming through the time portal soon," she said.

"I have diverted it, so she will have to come by alternate means," he said with a cunning grin. "I am in control of everything now, and this universe will soon be mine."

"So much for kindness and hospitality," Shanice said angrily.

"Take her away," Merek ordered his guards to escort her to the cells.

Shanice sat in her cell realizing that she had made a mistake by going through the time portal. She could almost hear her mother saying I told you so. She was warned so often not to be drawn by curiosity. There was an old saying that curiosity killed the cat. Now, she was facing a death sentence for her stupidity.

The hours passed and the hours went into days. She was being fed by the guards who explained to her that the cell would suppress her powers, and that she would remain weak. Shanice was helpless and confused.

One morning, she was visited by a goblin called Shimick. He

had brought her food and tried to talk to her. Shimick was short with a green body and outfit to match. He let the guards search him, and then entered the cell through an automatic door.

"Good morning. I am Shimick. I have brought your breakfast," he said in a strange voice.

"Go away, you little freak," she shouted at him.

"But I am only being friendly," he replied.

"Friendly like that wizard. I don't need friends like you," she played with the food with a spoon. "What is this slop? Is it poisonous?"

"No. Look, I will taste it," he said taking the spoon from her and tasting the food.

He pretended to collapse on the floor and groaned in pain. Then, he laughed and got up. "See? It is okay."

"You're funny," she said smiling.

"I know. That's me! I do like to entertain," he said chuckling.

"But why am I here? I have done no wrong," she insisted.

"The wizard wants Natasha and anyone else who may stop him from getting what he wants. He is a powerful wizard who is watching us right now."

She looked up and noticed a camera. She suddenly went into a rage and pointed to the camera.

"You are insane. You won't beat the white witches with your evil sorcery," she threw the dish at the camera, and all the contents dripped down the wall.

"It is futile trying to antagonize the wizard. He will win," Shimick said. "Just eat the rest of your food, and I will visit again."

Shanice began to cry, sitting on a bench with her hands covering her face, while Shimick patted on the arm and left the cell.

"You will come back, won't you?" she asked him.

"Yes, of course," he replied.

"I am sorry I said those things to you," she said, wiping the tears from her eyes.

"See you soon," he replied and smiled.

Shimick was true to his word and visited her three times each day. Sometimes, he brought games for them to play and they became very close. In fact, Shanice looked forward to seeing him, and felt alive when he was present.

THE WIZARDS OF ZENA

It had taken nearly a week for the time craft to reach Zena from Aspera. They landed in a dessert near the mountains where the modern castle of the wizards existed. It was time to plan Shanice's rescue. Natasha explained that she was going to see Merek, while Crystal and Foster searched for Shanice.

Natasha knew the layout of the castle and explained where the cells were, so that they could act fast. She also planned to diversion that would allow all of them to escape. Natasha entered the building through the main door while the others found an alternate method of entry. They went in undetected and managed to confuse the guards by using magic. Crystal used a spell that created optical illusions and the guards were spell bound, while Crystal and Foster took an uninterrupted trip down to the cells. It was there that they found Shimick heading towards the cell, so they stopped him. Crystal held her wand at his throat.

"Right, Goblin. If you want to live tell me where Shanice is," she said sharply.

"Happily," he replied. "Are you a time witch?"

"What of it?" she said suspiciously. "Who are you?"

"I am Shimick. I am Shanice's friend," he replied nervously. "Well, we will see. Lead the way, Shimick," she insisted. They arrived at the cell, and Crystal put the guards to sleep with a spell. She then used to access key to operate the door.

"Do not enter. The cell will take away your powers," Shimick advised.

"It is true," Shanice said. "I have lost mine." Shanice stepped out of the cell with help from Shimick. She looked at Crystal and smiled, "Are you a time witch?"

"Yes, and Natasha is here with Merek," she said.

"But he is going to kill her," Shanice said concerned.

"We are aware of his evil, and we have our own plans of escape."

Merek was entertaining Natasha pretending to be friendly and using holograms of the other wizards to convince her that all was well as he did with Shanice thinking she was Natasha. He even arranged a banquet keeping his guards at bay. His plan was to poison her, and let her die an agonizing death as he had done to all previous associates of the wizards. It may have worked if Natasha had not been warned by Crystal and her father. He had laced the wine with great subtlety using a drug, and then put more poison in the dessert to ensure that she died.

Natasha changed the goblin that had the poison in and

pretended to feel faint. He served the dessert and watched her start to slur her speech. She appeared to be eating her dessert but started to flop down. Merek gave an evil grin, and called the guards to the room. They carried her body out of the room and outside laying her on a slab. A group of starving birds swooped over her. They were large birds of prey hoping for a feast from her limp body lying on the concrete surface.

Once the guards left her, Crystal and friends were waiting to take her away to safety. Crystal sent the birds away by waving her wand and sending a bolt of lightning in their direction scattering them. They all headed towards the space craft before the wizard could follow them and destroy all of them. Shimick was with them as Shanice insisted on taking him along. He was now a friend of theirs and a valued member of the crew.

Once in the ship, they soon left the planet and had to plan a new course, but where would they go? Back home to the twentieth century for Shanice or another direction?

"Crystal, did everything go well?" Natasha asked.

"Yes, but we have another member of our crew, Shimick," Crystal said.

"He is my friend," Shanice said. "He took care of me when I lost my powers."

"Not good. I mean losing your powers," Natasha said.

"Can she regain them?" Shimick asked.

"Maybe," Natasha said. "Maybe if we go back to the origin of the witches, where it all began. Back in Scotland, with the cave dwellers."

"Back in time?" Shanice said excitedly.

"Yes, there is a chance that you could regain your powers from the meteors that landed in Scotland all those centuries ago," Natasha said confidently.

"I agree," Crystal said. "Let's set a course for that time."

IN THE BEGINNING

The time travellers landed in the sea just off the coast of Inverness, Scotland, back where the witches experienced the meteor storm and gained their powers. They all seemed relaxed after the long journey through time and space. The trip was calm and pleasant on this occasion.

Foster gave the crew a brief history lesson about where the witches were said to have got their powers. He began in space discussing the galaxy and how the super nova began.

"A super nova is described as a transient astronomical event, which occurs in the last evolutionary stages of a massive star, a progenitor collapses to a neutron star or black hole, or it is completely destroyed. So, the energy stems from the nuclear fusion and explosion. Fragments travel in many directions as meteors. Some of the energy is still present propelling these rocks travelling at great speed through the galaxy. Some of these meteors rained upon the Earth, falling on Scotland. The energy gives off gamma radiation which the cave dwellers were exposed to this would normally be dangerous, but it was said to have altered the DNA in the people and caused them to obtain their great powers. And then, as you well know, the tribe split and they called themselves witches. The white witches used their powers for good, but the dark witches used their powers for evil, by killing and destroying those who opposed them." Foster provided a detailed account with a simulated demonstration of each event on the monitor, with three-dimensional graphics. It was so effective it made the viewers jump in places such as when the explosions occurred.

"Well, here we are at the beginning of the witches' rise to power."

"So, what happens now?" Shanice asked.

"We join the festival of Samhain with the cave dwellers," Natasha explained.

"We can expect the fun to take place this evening," Crystal said.

"This is where they gained their powers from space after a meteor storm," Natasha continued. "It must have been a spectacular event and we have the chance to see it tonight".

"Foster, you need to stay here with Shimick. Make sure all is well for a fast take off later before the battle of the dark and white witches," Crystal said. "That is what is going to happen, isn't it Shanice?"

"Yes, I am afraid it is. The dark witches will win and kill most of the white witches," Shanice replied.

"So, we need to make a fast exit before being caught up in this war," Natasha said concerned.

"We need to blend in with these cave dwellers. I have costumes in the dressing room. Come with me," Crystal said, leading them through a door.

Each of them tried on costumes. It took a while to find suitable clothes from the masses of costumes that Crystal had collected over the years. She was well prepared for various ages of time; from the ancient Egyptian times, medieval times, and back to the Celtic ages. Foster had researched through computer data on the authenticity of each costume for accuracy. Not a thing was out of place.

They had to get used to not wearing make up and appearing quite dull compared to their modern dress. Shimick seemed concerned about them especially Shanice who he had befriended.

"Be careful all of you, and look after Shanice," he said. "I wish I could come but I would stand out in that place being a Goblin."

"Shimick, I must go in order to restore my powers, but I will miss you," Shanice said, kissing him on the forehead. Natasha and Crystal did the same, and Shimick began to blush. He turned his little face away as he started to get upset.

The three women left the craft through the hatch when they went outside. They swam a little way to the shore. They walked through the rocks and looked up at the cliffs above. They travelled down the beach a short while until they reached a pathway up the side of the cliff. Gradually, they walked up looking back noticing that the ship was no longer visible; it was camouflaged. This was in order to protect the ship and its secrets from view. It blended into the scenery; in this case, the sea with a cloaking device controlled by the ship's computer. This was a great advantage for Crystal as she travelled through all kinds of worlds. The travellers continued across the rough terrain until they reached the caves where the cave dwellers lived. People were everywhere in large groups. The three blended in nicely with the crowd. They felt free to wander around, but Natasha advised Crystal not to speak as these people spoke Gaelic. Only Natasha and Shanice knew the language, and they could interpret it to Crystal. But she needed to act dumb in order to be safe. Crystal agreed but found it awkward not speaking, but she felt it was wise to act dumb in order not to endanger the mission. They just needed to remain in the area until the meteor storm had occurred, , and then to escape before the battle began between the dark and white witches. They looked around and noticed the tall rocks at the edge of the cliff which were arranged in a large circle with a flat slab in the centre. It looked quite impressive in the day light. It must have looked even more so at night with under the moonlight. Shanice recognised Murdina from her encounter in the twenty first century. Here she was before she gained her powers and become a powerful dark witch.

"That's her, Natasha," Shanice said. "Murdina, the evil witch," Shanice was speaking in Gaelic.

"Really?" Natasha replied in Gaelic. "The leader of the dark witches. We need to watch her."

Natasha listened to a conversation between Murdina and her friend Fenella. She had used her powers to pick up every word even though she was a short distance away, and in order not to be detected, transformed herself into a bird.

"Fenella, you must remain silent until the right time. I will tell you when," Murdina said.

"But Murdina, why do we need to sacrifice a human? Why not an animal?" Fenella asked.

"Because human flesh would plcase the gods," Murdina explained. "Gabbran may be the chieftain, but he fails to understand the importance of human sacrifices and pleasing the gods. He is weak as a leader. He needs to be ruthless and in control of these people."

"I agree. You are right, Murdina," Fenella agreed. Natasha transformed herself back and led the other two into a cave. Shanice recognised the cave from her journey. There in the twenty first century when she battled with the spirits of the witches.

"This looks familiar," Shanice said. "Recognise this cave. I never thought I would see it again."

"Crystal, you can speak freely. We are alone," Natasha said in English.

"Of course. I am sorry, Crystal. It must be hard for you,"

Shanice said.

"I was beginning to think I had lost my voice forever," Crystal said.

"Murdina is the evil witch who eventually leads the dark witches. She is already rebellious. Gabbran is the chieftain with Barra, his friend, and his wife Alana. They make sacrifices of animals on this festival of Samhain," Natasha explained.

"But Murdina wants to sacrifice a human instead," Shanice said.

"So, there may be conflict before the battle if Murdina has her way. She is powerful even now, and tries to take charge of a small group of women." Natasha said concerned.

"Can't you stop her, Natasha? You have powers, and so do you Crystal. You can stop this," Shanice said anxiously.

"No, Shanice. We cannot meddle with time. We are merely observers," Crystal said. "We are here to get your powers back. That is all."

"Crystal is right. We cannot mess with time," Natasha agreed. "Once your powers are restored, we are going; ever to return."

That evening Murdina was restless. She had gathered her followers together, and plotting to take over the tribe. Fenella encouraged her to rebel by discussing Gabbran, and how he was a weak leader. The time travellers listened intently, all but Crystal, who had to rely on Natasha translating the language to her. It was difficult as they were now in the crowd and could be easily heard. They walked further towards the altar, so that they could get a better view.

Burning torches were placed strategically around for lighting as it was getting dark. The moon appeared. It was full and bright silhouetting the large stones around them. As the three-time travellers pushed through, the crowd Crystal felt someone grab her arm and pull her along; it was Murdina as she resisted another woman stepped forward, it was Fenella.

"She will do," Murdina said, tying her wrists with a rope.

"Perfect," Fenella agreed.

Shanice noticed Crystal missing, and alerted Natasha discreetly.

Crystal was reluctant to use her powers at this point in case she exposed herself or her friends. She decided not to struggle, but to allow Murdina to take her to the altar. Murdina lay her on a long slab type rock, and then pulled a knife from her clothes. The knife was long and very sharp. She slit a lamb's throat demonstrating how sharp it was. The lamb fell to the ground and bled to death.

Murdina chanted and looked up to the moonlit sky, and then she held the knife to Crystal's throat.

Shanice screamed, "Stop her! Somebody," but spoke in English. Realizing, she repeated herself in Gaelic, "Cuir stad oirre."

At that moment another voice was heard shouting above Shanice. It was Gabbran who was very angry with Murdina.

"Stop this at once," he shouted. "Let her go," he insisted. Everyone was silent Murdina helped her from the stone and Barra took the knife from Murdina and cut the ropes. Crystal was about to move forward towards Gabbran when Murdina pulled her back.

"Why are you doing this? You will anger the gods," Murdina shouted.

Sprays of saliva hit Gabbran in the face. He wiped it away and walked forward towards her. She stepped back and pushed Crystal further back. At this point, she was on the edge of the cliff. The soft soil gave way beneath her, and she fell down towards the rocks. It was dark, and so they could only hear her scream as she fell. This was followed by a strange light.

"Crystal," Shanice shouted. "O mo chreach," or *oh my god* in English. She buried her head into Natasha's shoulder and wept.

"I have my human sacrifice now," Murdina shouted with joy.

Shanice slapped her on the cheek, and went to scratch her face, but Natasha pulled her away. She began resisting, hitting Natasha.

"Stop, Shanice. Look at the sky," Natasha said, alarmed; meteors were falling from the sky.

"The gods are angry with us," Gabbran shouted. "They send fire from Heaven."

The meteor storm had begun. The whole sky was lit up and hundreds of meteors were heading in their direction.

"Run for cover," Gabbran shouted. "Run for your lives." "Head for the caves," Barra shouted.

Everybody ran and some fell to the ground. There was shouting and screaming; some fighting to get into the caves. Some were killed instantly by the falling rocks, some were set ablaze, and some panicked. The whole situation was horrific. Men, women, and children were either injured or killed by this storm. Murdina was beginning to regret her actions, believing that the gods were angry with her.

Eventually Natasha and Shanice had found cover in a smaller cave. They knew this was going to happen, but to witness the event first-hand was spectacular and very frightening. However, the events to follow were much worse as the cave dwellers that had survived began to discover their new found abilities and powers. Natasha and Shanice needed to stay long enough for Shanice to restore her powers. It took days to restore them completely.

By this time, Murdina had become powerful and had formed her army of dark witches. They were seen to fly on broomsticks at night. They produced magic spells, and began to document their finds on parchment. They used divination and created wands firing lightning bolts in every direction. Some levitated and some transformed themselves into other creatures.

Gabbran led his existing followers away from the caves, calling themselves white witches. This was the start of the witch wars; more was to follow, much more.

As Murdina grew stronger, her army were fearless and cruel. She wanted to conquer the world with her army, while Gabbran only wanted to use his powers for good. Shanice was showing progress as she transformed herself into a grey cat. She levitated a few times, and used her wand to send a lightning bolt across the cave.

"Time for us to go, I think," Natasha said. "You have your powers back."

They slipped out at night, so they would not be seen. They followed the same path back to the beach. Shanice noticed the rocks where Crystal had fallen to her death. She stopped and stared at them. Natasha stood silent, knowing what Shanice was thinking. Shanice looked at her with wild eyes.

"We could have saved her," she shouted. "You could have saved her."

"No, we couldn't," Natasha replied. "We would have exposed ourselves."

"Yes, we could," Shanice said, feeling the rain coming down. "You had the power to save her."

"I told you, Shanice, it wasn't possible," Natasha replied wiping the rain from her face.

"You let her die, and stopped me from killing Murdina," Shanice continued.

"Crystal had the power to save herself," Natasha explained. "I would have done."

"Oh ,yeah? That was possible?" Shanice said sarcastically. "We have to go, Shanice. The dark witches will find us," she said.

"Well, I won't count on you rescuing me," Shanice shouted angrily.

"That's not fair. I have looked out for you," Natasha shouted back.

"You are just like Murdina; crafty, selfish and cruel, and I hate you!" Shanice said bitterly.

At that moment, two dark witches swooped over them on broomsticks. Both Natasha and Shanice jumped back. They watched as they came back. One of them was Fenella. She headed straight towards Shanice, knocking her to the ground. Natasha drew her wand from her cape, and aimed it towards her. She fired a thunderbolt but missed. The other witch approached heading towards Natasha, but she was ready to defend herself and fired another thunderbolt this time knocking her to the ground. Fenella disappeared for a while giving Natasha and Shanice time to run towards the rocks, but Fenella soon returned with two more witches, and attacked them once again. Shanice remembered what her mother Rosa had taught her about combat, and fought for her life. Natasha stood nearby and battled with the dark witches. After a while, the dark witches were defeated but Shanice was injured during the attack. Natasha struck Fenella and she fell to the ground next to the others.

Natasha ran to Shanice and helped her get towards the ship which had appeared in front of them. Shanice was helped into the hatch by Shimick, and Natasha followed. Once inside, Shanice looked shocked as Crystal was standing in front of her. She ran towards her and hugged her.

"Crystal, but how did you survive?" she asked.

"Just like magic," Crystal said. "I slowed down my fall with a spell, and directed myself onto the beach where I made a flash of light with my wand to signal the ship."

"I saw a light," she said excitedly. "That was you?"

"Yes, it was also a way of signalling Natasha to tell her I was safe," Crystal explained. "She told you that shortly."

"No, but I have been an absolute bitch to Natasha," she turned and looked at Natasha with puppy eyes, "Sorry, Nat."

"Forget it," Natasha said. shrugging her shoulders. "Worse

happen at sea."

"We must get you home, Shanice. Your mother will be worried," Crystal said. "Foster, set course for England in the twenty first century."

"Very well. Course is set," Foster said confidently. "Let us sort out your wound, Shanice," Natasha said, taking her to the medical quarters to examine the wounds.

"Superficial burns, Shanice. You're lucky it wasn't worse," Crystal said.

"Can you fix it?" Shanice asked concerned.

"Yes, of course," Natasha said. "Well, we are witches."

"Let's go then, girls," Shanice said.

THE WITCH TRIALS OF NORTH BERWICK

In 1590, King James of Scotland, who was also King James the 1st of England, had returned from Copenhagen with his new wife Anne. He had crossed the channel through rough seas and storms arriving in Scotland in time for the witch trials at North Berwick.

North Berwick was once a quiet fishing village on the east coast of Scotland, not far from Edinburgh. Men and women were brought to Berwick from various parts of Scotland by witch hunters in order to stand trial, and to be either burnt or hung for witchcraft. This put the entire country under fear of condemnation or the fear of witches themselves. King James ensured that this took place especially after his ordeal on the ship as he blamed that on witchcraft. They created the storms of the sea and death of cattle. He went on to blame them for still born babies and other catastrophes. He meddled in the occult, but feared witches. His fear was shared by many people, and spread across England and Europe.

The time travellers took another portal in space, and hit a lot of fragments and waste on their journey. It was as if they had been purposely attacked by something strange, or someone was planning their demise. They made an exit out of the time portal, into a storm by the North Sea. They landed inland for safety hoping to be discreet, so that the people of the time wouldn't notice them. The cloaking devise was quite effective as it sheltered them making the craft appear invisible.

"This is the 16th century. We must be aware that during this time, the witch hunters were busy searching for poor souls to torture, put on trial, and execute them for witchcraft," Foster explained.

"So, we are not home then?" Shanice said, disappointed.

"Not exactly," Crystal said sadly.

"We have unfortunately missed the time zone for some reason, and arrived during the reign of James the first of England, who is also James the fifth of Scotland. He feared witches and ordered this big witch hunt across Scotland fearing for the lives of many," Foster explained.

"Do we really need to go?" Crystal asked.

"Yes, of course," Natasha said. "We need answers."

"It will be fun," Shanice said. "I am up for it."

"We need to understand why they did this, and see if it is connected to our ancestors," Natasha said eagerly.

"Very well. We need to be careful and no foolishness," Crystal said, looking at Shanice.

Shanice was aware that Crystal was referring to her, and gave a smug smile. "I suppose you mean me as the young reckless teenager?" she said.

"Well, if the cap fits, wear it," Natasha hastily replied.

"Foster and Shimick, stay here and guard the ship. We don't want to look suspicious, do we?" Crystal ordered.

"Be safe all," Shimick said, watching them leave.

They had dressed according to the age, covering up any marks on their skin and hiding tattoos. Each one checked each other for any mark that may be interpreted as a devil's mark like a scratch of a claw or hoof.

They walked through a quiet town in Berwick. The streets

seemed deserted. But in the distance, they could hear a crowd shouting. The travellers decided to follow the sound of the crowd which took them to the guildhall and local market place. The sight they saw would inevitably stay with them forever. The horror of the moment was people being hung; men and women swinging from ropes. These ropes were secured by scaffolding and the necks of the victims were broken, and they endured a slow agonising death. The crowds were excited by such things, and cheered as one more victim died. It was almost like a special occasion for them – a day at the hanging or execution. Some of these people were burnt at the stake with gunpowder tied to them to ensure they burnt quicker.

Shanice went very pale and seemed to be passing out. Crystal caught her in time, and they decided to find a hotel or inn. Fortunately, there was one close by, and so they settled there for the night. Shanice was in shock. She couldn't believe how cruel people could be. But Natalie and Crystal were not shocked as they had seen such things before. It was tough on Shanice but a valuable lesson in history regarding witchcraft and treating people badly.

The next, day Natasha ventured out on her own, leaving Crystal to care for Shanice. Natasha was eager to find out more about the way people were treated, picking up survival techniques. She was walking down a street when she saw a prison wagon with a young girl inside it. She had long dark matted hair and torn clothes. She was covered in mud and blood, held down with chains. Natasha stopped to speak with her expecting her to shout or scream due to madness, but she gazed at Natasha's hair blowing in the breeze and her pale but smooth complexion. Natasha was very attractive. Her large eyes sparked in the sunlight.

"Who are you?" she asked.

"I am a friend," Natasha replied.

"A friend of a witch?" she asked trying to touch her hair.

"Are you a witch?" Natasha asked. "Do you possess any powers?"

"Only to heal the sick and help people," she said smiling.

Suddenly, a guard rushed forward and pushed Natasha aside. He then prodded the girl with his pike.

"Be careful. She is a witch. She will turn you into a frog, or curse your children."

"I am careful, sir, and know when I am in danger," Natasha said addressing the soldier.

Natasha winked at the girl and walked away. She wanted to help her, but it was impossible at this time. Instead, she ventured on not realising that she was being watched by two soldiers as she moved on. They followed her.

Shanice was not feeling well which Natasha put down to time travel. She also felt ill after she saw people being hung and burnt to death. She found it difficult to understand such cruelty. It's probably a good thing that she never saw the horrific tortures that were taking place in order to make the people confess to being witches. Crystal stayed at the tavern with her while Natasha went to explore and try to find out whether some of the people actually were witches. She had been talking to a young girl who had just arrived in the town. She was bound by ropes and thrown inside a wooden cage on a cart. She appeared dirty and wild. She had all her teeth but her dark hair was long and matted. She was a pretty girl around eighteen, maybe younger. Soldiers stood nearby, laughing and joking. They're discussing how they managed to capture the so-called witches, including this one.

"I am Rebecca," she told Natasha. "Captured in the woods, near my home."

They were disturbed by the guards who pushed Natasha aside, and told her to go away in a very impolite manner. Natasha left the square and began walking back towards the tavern. It was at that point that she was abducted by two soldiers who took her to the dungeons.

Crystal could sense that something was wrong, while Shanice felt guilty for letting Crystal remain behind, and take care of her.

Natasha was not in the cell long before the prison guards took her to another room that smelt as equally disgusting as her cell. She noticed the blood on some of the instruments of torture. The guards held her down, and tied her to a board. She felt it was pointless struggling and remained calm, but the sweaty smell of the guards made her nauseous, and she began heaving. A man came in some sort of religious garment and spoke to her.

"Are you a witch?" he asked.

"Yes, I am," she replied casually

"You admit it? You confess to practicing witchcraft?" he said, surprised at her response.

"I have no secrets, and tell it as it is," Natasha said boldly.

"Even though you will die?" he said in a threatening manner.

"Yes, even that," she replied.

"Then, there is nothing to be said," he said dismissively. "Take her back to her cell. She can await trial."

The guards led her out of the room and back to the cell, securing her in chains and left the room.

Later that evening, the guards brought her food, or so they called it. It appeared to be a stew that hardly looked edible, and a battered spoon.

"Wonderful room service with the finest crockery and preparation," she said sarcastically.

"Enjoy witches," they said laughing.

She tasted it, spat it out, and then emptied it on the floor.

"Disgusting slop," she shouted. Even the water was undrinkable. "Remind me not to book you for my wedding," she shouted.

She sat for a while thinking. After all, what else could she do? She reflected on past experiences trying to find a way to escape, she had small pockets in her clothes where she kept small potions and ointments, another compartment had her wand. Time passed as she began to drift off to sleep.

The dungeon was dark. The only light was coming from the gaps between the bars on the door. Suddenly, the door opened, and the guards dragged a young girl covered in bruises and blood stains on her dress. It was Rebecca. She had been tortured, and could hardly move. Her legs dragged along across the filthy floor. The guards didn't even chain her up just left her lying on the cold floor. She was staring at Natasha trying to smile, but her dry lips just cracked as she did so.

"Rebecca!" Natasha shouted. "It's me, Natasha. Can you speak?"

"Yes," came a weak voice. "Natasha."

Natasha stood up but could hardly move due to the chains. She took out her wand and pointed it towards the chains, and a spark hit them strong enough to blast them off. She rushed over to Rebecca and hugged her, and then began stroking her hair.

"You precious, poor child. What have they done to you?" she said.

Rebecca tried to smile again, and then began to cry. Natasha caught her tears with her fingers, and held her head close to her chest. She was cradling her like she was her own child.

"I must help you," Natasha said. "So, you must trust me."

Rebecca looked puzzled at her. Uncertain of what she meant by trust.

"I am a witch. I mean a real witch with powers to heal, and to do many things; but I work for the good of mankind. Do you trust me?"

"Yes," she said hesitantly.

Natasha made a circle on the floor. She produced a bowl of water, did the same with a cup, and slowly poured the water from the cup into her mouth. She made a plate of bread appear with honey, and gave her a taste. Once she began eating, she prepared herbs and ointments for her wounds. She gave her a blanket and settled her down to sleep.

The next morning, Rebecca stood up and began walking about. Natasha awakes with Rebecca at her side. She appeared brighter and could speak better. Natasha set a fire in the centre of the dungeon, and made breakfast.

"Will we be executed?" Rebecca asked.

"No. I plan to get us out of here," Natasha replied.

"But how? They have hundreds of guards," she said curiously.

"Just like magic," Natasha replied smiling. "Remember, trust."

"How long have you been a witch?" she asked.

"Always. I was born a witch and it goes back generations," she explained. "Mother, grandmother, way back."

"So, you have many powers?" she asked.

"Many. I am also a time witch, so I travel back and forth in time and space helping others," she explained, "including you."

"I am honoured, Natasha," Rebecca said smiling.

At that point, the guards came in and tried to take Rebecca away. One guard attempted to grab her. Natasha picked up her wand and held it at his throat.

"Leave her alone," she commanded.

Both the guards laughed at her as if she were mad. The other guard tried to grab Natasha, and she shot a bolt of lightening from her wand sending him flying across the dungeon. The other guard drew his sword, and Natasha forced it out of his hand; it floated in mid-air. The other guard drew his sword, and Natasha sent the other sword towards him catching the flesh on his left leg. She pulled Rebecca out of the way, and then formed a circle of fire around them. It was enough to hold them back while they made their escape. But as they reached the doorway, two other guards appeared. Rebecca picked up a sword from the floor and charged at him.

"Stop!" Natasha shouted, holding her back.
The two guards transformed into Crystal and Shanice, and then back into guards.

"She is with me," Natasha said. "Rebecca, we need to disguise ourselves."

Crystal heard her and changing them into dogs, so they would not be recognised.

When they had dropped Rebecca off home, they programmed the computer to find their next destination – Earth 2021, in order to drop Shanice off.

After taking off, the ladies decided to discuss their experience with Foster and Shimick. Shimick liked hearing about the magic and transformations.

"So, you are able to transform yourselves into anything?

"Yes, birds, dogs, rabbits, and cats," Natasha said.

"Not cats," Shimick said. "I hate cats."

"Why, they are lovely, Shimick," Crystal said, agreeing with Natasha.

"Why don't you like them?" Shanice asked him.

At that moment Natasha transformed herself in to black cat. Crystal transformed herself into a white cat. They both approached Shimick and began rubbing their bodies against his legs.

"No, stop it," Shimick cried out.

Shanice transformed herself into a ginger cat. She rushed forward knocking Crystal out the way, and began licking his face.

"Now, why do you hate cats?"

"They have sharp teeth, furry bodies, and they smell horrid."

"Oh, Shimick, you must be loving this," Shanice said.

"No, go away, you flee infested creatures," Shimick shouted.

After a while Shimick's face began to develop lumps, and he began to sneeze uncontrollably. Evidently, he must have been allergic to cats. They all transformed back into humans, and Crystal went to search for a first aid pack. She returned with a syringe, and some kind of potion. Crystal prepared an injection of adrenalin, and Shanice rubbed the antihistamine cream on to his face. Before long, the sneezing stopped and his skin improved. He was soon cured, but remained grumpy. He was now sulking, trying to avoid the ladies.

"Aww, Shimick, please don't get upset. We are only teasing you," Shanice said.

"Yes, we all love you really," Crystal said.

"Even I sort of like you," Natasha said smiling.

When they had dropped Rebecca off, they programmed the computer to find their next destination: Earth 2021, in order to drop Shanice off. After taking off, the ladies decided to discuss their experience with Foster and Shimick.

Shimick liked hearing about the magic and transformations. Not long after Shimick's ordeal, Foster announced that they had arrived in the 21st century, but there was one small problem, they had arrived in America, just outside New York. Shanice was disappointed as she had set her heart on returning home to her friends, and was missing her boyfriend, Arnold. Of course, she also missed her parents, Rosa and Andrew, since she had been missing for some time now, venturing across time and space.

THE ADVENTURES OF THE TIME WITCHES:

THE VAMPIRES OF DELUS

The crew had landed just outside Manhattan in New York, convenient with the south region near the statue of liberty. Something had obviously gone wrong again as they had set their course for England. Not that New York wasn't a good place to visit, and it did give them opportunity to visit the sights. But Shanice was eager to return home and see everybody again. She wanted to discuss her adventures with friends and family. She also needed to return to studies.

The crew took it in turns sight seeing so that each one saw various places of interest, such as the empire state building, central park, and other attractions. Much caught the eyes of the crew as they ventured across Manhattan, but the girls were most intrigued with shops that sold suitable outfits like Bloomingdales. Each of them had communication devices on them in order to keep track of their locations, neither Foster nor Shimick were interested in clothes shopping, and explored toy shops and museums. Shanice was really in her element looking at items of clothes. She grabbed a pile of outfits, and headed for the changing rooms.

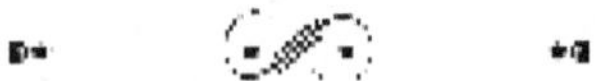

Meanwhile, far away from this place, in a bohemian type of castle, was a race of vampires led by a tall thin dark man called Thanatos. He spoke to the others around him.

"My children, I know you grow thirsty but I have to advise you that we have to travel through the time portals in our special suits through daylight in order to reap our harvest. We must risk our lives to gather up humans for their blood. Then, we can feast not before. You must bring me live humans from various locations in time, but if you find witches, bring them to me for they belong to another, and are poisonous to you. Orazio, you must lead the men. Delia, you must lead the women in the harvest. Now, go and come back with many," he instructed.

Tacito, a mute vampire, went through the time portal, and came out in the changing room behind Shanice. He covered her mouth. His helmet rose up, and his fangs appeared. He plunged them into her neck, and she instantly passed out. He picked her up having sucked blood from her neck and returned through the time portal.

On his return, he met Thanatos who was very angry with him. He put her limp body down on a bed, and looked at his master.

"What did I tell you?" he shouted. "You were only supposed to kidnap her and bring her back safely."

Tacito suddenly collapsed, and started to froth at the mouth. He was jerking about as if he was experiencing a seizure, and then, he remained still. His eyes were gazing up at the ceiling.

"She must be a witch," he said. "Put her in the cells with Siena.

She may be able to help her." The guards took her away to the cells.

Natasha and Crystal searched the changing rooms for Shanice unaware of what had happened. Foster and Shimick were asked to join them. They found blood on the floor and on one of the walls, and clothes everywhere.

"Look, a blood trail," Natasha said.

"She's been abducted. But how and why?" Crystal asked.

"A time portal," Foster said. "The blood trail comes to a stop at this wall. I am receiving reading from beyond this point."

"Can you program them into the computer on the ship?" Crystal asked.

"Yes, of course," Foster replied.

"I hope she is still alive," Shimick said sadly.

"I have found a location for Shanice, but you really won't like this," Foster said.

"What is it, Foster?" Crystal asked.

"Shanice has been abducted, and taken to Delus," Foster informed her.

"Where have I heard Delus before? Please remind me," she instructed.

"The planet of the vampires," Foster paused to gather information. "The master of the vampires is Thanatos. He is using time portals to kidnap humans from various locations of time and space, and then harvesting their blood to feed his vampires."

"So, are you saying that Shanice could have been killed for her blood?" Natasha asked.

"A witch's blood is poisonous to a vampire, so if they have bitten her, it will be fatal to them," Foster explained.

"Wait a minute. Don't they kind of shrivel up in daylight?" Natasha asked.

"Yes, apparently they disintegrate in daylight. However, they wear protective suits and a helmet with a type of tinted glass by day," Foster explained, showing them a suited vampire on the screen.

"I remember now, Foster. One of those creatures bit me and died," Crystal said holding her neck.

"That's correct, a few years ago," Foster recalled.

"So, is Shanice safe or not?" Shimick asked anxiously.

"Let is wait and find out when we reach Delus," Crystal replied.

Meanwhile on Delus, Shanice taken to the cell to join Siena. She seemed so weak and had to be carried there and placed on the bed.

"Take care of her, Siena," the one vampire said. "She is a witch, so don't get biting her," he paused. "Oh, sorry, you are no longer a vampire, are you?"

Siena remained silent. She went over to Shanice, and checked the puncture wounds on her neck. She touched them and thought for a moment.

"What are you doing?" Shanice asked. "Are you a vampire?"

"I used to be," she replied.

"Well, don't even think about biting me or you will die," Shanice warned her.

"Relax, I don't do that anymore," Siena said.

"I am cured."

"An ex-vampire? That's novel," Shanice replied. "Why am I so damn weak?"

"Loss of blood," she replied. "My name is Siena. I am a vampire slayer."

"I am Shanice, a time witch," she said trying to lift her head up.

"Well, Shanice, you're a prisoner at present," she said while helping her back down.

"My friends will rescue me soon enough," Shanice said confidently.

"Are they time witches?" she asked.

"Yes, Natasha and Crystal," she recalled. "And a robot called Foster, not forgetting the goblin called Shimick."

"A goblin? Those green creatures not to be trusted," she said disgustedly.

"Shimick is fine," she said defensively.

"They are horrible, spiteful, wicked, and untrustworthy creatures," she insisted.

"Well, my Shimick is kind, considerate, and trustworthy," Shanice said.

"Watch him. He may well betray you, Shanice," Siena warned her.

"He helped me escape from the wizard of Zena," she explained. "I am so glad we got away from him."

"Listen, Shanice," Siena said. "No one gets away from the Wizard."

"We did," she insisted.

"Merek is his name. He will be tracking you and find a way to get you," she said. "He was said to have killed his brothers and is seeking power of the universe."

"You know him?" Shanice said, concerned.

"I know of him," she replied. "And his evil ways."

Thana and Ballari were listening to the conversation with great interest these vampires were led by Delia.

"Come," said Thana. "Let's find the master."

"Wait! I want to know more about this witch," Ballari said.

"Siena was once my friend. Now, she is a vampire slayer."

"She was your friend? Thana asked.

"She was, when Count Vermont was my master. We used to hunt together," she said. "She used to choose her prey from the wickedest villains alive."

"It's a shame she isn't with us now," Thana said.

"Maybe I can convert her back, and she can lead us instead of Delia," Ballari said. "We could be powerful vampires if we can get that witch on our side," Thana said, looking at Shanice.

Thanatos stood in a quiet secluded part of the castle, staring at an empty wall. Suddenly, an image appeared. It was Merek from Zena.

"What news have you got for me?" he said with his powerful voice.

"I have one of your time witches called Shanice," Thanatos replied humbly.

"So, Natasha is not yet with you?" he asked, disappointed.

"She will come to rescue her, Merek," he replied appearing nervous.

"I have been tracking them since they left me," he said. "I want all of them, do you understand? Unharmed and well," he insisted.

"We are your servants and obey you. They will come to no harm," he said. "I promise".

Shanice was falling asleep and waking a various time of the night. Siena watched over her as she began talking in her sleep. She was muttering about being kept safe and free from the vampires. She awoke at one stage and complained about her stiff neck. She was concerned about the puncture wound and whether they would leave a scar.

"Do you have a mirror? I bet these wounds look awful," she said. Siena passed her a small mirror and she held it up beside her neck. "It is awful. Honestly, so grotesque," she said sadly.

"Don't you have potions for that?" Siena asked.

"Yes, in my coat," she said, "but I left it at Bloomingdales fitting room."

The time travellers landed close to the castle. They watched on the monitor for a while, checking the planet for Life forms, radiation, and breathable air. Any abnormalities would be picked up by the computer and relayed back via Foster. The system kept picking up some kind of tracking device but could not locate its source or origin. All they could determine is how long the device had been activated which led them to the Wizards of Zena. He has been with them all the time, and has been causing all their problems to date.

The time travellers looked out into forestry, and had landed in a clearing. They didn't exactly know what they were searching for – would it be a modern building or an historical castle. They all decided to go out and search the forest for signs of life. It wasn't long before they came across a modern building that appeared like a large dome. They searched for an entrance each armed with weapons in case they encountered trouble. They entered a doorway and travelled down a long corridor. It seemed very quiet with no one in sight, until they reached a large room like a hanger. At this point, they were aware of the presence of others – soldiers were hiding behind pillars that supported the main structure; some were on balconies.

"We see you," Natasha shouted. "Come out from your hiding places."

A single shot narrowly missed her. She returned the fire using her wand. By this time, several shots took place. Each of them dived for cover. Foster took a shot at the balcony, and a man fell down. Crystal used her wand and disarmed another man.

"Hold your fire," a voice commanded.

Both sides stopped and the person appeared on the Balcony.

"I am Carina. Who are you?" she shouted. She was dressed

in black armour with long black hair.

"We are the time witches," Natasha said. "We seek Shanice."

"Who might that be?" she asked.

"A friend taken by vampires," Crystal said.

"We are vampire slayers," she said. "We also have a friend captured at the castle."

Suddenly, one of the large soldiers rushed at Natasha. She responded by pointing her wand and turning him into a pig. Carina laughed and the rest joined in watching the pig run round in circles around the hanger.

"Nice move, Natasha," she said.

The leader of the slayers was still laughing when she leapt down to join the witches, "Is that how you fight your enemies?"

"We do what we have to defend ourselves," Natasha replied.

"Good answer," Carina said. "Now, can you please change Gareth back? Not that it wasn't an improvement."

"Certainly," Natasha said, turning Gareth back to his former self. Gareth seemed most displeased and stood in silence.

"We have a common enemy, Natasha" Carina said.

"Then we can fight them together," Natasha said.

"You are too trusting," Gareth said. "First, Siena; now, Natasha."

"Shake hands as I do, Gareth, and fight the true enemy," Carina said sharply.

Reluctantly, he did so. He wrapped his large hand around her dainty hand.

"My word, Gareth. If I had realised that you have such big hands, I would have turned you into a gorilla," she said smiling.

Unfortunately, he didn't appreciate her joke, and ignored her. At least he appeared to by his response.

"Let us plan our attack," she said, calling to her army to gather together.

Gareth set out the map of the castle across the ground using computer graphics. A hologram appeared showing the castle in 3D with details of the interior of the castle. He had obtained the images through spies over the years, and knew one day, they would be affective. It took years to perfect it and make it possible to view in such an amazing way.

"Now, a group of you will enter at the north side or main entrance as they expect," he instructed. "Two other invading parties will take the east and west."

"I will take the east," Carina said.

"I am going west," Gareth said.

"We will go through the main entrance," Natasha said.

"I must get some armour for you, people," Carina said. "You will need it."

Later that day, everybody was ready to travel to the castle and attack the vampires. They assembled, ready to leave the base. Meanwhile in the castle, Ballari went to visit Siena. She opened the cell and entered. Siena stood to her feet and looked at Ballari.

"Siena, we were friends. What became of you?"

"I grew up," Sicna replied.

"I heard that you made a pact with god," she said.

"I promised to be true to god and do as he instructed ridding the world of evil," she replied.

"But my dear friend, you had everything you wanted with the Master Count Vermont," she insisted. "Why would you give that up?"

"But I didn't have god to guide me. I need him, not a vampire race," she said staring at Ballari.

"You must join me. I can save you, Siena," she said staring back at her trying to hypnotise her. "Trust me," she said walking closer towards her. She had got close enough for Siena to feel her breath on her naked neck. Slowly, she touched her, stroking her hair. Siena put her head to one side while Ballari showed her fangs and was about to puncture the skin on her neck when she was pushed back against the wall. She instantly retaliated by grapping Shanice by the neck.

"Back off, witch," she said, throwing her onto the bed.

At that point Delia, entered the cell and took Ballari out. She chastised her and sent her away in order to keep the witch safe. Shanice was protected by Merek.

"Are you alright, Shanice?" Siena asked.

"Why does everybody go for my neck?" she said, still weak from the previous vampire attack. "I thought my neck was nice," she continued.

"Did anyone ever tell you that you moan a lot?" Siena said smiling.

"All the time," she said. "I don't know why."

The vampire slayers assembled at their positions outside the castle, making ready to enter at the various locations. Carina waited for Natasha to enter through the main doors, and then she entered from her side receiving a radio signal from her; Gareth did the same. The vampires expected those coming from the main entrance watching them walking down the corridors on a monitor. Natasha was in front clad in armour holding her wand, followed by Crystal, who caught up with her, and some of the vampire slayers at the rear with Foster and Shimick, who kept looking back nervously. Eventually, they reach the main hall where the majority of the vampires were; including Thanatos and Orazio. They were higher up looking down at the rescue party.

"Surrender now, slayers. You have no chance of beating us," Thanatos said. "We just want the witches for Merek the wizard."

Natasha stepped forward and Crystal joined her looking around them.

"We are the time witches, and we do not surrender," she said.

"Do you really want to take on time witches?" Crystal said, producing her wand.

"Do not be foolish, time witches. The wizard needs you," Thanatos said calmly.

"Come and take us, Thanatos, if you dare," Natasha said confidently.

Both Natasha and Crystal formed a circle around them with their wands, and waited for the attack. The first few vampires flew forward and were knocked back by an invisible force field. The vampire slayers stood outside the circle, and fired their weapons. This was the start of a long battle between the vampires and slayers.

During the battle, Natasha and Crystal took Foster and Shimick from the circle and into the area of the cells. The vampires didn't notice them vanish and thought they were still under the protective bubble canopy that the witches had created. They reached the cell, and forced open the cell door. At first, Shanice thought they were vampires, and raced forward to attack them. Crystal removed her helmet.

"Wait," she said.

Shanice was delighted to see them. Natasha held her wand to Shanice's neck, and began to heal it. She followed by hugging her.

"Thank goodness you're safe."

"Thank goodness, my neck is back to normal," she said.

"Siena, these are my friends, Natasha, Crystal, Shimick and Foster."

"Siena is what you might call an ex-vampire," she said, looking at confused faces.

"I will explain later," she said dismissively.

"Shanice, you need to go back to the ship with Shimick."

"But I want to fight," she said disappointedly.

"No, sorry," Crystal said. "You are too weak."

"Show her the way out, Shimick," Natasha said.

Shanice reluctantly went with Shimick and Foster, while Natasha and Crystal returned to the battle. They proved effective producing thunder bolts from their wands stunning the vampires so that the slayers could kill them. It was a long hard battle with many casualties and deaths on both sides. Both sides were reluctant to surrender.

Carina arrived in the main hall having defeated vampires from the east side, and Gareth arrived having done the same from the west side. At one stage, the vampires appeared to be winning as they killed one slayer after another, but as Carina and Gareth arrived, the slayers began to fight back.

Shanice sat in the ship, relaxing, when Foster decided to show her his new room. It was designed to restore powers back to the witches as it contained fragments of the meteor that gave the powers to the witches all those years ago when they were cave dwellers. Foster collected it when they ventured back in time to restore Shanice's powers. Now, they can do it whenever they are weak. Shanice rested in the room for an hour, and then came out bouncing with energy. She went to the slayers' base for armour and weapons, and took a small group of slayers with her.

"But Shanice, you can't go back."

"Watch me," she said confidently. "Let's finish this."

They used the main entrance back into the castle, and walked down the corridors. Shanice led them into the main hall and went straight into battle. She noticed Thanatos trying to escape and followed him. He was travelling up a tower so she aimed her wand. She taught about how Natalie had trained her, and shouted Obliterate catching his leg. It was blown right off in an instant.

"Wait, Shanice," a voice came from behind her; it was Natalie.

Natalie passed her flying at great speed. She pinned him down and Shanice joined her.

"I need my wand," Natalie said.

"Where is it?" Shanice said.

"In my coat," Natalie said. "But hurry, he is so strong."

"What do you need your wand for?"

"To get a stake," she replied.

"Why are you thinking of food right now?" Shanice said confused.

"Not a steak, a stake – piece of wood," Natasha said. "For his heart."

Crystal arrived to see the commotion and produced her wand. She waved it about and produced a stake and hammer. Meanwhile, Natasha and Shanice were wrestling with him.

"I got him around his neck," Natasha shouted.

"That's my neck, Natasha," Shanice said choking. "Always the neck."

"Hold him still, girls," Crystal said, taking aim. Thanatos managed to break free from their hold, and tried to get away from them.

"Out the way, all of you," came another voice. They all stood back, and a steak was shot from a crossbow, and went straight into Thanatos heart. He began to disintegrate. Siena had fired the fatal shot, and took a ring from his ashes.

Carina had battled with Delia and defeated her, while Gareth killed Thana; Siena was now battling Ballari. There was a lot of shooting of weapons until Shanice took aim once again with her wand, and caught Ballari in her head. Siena saw her opportunity, and fired her weapon. Ballari fell to the ground and disintegrated. After this, the battle soon ended and the slayers were victorious. Some of the vampires escaped including Orazio.

The time travellers said goodbye to Siena, Carina, and the remaining vampire slayers. They were about to travel again, hopefully to Earth taking Shanice home.

"Siena, we will miss you. Thank you for looking after Shanice," Natasha said.

"Yes, thank you for looking after me," Shanice said, smiling.

"Thank you for helping me, Shanice," Siena said, smiling back.

"Carina, you are a true warrior. You fought so well," Crystal said. "You saved us all."

"You witches took your part in the battle, and helped our victory."

Carina said hugging each of them. Siena did the same, and told them to keep the armour and weapons in case they encountered more vampires.

THE V.R. COMPLEX

The time travellers left the planet Delus, and travelled once again through the time portal expecting a smooth journey to Earth, instead, they encountered a rough storm like a mighty tornado or twister. The ship entered it and was being tossed about the outward pressure. It was causing the vessel to cave in and get crushed like a can of pop. The crew were feeling the pressure too as they rolled about in pain; blood was dripping from their ears and nose.

Foster was malfunctioning; was this the end for the time travellers? The ship was vibrating under the pressure and causing the passengers to become violently sick. It was at this point that Natasha woke up from a very disturbing dream. The other crew were disturbed by how she was reacting and tried to help her.

"Natasha, wake up!" Crystal shouted. "You are dreaming."

"We have experienced turbulence," Foster explained. "It has been a rough journey, but it's over now."

"Have we reached Earth?" Shanice asked.

"Not exactly," Foster said. "This is XMFT 1 or Cryrotario to be precise, a planet that contains a city fully automated run by robots. Its function is to research local planets and find a suitable place for human inhabitancies. The outward atmosphere is highly toxic, therefore, I suggest you get into space suits for protection. The androids are protective over their automated city, and I suggest you take extra care while you are here."

"Thank you, Foster," Crystal said. "Now, who wants to explore?"

"Well, as we have been blown adrift once again, I suppose it would not hurt to explore this planet," Shanice said. "Cryrotario interesting name."

"Okay, count me in," Natasha said. "How about you, Shimick?"

"It's dangerous," he said. "Life threatening?"

"Yes," they all responded.

"Okay, I will go," Shimick agreed. "God help all of us."

"I was thinking," Natasha said, "Arthalo tried to warn me about Merek. He said that he wasn't to be trusted. I could tell you many tales about him. I know he had a temper. He once had an argument with Saden. I saw his eyes staring at the Goblin looking so evil that it should have told me not to trust him. Now, I feel sad that I didn't protect Doran as I promised I would. He would still be alive today."

"What made you bring that up?" Crystal asked.

"Because, I have a feeling he has been after us ever since we left his miserable planet," Natasha replied.

"You mean tracking us?" Shanice said.

"Yes, I don't know how, but he has been tracking us," she replied.

"All instruments indicate that there is no such device in the system but from an outside source, not connected with the ship," Foster explained.

"So, in other words, it is coming from one of us?" Shanice

asked.

"Yes, it appears to be so," Foster replied. "I need to scan all of you."

Foster prepared the scanner, and then began to scan the crew one by one starting with Natasha, and working through to Shimick. Eventually, Foster had the answer.

"I have the answer to your question about the tracking device," he said.

"Well, tell us, Foster," Crystal said impatiently.

"I am afraid, it's you, Shimick" Foster said. "You have an implant in your wrist."

"That's impossible," Shimick protested. "How have they done this?"

"The Gizalians have done this to you. They are evil creatures, and they are green ugly things known as changelings who can alter into blobs of mush," Crystal explained.

"Doran hated them," Natasha explained.

"So, you and Doran had a thing going?" Shanice asked inquisitively.

"Doran and I were friends," Natasha insisted.

"An item," Shanice teased. "He was your boyfriend."

"Yes, okay. We had wonderful time together," Natasha agreed.

"You mean you had magical sex together?" Shanice said.

"Shanice, just who is telling this story?" Crystal asked.

"Sorry, go on, Natasha," Shanice said, smirking.

"Well, Merek was against me and Doran being together, and made it obvious." Natasha said sadly.

"Why would he object to you being together?" Crystal asked.

"He considered time witches were inferior, not in the same class as wizards, and considered time witches as drifters in time and space," Natasha explained. "Merek was head of the family, and what he said was final, and so we eventually parted, and I continued my time travelling alone. I have not seen him since this time. I was supposed to look out for him as he did with me, but now, he is dead because of Merek."

"How sad," Shanice said. "You must be devastated."

Shimick stood to his feet and jumped up and down. "How is that helping me?" he said furiously.

"Shimick, chill, man. They will help you," Shanice said.

"Yes, we will remove and destroy the tracker for you," Crystal said, reassuring him.

"I feel like the enemy having this thing in me all this time," Shimick said frustrated.

"You are not the enemy, but the victim being used to let Merek know where we are," Natasha said sympathetically.

Foster operated on his arm; removing, and destroying the device which took only minutes to do. Shanice held his other hand while he was undergoing the procedure, and then Crystal used the healing potion on his arm.

"There, there," Foster said tapping him on the shoulder.

"There, there, Foster? Really?" Natasha remarked.

"As you Crystal, I have an emotional chip in my head that enables me to empathize with someone in pain or discomfort. It is designed for me to understand human emotions and feelings such as loss of loved ones saying there, there, and what a shame or deepest sympathy. I even respond to students who fail to make their grades or reach their targets in an examination; there, there. I can offer comfort or produce tears of sympathy."

"Can you make love?" Shanice asked.

"No, I am not programmed to do that or have the relevant parts to complete this task," Foster said.

"You have no willy?" she said with her fingers to her mouth.

"Shanice, really?" Natasha said. "He is an android."

The crew prepared to go out onto this planet Cryrotario to explore wearing spacesuits. Each one wore the appropriate clothes for the journey to the android city not knowing what sort of reception to expect. They travelled for a while across a dessert-like terrain until they reached the outskirts to this vast city. The city consisted of massive metal domes that shone under the sunlight and monorails connected to each dome.

Above the city were drones flying overhead to watch the outer areas. It was an incredible sight like something from a science fiction movie. Each of the crew were astounded and made comment to this fact.

The crew struggled to find an entrance, and eventually, a metal hatch opened allowing them to enter. Cautiously, they walked in and found the crew in a corridor as they walked along. They could feel eyes on them.

"This is creepy," Shimick said. "Can't we go back?"

"Hush, Shimick," Shanice said. "Be brave."

"Easy for you to say with all your powers," Shimick replied.

"Powers are nothing without courage," Natasha replied.

"That's true, Natasha" Crystal said.

"Let us be logical about this. This is an unknown environment nobody can determine whether or not it is indeed hostile," Foster said.

"Stuff your logic, you mechanical fact finder," Shimick said rudely.

"This place is giving me the creeps."

"Can I suggest, my little green friend, that you remain calm and exercise tolerance?" Foster replied none expectantly.

"Can I suggest you keep your opinion to yourself, and shut down for a while?" Shimick replied. "Give your circuits a rest."

"Shimick, how rude!" Shanice said sharply, "Show some respect."

"To a robot, that's rich," Shimick replied grumpily.

Suddenly a voice was heard. It seemed to come from all

around them, and sounded mechanical, like a recording of a human voice echoing from a tin drum.

"Identify yourself," it said.

"We are the time witches: Natasha, Crystal, and Shanice," Natasha said.

"Why have you come here?" the voice continued. "What is the purpose of your visit?"

"We are here to explore your planet Cryrotario, and find out about your city and its function. We are peaceful people. We also have Shimick, a goblin, and a robot called Foster," Crystal said.

"Enter the next section, and remove your space suits," the voice instructed.

"Is the environment safe for us? Crystal said.

"Yes. We provide oxygen to sustain you humans," the voice explained. "Please do as instructed."

The door opened automatically, allowing them to enter a changing room. Each of them removed their suits, and walked into the sanitation area shower cubicle, where at their disposal, with cleaning gels, and towels. Fresh clothing was also at hand consisting of one-piece suits in yellow.

"Very stylish," Shanice said, laughing.

"It must be their idea of fashion, Shan," Crystal said.

"I feel like a right cabbage in this," Shimick said.

"Don't you mean a banana?" Shanice said, laughing. They entered the main control room and were greeted by an android who called himself Waverley. He escorted them to a monorail, and instructed the android that was driving to give them a tour of the city. The monorail set off, and a voice introduced them to each aspect of the city and its function, starting with the entertainment section. This was displays of robot artists mimicking real celebrities from Earth. The voice explained that they had discovered a damaged satellite from Earth that contained messages; data about life on Earth, and music through the ages. The

Elvis Presley performance from an android was particularly entertaining with virtual reality movements that could astound anybody. The voice was Elvis's programmed in singing his hits over the years. Adele was an android who did the same but was programmed to do other things too apart from entertain. They moved from this to the research laboratories conducting research into rock samples and poison gases from the planet. This was their primary function. This section consisted of eight laboratories and a human section which was empty. The human section had a hologram room for relaxation purposes, simulating a bar room with people from Earth acting out a social evening. They left this dome for the security dome with androids armed with weapons and patrolling this section. The inner rooms were out of bounds and had notices on them saying private restricted area. Needless to say, the whole complex was impressive, highly automated, and germ free, which is why they had to wear the suits. They were taken back to the control room after the tour and greeted again by Waverley who led them to a room with a long table filled with various foods and drink.

"Help yourself to the food and drink," he said.

"Thank you," Natasha replied.

The others responded in a similar way, and then started to fill their plates.

"They seem very obliging," Crystal said.

"I can't help suspecting something is wrong," Natasha replied.

"The food looks good," Shanice said. "Why are you being so negative, Nat?"

"This is all too good," Natasha explained. "Something is wrong here; I can feel it."

"You see menace in your own shadow," Shanice said. "Relax."

"Why have we landed here?" Natasha said concerned, "It doesn't add up."

"I fear she may be right," Shimick said. "I have a bad feeling about this."

While the crew were eating, Foster had gone to see Adele and conversing with her. He seemed to be communicating well with her, and despite suspicions, everything seemed to be fine. After lunch, all of them were shown to their sleeping quarters, and were advised to remain in their rooms during the night as security would be watching the building and maintaining safety at all times.

Natasha was unable to rest due to a nagging concern about the androids and their true intentions. She used telepathy in order to communicate with the other time witches, sending her thoughts through to both of them. Crystal responded first and replied telepathically advising her to sleep, and the security was to protect the city and its occupants as well as them. Shanice wasn't used to telepathy and thought she was imagining hearing voices. This was until she heard things about exploring the city. She concentrated hard focusing on the conversation and tried to reply to them. It took a few attempts to get through to them, but eventually she was heard.

"Join us, Shanice," Crystal said.

"Come to my room," Natasha said.

"Okay," she agreed.

Shanice left her room and crept along the corridor until she reached Natasha's room. She entered cautiously and found Natasha and Crystal in the room.

"Well, that worked," Crystal said. "Welcome, Shanice."

"So, what's wrong?" Shanice asked.

"Satisfy my curiosity, Shan," Natasha said. "We need to find out what is going on here. If I am wrong, no harm done, but if I am right, we are in danger."

"Okay, but I think you are wrong," Shanice replied.

"So, what do we do now?" Crystal asked.

"Cloak ourselves and make ourselves invisible to the androids," Natasha explained. "We need to go to the restricted section."

The time witches created shrouds that made them appear invisible. They had conjured up replica dummies of themselves for their beds, and made their way down the corridor undetected, passing the guards who were patrolling the complex. They managed to reach the secure section undetected using telepathy to communicate with each other until they arrived at their destination. At this point, they waited for the door to open and two guards to enter first through the door, and there was another long passage that was brightly lit and rooms either side of them. They continued walking down the long corridor until they reached another door. The androids opened it, and a man stood in the middle of the room. It was Doran.

The android guards spoke to him. "We have the time witches here in the city."

"Natasha?" he asked.

"Yes, as your brother Merek ordered," one replied.

"He wants them to return to Zena and face him," the other android said.

"He will kill them," Doran said. "You can't do that."

"We have our orders, Doran. Just as we were told to keep you here," they told him.

Natasha tried to communicate telepathically with Doran but to no avail. He would also have been aware of their presence, but he had obviously lost his powers. He appeared weak and lethargic as if he had been sedated. He was standing but leaning against the wall for support.

The guards left the room, and he began to slide down the wall until he was on the floor. The witches revealed themselves and helped him to his bed.

"Am I seeing things?" he said staring at them. "Are you real?"

"It's me, Natasha," she said gazing into his eye.

"Natasha is that really you?" he asked gazing back at her.

"Yes, my dear Doran," she said hugging him.

"But you are all in danger," he warned them. "Merek tried to kill me and then sent me here. He took away my powers."

"We must get you out of here," Natasha said. "We have to get you back to the ship, and restore your powers."

"Natasha, you cloak him and take him back. We will return to our rooms," Crystal said.

"Yes, okay," Natasha said. "I will help him."

Natasha and Doran left the city undetected, and returned to the ship. They had worn the space suits on their journey across the planet surface. She took Doran to the recovery chamber, and left him to rest while his powers were restored by the meteors that Foster put in place when they were back in time following the meteor storm.

Natasha slept in the room next door until morning. As she woke up, she could hear activity outside her room. Doran was up and searching for food. Natasha went to find him, and eventually found him in the cockpit with a mushy kind of food in a dish and a spoon in his hand.

"Good morning, Doran," she said. "I see you have breakfast."

"Yes," he said. "I feel amazing."

"Are your powers restored?" she asked.

"Yes," he said levitating. "I am back to health and strength."

"I think we need to rescue the others," she said concerned.

"Of course," he replied. "Let us do this."

Natasha and Doran re-entered the city, and remained cloaked until they had found Crystal's room, and then they appeared in front of her. They explained about his powers being restored and his willingness to fight. At that point, the android guards entered the room. They surrounded them all and Waverley entered the room.

"Who is this man?" he asked.

"This is Doran, brother of Merek," the android replied. "Merek wanted us to keep him here and take the time witches to him."

"Why hasn't the wizard come here?" Waverley asked.

"I can answer that," Doran said. "He is powerful but not able to leave the planet of Zena due to being acrophobic."

"Really? Is that true?" Natasha asked.

"Yes, it is true," Doran said. "He cannot leave his home."

"This explains a lot," Crystal said, "on why he didn't pursue us around the galaxy."

"Yes, he could have tried to destroy us long ago," Natasha said.

"So, what happens now?" Crystal asked.

"You are obviously wanted back on Zena," Waverley said. "I can only suggest you go with the guards immediately."

The time crew got together and followed the robots to the prison area. Foster was oblivious as he was dancing with Adele increasing his understanding about human emotion being taught by Adele. The androids took them past a room which was out of bounds. It was the robot repair shop and reprogramming room. All the input and data must have come from this laboratory. This room could be vital to the time crew in adjusting their thought pattern. They were taken to individual rooms, and left to await to be transported to Merek in their vessels. They decided to communicate telepathically making plans to escape. It was time for the witches to reveal their powers and overthrow the androids.

"The androids will be taken by surprise," Natasha said.

"Doran, you can cause a diversion," Crystal said. "Keep Shimick with you."

"My old friend, Shimick," Doran said. "My loyal servant."

The witches broke out of their cells at similar times blasting the doors using their powers and causing the guards to fly down the corridors with the force of each blast. Shimick joined Doran. He had obtained a laser gun from one of the androids. They continued to fire on the android guards, while the witches entered the laboratory. They noticed experiments with humans providing them with cybernetic organisms, where some seemed quite hideous according to how they replicated their physiology. Some of the android guards entered the room, and the witches went into battle using their powers to disarm and disable them.

The androids fired weapons on the witches while they returned the fire using lightning bolts, and levitation forcing them to rise and go crashing into equipment. Natasha turned into a rhinoceros and charged the androids smashing them up; Shanice became a tiger, while Crystal found the main computer that programmed the androids. She managed to adjust the program and cause the androids to stop for a while. She worked on the program for a while before managing to disable them.

When they returned to the main function room, Foster was kneeling beside a shattered body; it was Adele. She had been attacked by one of the guards who had blown her up with his weapon. She lay with oil coming out of her body. She had lost her legs and part of her head.

Foster was sad and had tears coming from his eyes, and was patting her saying, "There, there."

"We are sorry for your loss, Foster," Crystal said. "My condolences, Foster," Shanice said.

"And mine," Natasha said.

"We must make readjustments with our lab and with those androids." Waverley said. "What about Merek?"

"We will deal with him. Don't worry," Crystal said.

THE FIRE OF JANUS

The time travellers continued on their journey. This time, they decided not to set a course home but to reach the wizard Merek on the planet Zena. But once again, they were off course as a distress call was picked up by Foster while he was tuning into the space radio signals.

"Foster, what is that?" Crystal asked.

"It is coming from the planet Janus. They appear to be in trouble," Foster replied.

"Janus is right near Zena. Maybe we can help," Doran said.

"Yes," Shanice said. "We need to help them."

As they approached the planet, the temperature in the ship warmed up, and they could visibly see eight fires on the planet surface which encircled the mountain.

"Things are going to get hot down there," Natasha said concerned.

"Let's hope we are in time to rescue them," Crystal said. "What do you think, Foster?"

"We need to gauge the heat, and probably wear the protective suits."

"I don't understand. Janus used to be a cold planet," Doran

said.

"Like Earth's arctic?" Shanice said.

"Very much so, Shanice," Foster replied. "Something is radically wrong."

"This could be something to do with Merek," Doran said.

"He must be angry at the Janusians and is punishing them."

"The Janusians is a holy order who live in the mountain regions of Janus."

"Yes, much like Earth's monks," Doran said. "They wear shrouds and worship their god Husharelis."

"A peace-loving race who have helped many travellers," Foster explained. Foster contacted the Janusians by video call on their large monitor. "I have them on screen now," Foster said.

"Very well, Foster," Crystal replied. "Greetings, Janusians. We have come in respond to your distress call."

A man in a red hooded shroud came on the screen. His face was barely visible, and only his eyes were seen clearly.

"I am Oval, the Janusians leader and high priest."

"We are the time witches and friends," Crystal said, introducing everyone. "Greetings, Oval. May we land?" she asked.

"Yes, we will open the hatch to the docking bay," Oval said.

"Thank you," she said.

"We are expecting you," he said, instructing the crew to open the hatch.

Crystal steered the craft onto the platform with a vertical landing, and then, the platform moved under cover in the landing bay. The crew stepped out, but Doran, Shimick, and Foster remained on the ship.

The time witches were greeted by the Janusian people. Each of them dressed alike. They were a kind of holy order fixed in time period and never changed on this planet. Pilgrims travel from other places and volunteer their services to help physically and mentally. They were escorted through the chapel, and past a few rooms until they reached the conference room. Oval opened the door and asked them to sit down at a long table. Oval sat at the head of the table with his colleagues beside him.

"Let me introduce my friends and colleagues to you. On my left is Robert, Simon, and David; and to my right is Paul, Andrew, and Daniel. There are others about the building, some in prayer, others cooking our food," Oval said.

"Pleased to meet you," Crystal said, and the others agreed.

"We called for help following a really bad incident involving the Lamians. These are from a Greek mythology conjured up by Merek the wizard to destroy us. These Lamians are creatures with snake heads and human bodies, although they take different forms according to their environment. They immerged from the eight fires that suddenly appeared around our mountain. They climb up the mountain and linger outside waiting to capture us. They have long fingers with sharp claws that penetrate the flesh like knives. They sometimes bite their victims, tearing into their throats, but they won't enter this building as it is sacred ground. They have taken thirty men so far. Until we made measures to remain indoors, they are afraid of the godly atmosphere, and especially the cold weather on this planet which is why they live in these fires. Then, we have the demon child Lamia, Queen of the Lamians, or should I say, the child possessed by Lamia locked away in our prison. She is wild. She throws herself across the room, levitates, curse, and is generally disruptive. We have seen possessed children before but not quite like this girl."

We were given food and then led down to the prison to see the girl. It seemed very quiet at this stage until the girl noticed the Janusians and the time witches. She snarled at them and spat in their faces.

"Let me go, you motherless beings! I spit on your fathers' graves."

She began to levitate and make everything in the room shake. "Bring me my children, and let them defile your bodies, cut open your flesh, and hold your heart in their hands." She spun around and clutched at the prison bars. Everybody jumped back as each one of them startled by her actions.

Crystal could see that the child was in pain, probably from the pressure she was in being possessed by Lamia, a powerful demon. It was obvious that the girl was dying inside. Her body was no longer able to house such a powerful host. Her heart would surely fail, and her mind was confused. Death would free her from this evil and rest her soul, but their must be another way, less drastic with the ideal goal of freeing her forever.

Natasha stepped forward and looked her in the eyes. She could see the creature. "Crystal, Shanice, we can save this girl," Natasha said confidently.

"Yes, we can," Crystal agreed. "Let Shanice and I speak the words of our ancestors from Scotland."

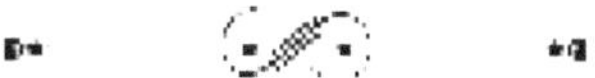

Meanwhile, the rest of the crew watched activities outside the building as the Lamians climbed the mountain, and prepared to battle the men of the sacred order. They began to wander the courtyard.

"We have to do something," Doran said.

"What do you suggest, Doran?" Foster asked.

"I am not going out there with those creatures," Shimick said.

"We have to save these people," Doran insisted. "Where can we get ice from?"

"The Great Lake is a short distance away," Foster explained. "It is on this map."

"Let us contact the time witches, and let them know," Doran said.

But the time witches were occupied with saving the girl, and destroying Lamia. They had already marked out a circle near the prison bars and beginning to perform their magic. Natasha spoke the magic words in Gaelic, and already, the creature responded.

"Glacadh spicrad nan deamhain," meaning 'capture the spirit of Satan'.

"Tilg air ais egu ifrinn," Shanice said, meaning 'cast it back to hell'.

Smoke rose from her body and the creature separated from the girl, it shot past them at great speed and vanished. The prison door opened and the girl ran to Natasha with open arms, she seemed to be so calm and secure; Natasha kissed her forehead and spoke to her.

"Your safe now, child," Natasha said.

"My name is Tristana," she said softly, "It means sad child."

"Where are you from?" Natasha asked inquisitively.

"From Sabira, I was kidnapped by Merek, the evil wizard," she explained.

"Well, Tristana, you can come with us," Crystal said.

"But first, we need to rid this planet of the Lamians," Natasha said.

"The Queen has vanished but could return," Shanice said.

The time witches rushed into the ship with their new companion Tristana, once inside the craft they planned how they were going to deal with the Lamians.

"What's the plan, Doran?" Crystal asked.

"To find enough frozen water to put the flames out," Doran replied.

"Where do we get it from?" Natasha asked.

"There is a lake, a short distance away with ample water," Foster replied.

"My word! You have an android," Tristana said. She looked at a seat beside him, "And a goblin?"

"Yes, Tristana. This is Foster the android, and Shimick the goblin," Shanice said.

"And I see you have Doran, one of Merek's brothers," Tristana said, frowning.

"He is fine, Tristana," Natasha said. "Only Merek was bad."

"Did he banish you, Doran?" she asked.

"He tried to get rid of all of us, replacing us with holograms," Doran explained.

"But you survived," Tristana said. "You are here to tell the tale."

"I was sent to a planet with robots running a research complex," he explained.

"Let us deal with the present situation, guys," Natasha said. "We have demons to destroy."

"Could I suggest that we split up and deal with these demons?" Crystal said.

"Go ahead, Crystal," Natasha said.

"I propose that Natasha and Shanice use spells to send the Lamians back to the fires, while the rest sort out the frozen water to rain on the fire," Crystal explained.

"Excellent idea, Crystal" Shanice said. "Both Natasha and I will exit the ship and meet the Lamians in the courtyard, and use our spells there."

"We will head to the lake with the ship, and gather as much water as possible." Doran said confidently.

Natasha and Shanice went back to the chapel while the rest stayed aboard the ship. Crystal piloted the ship on a course towards the great lake. They gathered up the ice using their magical powers, and brought it back to the fires. Meanwhile, Natalie and Shanice waited for the signal to go out into the courtyard and use their spells on the Lamians. They left the building out of the main door having practiced their spells ready for their encounter with the Lamians. It had to be word perfect and in unison with each other for the spell to work effectively. They drew their wands and aimed them at their enemy and began the chant.

"Falbh as an seo cruetairean a ifrinn," they both said. "Till don aite a bn'agad roimhe."

"Bi air Falbh, bi air Falbh an seo tuilleadh," they continued, "vanish a-nis."

After they finished their spell, the Lamians disappeared back into the fire.

Meanwhile, the queen known as Lamia appeared from the shadows.

"So, you thought you had got rid of me?" she said, catching Shanice around the throat with her long black claws, puncturing her neck and making it bleed.

Natasha turned to face her realising what had happened. She had to think fast because Lamia was about to bite Shanice's head off. At that moment, the ship returned, and they were dropping the ice on each of the eight fires. Screaming came from the flames as each of the Lamians died slowly from the cold. Lamia responded by letting Shanice go, and Natasha conjured up some ice, and sent it towards Lamia in the form of icicles. They penetrated her body like spears. Lamia cried out and disintegrated. Shanice remained on the ground curled in a ball. Natasha ran towards her, and knelt beside her. Shanice looked up at her holding her throat.

"Are you okay?" Natasha asked her.

"Do I bloody well look okay?" Shanice replied choking. "What is it about my neck? First, the vampires, now, demons? For god's sake! Does anyone else want a pop at it?" she went on. "I think my neck is nice."

"Yes, you are okay," Natasha said jokingly. "Let's head inside and I will see to your wounds."

The ship landed on the launch pad, and the crew waited to enter the hatch. The air outside was beginning to get very cold and it began to snow. Inside the building, the Janusians were celebrating their liberation. Natasha was tending to Shanice's wounds, and Tristana was having a discussion with Doran. Everything seemed fine until one of the holy order, Simon, rushed over to Oval, and whispered in his ear. Oval seemed alarmed, and walked across to Crystal and spoke to her.

"I think everybody should be aware of this," Crystal said, concerned.

"What is it, Crystal?" Natasha asked.

"Look at the large screen," she said while pointing. Merek appeared on the monitor large as life. He seemed angry and began waving his finger at them.

"I want you, meddling time witches!" he shouted. "Come and face me."

Doran hid from view so that Merek was unaware that he was there.

"Tell Shanice I have a surprise for her," Merek said. He showed her mother Rosa confined in a cell. "Come and get your mother, Shanice," he proceeded to laugh wickedly, and then turned the monitor off.

"Mother!" Shanice shouted.

DILEMMA IN SPACE

The crew set course for Zena. They were planning to see Merek before hearing the news that Shanice's mother, Rosa, was there. Now, they knew they had to go and rescue her from Merek.

Shanice was understandably upset, and was consoled by the crew. Foster offered his usual pat on the shoulder, and comforting words.

"There, there," he said.

Shanice went to lie down. She felt that she needed to be alone for a while; everyone understood at the time. They all offered a comforting shoulder and words of reassurance, but who knows what Merek had planned for her.

The journey was quite short, and soon, they could see Merek's home – the castle like building with the wizard's family crest above the main entrance. Inside, it had Bohemian decor with oak furniture, and satin curtains in yellow and white.

Merek's little army of Gizalians met them at the door, and escorted them to the main hall. Doran stayed in the ship with Foster and Tristana. He wanted to be discrete for now, while negotiations were going on for Rosa's release.

Merek stood in front of them, and looked at each one of them in turn as if he was conducting an inspection.

"Natalie, you are back," he observed. "And you, Shanice, I have your mother."

"If you have harmed her, I will…" Shanice shouted.

"She is quite safe with me," Merek interrupted her. "Just powerless. I am sure you know exactly how that feels."

"Yes, I do know," she said.

Merek's eyes widened as he looked at Shimick.

"As for you, Shimick, you traitor! I have a short memory that is nagging me saying remember Shimick, the one who let me down and allowed Shanice to escape."

"You would have killed her," Shimick said in his defence.

"Maybe or maybe not," Merek said cunningly.

Natasha spoke telepathically to Shanice speaking in Scottish Gaelic. "Feumaidh sinn an draoidu a mheallada," she said, meaning 'we must trick the wizard'.

Shanice replied with these words, "Faigh e anns a 'chill sin agus an umirsin gheigh sinn cuidhteas na cumhachdan aige," 'Get him in the cell, and rid him of his powers'.

"I want to see my mother," Shanice said.

"Very well. The guards will escort you;" Merek said, "my trusty Gizalians."

This left Natasha, Crystal, and Shimick wondering what he had planned for them. He certainly showed no mercy with his brothers. He wanted power and superiority, and he gained it.

As Shanice was escorted to the cell, she was seen on the monitor. She entered the cell, and joined her mother. They embraced and the door was shut on them both. But surely, Shanice knew that entering the cell, she would lose her powers and not be able to leave.

Suddenly, Merek turned on the witches sending lightning bolts to knock them off their feet. He then turned into a dragon, and spat fire at them. They headed in separate directions and changed themselves into dragon creatures in order to combat him. Shimick ran for the door and down the long corridor to the cells. He reached the cell that Shanice was in, and tried opening the door.

The dragons continued to fight clawing at each other, but Merek stopped when he saw Shanice use her powers to open the door, and escape with her mother.

"What trickery is this?" he asked.

"The power has reverse, and soon, you will lose yours," Natasha said.

He stunned both witches, and put them in a large basin, and filled it with sand, and then sealing the lid. "I will deal with you two later," he said.

Meanwhile, Shanice was heading back down the corridor with her mother Rosa and Shimick. They reached the main hall combating the Gizalians on the way. They arrived just in time to rescue Natasha and Crystal. At this time, Doran had arrived in the area of the cells only to meet Merek.

"Doran! You are alive," he said shocked.

"Yes. I survived from the androids in one piece, and guess what, I have my powers."

They both transformed into dogs and fought, tearing at each other with their sharp teeth rolling around until they were both weak. Merek managed to crawl into one of the cells, and lay down waiting for Doran to lose his powers; but to his surprise, Doran demonstrated that he still had his powers by making objects appear and disappear.

"You have been fooled, Merek. The cell's energy was reactivated removing your powers," Doran said as he was leaving.

Tristana went to visit him outside his cell. "Remember me?"

"Yes, I do, my trusty child," he said, clinging hold of the bars.

"You kidnapped me from my family, and then made that demon possess me," she said. "Now, you can burn," she said; her features suddenly changed, and had an evil expression on her face. She caused a fire to occur in his cell.

He began to burn, and the girl just stared at him. "The fires of hell are upon you."

Doran raced back to the cell, "No!" he said as he put the fire out. "This is evil."

Tristana changed back before Doran noticed her face, and remained silent. She continued to stare from her prospective. She had done nothing evil; it was an act of justice and revenge.

"I am sending you to the research facility at Cryrotario with the androids," Doran told Merek. "You will do no harm there."

"Good idea," Natasha said.

"As for the Gizalians, they will be sent to their own planet," Doran said.

"We must go too," Crystal said, "back to Earth with Shanice and Rosa."

"Shimick, what are you doing?" Natasha asked. "Staying here with Doran," Shimick said.

"What about Tristana?" Crystal asked.

"Can I travel with you?" she asked. "I will be no bother, honestly."

"If you want to come with us, you can; but what about your home on Sabira?"

"I am not in a hurry to return home," she said.

Everybody said their farewells, and Crystal told Foster to set a course for earth in the 21st century.

Once they arrived on Earth, the time witches said goodbye to Shanice and Rosa. Rosa had regained her powers on the ship in their special room. Once they were home, Shanice contacted her friends, Kayleigh and Jessica, and told them all about her adventures with the time witches.

A week later, Doran was contacted by a forty-year-old lady called Ramona. She was poorly dressed, and said to have travelled from Sabira to find her daughter Tristana. Doran explained about her ordeal, and said that she had gone travelling with the time witches. He fed her and she continued on her journey to find her. But when she entered her ship, she changed her appearance.

"Well, my friends, it seems that Tristana is with the time witches," she said.

"Where have they gone?" said another woman.

"Guess what, Divina?" Ramona asked. "She went to Earth."

"But Tristana is a dark witch like us. Why would she mix with them?"

"My dear Cursida, I don't know; but it won't be for anything good." Divina said.

"Helga, set a course for Earth, in the area of Manchester, England," Ramona said.

"What about Doran?"

"We will deal with Doran soon," Ramona said. "His death is imminent. The time witches must be dealt with first. My daughter Tristana is a dark witch, and needs to be with her family."

THE DARK WITCHES OF SABIRA

It was nearing winter time in Manchester, England. Rosa and Shanice had returned home to Earth for a bit of normality. Shanice had returned to school, and was as if she had never been away. She was seeing her friends Kayleigh and Jessica, and by now, they were fed up of hearing her adventures with the time witches travelling in time and space. Instead, they wanted to plan a Halloween party dressed as their favourite monsters or freaky creatures – from vampires to zombies, walking down the street to Kayleigh's home. Jessica was a zombie, with a pale face and torn shirt and trousers. Kayleigh was a devil woman dressed in a red dress, a tail, and horns. Shanice was dressed as a traditional witch wearing a traditional witch outfit, with a pointed black hat, a long black dress, and a broomstick. The party went on to the early hours of the morning, and everybody enjoyed it; lots of food was eaten, and drinks consumed, after which the girls walked home. They were unaware that they were being watched from a van across the street.

Ramona and her coven of dark witches were close by. Cursida, Davina, and Helga were discussing Halloween.

"So, what is this all about Ramona?" Davina asked.

"Do you mean Halloween?" Ramona replied. "Some traditional Earth thing about the spirits coming to life on this day in the year, on Earth's calendar 31st October."

"So, it is our day to celebrate, is it?" Helga asked.

"Let's drive on and see Shanice tomorrow," Ramona suggested.

"Why do we trust Cursida to drive?" Davina asked.

"She has the most experience," Ramona replied.

"She is reckless, and she will have us killed," Davina stated.

"Davina, have faith in her," Ramona said, hiding her face from seeing what was ahead.

"My frog could drive better," Davina said cringing.

Kayleigh was leading the girls up the street singing typical Halloween song while laughing. Jessica lagged behind with Shanice.

"Come on, girls; join in. Let's have fun," Kayleigh said, turning to face them.

"Wait, Kay. These heels are killing me," Shanice replied.

"Then, why don't you fly like a witch, Shan?" Kayleigh said mockingly.

"Okay, I will," Shanice agreed.

"Shan, don't. People may see you," Jessica said.

"Yes, Shan, you better not in case you are seen," Kayleigh agreed.

But Shanice loved a challenge, and proceeded to mount the broom; no sooner was she on it. She began to levitate, and she was soon flying about in the air. Unfortunately, she had never practiced flying on a broomstick, and lost control flying into a tree, and hitting her head on a branch.

"Ouch! That hurt," she said, rubbing her head and floating down to her friends.

"That man saw you but I think he was drunk," Kayleigh said, pointing to a man staggering across the street.

"Good job, too, Shan. That was reckless," Jessica said.

The next day, as Shanice and her friend were coming out of school, the witches arrived in time to kidnap Shanice. They parked in a van close to her house.

"So, Davina, you know what to do," Ramona asked.

"Yes, knock the bitch out," Davina replied.

"Use the tranquilizer; inject her neck," Ramona explained.

"Can I strangle the white witch bitch?" Davina continued.

"No, Davina. I want her to trade with my daughter," Ramona said sharply.

"Are you sure it is Shanice?" Cursida said.

"Yes. When I spoke to her mother yesterday, I saw a photograph of her," Ramona said. "And what is also useful is that Annabella is her grandmother."

"Who is she?" Davina asked.

"The daughter of Albelenda, one of the most notorious dark witches of the sixteenth century, killer of the witch finders," Ramona said. "My cousin from that distant age on Earth."

"I am sure that Rosa knows about the resurrection, and the true meaning of eight," Cursida said. "Shouldn't we take her too?"

"Rosa will insist on going with the time witches, and rescue her daughter on our planet. We will leave a trail directing them to Alba Two."

"She is coming now," Helga said.

Shanice passed the car walking casually down the street. Ramona stepped out of the car and approached her. She had changed back into the innocent woman that Rosa had met.

"Hello, you must be Shanice," Ramona said.

"Yes, I am," Shanice said apprehensively.

"I am Tristana's mother. I have been looking for her," Ramona said slyly.

"She is with the time witches," Shanice said, and then thought for a moment. "How did you know who I was?"

At that moment, Davina plunged the needle into her neck, and she soon collapsed. Kayleigh and Jessica saw what had happened from a distance, and raced down the street; but before they could reach the van, the witches had put Shanice inside, and began speeding up the road.

"Did you see those people?" Kayleigh asked.

"That woman's face changed," Jessica said. "She was a witch."

"Quick! Let's tell Shanice's mother," Kayleigh insisted. They ran across to Rosa's house and knocked on her door. They continued knocking until Rosa answered. Rosa let them in, and then ran outside. But the van had long gone; Shanice had been kidnapped.

During the time that the kidnapping took place, the time witches were answering a distress call from Zena; a faint bleeping came from their transmitter. When they finally arrived on Zena, the building was in ruins as if it been hit by a meteor storm. The time witches searched amongst the rubble, and eventually found Doran's body crushed beneath the earth. Later, they found Shimick alive but unconscious. They decided to take them both aboard their vessel. They left for Crystal's planet, as it was the closest to them.

No sooner had they arrived when they received a distress call from Rosa on earth. Crystal left Doran's body in a frozen state, and continued to Earth to Rosa. It was a long journey to earth, and the time witches were tried. Shimick was resting in one of the bays, unaware of his journey, and that he had been rescued.

Shanice awoke lying on a bed the dark witches castle. Her arms were secured together with wristband-like handcuffs. She awoke slowly and struggled to move properly. Her eyes were focusing on the ceiling. She looked around the dark and gloomy room with gothic pictures on the walls, each one told its own story of darkness and misery. She suddenly started coughing followed by a sneezing fit, induced by household dust which she disturbed on movement.

"I see you're awake," Cursida said, sitting in an armchair observing her. "You can get up, and we will visit the others."

"Where am I?" Shanice said, struggling to speak. "And who on Earth are you?"

"I am Cursida," she replied. "You are on the planet Sabira, at a place called Alba Two," she said, helping her up.

"Ouch!" she shouted. "My neck hurts."

"It will get better," she reassured Shanice. "You were sedated."

"Wait! Alba is Scotland," she looked around again. "Am I in Scotland?"

"No, you are on the planet Sabira; far from Earth," she said, leading her to the mirror.

"So, have I been abducted?" Shanice asked, then saw her neck. "Look at my neck! Why does everyone attack my neck? Vampires, and Lamia's, and everybody else. I am sick of it," Shanice continued to moan as she was getting cleaned up, and walking along the long dark corridors. "Catch you lot afford to pay your electric bill. It's so dark and dingy."

"Don't you ever stop moaning, girl?" Cursida asked. "You have been abducted, and you are being exchanged for Tristana, who is with the time witches."

"Why do you want Tristana?" Shanice asked.

"She is the daughter of Ramona," Cursida replied.

"Who is Ramona?" Shanice asked, puzzled.

"She is only the greatest and most powerful witch known around the universe," Cursida explained. "And the most dangerous, too."

"Of course, she is," Cursida said. "We dark witches rule supreme in this universe."

"So, Tristana is a dark witch?" Shanice asked. "That would explain her trying to burn Merek to death. A white witch would not do that."

"That's because you, white witches, are too soft and gentle. You people fear what is said to be bad, instead of embracing evil as your friend."

"You speak like the ancient witches who were ruled by Murdina," Shanice said angrily.

They arrived in the main hall, and Shanice was escorted to a chair at the head of the table next to Ramona and Davina on either side of her.

"Sit down, dear," Ramona ordered. "Help yourself to a drink."

"What is it?" she said, sipping from the goblet.

"Sheep's blood with the odd eye floating about," Ramona said laughing.

Shanice spat it out, and looked over to the cauldron that Helga was stirring. "I dread to think what's in there. Some sickly concoction, I suppose."

Shanice was awaiting a horrible reply to her question but she could detect an horrendous smell like vomit, smelly feet, and anal gas all together. No imagination required there with her sensitive nose.

"Toad stew with crushed beetles and spiders, bats' wings, and goblins toes," she said, laughing along with Davina.

"So, who bruised my neck?" Shanice asked.

Cursida sighed as if to say here we go again.

"I did, and what's more child, I would have done more if I could," Davina said, wagging her finger at her, poking her in the face with her long pointed nail.

"Charming," Shanice said. "Remind me not to invite you to my next party."

"What makes you think you're having a next party bitch witch?" she said, grabbing her neck.

"Davina, let go of her," Ramona insisted.

"Again, the neck is a target," Shanice moaned.

"Shut up, Shanice," Ramona said. "Watch the show."

Shanice was puzzled until she saw the stage curtains open, and performers enter the stage. She was pleasantly surprised at the acts, such as magicians, jugglers, and dancers; the music was a little freaky but entertaining all the same. With strange creatures performing, and being waited on by the Gizalians, who were known to shape shifting into various forms, but they had difficulty with humans as they remained green and florescent.

"Where is that soup, Helga?" Ramona shouted above all the music.

"It's on its way, Ramona," she said, tasting it with a ladle. "Tasty."

"Stop drinking it, and bring it here," Ramona said impatiently.

The next performance had to be the best as a girl was introduced on stage. She was known as anger girl or Tempesta. She was brought onto the stage in shackles and chains. She shook her short blonde hair, and a type of gothic dress. She had strange staring eyes and a slim figure. The band were similarly dressed; some were transsexuals who looked as attractive as the female performers. They sang and danced provocatively amazing to the crowds of dark witches and followers. The Gizalians clung to the witches like leaches, sucking them dry of evil thoughts and wicked ideas. No wonder they were known as the lowest form of life in space.

Shanice was enjoying the performance although she felt sorry for the girl dragging her chains along and cutting her wrists as she pulled at them. Shanice did try this awful stew, and thought it might be a good way to lose weight; a few bowls, and she would be vomiting for sure. Davina said that one of the male dancers was annoying her, and transformed him into a toad. Shanice was trying to perform magic but realised the handcuffs were dampening her powers.

"My dear, Shanice," Ramona said, "These cuffs are powerful and are preventing you from using your powers while you're here."

"Yes, bitch witch. You need to chill, child," Davina said with a sly look on her face.

"Charming as ever, Davina," Cursida said, laughing.

"You have your fun, Davina," Shanice said. "I will have mine when the time witches arrive."

"Oh, I am scared, child," Davina replied. She spoke to Ramona in Scottish Gaelic and then became shocked when Shanice replied in Gaelic.

"Tha I na nighean spaideil airson dana – bhuidseach geal," Ramona said. 'She's a smart girl, for a white witch.'

"Tha mi nam nightean glic," Shanice replied. 'I am a smart girl.'

"A bheil gaidhlig na hi – Alba agen?" Ramona continued. 'Do you speak Scottish Gaelic?

"Bha, theagang mo mhathair mi dhomh bruidhinn Gaelic," Shanice replied confidently. 'Yes, my mother taught me to speak Gaelic.'

"How do you know our language?" she asked in English.

"Because my grandmother was from Scotland. She was brought up by dark witches, and became a white witch," Shanice explained.

"What was her name? Ramona asked.

"Annabella, but she used to be known then as Lamia," Shanice continued, showing that she was proud of her grandmother.

"I know of her. She had knowledge of the Resurrection," Davina said. "Enough about her. She was a traitor and a fool," Ramona said.

Shanice stood up, and Davina expected her to fight with her; but Shanice turned her back on them, and said, "I am going to dance."

Shanice did dance to the band, and used her acrobatic skills to show what she was capable of. She danced amazingly well, and applauded by the witches at the end. She made it a colourful performance using her powers to omit light from her body and glowed brightly.

Once the party ended, Shanice went off to her room, and slept almost immediately. She began to dream about her mother and friends. She missed her life back home, but missed her life with the time witches even more as she dreamed about her adventures in time and space; battling robots, vampires, and the Lamians. Her mind drifted back to Foster and Shimick, her time travelling buddies. Foster the android made her laugh with his research-based explanations, and Shimick the green goblin, who she loved to tease. She wondered whether Natasha and Crystal the time witches were missing her with her cheek and constantly moaning about her problems.

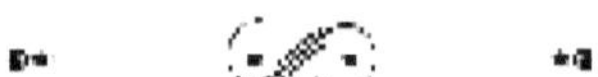

The next day after breakfast with the dark witches, Shanice was given her freedom while they allowed her a chance to race with some of the younger witches across Alba Two's terrain, but Davina was keeping a close watch on her. They were racing on broomsticks even though Shanice was not very confident flying on a broomstick. She made every effort to compete with them. Colosia, Musette, Hesperia, and Emmerame were the main competitors, but Niamh, Sinead, and Saairse were the fiercest competitors who stop at nothing to be the best and win this race. Tempesta was the champion. Davina had trained the witches to reach their standard. She had also listened in on a conversation between Ramona and Shanice that she was not very happy about it was concerning. Shanice becoming a dark witch, and sitting at Ramona's right side. Surely that was her place with Tristana on her left side. This made her jealous and angry to think that Shanice was going to be so close to Ramona so much. So, she planned to make sure Shanice never finished the race, and to have a nasty accident during the race, bad enough to kill her.

Shanice had been practicing on a broomstick since her unfortunate accident on Earth, flying into a tree. Hesperia had befriended her, and took around the canyon to practice her latest skill. Hesperia was exceptionally good at flying on brooms, and hoped to win the race. But Tempest was the champion that no one could beat.

The witches got ready for the race by lining up at the starting post. Davina saw her opportunity to disappear at this point, four witches were ready to follow the competitors in case of any accidents during the race. If someone was injured, they would send a signal into the sky alerting other witches; by firing a lightning bolt into the sky. Ramona started the race by sending up a flare. She turned and winked at Shanice which was her way of wishing her luck. The witches set of to the mountains in one group. Shanice was astonished that the dark witches seemed so friendly travelling high into the sky. However, when they were out of sight of Ramona, they began showing their true colours. Sinead was the first to barge through the ranks of witches knocking others out of the way, but at this point, there were no casualties. They entered the canyon and things became very different. Sinead knocked Musette off her broom, and took the lead. Musette rolled about the ground in pain. Shanice wanted to help her, then she remembered about the four witches who were looking out for injured racers. Hesperia gave her a wave, and continued in front of her. They turned a bend, and Davina appeared from behind a rock. She used her wand to send a lightning bolt towards her. Unfortunately, it caught Colosia, and she fell to the ground. Davina was angry, and hid again. She gathered her thoughts, and then vanished. Tempesta and Hesperia were catching up with Sinead. They were followed by Emmerame, Niamh, Saairse, and Shanice all in a group. Davina tried another attempt at stopping Shanice by using the same tactic. This time, she caught Shanice's shoulder, and hit Saairse who went straight into the canyon wall. Shanice had to adjust herself on the broomstick. It was fortunate for Shanice as Saairse was trying to knock her off her broom. She was one of the most vicious witches. They finally left the canyon, and headed for the forest. Sinead remained in the lead followed by Tempesta and Hesperia, who followed the trail back towards the castle. Shanice was now catching up with Tempesta she had almost reached her when she noticed Hesperia speeding ahead catching up with Sinead. Davina made one last attempt to stop Shanice setting trees on fire, and securing a rope for her to stumble into tied around two trunks. But Shanice was quick to react, and broke the rope with a magic spell, and then sending a spray of water into the air in order to put out the fire. Tempesta had witness the event, and stopped to make sure Shanice was alright. Niamh and Emmerame were close behind to also witness the event. They left the forest with Sinead and Hesperia beside each other. Tempesta and Shanice were getting closer. Suddenly, Sinead kicked Hesperia, and cast a spell on her that caused her to hit the ground. Tempesta moved forward, and did the same to Sinead, and then, she fell to the ground. Shanice stopped to make sure Hesperia was alright. She looked up at Shanice, and waved her on.

"Go on; I am fine. You can win this," Hesperia said.

Shanice continued, and caught up with Tempesta. It was now just about them, but to Hesperia's surprise, Shanice seemed to slow down, and crossed the line in second place.

After the race, Hesperia went over to Shanice, and questioned her.

"You could have won. Why didn't you?" Hesperia asked.

"It isn't my place to win as a white witch, but it was fun,"

Shanice replied.

"I can't believe you're a white witch," she said.

"But I am," Shanice said, "and it goes back generations too."

"Join us, Shanice, and we could be friends," she said pleading with her.

"My destiny lays elsewhere. Sorry, Hesperia," Shanice said.

During the time that Shanice was with the dark witches, the time witches were making their way over to her from another galaxy. Tristana was enjoying her adventures with the time witches, but knew that she had to return home at some point, and face her mother, Ramona. But Tristana was confused by two very different ways of life. The one that the dark witches followed based on cruelty and treachery, or the route the white witches followed that consisted of kindness and helping their fellowmen.

When they arrived on Sabira, they made their way to Alba Two where the dark witches lived. They were greeted by Ramona and Shanice. Natasha was very cautious, and led her crew into the castle looking all around her suspecting a trap. Davina was watching them from a security camera. Crystal was walking along side Shimick, Tristana was next to Natasha, and Foster remained in the vessel. When they met up with Ramona, Tristana went to stand beside her mother, and Shanice stood beside her mother, Rosa. The atmosphere was tense. No one wanted to speak, but finally Ramona did.

"So, I finally meet the time witches." She looked them up and down. "I need to decide what to do with you all."

"Let them go, mother," Tristana said. "You don't need them."

"Oh, Shanice has been a great asset," Ramona replied. "I think I will keep her."

"No, you have me. So, let her go," Tristana insisted.

"Very well," Ramona replied reluctantly.

She led everyone to the banquet hall. Many guards stood around the doorways. Tristana watched as Shanice went down the corridor in the direction of the toilets, and then, she followed her. Shanice turned back to face her.

"Can I help you?" she asked.

"Yes, you can. Stop trying to get in my mothers' good books."

"That is not my intention," Shanice replied innocently.

"Davina told me of your cunningness. You want to be a dark witch, and stand at my mother's right side."

"That is not my intention. I am a time witch, a white witch."

"I am warning you, witch bitch. Stay away from her, or I will harm you," Tristana warned Shanice.

"Don't you dare threaten me, girl," Shanice replied. "I am not scared of you."

"You should be. I can destroy you with one swoop of my wand," Tristana said.

"Let's see you try," Shanice replied with her wand in her hand.

At that moment, Natasha appeared, and spoke to them both. "Stop this nonsense now," she insisted. "Return to the hall at once." She pointed down the corridor. "We are leaving."

While this event was taking place, Tempesta caught sight of Crystal standing outside as if she was up to no good. She took out her wand, and sent a bolt of lightning at her. Crystal pleaded for her life but was too late. Tempesta had killed her. Ramona used her wand to destroy Tempesta.

"We are not at war with these white witches!" she shouted.

Natasha and Shanice stood shocked and saddened by the event, and cried at the loss of their friend and fellow time witch, and then decided to leave.

"Wait!" Ramona shouted. "I did not ask you to leave."

"Mother, let them go," Tristana said. "They have lost enough."

The time witches left, minus Crystal. They were on the way to the ship when they found a body by the rocks. When they turned the body over, it was Crystal. Her head was bleeding, and she had a bump to the left side. She was awake but confused and disorientated. She had lost her memory.

The crew managed to carry her onto the ship, and took her straight into the treatment room laying her on the bed. Once her wounds were attended to, they allowed her to rest. Each of them was confused about finding her as she appeared to be killed by Tempesta. They even questioned whether or not she was really Crystal, and not a witch in disguise. After all, they seemed to get away relatively easy.

The ship had taken off just after they got aboard, and they were heading for Crystal's planet. In the days it took them to reach the planet, Crystal was recovering. They had questioned Crystal about events at the castles as her memory gradually returned. She answered questions that only knew about, and seemed to be herself again. They discovered that the other Crystal was the impostor trying to cause trouble for the witches. Shanice seemed to think it was Davina who was killed using a spell to look like Crystal. Making out that Crystal was a spy, she had knocked the real Crystal out with a rock but didn't expect Tempesta to react the way she did, and kill her.

FURTHER ADVENTURES OF THE TIME WITCHES

RETURN TO ASPERA

The time witches travelled to Crystal's home planet, Aspera, to meet her Father Zenith, but also to surprise Shanice at the same time. When they arrived, they were greeted by the servants who led them to the main hall. Zenith was sitting, and struggled to stand when they entered the room.

"Crystal, my child," he said with a smile on his face.

"Father," she replied, ignoring him referring to her as a child. Who could be offended by the man with sparkling eyes who loved her so much? Crystal felt the same as she considered him to be her closest friend, as well as a father to her.

After they had caught up with all the events from the past and enjoyed their refreshments, Zenith led them to the place where they had frozen Doran. He was travelling on a hover device like a floating wheel chair. He revealed his body which was in a special container Shanice was shocked at the sight of him in this condition.

"What has happened to him?" she asked.

"The witches attacked his castle and completely destroyed it. As you see, Shimick survived, but Doran was crushed by the rubble," Natasha explained.

"So, why is he here?" Shanice asked.

"We were hoping that we could resurrect him with your help," Crystal said.

"But how can I do that?" she asked, confused.

"You are the most powerful witch I know. You can do it without our help," Natasha said confidently.

Shanice looked to her mother for reassurance. Rosa nodded and smiled at her.

"Shanice, you can do it; you have the power to do it," Rosa said, holding her shoulders, and then hugging her.

"Are we performing the resurrection here?"

"No, we are heading for Earth to the caves where we went before in Scotland. Your father and Professor Graham Stokes, one of the leading archaeologist's from Manchester University, will go with us. We can pick him up from the Manchester area, and go on to Scotland," Natasha said. The course was then set for England.

Meanwhile, the girls were catching up with events from Alba, and the planets history to the recent adventures of the time witches. Natasha explained to Shanice about being wary of Tristana as she is a dark witch, and Shanice warned the others about the dark witches and their plan to rule other planets in the future. They eventually touched down in a field near the university, and soon found Professor Stokes. He was delighted to meet his friends, Rosa and Shanice. His son Andrew was also present with Professor Erickson.

They continued to Scotland with the surprise food and

medication on board flying over the Thames. They needed the Book of Shadows and their wands, so that they could perform the ritual.

They entered the cave leaving Foster in the ship. Stokes and his son, Andrew, remained near the entrance while the rest walked further into the cave until they reached the part where the archaeologists met Rosa years ago. They had explained about this jelly-type substance that her body was preserved in, and found the very same substance still there, and so they dropped his body into the substance and began the ritual.

Shanice stood behind a rock which came up to her waste. She put the Book of Shadows, opened it, and put it on top of the rock placing her finger under the words, and speaking out loud.

"This is taken from the Book of Shadow, calling on the spirits to help and resurrect the body of our friend from permanent sleep. Awaken his soul and revive his spirit in order that he may live again. Open his mind to thoughts and liven his heart. Let the blood flow; listen to my voice as it echoes through the cave. Let me feel your presence like a breeze from the ocean. Let my wand conduct the power to restart your heart, and you will be a living being once more." The word she used was in Scottish Gaelic and these were encouraged by the other witches. "Le bhith a'gairm spioradan ar sinnsearan bidh e a'cwideachgoth le bhith ag. Ath-nuadhachudh a'chuirp. Seo bho chadal maireannach a'dihgadh a spiorid. Agus ag ath-bheothachadth a chuip gum bi ebeo arithist leig leans a bhith a'faireach dainn do. Lathaireachd mar a'ghaoith bhan chlian, eist ri mo gihuth mar a tha e a'tighinn tron waimh seo, leig le mo shlat cumhachd a thoirt air als gus athbheothachadh." She lifted her wand, and the other witches did the same, discharging lightning from it towards his heart. After a while, Doran's body began to respond by jolting. They made one more attempt, and he began to awaken.

"So that's it," a voice was heard which echoed through the cave. Everybody looked around. Eventually, they saw the spirit of the former mayor, Malet, standing behind them.

"Where did you come from?" Rosa asked.

"Who is he?" Natasha asked.

"This is Mayor Malet of Teversham," she explained.

"Yes, I have been watching you for years. I was in Arnold's body for years."

"Who do you mean? My boyfriend Arnold?" Shanice asked.

"Yes. I took over his body," he said with an evil cunning grin.

"Yuk! That's gross," Shanice said. "Imagine you inside him looking at me."

"So, I can be immortal," the mayor said. "You can resurrect dead people."

"Sorry, mayor, but you need a body," Rosa said.

"I will be back. Fear not," the mayor said, disappearing.

"What is he up to? I don't trust him," Rosa said.

"I can't believe he was actually inside Arnie," Shanice said.

The time witches dropped Rosa, Andrew, and Graham Stokes off in Manchester, and continued back to Aspera with Doran. Shanice insisted on going with them as she wanted to venture more in time and space. Rosa knew she was in good hands, and that she could now defend herself in times of trouble. Her powers had increased at this point and she was a powerful witch.

FURTHER ADVENTURES OF THE TIME WITCHES

REVENGE OF THE VAMPIRES

It was the winter of 2026 in location outside New York City. Cold breeze was sweeping across the land; thick snow was blowing everywhere swirling in the distance in a blizzard. A large group of people were travelling through it, dressed in armoured clothing with protective helmets. Their silhouettes could be seen.

As they marched forward, the closer they got, the more detail was shown on their suits, such as identity badges and coloured braids. Suddenly, they were surrounded by another army with similar suits. They started to attack them wildly, showing no mercy; swords were mainly used. The first army were vampire slayers, and ones ambushing them were vampires. The whole bloody battle took an hour, and the slayers were defeated. Soon after, the vampires disappeared taking some of the slayers with them.

Shortly after, the time witches arrived. They were horrified with what they saw; mutilated bodies all around them with arms and legs missing. Shanice was physically sick at the sight of them. Some of them were so young, drained of blood and life. They heard a whirring noise and all looked up to sky; above them was a space craft with more vampire slayers led by Carina, who they had met before at some point in time, wearing her black armour and long flowing black hair.

"What has happened here?" she asked.

"We have just arrived, Carina," Natasha said. "This is how we found them."

"We have just arrived, Carina," Natasha said. "This is how we found them."

"How do you know my name?" she asked.

"From a different point in time," Natasha continued. "We have fought together."

"Why don't I remember this?" she asked suspiciously.

"It must have been in the future. You were with Siena."

"Who is Siena?" she asked impatiently, awaiting a reply.

"A friend in your future," Natasha explained.

"These people are vampires," Gareth said. "I can see it in them. They killed our people."

"No; see for yourself. We are time witches," Shanice said, showing her wand.

"But they were obviously vampires who killed them," Crystal said, pointing to one of the bodies. "Look at the bites on her neck."

"Carina!" one of the slayers shouted. "It's Judith, your cousin."

"Judith!" Carina shouted, running over to where she lay.

"How did they know where your slayers were?" Crystal asked.

"I don't know," Carina said. "This was not a planned exercise."

"So, they would have had no way of knowing they were them?" Crystal continued.

"Not at all," Carina said.

"Unless they were from the future, and knew about the slayers plan to find them here; came back in time to just before the slayer killed the vampires here," Crystal said, working things out in a logical way. "This was a planned revenge attack by the vampires. Possibly the battle that we won Orazio fled with other vampires."

"She is talking nonsense," Gareth said. "This is so unbelievable."

"Can you offer a more logical explanation Gareth?" Shanice asked.

"They are right. So, how do we find out the facts?" Carina asked.

"Well, we are time witches. We simply travel back to an earlier point in time just before the ambush, and then defeat them," Crystal said. "You can all fit into our cargo bay."

"Okay. Let's go, slayers," Carina said, leading her army, and following the time witches to their craft.

Once inside, most of the slayers went into the cargo bay. They could communicate on the intercom straight through to Crystal.

"We are all ready, Crystal" Carina said.

"Okay, hold tight. We are heading back in time before the ambush," Crystal replied.

"We will be ready for them," Carina said, adjusting her black suit.

Crystal took off and headed into the time portal. She was determined to reach the right period of time, allowing half an hour difference, so that they could arrive earlier and surprise the vampires. She was accurate with her timing thanks also to the navigation of Foster. They landed the vessel and both the time witches and the slayers were there to save the other slayers.

As soon as the slayers arrived, the vampires headed forward to ambush them, not expecting Carina's slayers behind them. Her slayers advanced and began firing their weapons. The witches used their wands to attack them, firing thunderbolts, and managing to shatter their helmets. Between the slayers and the witches, they managed to destroy most of them, but some vampires were trying to escape, heading to their space craft. The witches were on broomsticks attacking them from the sky, but still a few escaped.

"They must not get away," Carina said, "or they will alter the time pattern again."

"Let's get in the ship quickly," Crystal shouted.

"Good call, Crystal. We can stop them with the ship," Natasha said.

They collected their wounded slayers, and headed for the ship. The slayers went into the cargo bay, but Carina went into the cockpit.

They followed the ship into space, and waited for the right moment to fire on the vessel. Shots were fired both ways until Carina fired the most crucial blow on the vessel, and it exploded.

Carina asked if they could head back to their planet, and treat the wounded; but Natalie and Shanice had already started treating them. Judith was fine and very talkative unlike her cousin, Carina, who was still puzzled who the time witches were. Eventually, they arrived on the slayers' planet, and stayed briefly at their base before heading back into space.

NATASHA

FURTHER ADVENTURES OF THE TIME WITCHES

THE INVASION OF THE ANDROIDS

Various planets were colonised by earth-based research that became established in since 2126 AD, accommodating androids and humans. They were classed as fully automated systems. The humans were used in case the robots malfunctioned, and they were required to reprogram them.

Everything ran smoothly, until one day, a group of androids did malfunction. They destroyed one base, and were targeting other establishments. Suddenly, no one was safe, and it was clear that someone was responsible for reprogramming them for destruction.

They entered five establishments, attacked the armed guards, and captured the humans. Mechanical voices could be heard over speakers throughout the establishments, sounding out instructions to destroy the humans and their technology. No one was safe from these androids who were equipped to kill humans, and destroy machinery. Whoever was behind the attacks had to be evil, and have no regard for the research stations.

The time witches had been travelling in space for a while, and contemplated visiting various places in history. They were interested in just observing the time, and not participating in any events. It would just make a change to just look at what was going on around them.

"I would like to visit Cleopatra," Shanice said.

"That would be fun," Natasha agreed.

"They worshiped cats," Shanice said.

"Not cats again," Shimick objected.

"Why, Shimick? Don't you like cats?" Crystal said, teasing him. "Big furry creatures with sharp teeth and big tails."

"Stop it," he insisted. "Let's go somewhere else."

"Where do you want to go, Shimick?" Shanice asked.

"The blue planet that glows like a pearl," he said, looking out into space.

"I would be inclined to seek adventure and mystery," Natasha said. "New adventures every time."

At that moment, they began receiving distress signals from the research bases; each call was similar, wanting help after being under attack.

"There is our answer to where we are going," Crystal said. "Someone needs our help, and we must respond."

"I agree, Crystal; all lives matter," Natasha said.

"That knocks Cleopatra on the head," Shanice said, sulking.

But Shanice soon got over her disappointment when she discovered that the bases were being attacked by androids, and she would have her opportunity to use her powers once again. She was eager to challenge the androids, and help restore the bases to their former glory.

It took hours to work on each base and get to the next base hoping to find clues to where the androids were, and where they would strike next. Eventually, they found a pattern of attack, and continued to the next location just a short distance behind the androids. The attack formation was the same: enter the building by two sides, and attack the laboratories one by one killing the humans.

This time, the witches had arrived in time to stop them, and find out who had programmed them. Shanice was in such a hurry to stop them. She went through the wrong hatch, and landed at the food of the android leader. The others were more cautious, and made a tactical assault on them using their wands to destroy them.

Shanice had been secured with a type of hand cuffs as the android gripped her neck. She yelled out, "My neck! Always my neck!"

"Who are you?" he asked.

"Shanice. I am a time witch," she replied.

"What do you want here, time witch?" he said, increasing his grip.

"To destroy you, androids, and find out who is programming you," she replied, choking.

"How disappointing that we captured you," he said, releasing his grip. "So, what do you think now? We have the power to kill you."

"I may die, but my friends will destroy the rest of you," she said bravely.

"Then die, witch," he said, gripping her throat again.

At that moment, he stopped and listened to a voice shouting out to him.

"Hey, metal Mickey! Let go of her or die," Natasha shouted.

The android turned to face her, lifted his arm to fire his weapon, and was blasted away by her wand.

"You only get one chance from me," she said.

Shanice picked her wand up from the ground, and used it to kill another android behind Natasha. They both ended up fighting other androids, and were soon joined by the others. They took some of the heads from the androids, and searched for clues of the person who programmed them. Each android was taken apart. Their circuits were checked for abnormalities. Eventually, after hours of work, a small chip was discovered containing detailed instructions of each base, including maps, names of humans, and locations. It was hours later when the name of the man who programmed it was revealed as Adam Granger, and what followed was his location on the planet Hydroxa, the first planet to have a research base because of its location within the solar system.

Doctor Adam Granger programmed the first androids, and the research team. Unfortunately, he had a bad accident in a laboratory that led to brain damage. Granger had episodes of paranoia, frequent headaches, and loss of memory. It was his paranoia that caused him to suspect that the company he worked for was out to destroy him; that he was regarded as useless at his work by his colleagues. He was no longer master of his trade as he watched new scientists taking over his research. In the passing months, he was becoming the assistant to other scientists cleaning up after them, so Granger became bitter, and programmed the androids to obey him and nobody else. This was the assumption of others as they noticed his decline. It was the only explanation for his actions, and for the destruction of the bases.

Shanice was looking at the bruises on her neck and cussing, "Why my neck? Look, Natasha, more bruises."

"Well, Shanice, you would wade in not thinking," Natasha said.

"I know," Shanice said. "But somebody has to jump in and save others."

"Foolishness! A reckless pursuit, if you ask me," Natasha said angrily.

"Come on, Natasha. Have you never been reckless?" Crystal commented.

"Maybe once or twice at Trafalgar, and the journey to the French revolution; not my finest hours, I must admit," she confessed. "But I was younger then."

"Were you about Shanice's age?" Crystal asked.

"Yes, I was," Natasha admitted. "Okay, I am sorry, Shanice. I was just trying to guide you in my own way."

"I understand," Shanice said. "I have a lot of growing up to do."

"Now, you have kissed and made up; what do we do about Granger?" Crystal asked.

"He has to be stopped," Natasha said.

"We must inform the space authority," Shanice said.

"Foster, contact them, please," Crystal said. "Immediately!"

Everyone was apprehensive about contacting the space federation, but it had to be done in order to save the other bases. They remained silent for a while just waiting for a response. Once they were acknowledged, Foster put them on the main screen. A man in a formal uniform stood in front of the screen. He has grey hair, blue eyes, and a grey moustache.

"I am Commander Shepherd," he said with a gravely voice. "How can I help you?"

"We are the time witches. We're here to bring you bad news," Natasha said.

"I have heard of you, time witches. What is your news?" He

continued, "I have heard about the distress calls from our research bases and how you assisted in restoring them."

"Yes, commander, and about the lives lost due to the androids," Crystal said.

"It is all down to one man, Doctor Adam Granger," she continued.

"He programmed the androids to destroy your bases."

"Do you have proof of this time witch," Shepherd asked, "or is this just pointing the finger?

"We have plenty of proof or do you think we are lying?" Shanice said abruptly. "Just because you have authority, doesn't mean you can insult us."

"Shanice," the others said at the same time.

"Well, we don't have to answer to the space federation."

"We do," Crystal said. "We must answer to federation law."

"We will forward all proofs to you, Commander," Crystal said.

"Thank you, time witches. I will speak to you soon," Shepherd said, ending communications.

Crystal and Foster began sending the relevant information, and then waited for a reply from the Commander. It seemed to take hours before he contacted the ship.

"Time witches, could I perhaps ask a small favour of you?" he said. "Could you distract Adam Granger while we get our men together?"

"Sure," Crystal agreed. "We will visit him and keep him entertained."

"Good. I will alert my men that you will be there," he said, satisfied with her answer.

"I am Crystal, this is Natasha and Shanice. We are the time witches. Shimick is a goblin, and Foster is an android."

"I will contact you when my men are in position," he said before leaving.

The time witches took a journey through space to where

Dr. Adam Granger was last located on the planet Hydroxia. It was a very strange planet with a cold and lonely surface. The base could hardly be seen for the snow and frequent blizzards that caused a series of domes immerged. They landed close by, and made efforts to communicate with the base. Eventually, a mechanical voice answered.

"Please state your name, and reason for your visit," he said.

"My name is Crystal. I am a time witch. I have come to visit your base in the hope to locate some lost files."

"Come in when you are ready, time witch."

"Thank you," Crystal said politely.

Most of the bases had a similar layout with domes and tunnels with a monorail leading to each dome. On entry though, the main hatch begins the sterilization process before going into the main research area. The time witches entered the base, and completed the sterilisation process. They were escorted by armed android guards to the main area.

Doctor Granger sat at a desk peering over his silver spectacles. He had dark receding hair that had natural grey highlights, and a matching moustache.

"Welcome to my base," he said, offering to shake their hands.

Each of the witches did so, and smiled politely at the doctor. It was hard to believe that he was capable of killing innocent people. Even if he didn't do it directly, this man had a great mind that was affected by his accident.

"What an incredible place," Natasha said.

"Outstanding," Crystal said.

"But, is it not a fact that witches are usually old and ugly,"the doctor commented.

"It's not true as you see," Shanice replied. "Some of us are beautiful."

"It is said throughout the universe that witches cause fear to spread across the planets," he continued.

"That would be dark witches. We are white witches," Crystal said, defending her kind.

"Are you Doctor Granger?" Shanice asked. "My word! You're skinny."

"Really? I hadn't noticed," he replied.

"Really, Shanice?" Natasha said bluntly. "That was rude."

"It's true," Shanice said. "No offence, but you're like a walking skeleton."

"Ignore her, doctor, she's from earth," Natasha said, trying to excuse her.

"I understand," Granger said smiling. "So, let me give you a tour of the labs."

"Splendid," Shanice mumbled under her breath. "Lead on, doctor," Crystal said. "Let us see the wonder of science."

"That's what I like to see, science at work," Natasha said, looking at the equipment and facilities.

Dome One was the main central dome. This was surrounded by Domes Two to Six, each had their own laboratories, sleeping quarters, and security units. They also had a holding bay containing prison cells which were very rarely used.

The doctor seemed calm and relaxed when they met him, and certainly no concerns at this point. He was friendly, courteous, and kind. Was this the man who programmed androids to kill humans and destroy bases without a conscience? His face seemed scarred and disfigured from his accident, and he did seem to have trouble walking. He explained about the importance of research and its benefits. His words seemed genuine, and he appeared to be dedicated to his work. They questioned between themselves whether or not the information was accurate or not.

Hours passed by during the extensive tour, and the doctor

was showing signs of becoming tired. His speech had begun to slur, and he was more unsteady.

"You are tired, doctor," Natasha said. "Why don't you rest"

"In good time," he replied. "So, are you impressed with the base?"

"Yes, I am, doctor," Shanice said. "Most impressed, such creative work."

"Spoken by a true artist," he said. "I can tell by your hands. You are gifted."

"Do you think so?" Shanice grinned. "Wow! Imagine that; me, an artist."

"Yes, you are," Natasha said. "Even though you're reckless at times."

"Excuse me, ladies, but I must rest. Any questions will be answered by the androids in the base," he said, escorting them off the monorail. He continued on the monorail to his sleeping quarters.

Two androids escorted them to the main area. Nobody spoke. There was an eerie silence like the moments before a disaster. The girls had been conversing telepathically during the tour, and continued to do so.

"Well, that was educational," Shanice said.

"Something isn't right," Natasha said. "I have a really bad feeling about this."

"I feel as if we are in danger, but not by the doctor," Crystal said. "By the space federation."

"Do you think we have been used by them?" Natasha said.

"The federation used us to find the doctor, and keep him occupied while they prepare to attack," Shanice said.

"What about us?" Crystal asked.

"They don't care as long as they have their scapegoat, namely us," Natasha said. "We are dispensable."

"Are we?" Shanice asked.

"Yes, we are time witches. We are no use to anybody,"

Crystal said.

"But we have incredible powers," Shanice said, concerned.

"That's what makes them fear us, and hate us even more," Crystal said. "I know them, and what they are capable of."

"Also, the dark witches don't do us any favours with their want and destruction," Natasha said, thinking about the evil things they had done in time and space.

"I can sense the hostility," Shanice said, turning her head to look at the androids.

"We need to decide what we are doing," Natasha said. "Remain here or flee."

"But what shall we do to the doctor?" Crystal asked. "If the federation programmed the androids and is blaming the doctor, both him and us will die."

"Why us?" Shanice asked.

"Because we will know too much, and expose the real villains," Crystal said.

"Is there a happy ending here, ladies?" Shanice said, concerned.

"No," Natasha and Crystal said in harmony.

"Let's get out of here now," Shanice said. "I certainly don't want to die."

"None of us do, Shan," Crystal said. "But we have to leave safely and discreetly."

At that moment, three ships arrived in space, and began to contact the space base.

"Calling Hydroxia," came a mechanical voice.

"Hydroxia receiving. Go ahead."

"We are an inspection team. Can we come down to you?"

The voice continued, "You are welcome," an android replied. "Beam down."

A party of androids beamed down to the main bay all armed for battle. No sooner had they landed, they began to fire on the androids in the bay. The alert was sounded that warned the base that it was under attack, and to take action. The time witches had seen humans working in the base, and went to find them. The invading androids were ordered to seek and destroy all humans. This would obviously include the witches. They had retrieved their wands earlier, and were ready for the invasion.

Meanwhile, more androids beamed down offering reinforcements to the first invasion. This continued until the base was full of androids. Lasers were being fired along with sharp metal swords used to cut down the enemy. The unexpected attack confused the androids, many were defenceless.

The time witches led the humans away from the battle area hoping to find the doctor on the way, providing him with a safe passage off the planet. They all got on the monorail and went to Section 2, searching for the doctor, but Granger was actually in Section 4. Some of the humans were getting tired unable to keep up with the others, but the androids were not far behind them. A warning came over the speakers for the humans to surrender, but they knew that if they would do this, this would mean death, so they continued. It was at this point that Section 5 was invaded. The humans were now in Section 3, and it was obvious that the androids were now heading for Section 4. After a short while, they finally met in that sector.

The witches fought alongside the security androids. All three witches sent out lightening bolts from their wands, disarming the androids at a fast rate. Fortunately, there were few robots being made that could destroy humans, and wipe them all out completely.

"I think it's time for some girl power, ladies," Shanice shouted, attacking the androids.

The other two agreed and joined in. Mechanical body parts were flying in all directions. The android guards were defending the witches until they finally scored a victory in this section.

During the time that they were under attack in the domes, federation ships had arrived to fire on the three ships that menaced the base. Before long, two of the ships were destroyed, and the third surrendered. Doctor Granger was discovered in his sleeping compartment as Shanice burst into the room after blasting the door. The doctor rose from his bed in shock.

"Have you come to kill me?" he spoke.

"Like I said before, Shanice is reckless," Natasha said.

"I would say she is very keen," Crystal said in her defence.

"So, what now?" the doctor asked.

"We see what the federation say," Crystal said.

"Someone set you up, doctor," Natasha said. "You and these poor humans."

"Evidently, and I suppose it was something to do with the federation," he replied.

They proceeded to walk towards Section 5, which was now in the hands of the federation. After walking a while, what looked like a robot guard was coming towards them. He befriended Crystal and by surprise, stabbed the doctor in the side. Shanice immediately responded by magically producing her broomstick, and chased after the guard by flying above the humans, and entering the main dome. Crystal and Natasha tried to stop her by shouting her name, but she was too fast, and she had taken off before they could reach her.

The guard began to run down a tunnel, and shooting at the wheels of the monorail derailing it, and successfully blocking the tunnel. Shanice sent a bolt of lightning towards the front of the train and moved it enough to get past it. Her slim body could get through easily. However, the guard stopped and began to face his enemy, and shot at her a few times. Shanice returned the fire making impacts on his armour until it split apart, and he fell to the ground with a thud. A small crowd had gathered around him, and Shanice knelt beside him, and began to remove the mask. People were surprised to see a human face looking at them. It looked like Arnold, Shanice's boyfriend at first, and then changed into the federation commander. Shanice was upset and confused by the ordeal, and was comforted by Crystal.

Natasha was angry. "Shanice, this is once again the result of your reckless behaviour."

The guards were ordered to arrest for attempted murder, and she was taken to one of the federation ships. She was taken to the main base on Earth in 2516, a vastly different place to stand trial. Crystal and Natasha followed her in their time vessel, and managed to land in close proximity to the court building. The doctor was taken to a hospital where he recovered, and he was waiting with anticipation to hear about Shanice.

The guard was discovered to be a changeling, able to transform itself into many forms. He worked for a splinter section of the federation who broke off and rebelled against them, leaving chaos in their pathway.

The doctor disappeared from the hospital without a trace which didn't quite fit the doctor's claim for innocence. Shanice was released and returned back to the ship.

Natasha greeted Shanice with a hug and said, "We all love you."

"I know," Shanice said with tears in her eyes.

"Just stop being reckless," she continued.

"Yes, Shan. Think about your actions."

"I will. I promise," Shanice replied with the tears rolling down her cheeks.

Foster patted her on the back and said, "There, there," in a matter-of-fact manner.

FURTHER ADVENTURES OF THE TIME WITCHES

LEGACY OF THE SPACE PIRATES

We are often told about the Caribbean Islands, and other places where pirates of the rough seas, who used to rob from merchant ships, sometimes from the ships full of treasure. They were often ruthless and cunning with little regard for others. They looked out for ships, and then attacked, killing innocent people back in ancient time, and continued to the 21st century, in some parts of Africa.

The time witches were contacted when a number of vessels alerted the space federation after being robbed. The time witches were playing games, creating elusions, and making tarot cards float in mid-air. Shanice had been chasing Shimick after transforming herself as her favourite animal, a cat. Shimick was running around screeching like car brakes, and Foster was listening and transmitting messages from distressed ships; this could only be described as the usual chaos on Crystal's vessel. However, the chaos stopped at the sounds of yelling and screaming coming over the speakers. This was followed by a sharp bang coming from outside the ship as particles of debris flew towards them through the time portal. The ship must have been completely destroyed by something. Foster gathered up information about the accident. One thing was for sure, it was no accident, and the people responsible should come to justice.

Crystal turned to face Foster, "Take us over there now," she commanded.

"Who are they, Crystal?" Shanice asked.

"Pirates," she replied.

"Space pirates," Natasha said. "Like the legendary pirates of the Caribbean."

They noticed a vessel drifting through space. It was damaged with dead people.

"God! Did they do that?" Shanice asked.

"Yes. The space pirates are ruthless. They cut throats."

"They are?" Shanice asked. "We need to stop them."

"I agree," Crystal said.

"Me too," Natasha agreed.

At that moment, the commander of the federation contacted them. He seemed a bit sheepish after the last time he contacted them.

"We need your help, time witches," he said, and then he continued explaining about the pirates.

"What makes you think we can trust you Commander, after the last time?" Natasha asked.

"Yes. You arrested Shanice," Crystal said, "after all we did for you."

"I am sincerely sorry about that, but then, she was proven innocent," he explained.

"Shanice, do you forgive him?" Natasha asked.

"Sorry, Shanice. You did a good job," he said. "The federation needs the time witches."

"Okay, I accept your forgiveness, providing you give us the credit for our work," Shanice agreed.

"Good. This is what I need you to do," he continued. The commander wanted them to set themselves up as bait for the pirates, so that they could finally be caught by the federation. It was risky, but at the end, this will give them notoriety for their good work across time and space. They would have recognition as the time witches, known as white witches, serving the universe for good unlike the dark witches.

The time witches reached Earth, and were greeted by the commander.

"You must be the notorious time witches," he said. "Please follow me to my office. I have refreshments laid on for you."

"Well, let's hope it is better than Shanice's accommodation which was definitely one star," Natasha said, tongue in cheek.

"Again, sincere apologies for that misunderstanding," he said.

They entered a large room with windows all around them, and a breath-taking view of the bay. A buffet was laid on for the witches, and those who attended the conference.

The commander spoke first addressing the council and people present. It was certainly not what the witches expected. Everybody headed to their allocated tables, where each place had their name on it. The time witches sat at the front table near the commander and other important people from the space federation. This was the first time any witch had appeared at such a conference which made them feel a little uneasy.

"Councillors, officers, and other people of nobility. May I introduce to you, the time witches. These Ladies have offered to help us with our space pirate situation."

A loud applause could be heard around the room, and the ladies bowed. This was prompted by the commander, but they were still concerned about his motive for asking for their help.

The ladies had dressed elegantly for the occasion, and listened intently to the commander. Crystal wore a white frilly blouse and a cream skirt to match. Natasha wore a black dress, long black hair, and black finger nails, while Shanice wore a dark green outfit which suited her large brown eyes.

The commander showed the audience how the pirates were crossing time and space to take control of ships. They kept most of crew alive to begin with. Their purpose was to destroy the ships, and leave the crew stranded on a lonely planet. Some places were a wilderness, and others not so bad. Whatever was near at hand, otherwise, they were destroyed by a volcano or murdered by the pirates.

Again, the witches were asked to take a grey figure with a number on the front and back. Natasha was number one followed by Crystal who is number two, and number three, Shanice. They were asked to take an old classic space vessel, and head towards another planet close by, and then allow his way was to make the pirates think they had won. But the pirates were no fools, and had expected a cunning plan to take place one day that would compromise their attack.

The pirates were still celebrating the success of their last conquest as they boarded a cargo vessel consisting of expensive equipment which sold on means a vast amount of money. They boarded the ship and killed everybody in sight. After this, they left the vessel to return home damaged and without cargo with a message of *We are the space pirates out to take what we want* sprayed on the walls inside, and *space pirates rule* on the outside of the ship. This was done everytime they raided ships in order to make

make their mark. Needless to say, the pirates were presented to be a huge problem to the space colonies.

The only thing left was for the time witches and crew of a cargo vessel to prepare them for a journey across space that could prove dangerous, but would result in the capture of the space pirates. During the conference, the ladies were able to meet up with some very interesting people from various locations of the universe. Some had heard of the time witches, and for others, it was a new experience. They were becoming legendary, and accepted the fact that they would be known by reputation as they travelled across space.

Natasha took Shanice to one side, "You need to be careful on this mission," she warned her. "These Pirates are ruthless and fear nobody. They will kill us if we become reckless."

"Natasha, I know what I am doing, and how to behave," Shanice replied.

"Just remember, it's not just your life on the line here," Natasha continued.

Dance music began to play in the background rock style from the 1980s.

`"Let your hair down, Natasha, for once in your life." She turned to Crystal dancing, "Come on, Crystal. You, too; let's dance."

Crystal and Natasha began to dance surrounded by other dancers who were all enjoying. The fun drinks began to appear on the tables. The commander joined in the dancing with other members of the space federation. Shanice suddenly decided to do her performance with the acrobatics using her wand for effects.

A man in the audience had been watching with great interest ever since the commander had been doing his speech. He was dressed in a grey outfit, and a matching cloak. His clothes stood out like a man from the bible. He made a discreet exit. Outside the door, he was talking to the commander.

"Do you realise these women might get killed tomorrow?" he said.

"Dexter, this no time for sensitivity or compassion," the commander said. "The girls know the risks they are taking. Besides, they have powers."

"You really don't care, do you?" Dexter asked him.

"Someone has to do it." The commander continued, "Why not the time witches?"

"They are extendable. Is that it, commander?" Dexter pointed his finger at the commander. "Just like the doctor?"

"Leave him out of this. I am warning you, Dexter."

"Or what will you do commander?" Dexter pushed his face in front of the commander's. "You will make me disappear?"

"Doctor Granger is safe, and will remain safe."

"Could you say that about your brother?" Dexter said.

"He turned his back on the federation and died for it," the commander said.

"But even he should not have died that way. Blown away in a federation ship? Your brother was brave," Dexter said.

"He was foolish to listen to Doctor Granger about the dangers of making androids for war purposes. The federation is about peace in the universe."

"Tell that to the council who arranged their programs," Dexter said.

"Believe me, war is coming; it is imminent, commander."

They were interrupted by one of the pilots. "Sir, we have been under attack by a pirate ship close to Neptune. The crew are dead, and the cargo is missing. It's just an empty ship."

"The sooner we take action, the better." He thought for a moment. "Contact the time witches, and tell them to prepare for action."

"That's suicide for those witches," Dexter said. "You must

see this."

"Dexter, you can help us or shut the hell up, and let us get these sons of bitches."

A member of the space team received the message off the pilot, and she approached Crystal who sat at her table at the conference room. Having received the message, she walked over to the others who were still dancing, and said that they were needed. They got their uniforms on swiftly and headed towards the hangers. Crystal called the commander on the radio.

"Commander, come in. Commander, it's Crystal and the other time witches; we're ready for action. We are in hanger two – the freight hanger, suited up, and ready."

"The crew will be with you soon, Crystal," the commander said.

"I will be joining them."

"Are you sure Dexter?" the commander said, concerned.

"Someone has to protect them," Dexter replied. "It may as well be me."

The time witches had never seen such a spectacular sight watching the crew coming aboard; all shaking hands with them as they entered the ship. Meanwhile, word got back to the pirates that a special freight ship was being launched from Neptune carrying fragile cargo and mining grain.

Captain Edward Welsh, better known as Red Beard due to his long fiery ginger beard, led the crew, and each occasion to attack the cargo ships. He was mean, cunning, and enemy of the space federation. But he recognised, and respected the pirate code of honour. He was slim but well-built, and colourfully dressed looking like he had come out of time from Earth's Caribbean pirates.

Red Beard arranged a meeting of his crew to plan the next attack on the cargo ships, chiefly the one from Neptune from information gained, but what he wasn't aware of was that it was a trap complements of the federation.

"I call you, motley crew, together in order to discuss our next raid," he said. "This may be worth a lot of cash and increase our riches."

"Tell us more," Flannigan replied, better known as One-eyed John.

"I have information that treasure is aboard. They are setting out tomorrow," Red Beard replied.

"Well, we had better prepare for the attack in our usual way," Harper said. Harper was a thin man with hardly any teeth and pale complexion, like a walking skeleton.

"I can't wait for the raid; in for the kill," James Hawkins, the Hawk, said. The Hawk meant every word. He spared no mercy and enjoyed killing as much as eating. He was known as the big predator with no conscience or affection for others – a cruel and savage creature. "Take no prisoners, and leave no survivors to tell the tale."

"We are after the loot, Hawk, and nothing else," Red Beard commanded. "We don't kill for fun just to protect ourselves."

The crew agreed with the captain not to shed blood, but to capture the crew of the vessel until the treasure had been removed. He would usually leave them locked in a room somewhere, and make his escape to his own planet.

The time witches had been briefed about allowing the pirates to board the vessel by which time the federation ships will move in, and attack the pirates. The commander advised the time witches not do anything at this point, not until they try to escape, and then take action. The truth is the federation does not like admitting that they are responsible for attacking anyone, but just take the credit for capturing pirates, and bringing them to justice.

On the cargo vessel was Captain Hayley Green, a twenty-nine-year-old pilot with a good military record; a brunette who was sharp and keen. Thomas was the youngest at twenty-two, strong and fearsome. Collins came next with his knowledge of weapons such as lasers, explosives, and daggers. Eccles appeared to lack the knowledge of weapons but he was good in combat. He had many strategies and trained teams of people to use their skills to fight. This was pleasing to Dexter who needed a good army to defend the vessel. At the start of the journey, Dexter spoke to the crew especially the ones previously mentioned, and to the time witches.

"Remember, we do not attack until the federation arrive," Dexter said. "We must be patient."

"You obviously have more confidence in him, Dexter." Natasha said.

"More than we do, Dex," Crystal said, agreeing with Natasha. "He has let us down before, why not now?" Natasha said, feeling uncomfortable.

"He is a man of his word," Dexter said. "He has a plan; just trust him."

"I have a bad feeling about this," Shanice said. "At least we knew where we stood with the androids."

The journey had continued with joyful song and dancing, on-board the pirate ship, and similar from the cargo vessel, although a little tamed down version. Hours passed before the pirates spotted the cargo ship, and the hawk spotted it was getting very excited.

"There it is, Captain, our treasure," Hawk said pointing to the ship. "It's all here."

Red Beard sent out a warning message to the vessel with a warning, "This is Captain Red Beard. I am about to invade your ship. Be prepared and surrender, or die. You are now my prisoners. My pirates will instruct you what to do from here."

"This is Captain Hayley Green, speaking," the Captain said. "We surrender."

At that moment, the hatch to the vessel opened, and the pirate crew entered the ship with his forty men. Some went to the engine room, some straight to the cargo bay, and the rest went to main cockpit area. Captain Green was waiting for them with the time witches and Dexter. They all seemed composed but Shanice, who appeared anxious, was fidgeting and trying not to have eye contact with Red Beard.

"Now, I aim to relieve you of your treasure. We have men already in the cargo bay. They will take it, and leave you without any loss of life," Red Beard said.

"Don't let us stop you, Captain," Green replied.

"I haven't finished yet," Red Beard said. "We will take one person as hostage while we make our escape. The question is who?"

"You mean that you want us to choose?" Green asked.

"One-eyed John will do that, I am sure," Red Beard said,

looking at each woman in turn. "He has an eye for the girls."

One eyed John took a careful look at each of the girls in turn, eying them up and down carefully. Eventually, he pointed to Shanice. "This one."

Shanice rolled her eye, "Great," she said. "Why me?"

"Wouldn't you like somebody more mature?" Natasha asked.

"Or blonde?" Crystal said, both trying to protect Shanice.

"I like her eyes," One-eyed John said, lifting her head from her jaw, and she pulled away.

"Well, you're not having them," she said angrily.

"So, its decided then," Red Beard said. "You come with us. We will let you go when we are at a safe distance." Red beard continued, "Prepare my ship to board the loot. One-eyed John, take this wench away."

"No! Unhand me, you filthy toad," Shanice said, struggling. "Natasha, do something please."

Shanice sent a telepathic message to Natasha that Crystal could understand. She wanted them to know that she was aware they had no control of the situation. But she was the victim yet again this time not because of her recklessness. Shanice then cried in frustration allowing the tears to flow down her cheeks in a way of reacting to the situation. Everybody stood shocked, simply stood, and watched the cargo exit the ship. No one could believe what was happening, and where were the federation ships.

Red beard and his crew departed from the ship with his pirates taking Shanice with them. She was still tearful, but did as she was told for the sake of the others. After they had gone, Natasha who was angry at the situation immediately headed towards Dexter with her wand in her hand.

"Dexter, you are responsible for this," Natasha said, holding her wand to his throat. "Where are the federation ships?"

Green pulled out her laser, and felt a prod at the back of her neck "Drop it now."

"Don't tell me you have a wand, too?" Green said.

"Yes, and I am not afraid to use it," Crystal said. "We have lost a friend because of you."

At that moment they heard sounds from outside the ship, followed by a massive invasion of federation crew piling into the vessel. Soon after, they appeared everywhere including the cock pit.

"Lieutenant Neilson, what a surprise," Dexter said with relief.

"Dexter, we have only just picked up your signal," Neilson said.

"The pirate must have been jamming it," Dexter replied. "So, what now?"

"What do you mean so what now, Dexter?" Natasha said angrily. "We go after them."

"Yes; find them and our friend," Crystal said, still holding her wand on Green.

"We need another cargo vessel and try again," Dexter said.

"And delay things longer while poor Shanice is with them?" Natasha said.

"We have no choice," Dexter said. "At least, she's alive, and we know what they did by jamming the signals."

"And what will happen when they discover she is a witch?" Crystal asked.

"Probably kill her" Natasha said.

"Poor girl," Green said, feeling the wand being removed from his neck.

Shanice was escorted by the pirates to a prison cell and remained there for a while. Red Beard was deciding his next plan. One-eyed John entered the room. He seemed eager to speak to the captain.

"Red Beard, can I keep the girl?" he asked.

"Certainly not," Red Beard said, displeased.

"But we got the loot. What's wrong?" he asked.

"Because it's worthless," Red Beard said. "All of it!"

"He's right. We checked it all, and nothing is valuable," Hawk said with dismay.

"So, what shall we do with the girl?" One-eyed John asked.

"Bring her to me," Red Beard insisted.

Natasha and Crystal sat down, discussing Shanice. In the sleeping cabin allocated to them, they were both shocked by the decision, and now had to face a further ordeal being on another cargo ship and using themselves as bait once more.

"Poor, Shanice. She must be scared to death," Crystal said.

"Yes, I agree. Nothing can prepare you for this kind of thing," Natasha replied.

"Let's hope she keeps quiet about her being a witch," Crystal said.

Shanice was led to the Captain, escorted by two pirates. She seemed composed with her head held high trying not to show her inner fear. The captain looked her up and down, and stood close to her. She could feel his breath on her face.

"Could I recommend another type of mouth wash?" she said, trying to catch her breathe.

"Are you not afraid of me, wench?" he said, touching her face.

"Afraid of you? I don't think so," Shanice said, feeling her heart beating out of her chest, and her throat drying up.

Red Beard gripped her throat. "I could kill you right now.

Break your scrawny neck with one hand. Is that what you want, pretty girl?"

"What the bloody hell is it about my neck? Vampires, androids, and pirates?" Shanice said, struggling. Suddenly her wand dropped to the floor. Both Red Beard and Shanice looked down at the same time. "Whoops!" Shanice said. "That's not good."

"You're a witch," Red Beard said with surprise.

"Surprise," she said. "A time witch, actually."

"A witch! We captured a witch," Red Beard shuck his head. "That's not good."

"Are you going to get me to walk the plank? No! We are in space… or burn me the stake?" she continued questioning him. "Hang me or send me out in space?

"Stop it now!" he insisted. "I need to think."

"Don't you let me stop you thinking," Shanice said.

"I am cursed," he said.

"Didn't pirates used to tie people to the crow's nest and put fish on their head for the seagulls to peck at?" Shanice asked.

"They used to peck head like you're doing to me now," Red Beard said. "God, why me?"

Shanice went to pick up her wand. It was knocked out of her hand by a bolt of lightning. A dark figure appeared out of the darkness.

"Tristana!" Shanice shouted.

"White witches are pathetic," Tristana said, laughing.

"You know her?" Red Beard said.

"This is Shanice, a time witch," Tristana said. "Where she is, the others must be."

"Why were you in the cargo ship?" he asked.

"Escorting the treasures, of course," Tristana explained, working for the federation. "White witches are known to be helpful and friendly."

"So, what do I do with her?" he asked.

"Let her go or better take her on the next raid," Shanice was puzzled by Tristana. She seemed to be helping her. *What was her motive?* She thought.

"You're right, of course, Tristana. She can come on the raid."

Shanice was unsure about Tristana. Why did she want her on the raid? Things seemed very wrong with this situation, and she definitely had a bad feeling about it.

That evening, the pirates organised a big feast as they usually did after a raid. Usually, it was to show off their new gained treasure, and had a few prisoners to humiliate as it was, only Shanice was taken hostage. So, the pirate made do with what they had by using each other as targets for knife throwing, and then chose the dimmest witted to make fun at. A band came on and performed in heavy metal style, and Shanice began to dance. Shortly after, Tristana joined her, and the pirates watched bewildered, then Tristana spoke to Shanice.

"My mother said you perform like me with acrobatics and magic."

"Yes, I do that," Shanice replied.

"Why don't we perform together?" Tristana said.

"Okay, sounds good," she replied.

Once the music stopped, they spoke to the leader of the group. They discussed their moves jumping, flying, and waving their wands about forming some kind of choreography in order to demonstrate their power as witches. The performance began and it was electric, colourful, and dynamic. Shanice was at her best, and Tristana matched her performance. The crowd cried out for more, even Captain Red Beard was impressed as he sat on the edge of his seat.

"They will do well in our raid tomorrow; fire and brimstone, I call them."

"We should gain our fortune with them," One-eyed John said.

"But then, they must go. Witches don't belong here," Red Beard said.

"Can't I keep, Shanice?" One eye said.

"No. We can't risk a curse," he replied. "Find another who is not a witch."

One eye walked away, disappointed, walking along a long lonely corridor in the pirate's den grunting as he walked and speaking colourful profanities. He was what can only be described as a loose cannon about to go off. He later approached Shanice to explain what he wanted, but Tristana intervened and dismissed him threatening to turn him into a slimy toad.

Meanwhile at space federation headquarters, another cargo vessel was being prepared to leave the docking bay by the afternoon with Natasha, Crystal, Captain Green, and Dexter on board. They had federation troops, but this time, advised to attack not surrender.

"I wonder how poor Shanice is getting on," Natasha said, watching the cargo going aboard.

"She will cope. She is a survivor," Crystal said. "Also, if the pirate knows who she is, they will fear being cursed."

"I do miss her presence," Foster said.

"Me too," Shimick said. "Wait a minute, how can you miss her? You have no feelings?"

"I do happen to have some," he replied. "I can say 'there, there' in response to a shock, loss, or a fall."

"Oh, wow! Impressive, tin man," Shimick said.

"He does have the right idea, Shimick," Crystal said, "having a sad tone in his voice, and using the correct words."

"But he lacks feelings," Shimick said. "Oh, please don't cry, Shanice. It will get better."

"There, there," Foster said in a manner of fact way.

"You see? No feelings in that metal body," Shimick said.

"Well, you have no feelings for him," Natasha said, "talking about him like that."

"He's a damn android," Shimick said, pointing at him. "Nothing more."

"I protest," Foster said. "I have many functions, and I do understand feelings, my green little pointed-eared friend," he pauses, "said with affection."
Shimick growled like a lion, and then began to sulk. The time witches laughed as they noticed Foster out smart Shimick.

The time had come to fly the cargo ship. Captain Hayley Green was at the helm with Dexter, Crystal, and Natasha. Two of the crew occupied the other seats. The ship left the docking bay and made its journey across space. The time witches were eager to find Shanice safe and well. They arrived in the same area as before, and slowed the ship down and waited. It seemed like a lifetime. Many thoughts were going through their heads. Some telepathically talk to each other about their adventures in time and space, comical moments with Shanice, some tragic events, and final triumphs.

Silence was broken as the pirate ship arrived. The usual warning from Red Beard came over the radio announcing his intentions. The captain acknowledged the call as she did before she allowed the pirates aboard. Shanice and Tristana entered the vessel first via a hatch, and travelled down on ropes. They arrived on the ground and were met by troopers who held guns on them.

"Don't shoot! We are time witches," Tristana shouted.

Natasha could see them on security cameras and rushed forward to the screen.

"They are time witches," Natasha said.

"Bring those two to me," Green demanded.

No sooner had they arrived at the helm, Natasha and Crystal made a fuss of Shanice, and acknowledged Tristana. Both seeming puzzled by her presence.

"How did you get here?" Natasha said.

"Usual route," she said. "Time portal."

"But what about your family? They will be looking for you." Crystal said.

"Let them. I just don't care," Tristana said, shrugging her shoulders.

"Who does she sound like?" Natasha said.

"Definitely Shanice," Crystal said.

"Quiet," ordered Green. "Here come the pirates."

"Right, witches, to your stations," Natasha said. "Shanice, you're with me."

"Tristana, you're with me," Crystal said. "Let's go."

Red Beard headed straight for the helm as before, sending his men in various directions of the ship. Suddenly, there was firing coming from lasers everywhere. Natasha and Shanice had their wands out and were firing thunderbolts at the pirates. Meanwhile, elsewhere, Crystal and Tristana were doing the same. This time, Crystal had prevented the signals to other ships jamming, and before long, the pirate ship was surrounded by federation ships. They all continued fighting; bodies were dropping everywhere. One-eyed John caught sight of Shanice, and went after her. He fired at her hitting her in the back, and she fell to the ground. Natasha was busy fighting another pirate to notice her fall. One-eyed John grabbed her by the arm and pulled her up, and then began to pull her along. Shanice was too weak to resist and tried to keep up with him. He was holding his laser on her.

"Don't you worry now, you are all mine," he said.

Red Beard was under arrest at the helm. Watching the monitor as the ships surrounded his vessel, he realised he had lost and admitted defeat. He had surrendered and expected his men to do the same. After a short while, he spoke to them over the ships radio and ordered them to surrender, to give themselves up peacefully. It was hard for Red Beard to admit defeat as a pirate. He now had to face the charges at a federation court with a possible view to execution by lethal injection. As for the other pirates, they also were facing charges of piracy, which covers a harsh penalty. Out of fifty pirates, ten were caught.

One-eyed John was still finding his way off the ship, hotly pursued by Natasha. They finally found an escape pod. Natasha stood with her wand in front of One-eyed.

"Don't even think about it," she warned him.

He fired a shot that missed Natasha. She fired a thunderbolt that hit in the chest. He let go of Shanice but hit a switch as he fell outside the pod saying, "If I can't have her, nobody has her", and then the pod launched. He got sucked out of the craft into space. Without thinking, Natasha found another escape pod and launched it with her inside, hoping that she would go in the same direction as Shanice, destiny unknown. Crystal saw the pods drifting away and contacted Natasha telepathically, and then spoke to Dexter.

"Are they going to be okay?" she asked.

"The pods will find their way to the nearest planet, and hopefully land safely," Dexter said. "I want to say yes."

"But you can't be certain," she said sadly.

"I wish I had a magic wand to make it happen," he replied.

"It doesn't work like that, Dexter," Crystal said. "Just get me home to my ship."

"Let me come with you, Crystal" Tristana said.

Red Beard witnessed all this before being taken to the ship's prison or brig. On the way home, they experienced a meteor storm that was so fierce it hit every vessel, especially the cargo ships. The brig was affected and enabled the pirates to escape in pods. Some were damaged, others survived to land on their own planet where Natasha and Shanice had gone.

Natasha landed in a jungle. She found herself surrounded by strange creatures peering into the pod.

"Hi," she greeted. "I need to open the pod."

They continued staring at her in disbelief.

"I need to come out but the door is jammed," Crystal had her language converter in her left ear but couldn't understand them. "Am I dreaming?" she asked. "Are you like munchkins from the Wizard of Oz?"

"Ah dibble," one said.

"Camma a lamb," said another.

"Wait, it must be damaged," Natasha said. She found her wand and cast a few spells.

"Dibble dibble," one said.

"You're so funny," Natasha said laughing, and then using her wand to escape from the pod. She gave a stretch and a yawn, and looked around her.

"Where are you all gone?" she asked.

Gradually they reappeared and surrounded her, feeling her clothes.

"Okay, enough. I am no celebrity," she said.

"Celebrity," one repeated.

"You understand me, so the device works," she said. "I am Natasha."

They looked puzzled at each other.

"Natasha," she repeated.

"Bless you," said one of them.\

"Dob," said another.

"I agree," said the first one. "That's what he says, nothing else."

We are the Cluffins," another said. "I am Moss."

"Petal," said another.

"Well, Cluffins, I have lost a friend. She was in a craft like this one," Natasha said.

"It landed over there," Moss pointed to distant trees.

"Can you show me?" Natasha asked. "Take me there."

"Very dangerous. There with Earth creatures, like giant snakes."

"Dob," Floss agreed.

"Don't worry, I will protect you. I am a time witch," Natasha said, holding her wand.

"A witch," Moss sniggered. "They are ugly."

"Only dark witches," she explained. "Bad people are ugly. They rot from the inside out."

"Let us find your friend, time witch," Moss said.

"Natasha," she said.

"Bless you," they all said.

There were twenty of them walking with her, all tussling for a place near her. She had gained many friends this day. It was a twenty-minute walk to the landing site in the whole of the journey. Each person had spoken to Natasha but nobody mentioned the pirates. Natasha thought it best not to say anything at this point. She spoke only about time travel to the Cluffins and her experiences.

TRISTANA

The continuing story of the time witches introducing Tristana, a dark witch who finds herself confused as a child as she is brought up by the evil dark witches, but questions their ethics having come in contact with white witches. She begins travelling through time and space within the time portals and experience many things about life away from her home planet, Sabira, or as the witches call it: Alba Two. Alba one being Scotland.

Tristana gets into trouble and sometimes causes havoc due to her upbringing. She demonstrates her powers in many ways, sometimes for the good of others which questions her loyalty to the dark witches. Her mother, Ramona, was always searching for her, and anxious about losing her child to strangers or enemies of the dark witches. This was a little strange considering the way she treated her as a child by not wanting to have anything to do with her and abusing her in many ways. Although it was common amongst some dark witches, they used the excuse that it made them tough and able to defend themselves against their universal adversaries.

THE BIRTH OF A WITCH

It was a cold winter's night and the moon was full. A cold wind was blowing and the snow covered the land like a white blanket on a bed. Dark figures were moving about around stone buildings each lit up by lanterns. This was on the planet Alba known to most as Sabira, inhabited by dark witches who had arrived here centuries ago from Earth, having discovered a time portal. They actually came from Scotland which was originally called Alba, which is why they named this planet Alba Two or the Second Alba.

When they travelled through the time portal, it closed up and vanished, and so they were forced to stay on Alba Two. In one way, they were relieved as they were hunted down as witches on Earth and tortured into confessing to be witches, and then they were executed by one means or another, usually by hanging or burning at the stake. But not all the dark witches were as innocent as they appeared, and kidnapped children or raided homes using their powers for bad purposes. Ramona was one such witch along with Helga, Davina, and Cursida. They all took part in raids and despicable crimes against humanity. When Ramona became pregnant, it was said that the devil had visited her bed, but this was the case for her friends, also who seemed to conceive at similar times. Ramona denied this and said she met an alien who had made love to her in a moment of weakness. But on this cold night, Ramona had got her friends running around for her while she was in labour. She yelled and swore as the labour got more painful, cursing the life within her.

"Will somebody get this thing out of me?" was the words that she partly said.

"Ramona, be patient. It's coming," Helga said, trying to encourage her.

"I don't care! I want it out!" Ramona said angrily.

"I see the head," Helga said. "Now, push!"

"What the bloody hell do you think I am doing? Flying or swimming?" Ramona said, causing the room to shake like an earthquake. Window began to crack and break, mirrors smashed, and finally, the baby was born.

By this time, a thunder storm came like a freak weather as if produced by the witches in their excitement. This was common during the birth of a witch as they make their powerful entry into the world.

"Do you want to see her?" Helga said.

"Is she like me?" Ramona asked.

"Not exactly," Helga replied.

Ramona took a look at her, and turned away. "She is ugly! Not a bit like me."

"She isn't that bad," Helga said. "She may change."

Ramona's perception of ugly was far different from most of us, but not of dark witches who had to agree with her; but certainly not this baby with its large brown eyes and beautiful features.

"What are you going to call her?" Helga asked.

"What do you call an ugly baby?" Ramona said. "Pig face or donkey's ass?"

"Magnolia, Charlotte, or Tempesta," Helga suggested.

"Tristana," Ramona finally said. "Now, let me rest."

Ramona had so much help raising Tristana from a baby giving

her very little attention. She had more time for older children and hated the cries of her own. Also, Tristana was ever more beautiful when she was growing, and her mother hated looking at her, making remarks about her face, calling her an ugly toad. She tried to conceal her from the outside world saying she was an embarrassment to her, and often covered her face in a mask or hooded garment. Tristana grew up self-conscious and lacked confidence in herself. She felt unloved compared to the other children who grew up with her. She was also taught by others as well as her mother in self-preservation and self-defence.

Tristana developed her magic powers from an early age, and often practiced her skills at home or in the canyons near home. She fathomed out the art of riding a broomstick, and developed a skill in acrobatics. She liked dancing and singing, finding that during her lonely times, she would entertain herself in song and dance. When she reached twelve years old, she was taken on raid with the other dark witches stealing items and destroying property from inhabitants in other areas of the planet.

Later in years, she would travel in the witch's space vessel and go further away to find places to steal from. The dark witches could be quite ruthless as they conducted their raids on the weak and feeble, using their powers to cast spells and even kill people, just like their ancestors who were the original dark witches from Inverness, Scotland (Alba).

The witches managed to keep part of their history so that they could pass it down the generations, going back to ancient times when the meteors hit the earth, and gave them the powers they have today. Originally from the cave dwellers as one tribe, they divided into two groups: white witches who used their powers for good purposes, and the dark witches who used them to do bad things. The dark witches thought that they had wiped out the white witches, and were surprised when they came across some in time travel. Tristana was always told that people feared dark witches because of their power and dominating personalities, not the fact that they could easily destroy them with one wave of their wand, was causing a massive burst of electricity as powerful as lightning to strike them or hurling balls of fire at them. Tristana had clearly been misinformed about this and about the good deeds of white witches, making out it was a myth and that they were the evil ones. It was no wonder that Tristana had grown up a confused child. She was also a bright child who could work things out quickly, and eventually, her acrobatics and dancing skills helped her to perform on stage to music each Saturday night, when groups were entertaining at the witches' castle.

Tristana was forced to do many chores from an early age much like child slavery. She was beaten if she did not meet expectations, and locked in a dark room with the spiders and rats. She had to clean wash clothes and cook for her witch family. One of the worst punishments was to make her sleep in the mortuary amongst the dead. Tristana's only crime was being born as a dark witch, and committing their crimes of stealing and destroying property. She was forced to be like them without the knowledge of goodness.

A WITCHES RAID

It was night time. The moon was full and a breeze was blowing the nearby trees causing a whistling effect. The dark witches gathered a small party of them together as a coven. This was to discuss a future raid on a village, a short distance away. Occasionally, they did this to demonstrate their power. Sometimes they travelled further, even left Alba to visit other planets.

Ramona felt it was time for Tristana to join them, and learn the art of the dark witches. She was already attending school, and quite capable of defending herself as she proved at school against other pupils. One girl stood out amongst the many at school. She was Musette who was a year older than her and disliked Tristana as soon as she saw her. She wanted to slap her and made fun of her in class and in the playground. Musette would trip people up; drop insects down their backs, and cause havoc everywhere. No one was safe at any time.

Tristana was keen on riding broomsticks and entered the annual races around the canyon and woods. When she reached eleven, she entered the tournament that was often spoken about all year round until October, around Halloween time. It was a rough event and very competitive where people got hurt often.

Occasionally, lives were lost through the fact that everyone wanted to win and were determined to cross the finish line no matter what they did.

Musette practiced on her broomstick everyday. She was very skilful and learned many trick and cunning movements in order to succeed. This year's game was only a week away, and everybody was excited about it.

Meanwhile, the witches were preparing for their raid upon the village. They wanted to let the villagers know who they were, and to fear them. The villagers were natives of the planet, appearing humanoid with thin bodies and a type of green skin, much like Shimick the goblin, that lived with Merek the wizard of Zena. The natives called the planet Sabira and not Alba. These inhabitants were widespread across this planet. They called themselves Sabiranites. They knew how dangerous and powerful the witches were and feared them. They had basic needs and led simple lives. They made their own clothes, and lived off the land. Everything was peaceful before the witches arrived and disrupted everything.

Witches were inclined to raid at night using their keen eyesight to travel and locate the villages from the air. They had hawk eyes and keen hearing making them challenging predators. The Sabiranites didn't have a chance against their hunting abilities and powers. The witches preyed on their vulnerability taking what they needed and discarding what they didn't need and destroying other things by fire or bolts of lightning.

This night was no exception as they gathered a small party, including Tristana, to attack the village. Tristana was excited not knowing what to expect, and they rode their brooms in the night sky keeping in a flying formation in order to stay together, watching that no one went astray. She watched as the witches at the front dived down towards the lights from the local buildings. This was it! The raid was on, and she was part of it. Tristana noticed that some witches had already began to throw fireballs at some of the buildings. People on the streets rushed for shelter. She was fascinated at this sight and did the same. By throwing fireballs, one set fire to a small building and she cheered. Some of the witches entered homes and remained in there long enough to steal food and blankets; others flew around watching for people to emerge from other buildings. The whole ordeal took an hour until the witches were satisfied. They had all they needed, and then left the village.

Tristana had become popular at school once the pupils knew about the raid. People spoke of how she participated. She was praised; even Musette seemed impressed, although she was jealous of Tristana, so she would never be seen complimenting her or being in her company. She considered her as a rival.

THE WITCHES RACE

The time had come for the race to begin. The competitors prepared their brooms for the ride. They were reminded of the route to take, although there were suitable markers along the way – sometimes signs, sometimes people standing at certain points. The excitement was clearly visible by the cheering of the crowd who were waving frantically at their relatives.

The witches competing stood in a line behind a rope, until Ramona fired her wand into the sky like a gun. The rope was dropped and the witches flew to the sky and down towards the canyon. Tristana was at the back of the racers to begin with, pacing herself. She watched as one person fell early in the race. She rolled over, and then after a while, she sat up. Evidently, she was fine, having been attacked by Musette who started laughing.

In the lead was Sinead, a confident young witch, the same age as Tristana. She was top of the school's chemistry class and art group, known for her dark gothic pictures of dragons, demons, and werewolves. Tristana preferred vampires and dark angels. She was fascinated by bats and other flying creatures, and those that drink blood. She was aware that her blood was poisonous to vampires which made her fairly safe.

The canyon was a long distance in the race. It ended with the beginning of the forest, now that had to dodge trees, at this point another few fell and Tristana was quickening her pace to find the person in the lead. Musette was a close second weaving her way through trees and competitors. She was confident that she was going to win, and made sure by knocking a few witches out of the way. Tristana could see the leader in sight; it was Tempesta, a worthy competitor, previous champion, and five times winner. It was almost a certainty she would win. She was so confident she had a place reserved for the trophy. After a short time and a few more casualties, they left the forest.

The end was in sight, but Musette was hiding to ambush Tristana. She hid behind a large tree trunk and waited. Eventually, Tristana turned up with another witch who seemed to be injured. She took her to one of the witches looking on, and then carried on. Musette was surprised at her act of kindness, and rather than ambush her, she decided to continue in the race. Tempesta was almost at the finish line; Musette was a short way behind, and Tristana was behind her. They both arrived at the finish post together making them a tie for second place; but this angered Musette as she wanted to beat her in second place. Tristana was happy with the result and celebrated her success with the other dark witches. They had a feast that night and Tristana did her usual performance of dancing and doing acrobatics in the air, waving her wand for affect causing a colourful display that people could admire. Dancing to a group from the Warlocks domain, a group of male witches and wizards, who all came through the time portal via Earth at a very bad time in history for witches, from the sixteenth and seventeenth century predominately.

A slim girl with short blonde hair was dancing in chains calling herself Wendy or her Goth name was Angel girl. She looked in a trance, but the dark witches kept her sedated because of how dangerous she was to them. But she had a fine voice, and she performed well on stage. She's moving quite well despite the chains; this was her freedom from her prison cell – to perform for them.

THE CURSE OF MEREK

The day after the big event, Tristana was walking down a corridor in the castle when out of the darkness, a figure appeared dressed in black wearing a hood.

"Tristana!" she shouted. "I am glad to see you."

"Musette, what a surprise," Tristana replied. "Why are you glad to see me?" she asked apprehensively.

"I am not exactly glad, but I wanted to see you," she explained.

"What is this about?" Tristana asked.

"The race. It was a total farce. I should have beaten you and Tempesta," she said crossly. "I am better than all of you, and I can prove it."

"How are you going to prove it? The race is over; Tempesta won," Tristana explained.

"God! You're dumb," she said, pushing Tristana against the wall and holding on to her clothes. She pushed her gripped fist up to Tristana's throat, and held the wand in her other hand.

"I don't understand, Musette. What do you want?" Tristana asked.

"A race, you idiot! Just us two tonight; same circuit, and with a time limit. The winner gets to do the other's homework, right?" Musette said, loosening her grip as the was dark witches approaching.

"Okay," Tristana said, adjusting her clothes.

"Is everything alright?" said one of the ladies.

"Yes, thank you, miss," Tristana said.

"We were just sorting our lessons out," Musette said.

"Then, get along to your classrooms immediately," said the other witch.

Later that night. the two girls met at the starting point of the race. Both were determined to win the race, and prove themselves as worthy competitors. They counted down to begin from ten to zero, but Musette kicked Tristana as she went, making her stumble. Tristana made a quick recovery, and soon caught up with Musette. There were no markers so they had no clear guidance. Both were travelling down the canyon, but had to guess the route. They knew the forest was at the end of the canyon, but it was not in sight; instead, they seemed to go on and on through this canyon, and both of them were confused. Suddenly, Musette vanished followed by Tristana, and they suddenly found themselves in a desert. Musette turned to face Tristana.

"What have you done, freak?" Musette asked. "Where are we?" "I don't know," Tristana replied.

"You did something to make me lose the race," Musette continued. "Tell me bitch or you die," she said, pointing her wand at her.

"Honestly, I don't know what has happened," Tristana insisted.

"You had your chance," she said, firing lightning at her.

Tristana dodged the attack, and returned the fire, narrowly missing Musette. They exchanged attacks a few more times, before they were stopped by a green goblin that had gone to meet them.

"I thought I heard people in the time portal," he said. "I am Shimick, the wizard's servant."

"Well, Shimick," Musette said, "show us the way back home or suffer the wrath of my mother, Helga, the dark witch."

"And my mother, Ramona," Tristana said.

"The portal is closed, sorry; and only the wizard can open it," Shimick said.

"So, where is this wizard, green man?" Musette asked.

"Follow me," he said confidently. He led them to the wizard's castle on a hillside.

They were walking a winding pathway with trees on either side, with a fragrant smell of flowers in strange shapes and colours. The only familiar flowers were orchids that grew tall with many colours. They arrived at this amazing building – a mixture of Gothic and ultra-modern design – never seen in any architectural designs before, but certainly magnificent. They entered the castle through the large main door, and started walking down a long corridor. They could feel eyes watching them all the way to the main hall. They arrived to see a man dressed in robes with a long beard. He gazed at them with menacing eyes, looking them both up and down.

"I am Merek," he said with a booming voice. "I am the most powerful wizard in the universe."

"You don't scare me, wizard. My mother is Helga, a dark witch. When she finds out you have me, she will kill you," Musette said.

"Brave words, girl, but I don't like or fear dark witches," he replied.

"I have heard of the Wizards of Zena," Tristana said. "You and your bothers, Doran, Saden, and Arthalo."

"And here they are; all assembled to greet you," Merek said, producing images of his brothers. Each one spoke, greeting the witches.

"I want to return to Alba," Musette said. "I insist you take us back."

"You will not return, child," Merek said in a patronising tone.

"You can't keep us here," Musette protested. "We will escape, and the dark witches will destroy you."

"I have heard enough," Merek said. "Guards!"

Musette raised her wand and aimed it at Merek, but before she could use it, he took out his wand and fired a bolt of lightning into her chest and destroyed her. Tristana stood speechless awaiting her fate. She was taken by the guards to a prison cell. Her wand had been taken off her, and she sat bewildered on a bed reflecting on Musette's death, reliving the awful event over and over in her head.

The Gizalians made up most of Merek's guards. They were evil little green creatures, slimy and scaly, with lumps all over their bodies like crocodiles. They were cunning creatures and well-known parasites moving from planet to planet feeding off people's misery. They feasted off Tristana's misery that night, leaving her without clear thoughts and logic. She was sad but couldn't think why.

Later the next day, Merek summoned Tristana to join him. She was nervous having lost Musette so tragically, wondering what her fate might be. Merek walked up to her, and began mumbling. He was casting a spell on her knowing how empty her mind was, and how susceptible she was at this time. What he was actually doing was laying a curse on her so powerful it was driving her mad. Before long, he successfully had her possessed by the evil Lamian's satanic creature from another planet Janus. She was taken away, and sent in a spaceship to this planet to be tormented forever. That's how much Merek hated witches.

Tristana was rescued from the Lamians by the Janusians. She

was wild, shouting, and screaming, attacking everybody in sight. The Janusians were forced to restrain her with chains and put in a dungeon. She remained there for months until she was finally rescued by white witches better known as Natasha, Crystal, and Shanice. They lifted the curse and broke the spell bringing her back to herself. She cried about Musette, and thanked the white witches, although she was baffled by their acts of kindness. This was very strange.

When she was free, she attempted to kill Merek by setting him on fire after he was tricked into losing his powers, but his kind brother, Doran, came to his rescue, and then banished Merek to another planet. Tristana remained with the white witches until her mother arranged for her to return home to Alba. Ramona was furious about what Merek had done to Tristana and Musette, and headed to his planet to destroy him and his castle. Unfortunately, Doran was there and not Merek, and so he was killed. Tristana had a taste of adventure, and continued to journey through the time portals alone. She was confident that she was no greater danger than Merek the wizard, and as he was no longer powerful, he would not harm her again.

THE GHOST

It was in a busy station that the emergency services were called at a popular railway station in London. The area had been evacuated after a number of people had collapsed, and some even died suspiciously. It was said to be a virus deadlier than any other that had killed them. The bodies consisted of men, women, and children. The only people present were wearing white overalls, visors, and gloves, each taking special precautions not to become infected.

One of these men knelt down to get a closer look at one of the bodies – it was a female body with odd looking marks on her skin almost like burns. He moved on to find the next body. This time, a young male with the same marks on his face and body, but his face was distorted with boils filled with puss. The man in the protected clothes started to retch. His breathing increased and so did his heartbeat. Never had he seen such a sight, and so many bodies that had fallen in this one-time busy station.

The emergency team set up areas to put the bodies temporarily, while they tried to clean up the area. Trains were cancelled, and nothing was going in or out of the station. It was an eerie sight for anyone who was in the area and observing, such as the police or ambulance service. One witness described the incident saying, 'They all fell down suddenly, like the pins in ten-pin bowling. People ran scared; it was like mass hysteria.' Others made similar comments as they waited outside the station.

The whole area was sealed off; barriers were erected, and police had arrived in numbers to help and control the crowd, all wary of the dangerous disease that had obviously killed these people. No one was safe and words could not comfort them or reassure them that they were safe from harm. Some of the bodies were taken away for post mortem examinations. Everybody needed answers and fast before it spread any further.

Tristana was with the time witches when they decided to travel to Earth. She wanted to see the planet in the twenty first century, as people had told her that this age was particularly fascinating, especially the people of this time. Crystal was curious about Tristana's need to see this age. She was like a child with a new toy, eager to find out about this particular time. Natasha was more warily about Tristana, as she was a dark witch, and brought up in the ways of wickedness, finding the dark witches to be cunning, crafty, and cruel without any good aspects to their personalities. But Tristana had grown up with the dark witches, and witness all these things, especially from her mother, Ramona. She was beaten and deprived of even her basic needs; unloved and neglected throughout her childhood. She was termed as ugly and humiliated often.

The time witches arrived on Earth, and landed in a quiet remote spot. The ship was camouflaged and they set off, leaving Foster behind to protect the vessel. They walked a short distance before getting a ride in a bus to the centre of London. Natasha knew Earth better than the others, and led the way to a train station. They noticed the crowd which by now had increased trailing down the street. The media were camped nearby, hoping to find a good story, based on someone's tragedy, providing the worst cynical angle possible, reporting on their sympathy stories. It was sensationalism at its best as they stood like vultures after their prey, causing further heartache to the victims' families and friends. These cold-hearted people were immune to sensitivity of the masses.

Natasha made herself invisible, and swept past the police into the station. She looked around having overheard that these people had some sort of virus. She managed to find a white overall and helmet with special gloves beside them, and walked amongst the emergency crew. She had a close look at the bodies, and then returned to her friends. She seemed sad and tried to hold back her tears. It was an awful thing to witness, and the images kept flashing back in her mind. She described everything to the others discreetly, so the media didn't hear her. They were understandably shocked.

"How did it start, Nat?" Crystal asked.

"I don't know," Natasha replied. "They just said that these victims just fell to the ground without warning."

"That's awful," Crystal said, shocked.

"Is it a virus?" Tristana asked.

"Yes, like the great plague of London," Natasha said. "The bodies were a mess."

"We need to know more before the human race is wiped out," Crystal said.

"Is it that bad that it affects the whole planet?" Tristana asked.

"Reports are in from other counties with a similar death toll. It's rising rapidly hitting the capital cities, airports, and train stations," Natasha said. "We need to save the human race."

"We need to find the laboratory where the post mortems are being held and get samples from the bodies," Crystal said, "and do our own examinations."

"Isn't that dangerous?" Tristana asked.

"Not, if we are careful," Crystal continued. "We must take every precaution."

It was Crystal's turn to make herself invisible, and enter the building where some of the bodies had been transferred. She was nervous, but she thought of what Natasha said about saving the human race. This encouraged her to keep going and get tissue samples. When the doctor cut with the scalpel, the skin popped and oozed with puss. He opened up the chest cavity and examined the organs inside the body. Crystal looked on fascinated with his technique. He was talking into a microphone as he was investigating the body. He was taking samples that Crystal needed, and then got disturbed by a phone call. He was abrupt on the phone as he did not want to be disturbed by anybody during his procedure. He was forced to remove his gloves and quickly put on another pair, taking care not to contaminate his hands. Crystal had acted fast to take the doctors samples. The doctor searched around the room wondering where they had gone. Eventually, he took more samples. Crystal left the building, concealing the samples. She met Natasha and Tristana, and returned to the ship. Tristana was not happy about these tissue samples being carried back to the ship, and protested.

"You're putting us at risk, Crystal," she said.

"The containers are sealed, and you are quite safe unless you remove the lid," Crystal replied.

No sooner had they got back to the vessel, Crystal suited up and began sorting out the samples. She put the items under the probe and watched it react to various lights and heat. Foster worked on the sample with the help of the ship's computer. It took hours for the analysis to be completed but the results were worth it. The components were not from Earth but of alien origin, which was interesting. Also, under a certain light, the skin tissue was green and was surrounded by a green mist.

"So, we have an alien virus probably come through a time portal," Crystal said.

"But there must be a carrier; a host, perhaps," Natasha said

"Yes, that's right," Crystal said. "Someone or something transported this over from another planet via the time portal, either unknowingly or even knowingly."

"Well, it wasn't us," Tristana said. "So, why are we bothering to help the Earth people?"

"It what we do, Tristana," Natasha said. "We help others."

"So, I hear," Tristana said. "Kind and honest white witches."

"It's is true," Crystal said. "We help others and fight for good defeating evil"

"So, am I your enemy?" Tristana said, concerned.

"We didn't say that," Natasha said, "but you must choose your own path based on what you think is right, and according to your own conscience."

Tristana thought about what she had said; but she was in conflict with herself and with the way she had been influenced by the dark witches, and how she was being raised to think their way was right and just. Crystal wanted her to choose her own pathway in life, and appreciate the good side of life and not just the bad, just as she had to choose and Natasha.

Meanwhile, far away was the laboratory where the ghost lived. Professor Hadrian Kingsley was working on ideas how to bring down the government and make society pay for his failed experiments, and lack of funding. Kingsley had discovered a virus when an alien, known simply as 'The Ghost' came through a time portal and arrived at his house. He was a carrier of the deadly virus called 'Turtle Spawn' due to its colour on the skin. Kingsley was apprehensive at first when he was told how deadly it was. He was taking precautions when dealing with the man. At this time, the man was visible to the naked eye. He was nursed for a while at this time. They discovered he was a carrier, and had not got the virus. The alien could communicate quite well as he sat and explained to Kingsley about his planet, and how the virus had killed many people there. He was sad because it took most of his family and friends, leaving him to survive alone until now. Kingsley listened to his woeful tale, watching the poor alien cry for his family. But he was only concerned with the virus, and how he could use it to his advantage.

"Oh, my dear friend," Kingsley said. "I will call you 'The Ghost', as you are the host of this virus. I will help you as long as you help me."

The alien agreed, unaware of the Professor's evil plan to use him to spread the virus across the country, and cause havoc to the Earth people, holding England for ransom. But even Kingsley was not aware just how deadly the virus was… Not until he unleashed it into society.

The alien was naïve and never suspected that he was doing any harm at first. Kingsley had experimented on a type of serum that makes people appear invisible. He used it on the alien who was now called The Ghost. Suddenly, The Ghost disappeared before his eyes, and that's why he was called by that name. Kingsley wore special glasses to see him, and convinced him he was cured, sending him on errands around London. The ghost went off believing the professor. At first, he was just sent locally, until he was used to travelling, and then went further to stations and markets. A camera was attached to him so Kingsley could watch people collapse and die. It was a horrific sight, and the green trail of fog that was left behind told him that these people would be fatally ill or die.

After a few days, Kingsley contacted the media and explained about the virus and his intensions if the government didn't pay a modest ransom of half a million pounds. But then, he got greedy, and sent The Ghost to various countries, until he had the entire world up for ransom. Terror had hit the streets, and the government were panicking. No one was safe, and the Prime Minister ordered a lock down. Everybody had to remain indoors, unless they were working people, such as nurses, who had a lot of pressure on them to carry on their work. Pubs closed as well, as shops and other establishments. Most people's life had changed but not for the better. Streets had become deserted, and things were very quiet. Schools also closed and children were being taught from home, known as home learning. Factories closed, and so were many businesses. People were advised to wear masks, keep two meters apart in public, and no parties or other forms of entertainment that involves crowds of people in close proximity. Due to what was by now a worldwide crisis, people had to abide by the rules.

Meanwhile, The Ghost continues to travel undetected. The time witches were aware of the activity of The Ghost through the media, and knew they had to stop him. The death toll was going well into the thousands by now, and nobody could stop it, as they couldn't see him. He could have been anywhere brushing against people. The government were waiting for a vaccine that would protect them from this virus, but it took time and the hospital beds were full of patients who thought they had contracted it. In most cases, they had and were quarantined.

Crystal was in her vessel working on a way of actually seeing The Ghost. She knew it was possible with a little magic. She was confident she could do it having done similar things in the past. Natasha assisted and Tristana looked on in amazement. Crystal used a cauldron and put a few potions in it mixing it up with water, and then added a few spells from her book of shadows. The pot boiled and sent smoke clouds into the air. She was a very gifted witch who was able to conjure up many things. She was also good at Psychometry: the art of being able to read something from objects, such as metal rings or crystal balls. She has traced people through items that they left behind, especially a watch or necklace.

Once Crystal had mixed the potion, she dropped some glasses into the cauldron and waited for a while before removing them from the pot. Natasha made herself vanish and hid while Crystal tried to find her. She gazed around the room until she heard a noise, and began to follow the sound. Suddenly, it stopped; then, she looked behind each chair until she found Natasha.

"Got you," she said.

"You can see me?" Natasha asked.

"As clear as day," she replied. "It works."

"My God, it does," Natasha said in astonishment.

"You could show a little faith, Nat" Crystal said.

"Sorry, Crystal," Natasha said. "Very well done!"

"Yes, well done, Crystal. That was amazing," Tristana said, looking.

Tristana was looking around the vessel, and came across a mirror. She looked at it, and suddenly screamed. Crystal and Natasha went running to her rescue finding her in one of the cabin rooms.

"Whatever is the matter?" Natasha asked.

"This mirror has a horrible face in it," she replied, shaking.

Natasha looked at Crystal, and she looked back at her. Tristana noticed them looking at each other as if they knew what was going on.

"What is it?" she inquired.

"I am afraid it is you," Crystal said, "your reflection."

"I don't understand. It looked nothing like me," Tristana said, afraid to look at it again.

"This mirror reflects your personality at present. Your inner self," Crystal explained.

"The badness shows in the mirror," Natasha added.

"But I am trying to be good," Tristana said, disappointed.

"Yes, this is noted, and it will show in here eventually when the badness goes," Natasha assured her.

"If this reflects me, goodness knows what my mother would look like," Tristana said, laughing, but produced an evil smirk on her face which suggested the mirror was telling the truth about her at this time.

That night, Natasha had a dream about The Ghost travelling through Edinburgh Station during rush hour. She dreamt that she saw him with a trail of mist behind him. People were falling to the ground in great numbers, and he just walked away unnoticed. The emergency crew were all over the station as they were in London. She woke up in a hot sweat looking around her cabin at bare walls with the faint light of a clock near her bed, which told her it was five AM, and certainly not time to get up. She stayed awake for a while thinking, and then fell asleep once more; this time dreaming about time travel and meeting the dark witches; this time she dreamt about Crystal getting killed by them. Again, she awoke. It was now nine o'clock in the morning, so she decided to get up and have a shower.

During the night, Foster keeps the ship on course with the aid of the computer. He alerts Crystal if there are any problems by sounding an alarm to her cabin which can be heard by the other witches too. Natasha got dressed and brushed her hair. She left the cabin and joined everybody else for breakfast, eager to share her premonitions with them. First, she sat and listened to an existing conversation involving the dark witches who had abducted Shanice, and were holding her for ransom in exchange for Tristana. They thought that the white witches had kidnapped her, and did suspect the wizard Merek at first. Crystal had reluctantly agreed to give Tristana up as she thought she had made progress with them, learning the good practices of the white witches, but she knew Shanice needed rescuing and she was priority. However, the virus and The Ghost needed to be sorted out first, which would save countless lives not to mention the survival of Earth and other planets infected by it.

The time witches agreed that the virus came from the Planet Delcara with its host known as The Ghost. He had infected all the inhabitants of the planet before entering the time portal. There was no trace of life on Delcara. According to the space federation, it's just deserted homes and wild creatures' immune to the virus, now called Delcara.

The Delcara virus spread across the human skin leaving an invisible green layer of gel on the surface than work through like acid destroying the skin cells and attacking the internal organs. Breathing becomes laboured and the blood vessels becomes thin restricting blood flow. This resulted of the body perishes rapidly; but what is interesting is that the virus soon dies after it kills that person. The reason is so far unclear, but the green substance dries into a powder, and by that time, it is no longer contagious. This is what the time witches discovered after revisiting some of the bodies kept for further analysis. They had also discovered a vaccine against the virus based on previous research from the Planet Delcara. It was almost ready to be tested when the last group of people contracted the virus and died before the batch was ready to go out.

"I had a dream last night," Natasha began, "concerning the virus."

"You mean a premonition?" Crystal asked.

"Yes," Natasha went on. "That The Ghost's next target was to be in Edinburgh Railway Station."

"Then, we must go there," Tristana said, "and catch the ghost."

"We shall go right now," Crystal agreed. "Foster, set a course for Edinburgh, Scotland."

The ship took off and began its journey to Scotland. Meanwhile, Natasha was concerned about telling Crystal about her other dream regarding her death. They were now aware that they would be going to Alba to meet the dark witches and exchange Tristana for Shanice, but only Natasha knew about Crystal's fate.

When they arrived at the station, many people were about

even though the government and media had announced the situation concerning the Delcara virus. No set rules and regulations had been decided concerning lock down. It was announced that precautions had to be undertaken like previous viruses such as lock down, not allowing people to visit relatives, two-meter distancing, and working from home if possible. Shops closed apart from those supplying essentials, and industries came to a halt. Hospitals restricted visiting as did doctors' surgery while this pandemic was present.

The time witches reached Edinburgh Railway Station. It seemed fairly busy considering the circumstances as if people were ignoring the health warnings from the government. Crystal was invisible and wearing the special glasses awaiting the presence of The Ghost, while London was sorting the ransom of two million pounds in cash. The witches had contacted them, alerting them of his intentions to attack Edinburgh, and that they would find him and bring him to justice. They never mentioned that they were witches – just well-respected ladies of the community, doing a good deed – hoping this would suffice without making a fuss. They stood waiting for hours watching all the activity. Nothing appeared to be out of the ordinary. They were beginning to doubt Natasha's premonition when suddenly, he appeared. Using telepathy, they communicated with each other. Crystal followed him around the station keeping a safe distance. He began touching people as he passed.

"We need to stop him. Quick girls," Crystal said. "He is standing by the entrance."

"Do we use the spray yet?" Tristana asked.

"I will guide you to the place where he is," Crystal said.

"Why don't we wait? He might return to his hideout," Natasha said.

"You mean follow him?" Crystal said.

"Exactly. He may not be working alone." Natasha said.

"I agree," Tristana said. "It could work."

"We must not reveal our true identity to the public or the authorities," Crystal explained.

Crystal followed The Ghost along through the ticket barriers bound for London. She sat close by hoping that the train would not be packed. However, very few passengers actually boarded the train. Some were questioned by police as they wanted to know why they were travelling during this pandemic. Few that were travelling were actually going to work as they were not able to work from home. A few of them had jobs as nurses or carers in the private sector; the whole atmosphere was not normal and things looked bleak. The media was continually reporting about the Delcara virus.

The time witches had put this in the heads of the government and media, explaining that it was an alien virus. The media sensationalised it and suggested that it was put in place prior to an alien invasion. When in reality, it came to earth by accident, thanks to The Ghost who wanted to explore Earth, little knowing at the time that he was a carrier. Professor Kingsley had convinced the alien that he had done no wrong. He was just travelling to stations and airports unseen, and thought that he was just exploring. He couldn't help bumping into people as they were unable to see him. Kingsley had befriended the alien and made him invisible for an experiment, but took things too far by using him, calling him The Ghost, spreading this virus around the world.

The Delcara virus is quick spreading and is classed as the most lethal virus known to man. However, it is short acting and only remains in the body for twenty-four hours after leaving the host. The time witches had this information and they had a formula which would immunise the population; it just needed perfecting. Meanwhile, they needed to stop The Ghost from travelling and deal with Kingsley. They knew the ghost would lead them to him eventually. The other problem would be whether or not the vaccine would work on Earth people as it was an alien virus.

All they could do was hope and pray that it would be a success, and reach the remainder of the world population.

Natasha and Crystal had come across the plague of 1665, and the great fire of London, when they travelled back in time in 1666. They reached London before the great fire had begun. They had experienced other viruses in time and on various planets. They called this one the invisible enemy. They used the vaccine on each other just in case they contracted the virus while dealing with The Ghost. Natasha was the only Earth girl, so she was effectively the first of her kind to be immunised. She suffered no side effects, and within days, protected against the virus. Tristana developed a rash and severe headache. She was weak for a while remaining on the vessel by the sick bay. While she was ill, she had time to think about her life with the dark witches. She was relatively happy with them although she couldn't help thinking that the white witches were good role models, who respected life and were kind to each other. She too wanted to challenge The Ghost and Kingsley, and stop the virus spreading, but she had a fiercer approach and just wanted to destroy them. The dark witches don't see any way but annihilation without mercy as people's lives mean nothing to them. They believe in destroying man and property as demonstrated with the wizard's castle. Although this was done because of what they had heard about Tristana being cursed, and Musette being murdered by Merek.

The Ghost had reached the building where Kingsley had his laboratory. She followed him closely as he entered through a secure door, and walked along a long corridor which appeared like a hospital with trolleys in the corridor. It was brightly lit with florescent lights and looked very clean, smelling of disinfectant, and cameras were high up on the walls. Eventually, they reached the laboratory, and there stood Professor Kingsley waiting for The Ghost. He used a spray in order to make him materialise. Crystal saw this and remained in the corridor for a while. She was still able to hear Kingsley with his booming voice and loud laughter as he boasted about how many deaths he had caused. The ghost was not amused being used by Kingsley in this way. A nurse was also present. They were masked up, ready to greet The Ghost, and tell him their news.

"My friend The Ghost, you have returned," Kingsley said. "Come. Be seated, and listen to what I have to say." The Ghost was all green from head to toe, and seemed to have no face; just a strange shape with no obvious ears, and a thin body. He was paying attention to the Kingsley and clearly understood him. "You have done well, but I need you to return to Euston Station for me, and pick up a parcel left by her majesty's government containing the ransom money. Is that clear?"

"I understand, Professor," he replied. "But can I ask you something?"

"Yes, of course," Kingsley replied. "What is it?"

"Can you get me home?" he said sadly.

"Why, my dear friend? Why do you want to go back there to a disease-ridden planet containing the deadliest virus?" Kingsley asked. "Are you not happy here on Earth?"

"I would rather be with my own kind," he said.

"But they are dying," Kingsley said coldly. "They could be all dead by now. Well, okay. Get my parcel, and I will find a way of getting you home." Kingsley was lying so that the ghost would stay and serve him. He knew that he still needed him, and if he got him home, he would never return. He would not be able to ransom the world without him as he was the host of the virus.

Crystal had heard enough and returned to a meeting point, and waited for Natasha so they could return to the ship. When they arrived back, Tristana was sat by Foster. He was attempting to teach her card games, but they may as well be playing frustration as Tristana failed to understand the rules or pretending to, so that she could tease Foster. Frustration was a board game popular in the twentieth century – dice in a plastic dome that you press down to move the dice, and then, travel around the board.

Obviously, there is more to it than that, but that's the gist of it. Crystal could sense the tension with Tristana as she tried to learn the rules and ended up making her own up. She was still frustrated, so she threw the cards in the air and offered a few profanities. Natasha gave her a look of disgust and sat herself down, avoiding eye contact with Tristana and addressing Crystal.

"So, what do we do now?" Natasha asked.

"You mean with The Ghost?" Crystal said puzzled.

"Haven't you killed him?" Tristana asked.

"No. The Ghost or the alien has been misled. He believes he is working for Kingsley in order for him to return to his own planet with a cure for the virus." Crystal explained.

"But he is a carrier of the virus," Tristana said.

"Yes, but he isn't aware of this," Crystal said. "Only that he gets sent to crowded places, and that he is invisible."

"I have a chemical which can be sprayed on him, and make him appear," Crystal held it in the air and showed them.

"So, you can make him appear?" Natasha said. "Can you use the antivirus on him?"

"Maybe," Crystal replied. "It's worth a try, and then we can save his planet."

Tristana was not impressed with the idea. She felt the best way was just get rid of the alien, and put an end to The Ghost. As for his planet, she considered it not worth saving; just let the virus destroy what is left there.

Crystal was aware that Kingsley had contacted the government asking about the ransom, masquerading as The Ghost. He was determined to get his money in exchange for the antidote which would immunise the human race, but he had no such thing. She waited at the station for The Ghost, hoping to stop him and take him to a safe place in order to discuss his situation, and find the right solution for him. As for Kingsley, he was not interested in saving The Ghost once he had got his ransom money. He was more concerned with holding the world to ransom with or without The Ghost.

Crystal didn't need to wait long before The Ghost appeared. Agents were in the vicinity watching the bag that contained the money. The atmosphere was tense. Crystal moved in close, and pulled The Ghost away. They were both invisible, and The Ghost went with her into a room.

"We haven't got much time," she said. "I am Crystal, a time witch."

"I am Jay, better known as The Ghost," he said. "And I have heard of time witches."

"I am here to rescue you," she said, "and to return you home."

"Professor Kingsley offered to do that for me?" he replied.

"Kingsley is using you. He wants to ransom the world, and dispense of you afterwards," she explained.

Crystal took the ghost back to her ship where the others were waiting. She sprayed him down and injected him with the antivirus once he became visible. This gave the other chance to see that he was genuine and sincere. He was all green from head to toe with hardly any features. It seemed very odd not seeing a nose or eyes, not even ears. He spoke to each one of us, but Tristana had her barriers up and refused to respond to The Ghost, considering him as evil and hideous to look at. His body glowed green after a while like it was some kind of alert but The Ghost reassured them that all was well. He did this in order to relax and conserve his energy. He was preparing himself for his trip back home.

The witches need one more task from him, to return to the laboratory where the Kingsley was waiting for him. The Ghost was not eager to return to Kingsley having discovered the truth about him and his plan to use him to kill so many people with the virus. The witches refused to call him The Ghost and addressed him by his name, Jay. He liked that and trusted the time witches due to their reputation for helping people.

"Jay, we must go back to the laboratory and expose Kingsley," Crystal said.

"Too many people have died from the Delcara virus," Natasha added.

"I understand," he replied.

"Of course, it would be selfish of you not to agree," Tristana said abruptly.

"You don't like me, do you?" Jay said.

"No, you remind me of the awful goblins," Tristana said, turning her back on him.

"That's not very nice, Tristana. Have you still got demons in you?" Natasha said. "Should we address you as Lamia?"

"No, I am sorry," Tristana sat, embarrassed by what she had said.

"Let's not fall out. We have a job to do," Crystal said.

They all prepared themselves to go to see Kingsley. Jay, The Ghost and Crystal entered the building first. They headed down the corridor and Jay walked straight into the laboratory. Kingsley was there to greet him. He looked angry and glared at Jay.

"You were supposed to pick up the ransom money and bring it to me! A simple task, but you have failed! One bag! That's all!" Kingsley said.

"I tried," Jay said nervously.

"Well, not hard enough obviously," Kingsley said, using the spray in order to make him appear. "You have ruined everything." He produced a syringe from the table that had been neatly placed on a silver tray. He held it up and got rid of the air bubbles by pushing the end with his thumb and flicking it with his finger, and then he approached Jay.

At that moment, Crystal entered the room and used the spray

making her appear. "Not so fast, Kingsley," she said. "Time to be accountable for your actions."

"Who are you?" he asked, still holding the syringe tightly.

"I am Crystal, a time witch," she replied. "Surrender now!" she said, pointing her wand at him.

"You must be joking coming here and ordering me about," he said. "I can destroy you in an instant, and you wave that toy Harry Potter wand at me."

"This is no toy," she said, remaining still.

"Do you know what is in this syringe?" he asked. "A new spawn of the virus." He launched at her with the syringe pointing the needle towards her.

At that moment, Jay rushed in between them, and the needle entered his chest. Crystal sent a lightning bolt at Kingsley knocking him back. Kingsley was shocked finding out the wand was real remaining on the floor. Meanwhile, Natasha and Tristana were fighting the security staff making their way to the laboratory. Eventually, they reached Crystal.

"Be careful! Jay has been injected with a different variant of the virus. It is man-made, in this lab," Crystal warned them. Kingsley got to his feet noticing the other witches appear. Both had their wands pointed at him. Jay left the room, and Tristana went after him.

"Stop right there, ghost," she said, pointing her wand at him.

Jay was frightened, but he stopped for a moment and turned towards her. "You can kill me. I am going to die anyway," he said.

"Do not tempt me, ghost," she replied.

Jay turns away and ran down the corridor. Tristana sent a bolt of lightning powerful enough to kill him and he fell to the ground. Natasha rushed into the corridor, but she was too late to stop Tristana. She knelt beside Jay with tears in her eyes.

"Why the hell did you do that?" she shouted.

"He has the virus. It could have spread," Tristana explained.

"What if I have the virus? Are you going to kill me?" Natasha asked.

"I don't know." She thought for a moment, "No."

"You wonder why my truth mirror showed you as evil, when you do things like this," Natasha continued. "You are a dark witch and always will be. You prove this by your actions."

"I am not all bad," she replied.

"Well, what about the old lady with the shopping breaking her bag," she reminded Tristana.

"I fixed that. I got her a stronger bag," she said, defending herself.

"Whoopee! Good for you," Natasha said sarcastically.

At that point, Crystal arrived and tried to calm the situation down. She wanted to leave the police and army with all the details concerning Kingsley and the virus, making sure they were unaware who the time witches were concealing their identity. When they arrived, Kingsley and the guards were tied up, and a detailed letter was typed out for the police to see. As for the anti-virus, it was all prepared with details of the formula and a detailed account about The Ghost, aka Jay, being an alien with photographs of him taken with Kingsley's camera.

Jay was taken away by the witches after they discovered that the syringe had been filled with green washing up liquid. The time witches decided it was time to take Tristana back to her mother, and exchange her as planned for Shanice. They considered, although Shanice was a little extreme and careless, she was at least a white witch and not a bad person. Going to Alba wasn't an option as they had to rescue Shanice, but it meant meeting the dark witches and that was not good. Tristana was jealous of her and discovered that her mother was fond of her, and wanted her to remain by her side. But once the exchange had taken place, the time witches departed and left for another time on earth.

Tristana had found herself on Alba, and she was bored after the excitement of time travel with Crystal and Natasha. So, she found a way of travelling in the time portals and had her own adventures. She felt that she was now different from the dark witches and genuinely wanted to help others like they did. Maybe one day, she would come out from the darkness and become a white witch, and then she could look in that truth mirror and see a good witch.

WHO'S AFRAID OF THE BIG BAD WOLF

It was a dark cold night in winter. The moon was full and the sound of howling wolves could be heard in the distance. A child was lying in a crib who appeared to be abandoned by his parents. He began making crying sounds but rather that the expected sound of a baby, he sounded like a wolf. Gradually, he began to change in form first of all his features, and then his body. The sound of bones crunching, and hair was forming all over his body from head to foot. It was odious to watch the eyes were yellow at first, and then changed into dark menacing looking beads.

The boy had transformed into a wild beast or werewolf. After a while, he was joined by other wolves. It had become clearly apparent that the child was abandoned because his parents discovered he had become a werewolf, whether by birth, or as he began growing; this was uncertain, but at some point, he must have come in contact with a werewolf or perhaps his mother who gave birth to him. Whatever the case, he was cursed and lives his life in a forest searching for food and sustenance amidst a hostile world. But as the boy grew into a man, he became a good hunter at night, and slept most of the day. Therefore, he was a nocturnal creature, and someone to fear as a werewolf.

Tristana began her journey and adventure in the time portal. It was certainly a strange experience drifting through time through the galaxies, and landing who knows where, unlike travelling in a time machine, where you could set the controls and navigate the vessel according to your desired destination, or at least that's the theory of travelling in the time machine. Sometimes, things do go wrong, and the elements dictate your destination or other bizarre explanations that help to misdirect you to another time or area in space, such as a hostile planet or a mysterious place in any galaxy.

Each journey has its own adventure; meeting aliens or conversing with robots, seeing primitive worlds or intelligent beings that are capable of thinking far beyond our comprehension, and have advanced technology. Tristana sometimes wished that she had been better behaved and continued on journeys with the time witches, but here she was, alone, having her own adventures. She was often warned about temporal displacement or time sickness. She had to be careful when travelling through time portals in case she experiences this sickness. People have died through travelling in time portals, bleeding from the ears or nose through atmospheric pressure. As Natasha explained it, it was like going down in a flushing toilet, and then coming out of the other end confused or dizzy, like going on a fast fair ride such as the super waltzes.

Tristana landed as most time travellers did by falling onto the ground in a daze, looking around in confusion, like someone who had been dropped from a plane into a jungle or desert. *My God! It's cold here* she thought, and proceeded to rub her arms with her hands. She looked all around her at the snowy winter's landscape. Strangely enough, she felt eyes on her. Somebody was watching. She had fallen in the snow and noticed her impression on the ground where she landed. She continued to rub her arms, and then heard the sound of hungry wolves. Close by was a forest, and all around her were mountains; it was a beautiful landscape.

The wolves' cries were getting louder as they were getting nearer. She was beginning to feel uncomfortable, so she lit a fire with wood that she had discovered. Her wand lit the fire and she produced or conjured up food and a drink. The fire was all around her to keep her warm and protect her from harm. Being a witch had its advantages such as the use of magic, having sixth sense, and other useful powers. She remembered the advice that Crystal gave her *'don't follow your dreams, chase them'*, and Natasha told her *'You only fail when you stop trying'* or probably an apt saying is *'Motivation is what gets you started; Habit is what keeps you going'* – Jim Rohn.

Now, it was up to Tristana to find her own way to happiness. She could now see clearly a pack of wolves with hungry eyes all staring at her, all salivating and snarling at her. She knew that she was in danger and stood completely still. Her heart was beating fast, and although she was scared, she tried not to show it. She did everything to stop herself from trembling in fear. But the wolves could sense her fear and prepared themselves for their attack. She prepared to use her wand, but accidentally dropped it into a bush down a bank. They began to run towards her, growling. She tried to run but got caught her foot jumping over a log. One dog bit her leg, another took a bite of her shoulder. She had run away from the fire that had protected her. She thought that this was the end for her – to die in a snowy wilderness without anyone to save her – until she heard the sound that was much more terrifying. It was a howl that seemed to travel through the air and penetrate her ears. She lay still and noticed that the wolves had stopped attacking her. They, too, were afraid of this sound and fled back into the woods. She returned to the fire and reached down for her wand. She managed to summon it up into her hand, and sat peering into the forest. Eventually, she fell asleep.

She awoke the next morning with a feeling of discomfort due to her wounds. After a short while, a figure appeared from a bush looking a little bit shabby. His hair was in a mess, but he was handsome and caught the eye of Tristana, who couldn't help but stare at him. She had never been in love before, but it felt like she was the happiest woman alive. He instantly took her pain away by his very presence. He was a creature of beauty that she kept in sight. He walked towards her. She was nervous but in a good way. Unlike her fear of the wolves, she remained still until he was close to her.

"Hello," he said. "Are you hurt?"

"Yes," she admitted. "I was attacked by wolves."

"Allow me to help you," he said kindly.

Tristana showed him her leg. She watched him as he pulled out some bandages from his bag, and poured a fluid into a small bowl.

"Fear not; I am a doctor," he said, soaking some gauze into a bowl, and then dabbing her leg.

Tristana winced as he washed her leg, and then applied a dressing and secured it with a bandage. He seemed so gentle in his approach, and felt at ease. She then revealed her shoulder with modesty. He repeated his cleansing of her wounds on her shoulder and dressed it appropriately. Once the procedure was over, he sat next to her and began a conversation in a charming manner, showing her respect. She was not used to it and felt flattered, and at the same time quite humbled. She wondered if a dark witch should feel like this and decided not to reveal her identity. He had the most attractive smile and his eyes seemed to sparkle like the stars at night. He was clean shaven with long side burns, as if he was from the Victorian times. Tristana suddenly thought that she had no idea where she was or what period of time, but neither did she care at this point for she was truly in love with this man. He took her back to his home which just happened to be a country cottage. She hoped that it would be a clue about white photographs, and oil paintings of the English country side. On a small table beside an armchair, it read: London Times Newspaper with the date January 2nd 1881. She sighed with relief, and followed the man into the kitchen.

"I am sorry; I didn't introduce myself. How rude. I am sorry," he said.

"I am Tristana," she said.

"Doctor James Wiggins," he said, shaking by the hand.

"Where are you from?" he asked inquisitively.

Tristana had to think fast before lying. What place did she know on Earth, and then she remembered the time witches talking about Manchester.

"Manchester," she replied.

"North of England, where the mills are," he said.

"Yes," she replied not completely understand his reference to a mill.

"I have never been, but I have read about Manchester," he said.

I wish I had, Tristana thought. She had also heard about London and its history, especially the bloodshed, like the executions at the Tower of London, the Great Plague, and Fire of London. It seemed that the history painted a bleak picture of life in London: with the murders that were committed by Jack the Ripper, as well as the previously mentioned events. But surely, if it was so bad, no one would live there.

"This is my country home. I lived in London most of my life," he said.

"Riveting," she replied.

"Excuse me?" he said. "Don't you like London?"

"It's a bit crowded for me," she said. "I like my space."

"So, where are you staying, Tristana?" he asked.

"Oh, close by," she said. "I forget the name."

"You can always stop here," he offered. "I have plenty of room."

"Are you sure?" she said with surprise.

"Of course," he said. "Are you superstitious?" he asked her.

"What do you mean?" she asked suspiciously, thinking he had discovered her secret.

"Ghosts, witches or werewolves," he tried to explain, "strange events?"

"I suppose so," she agreed.

"Only in the forest, there is supposed to be a werewolf," he began. "So frightening and more dangerous than the wolves there."

"I heard an eerie sound that scared away the wolves," she said. "It certainly frightened me."

"Yes, the forest is not safe. Animals are found torn to shreds," he said. "And people have died out there."

"Have you ever seen a werewolf?" she asked.

"Never," he said. "But I am sure they are real."

"Have you seen a ghost? How about a vampire or a witch?" she asked.

"No. I think vampires and ghosts are a myth," he said dismissively.

"That is bizarre," she said. "How can you believe in one thing and not the other?"

"Blood sucking vampires? Really?" he laughed, "And witches are old hags who claim to perform magic and ride on brooms. Really? How absurd."

Ugly old hags?" she said. "Honestly, how rude."

"Come, now. Do you believe in witches?" he asked.

"Maybe," she replied, still concealing her identity.

"Would you like a cup of tea?" he asked, not wishing to pursue the subject of the occult at the present time. "Do you need to fetch your clothes?" he asked.

"Yes, I believe I do," she replied.

"If you don't mind me saying so, you are dressed oddly," he

said, looking at her attire. "No offense."

"None taken. I am a little eccentric," she admitted.

"We are close to town, and you can get a carriage back," he said.

"I will go shortly," she said.

"You don't want to come back in the dark," he said concerned.

"Werewolves," she said.

"Werewolf. Singular," he replied. "Just one."

"No vampires or witches?" she said, teasing.

"No," he replied.

After she had her refreshments of tea and biscuits, Tristana set off walking to town. Dr. Wiggins stayed behind and prepared her room. Tristana was reluctant to use magic for fear of being seen and being exposed as a witch. However, she had to produce a trunk of close from somewhere. She reached the town and noticed a carriage for hire which would take her back to Dr. Wiggins' cottage, and so she made enquiries at the coach house. The driver enquired about her trunk, and she said that she would get it. She walked down an alley and watched people coming and going. When she thought the coast was clear, she produced her wand from under her clothes and caused a trunk to appear out of thin air. She had observed the style of costumes worn and replicated them in great detail, and then returned her wand. She had even changed herself into a costume fitting for the age. After this, she conjured up some money from what she had seen, and put it in a quaint purse. She dragged the trunk so far, and considered it too much effort, so she made it vanish and re appears near the carriage. Not bad for a so-called non-witch, she thought, or an ugly old hag. Damn cheek, she thought to herself. If he only knew I am a witch and not at all ugly or old.

Tristana arrived back at the cottage to see the Doctor looking out for her. He began to smile as he saw her appear. He was unsure whether or not he would see her again. He felt he had put her off with his superstitions. But she was determined to return and continue being with him, without a thought of the long-term plans, whatever the outcome brings.

Tristana spent the night alone in a single bed listening to the rapturous noise of the doctor snoring, which bothered her. Then. Suddenly, it stopped, and all was quiet until the howling began. Strangely enough, this didn't occur every night, and the longer Tristana stayed, the less she heard it. This is because werewolves only come out during a full moon; at least that's what the legend says.

Once Tristana went to bed, she stayed there until morning hiding under the bedsheets, like a frightened child hides from the boogeyman. Meanwhile, the doctor is either in his bed or pacing the room like a caged lion, thinking of Tristana and his love for her, trying to find a way to tell her how he feels.

That night, a full moon appeared, and the howling wolves began their cries, so menacing and yet somehow appealing to certain people. Tristana decided to venture out that evening. Her enthusiasm for trying to find the so-called myth of the werewolf had gripped her and driven her into the woods. But she was not the only one out that night. The villagers were determined to seek the werewolf, and destroy him in revenge for killing their family, friends, and animals. Guns were fired and there were a lot of shouting. Tristana hid from view until everything went quiet. People carried lanterns and anything they could use as weapons such as farm tools. As she continued to move, she tripped over something and discovered it was an animal, like a wolf. It's very hairy, and with sharp teeth. But as she watched the creature, it began to transform itself into a man. Gradually, the features formed until all she saw was a naked man with smooth skin, clean shaven, with scars on his body from recent injuries, and old wounds. As she examined him, the great crowd emerged from the woods. They were surprised by her presence. No one knew what to say to her, but then one man began to speak.

"Come away, child. Lest the beast is still alive," he said.

"He is dead," she replied. "You killed him."

"We had to. He was a werewolf," he continued. "We used silver bullets."

"I have heard the legend of the werewolves, but never met one until now," she explained.

"Come, girl. Let us escort you home," he said to her. "Do you live far?"

"I am staying with the Dr. James Wiggins," she said.

"Nice man," he replied. "A very good doctor."

Most of the crowd nodded in agreement, or made approving noises as their way of agreeing with this man, who obviously was the leader and spokesperson. True to his promise, he took Tristana back to the doctor's home. She crept in quietly so that she wouldn't disturb him. She got undressed and returned to bed just as if she hadn't been away and fell asleep, dreaming about werewolves.

Tristana dreamt that she was being attacked by one in the woods. They were about to claw and bite when she awoke in a cold sweat. She gazed around the room disorientated at first, and was alarmed by the scratches on her body and blood from these wounds. Was this real? she thought to herself.

At that moment, the doctor entered the room. He seemed anxious, and when he noticed the blood, he began to panic. This seemed out of character for him, in his profession as a doctor.

"Are you okay?" he asked her.

"Yes. Although, I am a little confused," she admitted. "I fell asleep and had nightmares."

"I heard you shout and scream," he said. "Let me cleanse your wounds."

Tristana allowed him to nurse her wounds, and felt relaxed in his presence, she suddenly felt the urge to kiss him but resisted. She was excited by his hands touching her body that her skin began to tingle. She had never felt like this before; this was all new to her. She wondered what was happening since the evil dark witch was responding favourably to stimuli, and what she considered was intimacy. She had no control of her feelings, and her body was telling her so.

"Did you go out last night?" he asked, oblivious of her present feelings.

"Oh, yes, I did," she admitted. "I heard a strange noise and followed the sound."

"Why?" he said concerned. "I saved you from the wolves, remember?"

"Yes, I know," she said gasping.

"Am I hurting you?" he asked, listening to her moan.

"No; sorry, go on," she said, trying to control her body.

"What happened in the woods?" he asked.

"It was a werewolf. He was hunted down and killed by villagers," she said sadly.

"How did they kill him?" he asked.

"With silver bullets," she replied. "But before he died, he changed into a man."

"It definitely sounded like a werewolf," he said, looking into her eyes.

"The villagers brought me back here," she said, covering herself up.

"Well, you're safe now, Tristana," he said, standing up.

"Yes. Thank you for your kindness," she agreed. "Doctor!" she shouted.

"Call me James," he insisted.

"Okay, James," she smiled. "Could I have fresh clothes and bedding, please?"

"Of course," he said, smiling back at her and left the room.

The next morning, Tristana got up refreshed from her sleep. With this overwhelming feeling inside the presence of Doctor Wiggins made her giddy, she was getting palpitations and had a sense of belonging like never before. Her body quivered in his presence, and she felt warm inside. If this was love, she wanted more of it. She hoped that he was feeling the same about her. This was more powerful than any spells that she knew or had ever witnessed. She had seen so much in the past, and realised the good witches were the white witches, and the love they conveyed was the right way to go. The moments she shared with the time witches proved to be worthwhile. They had influenced her to think in a different way, and guided her in a loving way unlike the dark witches.

Tristana sat at a long table in the dining room. She watched a middle-aged lady bringing food to the table. The lady smiled, and then left the room. The doctor entered the room with a welcoming smile on his face. Tristana sat confused at everything that's going on, but managed to smile back.

"You have met Alice, my house keeper, I take it?" he said as she re-entered the room with a tray of tea.

"Hello, Alice," she said politely.

"Good morning, Tristana," she replied. "Would you care for tea?" she offered.

"Yes, thank you," Tristana replied, remembering her manners.

The doctor seemed pleased that they were getting along. He encouraged Tristana to eat from his banquet of food. She was overwhelmed by all the choices of food on offer: freshly cooked bacon, eggs, sausage, and beans to begin with. Toast and marmalade with other fried foods, and cereals like porridge; so much for a morning breakfast, including fresh fruit juice.

"Really, James? I am not that hungry in the morning," she said, struggling to eat her porridge.

"It's the most important meal of the day," he said. "It sets you up for the day ahead."

"I can appreciate that, but I still struggle to eat at this time," she replied.

After breakfast, the doctor announced that he was going on

house calls as people required his help in health matters. This left Tristana to entertain herself all day. She spent the day reading science books and going for a walk around the nearby village. She was trying to avoid using her powers, aware of the risk of being found out as a witch.

Later that evening, the doctor returned looking tired from his work and somewhat troubled. He seemed lost in his own thoughts, and failed to acknowledge that Tristana was there.

"James, what's wrong?" she asked.

"It's nothing, really," he replied. "The villagers were talking about the werewolf."

"But he is dead. They killed him," she said, trying to reassure the doctor.

"I know, but the villagers are very superstitious. They believe in all kinds of nonsense, such as witches, goblins, and aliens."

"And you don't?" she asked, being a witch and an alien.

"No, I am afraid. I have a problem believing in these things," he said. "Ugly old hags and little green aliens? Not at all."

"Well, I like to keep an open mind about such things," she said. "Good for you," he said smiling.

Tristana decided to go for a walk, and decide what to do about the doctor and her love for him. Surely, he will open his heart to her just as she opened her heart to him. What was preventing him to express his feelings? She was eager to make the next step and thought that if he didn't make the first move, then she would. Her urges were telling her to do it; her body hungered for his love. She got excited each time she met him that it made her skin tingled. She entertained herself all day by reading and going for walks around the quiet village. Women were gossiping about the killing of the werewolf in shops and on the streets. Nobody knew who the young man was or how he became a werewolf, but they presumed, through the legend, that it was from another werewolf. It was so sad.

Later that evening, Tristana was talking to the doctor about his day: visiting patients, and then discussed the villages and their conversations. The doctor went quiet and decided to retire to bed. Tristana followed and went into her room thinking that was the end of the evening and again no romance. She lay on her bed gazing at the ceiling thinking of the doctor. It was driving her mad wondering how he felt about her. The mystery of not knowing was frustrating. She was becoming aroused by the thoughts of him touching her body and kissing her passionately. Suddenly, she became very excited and got up quickly, then rushed to the door. She stood outside his room and knocked gently on the door. She hesitated, wondering whether or not to go back to her room. She turned to face her room, and was surprised by the doctor's voice behind her.

"Tristana," he said. "What's wrong?"

She turned to face him, and gazed into his blue eyes. He gazed back at her and seemed to read her thoughts. Moving closer to her, he clasped her face between his hands, feeling her soft pale cheeks. He moved his head closer to him, and she moved forward at the same time until they were close enough to kiss. He kissed her, feeling her warm tender lips against his. He kissed her neck which aroused her more, and eventually, they moved into his room and continued to make love. This occurred most of the night until daylight.

Tristana was in ecstasy. She had finally found her true love, and he had found his. For the rest of the month, they were hardly apart. They were very happy, even the housekeeper, Alice, remarked about how happy they were and that they made a lovely couple. All was going well and Tristana never wanted it to end. But one day, she made a discovery.

Tristana walked as usual around the village. The gossip had changed from the werewolf to the romance of the doctor. She was now the talk of the village. But this worried her very much because they spoke about marriage and children. As if they would have a big feast and a christening for the child at a local church. She was a dark witch who feared churches, thinking that she would be damned. She was in a state of despair and just wanted to hide somewhere out of sight in order to think about what to do. She was afraid and confused with the situation. She also wondered if this was what the doctor wanted. He would need to know her secret, but what if he hated her for what she was and rejected her?

Tristana went into barn and sat on a haystack, continuing to contemplate her situation. It made her cry, and tears flowed down her face and began kicking the loose hay. Suddenly, she heard the sound of chains and felt them buried under the hay. She pulled them up. On the end were shackles with splashes of blood on them. She followed the chain back to the wall and discovered more shackles. These were obviously to chain something or somebody up, binding hands and feet maybe. Whatever were they doing in a barn close to the cottage, she wanted answers and she knew the doctor could be the only one to approach about this. She put the chains back and went to the door in order to leave. But suddenly, the door opened which made her heart beats faster. Then, a figure came in. She stood frozen in one position beginning to sweat. The sun was behind the person making it hard to distinguish him at first, and he was just a silhouette. As he stepped forward, she began to see him more clearly. It was the doctor and he looked angry.

"What are you doing here?" he asked, clearly not pleased.

"I was exploring," she said.

"No one comes in here," he said angrily.

"I am sorry," she said sincerely.

"You could have ruined everything," he said. "Now, I don't know what to do."

"What do you mean?" she said nervously.

"I should have told you not to come in here," he said, looking down and noticing the chains had been moved. "I need to decide what to do," he said, moving towards her and causing her to fall back over the hay stack onto her back.

"Are you going to kill me?" she asked.

He remained silent for a moment, deep in thought. "No, of course not," he replied, helping her up.

"Who were the chains for? Is it for that werewolf? Did you have him chained up?" she said, concerned.

"No, but I did know him," he admitted. "I tried to help him."

"What happened?" she asked.

"I tried to dress his wounds and he bit me," he pointed to his shoulder.

"So, you must be a werewolf," she said, thinking about the legend.

"Yes, I am," he admitted. "Every full moon, I chain myself up in here, so that I don't go out and terrorise the villagers."

"I see," she said. "So, you are protecting them from you."

"Exactly right," he admitted. "But what about us now?"

"James, I too have a confession."

"Really?" he said, puzzled.

"I am a witch," she said, watching his reaction.

He began to laugh. "Well, that cheered me up."

"I am honestly a dark witch, and an alien," she insisted.

"I don't believe you," he said dismissively. "They are said to be old and ugly with black cats."

"Well, we are not all ugly, and don't all have familiars like cats," she added. She produced her wand and conjured up a pig in the corner of the barn using a spell speaking Gaelic, and then, she produced fire from another corner of the room, then began to levitate. She then put the fire out with a spray of water. As she came down, the doctor was gone. She looked around the barn.

"James," she called out. "Where are you?"

The doctor came out from behind the hay stacks. He was a little shaky, bewildered by her actions, sweeping the hay off his clothes with his hands.

"You are a witch," he agreed. "But an alien? I am not so sure."

"Yes, that too. I'm from a different planet called Sabira. I call it Alba," she said. "So, we are both freaks, I guess."

"We both harbour secrets which must never be revealed," he said. "Whenever the moon is full, I must be chained up in here."

"And I must not use my powers for fear of being exposed," she said.

"Very wise," he agreed.

The month went by and their love grew stronger. The doctor and Tristana were popular with the villagers. They both helped many people. All seemed well until the night of the next full moon. The doctor knew it was approaching and dreaded it each month. Each time he would chain himself up in the barn hoping that nobody heard his howling. But the villagers were usually in the woods far from the village on the night of the full moon searching for werewolves; but they had killed one, and didn't expect there to be another one, and so they remained at home.

Tristana helped to chain the doctor up, and then left the barn and watched for villagers. All was well until darkness fell, and that's when the doctor began to transform into a werewolf. Tristana peeped inside in time to see him changing. She heard the sound of crunching bones and the sight of hair forming on his body. His clothing became torn, and his jaw was reshaped with a mouth full of sharp teeth. It was at this point he began howling and tugging on the chains. He was making so much noise that he was heard all over the village. Lights went on everywhere, and people went outside with lanterns, looking around for the cause of such a noise. Soon, a great crowd had assembled in the street.

"Did I hear a werewolf?" one person asked.

"I heard one," said another.

"It came from that barn," a woman said, pointing to the barn near the doctor's cottage.

A few men headed towards the barn with their lamps burning. They carried weapons of many forms. One man had a shot gun, another one had a pistol, but most had pitch forks or other farming tools. Tristana saw them approaching, and ran towards the doctor or werewolf. She was anxious for his life. She stood in front of him, and decides to unchain him so that he could run away. The werewolf looked at her with hungry eyes, but she continues to unchain him hoping that he would recognise her. He was about to strike her with his paw, with his long claws showing, but then he stopped, and stroked her face with the back of his paw; a single tear appeared in his eyes.

"Quick! Get out of here," she shouted.

He hesitated for a moment, looking into her eyes. She was also shedding tears.

"Go!" she shouted again, "or they will kill you." He escaped through a large hole in the back of the barn.

Meanwhile, some of the men entered the door. Tristana used her magic to send hay stacks in front of the hole, and then faced the men.

"Are you alright?" they asked, unaware of what she had just done.

"Yes, I am fine," she replied.

"Where is the werewolf?" another man asked.

"What werewolf?" she said innocently.

At that moment, a shout came from outside. The men turned and left the barn. When they opened the door, they saw some of the villagers rushing to the woods. Some of the women and children remain behind. Tristana ran outside and joined them. Judging from their conversation, the men had spotted the werewolf and were chasing after him. She decided to chase after them in an effort to stop them or even slow them down; just until she could think of a plan of escape. Some of the men managed to corner the werewolf, and were waiting for others to join them. The wolf made an attack on them scattering their bodies around the woods. By this time, Tristana had reached them and took out her wand. They stood looking bewildered at her, unable to believe what they were seeing. Just then, Tristana hold up her wand and sent a lightning bolt into the air as a warning shot.

"Stay away from the wolf," she shouted. "She's a witch," one cried.

"Get her," said another.

"Kill the witch!" another cried. They all started to come towards her.

The werewolf leapt in front of her in order to protect her, attacking each person who got close to them. Before long, others joined them and they battled with the wolf. Tristana summoned up a wall of fire between them and the villagers, hoping it would help them to escape, but one man took a shot at the werewolf with a silver bullet catching him in the chest. He fell to the ground in pain. The blood was oozing out, and Tristana rushed towards him and tried to comfort him. At that moment, he began to change back into the doctor. Gradually, his body altered and his features were back to normal.

"Don't die," she said sobbing. "Please don't leave me."

The doctor was trying to murmur a few words but struggled. He looked into her eyes, and tears tricked down his face. She stroked his right cheek to comfort him.

"I love you," he managed to say, and then took his last breath and died.

"It's Doctor Wiggins," a man shouted, looking through the fire.

"The witch has cast a spell on him," said another.

"Kill the witch!" a few shouted.

"You have killed the doctor," Tristana shouted. "Murderers!"

As the angry villagers raced forward, Tristana summoned up a whirlwind causing the fire to spread. Some of the people were caught up in it being thrown into trees, but a few managed to take cover and shot at her with guns and shot guns. Tristana fell back and the villagers ran forward avoiding the flames. But when they got to the area where she fell, nobody was there. She had vanished completely.

TRANSFORMATION

The sun was shining on a new day. The birds were singing and the weather was warm. The sight of a tractor was in a field, and a combine harvester was cutting the corn in a large field close by. The body of a girl lay in the corn field with blood over her clothes. She was not moving. She was lying in a fetal position. She was right in the pathway of the harvester. The driver had headphones on listening to music. He was humming to the tune, and oblivious to the body of the woman ahead. He was getting nearer and nearer; the sharp blades were turning and cutting at the corn. Suddenly, he stopped as a flash occurred in the sky and an unidentified flying craft appeared landing in another field. The man was startled and froze to his seat waiting for something else to happen. At that moment, the woman began to move and he caught sight of her. She was staggering about as if she was dazed. She looked around and noticed the man. He had climbed out of the harvester and walking towards her. He was wearing a t-shirt and tatty jeans with dirty shoes. He was young with short hair, and had unusually big nose.

"Are you okay?" he asked. "You could have been killed."

"I am fine," she said. "I am Tristana."

"I am Jason," he replied. "How did you get here?"

"I really don't know," she replied.

"You're covered in blood," he said, concerned.

"It isn't mine," she said, still confused. "I mean I don't think so."

"You don't sound sure," he said, looking at her clothes.

"I need to get cleaned up," she replied. "Is there somewhere I can do this?"

"Sure, I will take you in my car," he offered.

He walked her to his car by the gate. It was a green jeep. As they entered the jeep, he began to talk about the craft that landed in the next field, but when they passed the field, nothing was there. So, they continued to travel to the local farmhouse which was situated at the end of the field.

On arrival, Tristana was taken inside and introduced to farmer Joe Wilkes and his wife, Joan. They looked typical farmers with rosy cheeks, looking healthy. Joe wore a checked shirt and jeans, and Joan had a pale green blouse and jeans. Both of them were wearing Wellingtons. Joan took Tristana straight upstairs, and found some clothes belonging to her daughter who was roughly the same age. Tristana went into the bathroom hiding her wand under her clothes. She still had no idea how she arrived in the field, and could not remember her past trauma or the werewolf doctor, Dr. Wiggins. Her mind had blanked out everything. She had also not registered about the craft that landed in the field. It was as if the shock had wiped her memory of past events.

Once she had washed and changed, she headed downstairs. She did find cuts and bruises on her body, but had no idea how they got there. Joan put her clothes straight in soak. Tristana looked around each room for some clue regarding the time and place that she was at. Eventually, she found a newspaper with a date on it: 15th July 2020, and she was in a small village outside Somerset. She tried to explain to the family that she was in an accident, but due to the trauma, she was unable to recollect anything. This seemed acceptable to them, but they wondered why she had said it wasn't her blood. There was no report of an accident in the area, and although she had visible cuts and bruises to her arms and face, they were only superficial not enough to warrant all that blood. She was invited to stay overnight, during which time the family were hoping for answers. Their imaginations were working overtime as they thought of the many reasons for the blood; even to the point of the possibility of her being a murderer.

The next day, Tristana woke up to the smell of coffee and freshly cooked bacon. She felt hungry, and so she ventured downstairs to a busy kitchen.

"Would you like breakfast?" Joe asked, setting her a place at the table.

"Yes, please," she answered politely.

"Help yourself, my dear," Joan said merrily.

"Thank you," Tristana replied, taking some toast and placing it on her plate.

"How are you this morning?" Joe asked.

Jason entered the room and sat down at the table. "Have you remembered anything?" he asked.

"No, not a thing," she said. "Everything is fuzzy."

"Really?" Joe said.

"Yes, really," Tristana said sharply.

"Joe, stop interrogating the poor girl. She might be in shock," Joan said, pouring the tea from a stylish teapot.

"I was only asking," he replied, sulking.

"I thought I saw a flying craft in a field, but when we looked, there was nothing there," he said while eating toast. "Very odd it came from the sky."

"Have you been on that funny tobacco again?" Joan asked.

"No, it was there," he insisted.

"Did you see it, Tristana?" Joan asked.

"No," she replied.

"She was out cold," Jason said.

"So, it was you on weed then," Joe said. "We have one son and it has to be him."

"Joe, that's not fair," Joan said.

"He is just a bit special."

"I still think you need a doctor," Joan said, concerned.

These words seemed to jolt a memory in Tristana's brain. Joan's voice seemed to echo as she started to see the doctor. She remembers being in love with him and spending time with him while helping others. She kept looking down at a wrist band that was glowing, wondering what it was all about. She passed out and when she awoke, she was lying on a bed with a man looking over her.

"Tristana, I am a doctor. Are you okay?" he asked.

"Yes," she replied. "I just fainted, I think."

"You are suffering from amnesia brought on by a major trauma," he explained. "Can you remember anything?"

"I was in love with a doctor," she said. "We used to help people."

"What was his name?" he asked.

"James," she thought for a moment, "James Wiggins."

"Is that all you remember?" he asked.

"Yes, that's it," she said.

"I will get the family to look after you until you are well," he said. "If you remember anything, please contact me."

The doctor left the house, and the family took care of Tristana. She began dreaming about the dark witches and life on Sabira/Alba, but she didn't associate herself with them or their activity. She was beginning to change from the old life style of a dark witch to a more caring person. The former life had become detached from her as if it was someone else's memory.

While she was relaxing on the bed, she heard a knock at the door. At first, she listened as Joan answered the door. It was Natasha, but Tristana couldn't remember her voice, so she watched from the top of the stairs, but she didn't look familiar. She mentioned Tristana's name, claiming she knew her. She even had a photo of her in her hand and showed Joan. Joan was delighted and asked her in. They went into the lounge, and Joan offered her a drink. Joan shouted upstairs to Tristana and she came down to meet Natasha. Joan had explained about Tristana's memory before Tristana came down, in order to save any awkwardness. Natasha greeted Tristana as a long-lost friend. She hugged and kissed her on the cheek, and spoke warmly to her.

"Tristana, I knew you were in trouble, but had trouble finding you," she said.

"I don't remember you," she said.

"I am Natasha," she said. "Your other friends, Crystal and Shanice are here too."

Tristana suddenly remembered the name Shanice, and her mind went back to the dark witches, and how Shanice and her were arguing. She also had flashbacks of The Ghost, and how she killed him. After this, she realised who Natasha and Crystal were, and smiled at Natasha.

"I do know you. I also know Crystal and Shanice," she said. "But I am different now."

"What do you mean you are different?" Natasha asked.

"A kind person," she said. "Not like the former Tristana."

"Well, that's good, Tristana," she said, not wishing to divulge anything in front of Joan.

"Shall I take you back home?" she offered.

"Yes, please," she replied, eager to go.

"What about your recovery?" Joan asked. "What shall I tell the doctor?"

"Tell him I am with friends, that I'm going home to recover there," she replied. "Thank everyone for me, and I will miss them." Tristana packed some clothes and left the house.

Natasha took her across the field where Jason saw the space craft. Suddenly, the craft appeared, and they both went aboard. Inside, Crystal and Shanice greeted her. Although Shanice was reluctant to speak at first, Shimick nodded and Foster said hello in his robotic voice. Natasha explained about her wrist band signalling an alert suggesting that Tristana was in trouble, but she had vanished from the earlier time with James to the present via a time portal. Tristana was beginning to remember everything and explain it all to the others. After this, she looked in the mirror and found that she had transformed from the dark witch into somebody far different; she was now a white witch.

"I told you I had changed," she said happily. Everyone was delighted including Shanice, who never would have thought Tristana would be so different. They embraced just like sisters.

As for Jason, he saw the ship take off from the field, but thought he would keep this information to himself in case of ridicule. Tristana travelled separately but kept in touch with them from time to time. She wanted to avoid her mother, Ramona, and the other dark witches contacting the time witches. She also wanted to prevent the dark witches from harming her new friends, but Ramona still pursued them as she didn't trust them. She also liked Shanice, and hoped to convert her to become a dark witch, following their evil ways.

REVELATIONS OF THE TIME WITCHES

The time witches were last seen in Egypt during the reign of the beautiful Egyptian Queen, Cleopatra, and the Roman occupation of the land under the Emperor Julius Caesar. This was part of the Roman Empire that covered most of Europe including Britain. It was Shanice who wanted to visit this place having studied Cleopatra in history, but was unaware just how ruthless the queen was — having killed her brother and sister to gain power over Egypt. She also thought that she could outsmart the Romans by having an affair with Caesar himself, and then with Mark Anthony, his friend.

The Time witches transformed themselves into Egyptian cats in order to get close to the queen. Cats were said to be sacred, and so they considered that they were safe as maus cats. The three wandered about the palace as pets, fitting in as domestic animals known to be the first of their kind in the world. It was fun at first watching and listening to conversations. They conversed with each other telepathically carrying a translator in their ear in order to understand the language of Egyptian. All was well until Caesar found out about Cleopatra's plan to over throw the Roman Empire, and decided to put a stop to the devious queen of the Nile.

"Natasha," Shanice said telepathically. "The queen is in trouble."

"How do you know?" Natasha replied.

"I have heard the roman soldiers talking," she said. "She seduced Mark Anthony, and persuaded him to help her over throw Caesar."

"That puts us in danger," Crystal said.

"We have to go," Natasha said.

"But if I can be Cleopatra briefly, I can prevent it," Shanice said.

"That would be foolish," Natasha said harshly.

"I can convince the Romans not to do anything foolish," Shanice replied.

"You mean meddle with time?" Natasha continued.

"Wait. Shanice may be right in preventing a war," Crystal said.

"Then do as you wish, Shanice," Natasha reluctantly agreed.

Shanice cast a spell on Cleopatra causing her to sleep in her room, and then she made her invisible and transformed herself as the queen and went to talk to the Romans. They were convinced that she was going to make peace with them and agree to giving them treasure from Egypt as a peace offering, but Mark Anthony was furious with her and her plans as it did not meet with his desires. The Egyptians were also displeased with her and considered her a disappointment to them. Satisfied that she had made the peace with the Romans, she transformed back into herself and joined the time witches transferring herself as a cat once more.

The real Cleopatra awoke and reappeared looking for Mark Anthony, who asked her why she had betrayed him. Cleopatra was confused and instructed her army to prepare to fight. The Roman's were instructed by Caesar to advance on Egypt, and capture the queen, but before they could get her, she took a poison snake from a basket known as an asp, and killed herself. The time witches escaped from Egypt and lived to tell the tale.

The rest is history as we know it.

Following this, Shanice remained silent on the ship. She had been instrumented in the downfall of Egypt by trying to interfere with time, and had learned an important lesion through her actions. The other time witches did not have to remind her of her foolishness as she was ashamed.

Crystal set course for the federation as they needed to see the time witches. No doubt they had problems that needed their exclusive attention.

"Yet again, the federation needs our help," she said casually.

"Do we work for them now?" Shanice said, unhappy about returning to them.

"We help where we can, Shanice" Natasha replied.

"Why would they always put us in danger?" Shanice objected.

"We have to show willing as we might need them one day," Crystal said.

"Like when we needed rescuing from the pirates?" Shanice replied. "They were too late; we could have been killed."

"We need to be recognised as time witches," Natasha said.

"What do you mean, Tash? Like super girl or some other action hero?" Shanice replied sarcastically.

"We need our own identity," Natasha replied. "Something that represents who we are."

"So, super witch then," Shanice continued. "Girl power."

"Not exactly," Natasha said. "But on the right tracks."

"Natasha is right," Crystal said. "We do need to be known for our work."

"We need to wear something practical but stylish," Crystal said.

"You two? Stylish? I don't think so," Shanice said, laughing.

"What's so funny, Shanice? We can dress good without being teen," Natasha said.

"Forgive me, but I just can't see you pair in a super girl outfit; no offense," Shanice said bluntly.

"A nice blue dress with a logo TW, or time witch on a clock face; roman numerals of course," Natasha said, using her wand to make three dresses appear on her and the others.

"Not blue," Shanice objected, "and not long dresses." Shanice changed the dress length for something shorter on all of them, and made them all red.

"I don't mind shorter but red? Honestly?" Crystal said, changing them to purple."

"What do you think, Shimick?" Shanice said.

"Yellow," he said.

"Oh, Shimick," Shanice said, "defo not yellow."

"If I can intervene," Foster said.

"Okay, hit us with your ideas, Foster. You can't be any worse than these," Shanice said.

"Well, if I may suggest, various shades of green to represent conservation, and the love of mother earth. As for the logo, this needs to be central chest to protect the heart from attacks; therefore, it needs to be a logo and a shield TW. You should all keep your individual styles, but have long sleeves to conceal your wands. We can draw your designs in the computer and work from there."

"Thank you, Foster. That's a sound advice."

"Crystal, one thing to add," Natasha said. "A head band with a torch for night time or in a dark place."

"Perfect," Crystal said. "Let's get to work on our outfits."

The designs were soon drawn up allowing for their individual ideas, and various shades of green with white collars and sleeves. They had roman numerals on the sleeves, and the hems of the dress or skirt. The logo was made of special material that could deflect bullets or electric charges. The lights appeared as jewels on their foreheads that detected when it was dark, and switched on with an altering beam.

Each costume spoke volumes about each witch. Their personality shone through, and they all looked stunning. Shanice was pleased with all the outfits, especially her own, bright green top with an open collar, a skirt which was dark green with skulls, and the figure eight all over it. She has dark green tights and black fashionable lace up ankle boots. Crystal had a short dress and white trainers to suit her tennis style outfit, a sport she was fond of and played as a virtual reality game. Natasha was more classical and wore shoes with her outfit and a longer dress. She preferred a darker green than the others, and loved the time witch logo.

The time witches soon adapted to their costumes, and felt part of a team ready to face the federation and whatever they required of them.

IDENTITY OF THE TIME WITCHES

Space is sometimes described as a dark wilderness and a very lonely place. This is according to some people's perspective who have ventured through space. This was pointed out by a young student scientist called Fay Douglas, who was travelling through space in a small vessel piloted by Captain John Peters. Captain Peters was given the task of delivering Fay safely to her father, Doctor Edward Douglas, the well-known leader of genetic research – a wealthy man who had dedicated his work for the good of humanity. Captain Peters worked for the space federation under Commander John Shepherd, who had a high regard for Doctor Douglas.

The journey through space was anything but smooth, as the ship battled through storms and meteors. In fact, it was quite perilous and they still had a long way to go. Fay remained silent on the journey; whether this was due to the awful conditions or that she may have had something on her mind was unclear. She was never said to be sociable at university with fellow students that she was labelled by the class as a loner.

The captain announced that they were coming out of the storm and safe to travel to her father's home on Bendrulo, but as he made his announcement, they were contacted by a nearby ship. It was none other than Red Beard, the pirate leader who had notice the ship from a distance.

"This is Red Beard," he said. "Surrender your vessel or die."

"Pirates!" Peters shouted. "I thought he had been killed."

"No," Red Beard said. "I am very much alive," he paused for a moment. "Are you ready to surrender?" he asked.

"Fay, we have no choice but to surrender, or we get blown to pieces."

"That's sensible, Captain," Red Beard said happily.

"What are we to do?" Peters asked.

"Stay still and we will collect your ship," he said.

Captain Peters waited along with his crew for the pirates to secure the ship, and draw it up into the pirate vessel. Once they were aboard, they exited the ship and noticed the welcoming committee: a dozen pirate stood all around them, armed and dangerous. They were led out of the hanger along a corridor to the main control room where they were greeted by Red Beard. He looked at the crew, and then noticed Fay, who's looking young and attractive with a slender figure.

"Bless me! Who is this?" he asked.

Before anyone could speak, they heard a quiet voice who coughed and said, "I am Fay."

"Very nice," he replied. "But has anyone got anything worth money of value?"

"My father is rich," she announced.

"Well, we caught ourselves a big fish," Red Beard said. "I wonder how much you are worth."

"You must let the captain and crew go first," she insisted.

"I will let them go with a message to the federation about your ransom," he said, "which should be a considerable amount."

The time witches arrived at the space federation headquarters, displaying their new outfits so proudly. People had no doubt who they were and what they represented, from the Eco-friendly colour of green and the time witches' logo. They walked along the hangers from their ship to the main control area passing through security. All eyes were on them. The security cameras picked them up, watched by none other than the commander John Shepherd and Dexter.

"Well, would you look at that, Dexter," the commander said, clearing his throat. "The time witches are wearing uniforms, especially for us."

"Stunning," Dexter remarked. "They look really good."

"Contact Captain Green immediately," the commander instructed. "Let's get the team back in action."

The commanders' orders were carried out without question. Dexter contacted Captain Green, and the commander greeted the time witches.

"Well, I have to say, you all look splendid," he said, complimenting them.

"Why, thank you, Captain," Crystal said.

"We are touched by your remark, commander," Natasha agreed.

"The green represents the eco-warriors," Crystal explained.

"Friends of the environment. That's commendable, ladies," the commander said smiling.

"So, tell us, what you want from us?" Shanice said impatiently.

"The direct approach, Shanice. I like it," the commander said.

"I just want to know why you contacted us," Shanice replied. "It is usually for our help in some way. Is it androids or pirates?"

"The pirates still present a problem, and their captain, Red Beard, is still at large, but he has also taken up kidnapping. He has abducted an heiress called Fay Douglas," the commander explained, pointing to a large screen.

"This is her; seventeen-year-old daughter of Doctor Edward

Douglas, a well-known scientist specialising in cell reproduction in all forms of life."

"When did this occur?" Crystal asked.

"Last week as she was travelling to her father's laboratory on Bendrulo," the commander explains. "His work is crucial to our survival in the future."

"I have heard of his work," Natasha said. "He creates freaks, much like the Frankenstein monster that Shelley writes about."

"He deals with cell reconstruction and repair of abnormalities," the commander spoke in defense of the doctor.

"Whatever you want to call it, commander. We will rescue Fay from the pirates," Natasha agreed. "That is our mission."

The time witches all agreed to help rescue Fay, and then move on. They didn't want to get involved with federation politics, or experimenting with the human body. Captain Green arrived on queue delighted to see the time witches, surprised by their outfits and style of dress.

"I would like a change in uniform, commander, like the time witches," she said.

"These are special outfits for us," Shanice explained. "A form of protection."

"They are exclusive," Crystal said. "Unique costumes for time witches."

"I see," Captain Green said. "Unique."

The crew were ready to set off on a journey to meet the pirate ship in space with the intention to negotiate with the pirates, and bring Fay back safely. However, the pirates had other plans for their hostage and considered her more valuable than originally thought.

"If they think I am going to part with somebody so valuable, they can think again," Red Beard said to his crew.

"We could make a tidy amount, captain," Hawkeye replied.

"Riches, enough to retire me, thinks," Red Beard continued, "A handsome sum for the pretty one."

"She is certainly a beauty," Hawkeye said, running his dirty fingers down her naked arm.

Fay moved back and looked at him with disgust, rubbing her arm and making it obvious she didn't want to be touched. The captain noticed her reaction and smirked, knowing how Hawkeye smelt and was well overdue a good wash.

It wasn't long before the meeting of the space vessels at a certain area in space, Red Beard contacted Captain Green, and informed her that they would meet and discuss a deal. The captain came alongside the federation vessel, and he beamed aboard with some of his men. Unfortunately, they were beaming across as a storm occurred which disrupted to transference of some of the pirates and they perished. Red Beard had fear of being stranded on the federation vessel and captured as pirate.

"I am afraid we seem to be stranded," he said. "Which would be very unfortunate for Fay as she is relying on my safe return to my ship."

"There is another way you can return, but that, too, is risky," Captain Green said.

"And what might that be?" he replied.

"You could go alongside our ship and dock there, using a tunnel to travel through," she explained to Red Beard.

"That sounds like a plan. You see, it would be most unfortunate if we failed to return as I have instructed the men to kill Fay should I not return," he threatened.

"Captain, I will ensure you return safely," Captain Green said confidently. "My crew will sort out the docking of your ship and your safe exit."

The storm continued without abating, causing both vessels to rock fragments of debris narrowly missed them as they looked on in horror. It was at this time that the time witches intervened, starting with the reckless Shanice putting on a space suit, and securing a rope around her waste as a safety line. She jumped out of the hatch across to the other ship. Natasha and Crystal joined Shanice outside, also with suits on, keeping in contact with her telepathically, so that the pirates would realise it was them. Shanice had reached the pirate ship and waited for the pirate to open it. Meanwhile, the other two time witches held back the storm using their powers, and producing a protective shield out of view from everyone else looking on. They could only see Shanice.

"I have to say, you have brave men out there," Red Beard said.

"I would have to agree," Dexter said, watching Shanice perform.

Two of the federation crew were suited up, and sent the connecting tunnel across Shanice. She struggled to move it and slipped a few times.

"Are you okay?" Natasha asked her.

"Honestly, do I look okay?" Shanice replied.

"You would insist on doing this alone," Natasha said telepathically.

At that point the storm eased off, and Natasha helped to secure the tunnel with Shanice, while the crew secured it from their end. Crystal had entered the tunnel from the federation side and travelled through it to join her friends.

"Shanice, are you okay?" Crystal asked, knowing that only they could hear her.

"Yes, I am fine," Shanice replied.

"I wish you wouldn't keep taking risks," Crystal said, concerned.

"Somebody has to," she said in a matter-of-fact manner.

"We need to get out of these suits and make ourselves invisible, so that we can enter the pirate ship undetected," Natasha said.

The three of them used their powers to become invisible, and then they travelled along the tunnel unseen, but using their special light, they could make out each other. They fathomed out the route to the cells, and eventually found the one that held Fay. She looked well and she was relaxing, lying on a bed. Crystal opened the lock with a spell, and all three entered at that moment. Fay was startled and began to change her form into a green alien creature with sharp teeth and a hideous shape. The girls stood back realising they could now be seen, and afraid of being mauled by this alien creature. At that moment, Crystal shouted in order to make it realise that they meant her no harm. Fay reappeared as herself and calmed down.

"Who are you people?" she asked.

"We are the time witches," Natasha said.

"You people are legend," she said, "known across the galaxy."

"So, what's your story? What's with the freak show?" Shanice asked.

"Shanice," Natasha said sharply, and then addressed Fay. "Do excuse our friend. She is not familiar with things that are not Earth-bound."

"I am just saying, it's odd, that's all," Shanice said in her own defense.

"It is fine," Fay said. "She is right. It is freaky. My father is into genetics, and when I had a bad accident in space, I was so disfigured that he tried to help me by reconstructing me, and left me with alien parts. They only show when I am vulnerable or under attack," she showed them her arms which appeared scaly like a fish or snake. "I suppose I am part reptilian or something."

"Well, that's super freaky, Fay" Shanice said. "I thought being a witch was weird."

"Well, lets get you out of here, Fay," Crystal said. "We need to transform into pirates."

"Good idea, Crystal," Natasha said. "Fay will need to change too."

"I will conjure up a dummy replica of Fay, and leave it on the bed." Shanice said.

"Good thinking, Shanice," Crystal said.

"A compliment. I will bottle that," Shanice replied.

"I am the sarcastic one, Shanice," Natasha joked.

They all left the cell, and returned to the tunnel. No one questioned them as they just looked like pirate or part of the male crew. Some had beards for effect, one had a patch like Hawkeye. They certainly looked rough like the other pirates. Once they had entered the federation ship, they hid from view until Red Beard had returned to his ship with his men. Red Beard asked about Fay, and the pirates checked that she was fine. All they saw was the figure in the bed and took it to be Fay, resting.

Satisfied that the mission was a success, Red Beard told the pirates to get rid of the tunnel, and left the area for their home planet. The tunnel was removed by the federation crew and the hatch was secured while the time witches changed into their own outfits and transformed Fay back to herself. They dropped Fay off at her home, and she was reunited with her father. The witches avoided seeing the doctor, and returned to the federation. They considered that Fay would explain everything to her father about the pirates.

On their arrival to the federation, the commander insisted on a full report, but the time witches had something to say themselves in the privacy of the commander's office, away from listening ears.

"Commander," Natasha began, "was there something that you forgot to mention?"

"Such as what?" he said innocently, but in his usual brash manner.

"The doctor's daughter," Natasha said.

"What about her?" he asked.

"The freak show," Shanice said bluntly. "Part alien."

"Oh, that," he replied in a casual manner. "She was in a horrific accident on a space vessel. She nearly died, but the doctor saved her life, and had to use anything within his means at the time; this meant alien cells and such which seems awful, but it was affective and she is alive. Just a bit different, no big deal," he explained.

"Well, it would have been nice to be informed beforehand," Crystal said.

"Point taken," the commander said, "and nice outfits," he said, changing the subject, admiring the time witches in their matching outfits.

LUST FOR BLOOD

The time witches were on their travels again. This time, they decided to enter the time portal and take a random journey to see where they would end up. Perhaps Natasha and Crystal had become as reckless as Shanice. Although this would not be in their nature as responsible time witches, perhaps they just wanted adventure and take the occasional risk in life. Whatever the case, they were eager to see something exciting on their journey or at their destination.

Shimick was his usual apprehensive self, and Foster just did as he was told and navigated the ship accordingly. Foster would normally plot a course according to whatever time period or location in space. It depended normally on the said mission or distress call received. Shimick was still getting used to seeing the time witches in their new outfits, and relieved that he hadn't got to wear a male equivalent of some description. Foster was happy to provide his input by designing the protective badges and colour scheme in conjunction with the eco-warrior style.

They eventually arrived at their destination at a planet known as Vestari. It was a planet that had a desert-like surface, and according to Foster's instruments, it had atmosphere containing oxygen. The planet had two moons and no sign of life forms that could be detected, rather only an abandoned federation base, which was very strange.

"Shall we explore?" Shanice asked.

"This is no time to be reckless, Shanice," Natasha said.

"No, it's better to be safe," Shimick said nervously.

"Come on, Shimick, are you scared?" Shanice said, teasing him.

"There, there, Shimick," Foster said.

"Why don't you shut down for a while, tin man," Shimick replied.

"That was a bit rude," Shanice said. "Foster was showing you sympathy."

"You know what he can do with his sympathy, Shanice," Shimick said grumpily.

"So, who wants to visit the base?" Crystal said eagerly.

Shanice raised her hand in favour followed by Natasha and Foster. Shimick refused and sat folding his arms in defiance reluctant to move.

"Do you want to stay here alone?" Crystal said.

"No," he said, jumping onto his feet. "I will go."

They set out into the lonely desert walking through the sand and looking at the base in the distance about half a mile ahead. There was a mountainous region close by that followed the path to the base. It resembled the Arizona desert on Earth. It was a fairly a hot day with a calm breeze on their backs. They each carried a back pack containing supplies. Shimick struggled behind dragging his feet like a sulking child seeking attention. Everybody ignored Shimick, and continued walking ahead thinking that he would eventually change his attitude and walk with them. They soon reached the base. They were all apprehensive about entering the it. It soon became apparent that the place was deserted with no sign of life anywhere. They walked down the narrow corridors looking out for life and wondering why it was so easy to enter the building. All the monitors on the computers were switched off and all other equipment had no power. The questions were, why was the place deserted? What kind of dilemma had occurred? They searched for the main power supply. Eventually, they found the power room and switch the system on. The lights went on and all the instruments came to life. They played the CCTV and began to discover what had happened. The base had been invaded by many vampires capturing people, and taking them through a time portal. They were after one thing, which was to harvest humans for their blood. This was their prime purpose in their lust for blood. The time witches considered them their worst enemies apart from the dark witches, although the vampires feared them and their powers. But the witch's blood was poisonous to the vampires, so they usually avoided them for fear of being destroyed by them. It took half an hour to evacuate the base as the vampires swept through wearing their protective clothing. It was almost unbearable to watch seeing so many people being led through the time portal to their ultimate fates. Crystal remembered how to contact Catrina, the vampire slayer, and checked the details on one of the computers with assistance from Foster. She sent a message to her providing her with the coordinates of the base and then waited for a reply.

An hour passed before she received a message from Catrina through the time line with positive news.

"Time witches, good to see you," Catrina said, appearing on the monitor. "I see you have your own distinctive outfits now; all in green."

"Yes," Natasha replied. "A clear identification of who we are and what we stand for."

"Conservation springs to mind," Catrina said smiling.

"You guessed it, Catrina" Crystal said, smiling back.

"I see Shanice is with you," Catrina remarked. "Just as reckless, I presume?"

"Not so much these days," Crystal said. "She is getting better."

"I am here, you know," Shanice said. "I am quite sensible too."

"So, I suppose this call is not a social one?" Catrina said, concerned.

"I am afraid not. We need your help," Crystal said. "The base we are at presently has been under attack."

"I presume it has been under attack by vampires," Catrina said, "and you need our help?"

"Exactly," Natasha said. "They are up to their old tricks, harvesting humans."

"In that case, we will travel to you immediately," Catrina said. "See you soon."

Catrina stopped the transmission, and the time witches waited for the arrival of the vampire slayers. In the meantime, the crew looked around the base for survivors.

The vampires were not far away. This time led by Silas and Drusilla, who led the female vampires, and daughter of Silas, with Bianca and Lucinda close by her side. Silas kept Talon, Casius, and Lazarus with him. Each of them striving to please their master. Silas demanded to see the most recent humans that they had harvested from the base. This consisted of a number of men and women from a large base.

"Feast your eyes on our new harvest," Silas said. "Separate the group and take one each for your feast."

The vampires swooped in like vultures and separated the crowd of people taking the humans they wanted. The rest were taken back to their confinement. The vampires satisfied their lust for blood by biting into the necks of their victims and sucking them dry. Before long, all the chosen crew members lay limp on the floor while the vampires were satisfied with their feast and rested.

Catrina eventually arrived at the base with her vampire slayers. Gareth was with them as usual – the big strong military soldier who was faithful to Catrina. Catrina spoke with the time witches concerning the vampires. She was pleased to see them and spoke of Siena, their friend from the past.

"Siena wishes you well," she said.

"Siena was captured with me," Shanice remembered. "She was nice."

"Yes," the others agreed.

"She is in her own time at present," Catrina explained.

Once all the army were assembled, they planned an attack on the vampires using all the strategies at hand. They put together ideas of conquering the vampires, and hoping to free what was left of the crew from the base. The federation had been informed about the base, and they sent out a replacement crew to manage the base temporarily. As for the time witches, they were still annoyed with the commander for not informing them about Fay and her alien body cells.

Shanice located the time portal that the vampires had used to abduct the crew and led everybody through it. They arrived in a strange dark place that looked like an old castle or abbey building with wide corridors. Cobwebs were on the walls and high ceilings. The time witches had lights on their foreheads, and the slayers held torches, each were suited up for protection and carried the appropriate weapons. The corridor branched off into two directions, and so Gareth led one army, while Catrina led the others down the other corridor with the time witches and their crew. Shimick seemed nervous but tried not to show it, while Foster showed his reassurance in a rather patronising way.

"There, there," he said, not meaning to sound patronising but it curtaining sounded like it.

Shimick was aware that Foster was referring to him, although he never said. He just looked at Foster with a look of disgust. They soon arrived in a hallway with a long table and a theatrical stage in front of them. The place seemed deserted until a man appeared centre stage staring at them.

"I am Silas," he said. "What are you doing here?"

"I am Catrina, the vampire slayer," she replied. "What have you done with the crew of the base?"

"They are here," he replied. "You are foolish to come here."

"Silas, you are foolish to think you could get away with this," she said bravely.

"You are surrounded by my vampires. They will attack as soon as I give the order."

At that moment the time witches moved to the front of the slayers, and allowed themselves to be seen by the vampires.

"We are the time witches, and we insist that you let these people go," Natasha said.

"I have heard of you," Silas said. "The white witches who travel through time and space, helping people."

"That's exactly what we do," Shanice said.

"Well, not here child," Silas exclaimed. "We do not want your kind here."

"I am not a child," she replied. "I am a woman and a time witch."

"Then prepare to die, time witch," he said, raising his right arm. "Attack!"

The vampires swooped down upon them at the command of their master Silas. The battle began as the slayers began to defend themselves. The vampires targeted the slayers as they did not consider the witches as a threat. They concentrated on the ones they considered more dangerous. There were casualties on both sides. The witches created their protective dome and remained inside fighting the few vampires that were caught inside it like a spider's web. Bianca had led these female vampires in hoping to defeat the time witches, but the witches were prepared for them and destroyed each of them in turn. After a while, Gareth led his army in to trap the vampires and heavily reduce their numbers. Some vampires made a swift exit led by Silas.

The base crew were freed and transported back to the base assisted by the slayers through the time portal. Once they were back, the other crew helped them settle back into the base, while the time witches responded to another distress call from space.

BENDRULO EXPERIMENTS

A ship was travelling in space on a journey to the federation hom
base when they encountered a hostile ship that fired upon then
without mercy. It was a pirate ship hoping to capture the vessel an
steal the cargo. But as they attacked the ship, it narrowly escaped an
entered the atmosphere on another planet called Bendrulo. The shi
crash landed and only one person survived – a ginger haired girl in he
twenties. She was badly injured and trapped in the ship. A distress ca
had gone out and the girl who was conscious at this time sent
message out to whoever could hear her.

"Help me. I am trapped in this ship," she said as she began t
pass out.

The other messages were sent when they were under attack
The girl had crawled to the cockpit in order to send the last message
and then got trapped.

The time witches heard the message having just defeated th
vampires and returned to their ship. Foster located the ship and set
course for Bendrulo. They recognised the name of the planet from th
daughter of the scientist, Doctor Edward Douglas. Fay was the gir
who survived a crash and needed emergency surgery. The doctor wh
was an expert with human genes used alien genes in order to help he

survive, but the side effects left her as part monster. This was not noticeable until she became anxious or upset, and then she would transform into this creature and attack whoever had harmed or frightened her.

It took a while to arrive at the planet as they needed to avoid the pirate's pathway for the present time, in order to get to the planet quickly, and save the girl.

"I recognise that voice," Natasha said. "She sounds like my cousin, Elaina."

"Do you think it is her?" Crystal asked.

"It could be her," Natasha said. "I used to look after her."

"We will be there soon," Foster said.

"I hope she is still alive," Natasha said, concerned.

"There, there, Natasha," Foster said.

"I am sure she will be," Crystal said reassuringly.

"Maybe Doctor Douglas has rescued her already."

"That's worrying," Shanice said. "He could have changed her into a freak."

"Let's not go there, Shanice," Crystal said. "Think positive."

Meanwhile, on the planet Bendrulo, the girl had been freed from the ship by the scientists. She was taken to the science base and placed on a bed. Doctor Douglas was examining her body for injuries, and preparing her for surgery. The other scientists stood close by awaiting his decision.

"Cross match her for a blood transfusion, and have her body scanned. We can use the Delerite that we discovered yesterday. It will be a good match for her," he explained.

The scientist's looked at each other with apprehensive looks on their faces, but they followed his orders and did as he said. The girl was still unconscious, unaware that the doctor was going to operate on her using the genes from an alien species known as a Delerite. This creature was an unpredictable species that could easily become aggressive and attack anyone. It was also odious to look at with lumps and talons on its brown body. It had large yellow eyes and two holes in its nose in which to breath with, and holes for ears.

The doctor found the girls' identification card and copied her details on his form. One of the scientists recognised her name and commented.

"This is Elaina Jameson," he said.

"You know her, Clarke?" Douglas asked.

"Yes. She is a well-known herbalist," Clarke explained. "Some call her a witch as she has abilities or powers."

"Even better," Douglas said, clasping his hands together. "A witch and a Delerite. Perfect!"

"So, are we going ahead with the operation?" Clarke asked. "Of course," he replied. "Make sure she is sedated. Don't let her wake up."

The time witches arrived on the planet and immediately contacted the base alerting them of their presence. Doctor Douglas were aware of the time witches as they had rescued his daughter Fay from the pirates. So, Douglas agreed to meet the time witches, and discuss the missing girl, but he was reluctant to provide any details and hid the truth from them. He greeted them like an old friend offering refreshments and accommodation for the night limiting them to certain parts of the laboratory. This made them suspicious knowing that he must be hiding something, especially as he experimented on his own daughter. He had crossed her genes with Delerite alien, giving the excuse that he was saving her life.

The time witches sat at the dining room table with the doctor and other scientists. The other scientist seemed quiet and reluctant to offer conversation. But Douglas was more than happy to boast about his achievements, finding plenty of things to say and share with the time witches.

"So, you are the famous time witches who rescued my daughter," he said.

"Yes, we rescued Fay from the pirates," Crystal said.

"I do like your outfits," he continued. "They are very nice and suit you all."

"Thank you, Doctor Douglas," Natasha said, smiling. "When we have eaten, I will show you around and give you a tour of the various laboratories showing you what we are doing and our progress," he explained.

Shanice was already using telepathy so that she didn't speak out of turn. Crystal and Natasha heard her say, *Let's go and see the freak show'.*

So, Natasha responded to her by looking at her with a face of disapproval.

'What?' she said. *'He can't read my thoughts.'*

Natasha replied to her telepathically, *'Even so. Be careful, he is dangerous'.*

Shanice thought for a moment, *'Point taken,'* she said.

Crystal joined in, *'We will get to the truth later,'*

"So, where is Fay now?" Shanice asked.

"She has gone back to the Federation headquarters," Douglas replied.

"I trust she has recovered from her ordeal?" Crystal asked.

"Yes, she is a tough girl," he said. "I am sorry that I couldn't help you find your friend Elaina."

The other scientists looked at each other making it obvious that they knew something, but were afraid to comment for fear of exposing the truth.

The time witches looked at the expressions on their faces and communicated with each other using their powers of telepathy again.

'*Look at their faces, the look of guilt all over them,*' Shanice remarked.

'*They are making it so obvious,*' Natasha replied.

'*Keep calm and say nothing,*' Crystal said.

Douglas stood to his feet and the other scientists did the same. The witches followed suit and they waited for his instructions.

"Right, let me give you a tour of the labs," Douglas said, pointing the way.

The time witches followed Doctor Douglas as he walked towards a door. He used a card and opened the door revealing large reenforced glass containers, all containing live organs of all descriptions in a liquid. Some of the organs looked vile and odious, like parts of human heads and brains. Some were connected to alien parts. The witches continued to communicate telepathically, especially Shanice who seemed the most troubled of them all.

'*Ew, gross,*' she said. '*Welcome to freaksville! Everyone, welcome,*'

'*Not the prettiest sights, Shan,*' Natasha agreed.

'*Remind me not to sleep tonight,*' Shanice replied.

'*That reminds me, I must send the commander a post card saying, wish you were here,*' Natasha remarked.

'*We need to go exploring tonight,*' Crystal said.

'*This place is giving me the creeps,*' Shanice said, cringing.

"Are you alright?" Douglas asked Shanice, noticing her shudder.

"Fine," she replied pretending to act normally but inside she was feeling nauseas.

"This is my pride and joy," he explained. "The heart of my experiments into cross breeding and complex genetics using varied species."

"No shit," Shanice said rudely. "Oh, sorry. Did I speak out loud?" she said, correcting herself.

"I take it you are not impressed with my work," he said, sounding offended.

"I just have a sensitive stomach," she replied, holding her abdomen.

"Understandable, my dear," he said in a patronising manner.

'Not everybody likes freak shows, nob,' she thought.

Natasha picked up her last remark and smirked. This was what she would love to have said too, but managed to control herself.

The next room seemed worse as they had put their so-called more successful experiments in cages – sheep crossed with pigs, and monkeys crossed with bats. Many more specimens were roaming about seemingly distressed, making strange noises which certainly didn't match their breed.

In the next room, there were tanks filled with water with glass screens. These displayed the marine life with more creatures that had been altered genetically. Douglas explained what it was all about, but failed to justify why he had done such horrific experiments. Seeing such hideous creatures and calling it science, it was as if he had gone mad. Even his colleagues sometimes questioned his ethics. Some experiments seemed dangerous and cruel, but he continued in the name of science, and so-called progress.

It took over an hour to complete the entire tour. Even then, he avoided some rooms which probably had the worst specimens in. After the tour ended, the time witches were shown to their sleeping quarters. Shanice headed straight to the bathroom and was physically sick. Crystal followed her in in order to comfort her, showing a great deal of empathy and understanding. She was aware that Foster and Shimick were waiting for news on the ship, and so she communicated with them. Shimick was fed up of being left behind, but Crystal had said to him that he was safer there. She was concerned about the experiments that the scientists were doing.

Once Shanice had calmed down, the witches decided to explore the base without the doctor. They needed to see for themselves whether or not Elaina was really there. This was because they didn't trust Douglas and thought that he had plans to use her body for one of his awful experiments. This meant that they had to be invisible and communicate telepathically. They also needed to use their abilities to conjure up dolls that resembled them that could lie in the beds. The plan worked as they put the dolls into the beds and pulled sheets up, covering part of the dolls; and then, they left the room and travelled undetected down the corridor, unseen by the scientist who had security camera in various locations of the corridors and laboratories. They waited for each door to open when people went through them. The delay on each door gave them time to enter before they shut, although it was close and they nearly got stuck at times.

The place seemed eerie at night, passing all the same rooms, and seeing the hideous creatures for the second time. Although it was not so much of a shock, it still sent shivers down their spines. Lab Three, where they had not been, being even worse with half mutilated bodies lying in hospital beds. Some of them were sedated and others were awake, and in discomfort, tossing and turning, moving restlessly about some had bandages around their heads, and others had missing eyes or ears.

"Are you okay, Shan?" Crystal said, concerned.

"I think so," Shanice replied. "This place is horrible."

"Natasha, are you alright?" Crystal asked.

"Put it this way, I won't be recommending this place for a vacation," Natasha remarked.

The scientist had prepared Elaina for her operation, ensuring that she was asleep and bringing her to the theatre along with the creature known as a Delerite. It was like a cross between a monkey and a small dinosaur, with no ears, a large mouth, and two holes for nostrils. It was hairy like a monkey and the lower jaw was the same, but with long pointed teeth. The creature was being shaved by one of the theatre porters. It was sedated and very still at this time. Elaina was fastened to the bed with thick straps around her wrists and ankles. They considered that it was safer, knowing how powerful some of the witches could be.

The surgeons got prepared for the operation, while the anaesthetist checked that Elaina was still sedated and ready for this ordeal. She was wheeled on a trolly into the operating room close to the Delerite, so that they could transfer tissue and body parts over from the creature to Elaina. Douglas was passed the surgical instruments from one of the scientists. He cut into the creature and it started to bleed. It was an oily black substance that oozed out. Once it had opened up, he felt around for the appropriate organs. Fortunately, the biological structure was similar to the humans. So, he was able to find each organ easily, feeling around each part of the anatomy. Each piece he required was put into silver bowls, and taken over to Elaina. Douglas then walked over to her and covered her in iodine. This was a brown liquid that was used to keep the body clean and protected it from infection, an old method used on earth in the 20th century. After this, he took a scalpel from the sterile tray and went towards Elaina, ready to make the initial incision. At that moment, as he was close to the body, he noticed her open her eyes, the theatre lights began to flicker and the scalpel flew out of his hand and into one of the scientists. He held his stomach and yelled in pain. His blood began to gush out as he pulled at the scalpel. Elaina struggled to move trying to free herself from the straps, and the lights flickered again.

"Hold her down!" Douglas shouted. "Sedate her. Quick!"

The anaesthetist tried to sedate her but was forced back by a powerful energy.

"I can't do it!" he shouted.

A syringe was floating in the air. It flew into the anaesthetist's arm and the plunger went in, injecting the contents into him. He fell to the ground unconscious. The same happened around the room to the other scientists and theatre technicians until only Douglas remained conscious. He looked all around him in disbelief. At this point, all the time witches began to appear in front of him.

"What on earth is happening?" he asked.

"Doctor Douglas, you are a liar," Natasha said angrily.

"Yes, your freak show has been exposed," Shanice said. "You're busted."

"But I don't understand. You were all asleep," he said.

"All part of our magic," Crystal said. "We used dummies."

"You want to ruin my work?" Douglas said angrily. "I have spent my life helping people in this way."

"You have caused misery and chaos with your freak show," Shanice said, waving her finger at him. "Now, you can face the consequences for your actions."

Natasha removed the straps from Elaina and made sure that she was fully awake, before moving her off the trolly. Elaina looked at her and smiled struggling to move at first, stretching her arms and legs.

"Natasha, it's you," she said, hugging her.

"Good to see you, Elaina," Natasha replied, hugging her back.

"Where am I?" Elaina asked, looking around. "And what are all these bodies on the floor?"

"They are scientists and they were going to operate on you," Shanice said, guarding Douglas.

"What is that?" she said, pointing to the creature.

"Do you want to explain that, doctor?" Shanice said, pointing her wand at him in a threatening manner.

"It is an alien creature known as a Delerite," Crystal said. "The doctor was going to transfer some of his parts over to you."

"No, thank you," Elaina said. "Imagine the state that I would be in."

"Exactly! Like those other poor freaks in cages and containers," Shanice said.

"But you need help and I was doing that. You will become very ill if I don't operate," Douglas said. "You have internal injuries."

"We can help her," Crystal said, using her magic to help repair the creature.

"Sorcery is no replacement from surgery," Douglas exclaimed. "You can't replace science. Wait until the federation finds out what you have done. They will exile all of you."

"I have already informed them of your actions, and they are sending their people here to sort you out," Crystal warned him.

"I will call security!" he threatened.

"Don't you dare move," Shanice warned him, "or I will turn you into a toad and crush you under my foot."

"Listen! I hear the sound of somebody outside the theatre," Crystal said.

At that moment the security guards entered the room carrying lasers for weapons. There was a group of them stood in front of them.

"Arrest them!" Douglas ordered.

As the guards moved forward, the time witches aimed their wands at them and fired. The body count increased as they shot lightning bolts at the guards. This was before they were able to fire at the witches. The force was just enough to stun them and render them unconscious. Douglas was caught in the firing line and he too fell to the ground. The time witches rushed towards the door and down the corridor towards the entrance. Elaina used her powers to slow some other guards down by spinning them in the air. She was able to conduct her energy without the use of a wand, but through her hands and mind. She was able to throw a man fifty feet high, if necessary, twenty feet without any effort. The time witches encouraged her to change her clothes and she decided to simulate Shanice with her skirt and other design of clothes wearing black lipstick for effect. She too suited green and wore the time witch badge on her chest.

The federation ship arrived in time to take over the base with their own staff. Douglas was placed under guard, with all his scientists and so the time witches returned to their ship. On their return, they introduced Shimick and Foster to Elaina, who was now part of the time witch team. The time witch logo was activated on her costume to protect her from harm. Their job was done on the base, and so they set off to return to the federation, hoping that the commander did not need them for a while. However, on their return, the commander asked them to join him in his office. He had things to discuss with them. This usually meant a mission with the usual lack of details, like why they are going there and what monsters or crazy things they would find there. The commander sat in his office chair with the high back, like a gaming chair, swivelling from left to right in it with the fingers of both hands clasped together. His head was shaved at the back and sides with a spikey look on top, like an aged punk rocker or throw back from the late seventies. A knock came at the door which sounded like an exhausted woodpecker. This was repeated before he had chance to shout out.

"Come in," he managed to shout eventually.

The time witches entered. The four ladies followed by Shimick and Foster.

"You are all here," the commander said. "Good, please sit down."

"This is my team," Crystal said, "or my crew."

"Can I introduce Elaina?" Natasha said. "The rest, you will know."

"Elaina… yes we have met before," the commander said.

"Yes, we have," Elaina said.

"How was the mission?" he asked.

"Well, we rescued Elaina from the scientists before they had chance to operate on her," Natasha said.

"That Douglas guy nearly turned her into a freak," Shanice said, "like his pig-sheep, or monkey-camel, or dog-cat creatures."

"Really?" the commander said, pretending to look shocked.

"Yes," Shanice replied. "A proper freak show. Imagine a dog making a cat sound like a meow or a cat barking."

"I can't imagine that," he said.

"Cross breeding animals like this," Shanice said angrily. "It would be like me being crossed with Shimick. Can you honestly see me green with pointed ears?"

"Enough said," Natasha remarked.

"Is she usually so opinionated?" Elaina said in a low voice to Natasha.

"Always," Natasha replied.

"Well, ladies, the situation will change as we have the base under observation now," the commander said confidently.

"Do you think that will stop him?" Crystal asked. "After all, he is determined to create more monsters and has a lab full of them."

"His research is vital for the survival of our species in space," the commander insisted. "He must continue under supervision."

"I sincerely hope you're right," Natasha said. "He is a dangerous man."

"Yes, Elaina nearly died," Shanice said. "We rescued her just in time."

"Well, that's all for now ladies," the commander said. "I just wanted an update."

"Fine," Natasha said. "We will go, then."

The time witches left the office and entered their vessel. They were all relieved that they were not sent on a mission. After their last ordeal with the scientists, there was no mention of the pirates, and they believed that they had gone quiet, since the time witches rescued Fay from their clutches.

The time travellers made a fresh journey once they had left the Federation headquarters, based on a movie that they had been watching called 'The Wizard of Oz', where each of them commented on this old movie.

"What a place," Elaina said. "So bright and colourful."

"Whoever heard of a yellow brick road?" Crystal asked.

"Whoever heard of ugly green witches?" Shanice commented.

"Where was this film made?" Natasha asked.

"What's wrong with green?" Shimick asked.

"It was made in Hollywood in 1939, a very popular in cinemas with Judy Garland cast in the leading role as Dorothy," Foster explained. "It was taken from a book by the same name published in 1900."

"Let's go there," Shanice said excitedly.

"Go to Hollywood, you mean?" Crystal said.

"No, that place," Shanice pointed to the screen. "Kansas."

"Okay," Crystal said. "Foster, set course for Kansas, 1939."

THE ULTIMATE GIRL POWER

It was in the state of Kansas, U.S.A, back in 1939 during a very stormy period that homes were affected by a tornado commonly called a twister. People were sheltering underground in order to be safe. This tornado was very powerful and able to lift large objects such as cars, trees, and cattle into the air. The timber buildings were destroyed and this twister managed to cause havoc in its pathway.

It was a sight to behold and witness from a safe distance, but not as spectacular as the alien ship that entered the atmosphere at the same time. A small town had witnessed this sight and became very afraid in case this was some sort of alien invasion, like something from H.G. Wells, such as War of the World's novel published in 1897.

The movie came out in 1938, a year before The Wizard of Oz, causing anguish amongst the people who either read the story, or saw the movie. The fear was that aliens were real and would invade the earth one day. Hearing this story read out on radio made this seem so real. But now, people did feel threatened. After all, the movie did show hostile aliens invading earth. The alien craft that people called an unidentified flying object (U.F.O) was enormous, floating about in the clouds. People were alerted such as the Whitehouse in Washington DC. The president of that time was informed Franklin D. Roosevelt. The armed forces went on special alert, preparing for an alien attack. Everybody was on standby waiting for something to happen.

A little town in Kansas could see the spaceship in the sky and wondered whether it was – a hoax set up by the government or some type of conspiracy. No one could be fully certain of the situation, only that they could be under threat from some kind of attack, or perhaps an alien invasion.

A young boy was walking his dog when he suddenly caught sight of a strange figure. He followed it with his eyes until it vanished behind a bush. The boy decided to investigate the figure out of curiosity, because it looked so odd. His head seemed larger than its thin body, and his eye seemed large, with a pale grey complexion. It was nothing like he had ever seen before, such a rare specimen he had sighted. As he continued his search for the creature, a man was walking along with his dog in next field. He was armed with a shot gun. The boy stopped as he saw the creature again, followed by another one nearby; but the boy was nearer. His dog started barking and getting excited, and then, ran towards one of the creatures, they stopped and gazed at the dog. Suddenly, a shot was fired. It was the man with the shotgun who seemed to be aiming at the dog.

"Oscar!" the boy yelled out.

"Jimmy," the man shouted. "Be careful."

"Mr. Morgan, you have shot my dog," he said crying.

"You are surrounded by aliens!" he shouted back.

At that moment, a laser gunshot Morgan, and he fell to the ground. Jimmy saw him fall to the ground and became scared. He knelt down beside his dog and tried to move him, and then, he noticed one of the aliens lying beside him. He had been shot too, but he was wounded. Poor Oscar was dead. He saw tears coming from her eyes. The other alien came close to Jimmy and knelt by the other alien.

"We have come in peace," she said. "We mean you no harm."

"Is your friend alive?" Jimmy asked.

"Yes. He is alive, but hurt," she replied.

"I am Jimmy," he said, introducing himself.

"I am Vaska," she replied, "and my friend is Huskan."

"We have been observing your planet," she said. "My ancestors have watched this place for years, studying your culture and history."

"Do you want to come to my home?" Jimmy offered.

"That would be very kind," she said, tending to her friend Huskan.

Huskan managed to stand up, while Vaska offered to carry Jimmy's dog. They headed for the path that led to his family's farm house, across a field. Jimmy wondered what on earth he was going to tell his parents about the aliens, finding them in a field not far from home. Also, he had to explain about the dog, and Joe Morgan shooting him, and getting killed by the aliens. But as he approached the house, his mother came running out and suddenly stopped in her tracks. She saw the aliens and fainted, collapsing onto the ground with a thud.

"I never expected that," Jimmy said.

"Is that your mother?" Vaska asked.

"Yes, she is always doing that," Jimmy replied. "But she is fine."

At that moment, his father rushed out armed with a gun. He pointed it at the alien.

"Jimmy, get away from them!" he shouted.

"Dad, stop. They are friendly," Jimmy said, trying to reassure his father.

"They are aliens. How can you trust them?" Jimmy's father was very nervous.

"They saved my life," Jimmy continued. "Mr. Morgan shot at

me and Oscar."

"Where is he now?" his father asked.

"I think he is dead, lying in a field. Vaska defended me."

"I saw the man shooting at Jimmy and Oscar," Vaska said.

"You had better step inside," his father said. "But be quick."

They all entered the house, and Jimmy lay Oscar on the floor near the front porch. The aliens sat down. Huskan was checked over by Vaska. She was relieved that he only had superficial wounds. Jimmy's father was bringing in his wife. She had recovered and eager to see Jimmy. Once everybody was in the house, they discussed the situation about the aliens and the death of Joe Morgan. The aliens explained that they were not here long. They just needed to check if the planet was any different from previous visits. But nothing had really changed. The world was more polluted, wars were still happening, inequality and racism still occurring. It was not the type of world that they could live in. Things would drastically have to change for the aliens to call this planet home, starting with world peace and global equality in all nations. This was in line with the white witch's desire, to be at peace and bring about a liveable environment on earth.

Word soon got round that alien were on earth and staying in Jimmy's house. Troops were in the vicinity along with government officials. During the aliens' stay, they discovered that Jimmy was ill. He was suffering from an in operable brain tumour, and would probably only have months to live. He was deteriorating and had bouts of passing out. The aliens thought this was odd that they could not operate.

Meanwhile, the government officials who thought the family had been held hostage, planned a rescue mission. The time witches travelled past the big spaceship and made their way to this town that can't be mentioned. They went out to investigate what was going on. They had to be discrete, and so they used the invisible spell while they explored the town communicating telepathically.

They picked up the information about the aliens being at Jimmy's house, and the possibility the family were being held hostage. And so, they decided to go there first and see for themselves. As usual, Shanice rushed in without a thought. She entered the house without being seen, of course, and continuing to communicate with her friends outside. But the aliens who also used telepathy, picked up the conversation and discovered Shanice. They were firing their weapons at the figure believing her to be hostile. They hit her directly in the chest and she flew backwards with the blast. This startled the family who could not see Shanice. Her body became visible in response to the blast, and she lay on the ground. The aliens moved over to her and checked her body for injuries.

"She is a time witch," Vaska said. "Look at the logo on her costume."

"Have you killed her?" Huskan asked.

"We both shot our weapons," Vaska remarked.

"Yes, but is she dead?" Huskan said anxiously.

"She doesn't look as if she is breathing, Huskan," Vaska said concerned.

"You must contact the other time witches telepathically," Huskan instructed.

Vaska contacted the others, and before long, they entered the house. They rushed towards Shanice and examined her.

"She is not breathing," Natasha said and commenced CPR.

Crystal assisted her, and between them, started her heart beating. She made a full recovery despite the blast. The time witch badge saved her life along with the efforts of the time witches, who also used their wands to shock her back in to sinus rhythm. Everyone was astonished including the aliens. They seemed pleased as it was not their desire to kill her. All had turned out well, and the aliens continued their discussion about helping Jimmy, although his parents were sceptical.

The time witches had a long talk with the aliens. Some vocally and part of the conversation, using telepathy, so that they could get a clearer scientific discussion about the tumour. Medically, it was not advisable to operate using human equipment and technology at this time, but the aliens had advanced equipment and the capabilities to operate safely. So, it was decided that they should all be beamed aboard the alien craft as soon as possible. At this time, the house was surrounded by soldiers, awaiting instructions to enter the house.

The aliens on board the large craft beamed the aliens and guests aboard. After greeting them, the leader Dalius, arranged a special room for the alien surgeons to operate. Jimmy was prepared for the surgery, anaesthetised, and cleansed using a special tube-shaped pipe which he entered and came out the other end. He was asleep during this process and he would not be waking up until the surgery was over. It took about an hour for operation to be completed, having made sure all the tumour had been removed. He was taken to a recovery room and observed for a while, all his vital signs were monitored for any abnormalities. Jimmy was responding very well and made a rapid recovery. His parents were able to view everything on a monitor. They were very anxious, but when he was able to open his eyes and speak clearly, they were astounded. They were very grateful to the aliens and couldn't thank them enough. Their son had been saved by them.

Now, it was time for the aliens to make a decision whether to make contact with the humans on earth, or to just leave them to their own devises.

"I am not happy with the humans on earth," Crystal said. "No offense, Shanice, but they are not very hospitable."

"Judging by their history of wars and the cruel way some of them treat each other, I can understand that," Shanice agreed.

"It has a tainted history of racism, inequality, and homophobia," Elaina said.

"Don't forget the oppression of women. The female race was the lower of the species, and hunted down as witches, in some cases," Natasha stated.

"We are concerned about what they are doing to their planet," Dalius said.

"Pollution, environmental waste, and deterioration of the ozone," Vaska explained.

"I have looked at the starving people in various countries, the poor and helpless," Huskan said, showing these countries on a screen. "But I marvel at the different pigments of skin, so many colours and different coloured hair."

"Black, brown, blonde, and ginger, like mine," Elaina said, holding some in her hand.

"And yet, people dislike others because of their skin," Shanice commented. "They are called racists, because it is usually about ethnicity."

"They can't accept that they should all be equal," Natasha said. "A multi-cultural world or society."

"They need to get their act together," Shanice said. "Get eco-friendly."

"What about the homelessness?" Crystal asked.

"You have seen it for yourself, Crystal," Shanice said. "People walking the streets, sleeping in cardboard boxes, and no one wants to take responsibility for them."

"This sounds very bad," Dalius said. "We have had many discussions about the human race, and its crumbling society about poverty and greed. We speak about hunger and wars, racism throughout society, as you call it."

"I am embarrassed about my world," Shanice admitted. "Why can't they be like other world that I have seen, living in harmony?"

"You do good work, time witches," Dalius said. "Bringing goodness to the places you see, helping others and the environment."

"I was brought up to respect my planet," Crystal said. "But we are plagued by the dark forces of evil, such as the dark witches."

"They are the curse of our lives, and the vampires," Natasha said. "We do have other enemies, but they are not worth mentioning."

"We have heard of the dark witches and the evil wizard," Dalius said. "We carry weapons because of the other planets and their hostility."

Darius was disturbed by a report that tornados were occurring in Kansas, heading towards the time witch's craft. The aliens offered to transport them by the same means of teleportation back to Earth in order to rescue their ship. The time witches agreed, but Natasha and Elaina stayed behind to discuss the fate of earth. The aliens were eager to assist the humans to cleanse their planet, but were apprehensive about this due to their history. By this, they were referring to wars, famine, pestilence, and diseases, as well as racism, sexism, and inequality.

"There are countless of problems on this planet," Dalius said.

He pointed to the monitor. "This is evidence of what has happened on Earth."

A series of films appeared showing slavery, war, poverty, cruelty, and the holocaust, where Jews and others were gassed to death in concentration camps, such as Auschwitz – one of the worst camps ever known – for its experiments and tortures, especially known for the number of deaths in the gas chamber.

"Do you really think that we want to live on such a planet when our planet is pollution free and peaceful?" Vaska said.

"I can see your point, Vaska, but what of these humans? What are they to do?" Elaina said. "They have to breath oxygen to live."

"We realise their need to live and breathe in the right environment and we can provide this," Dalius said, concerned. "We are offering this family a home."

"We know nothing about any holocaust or death camps," Jimmy's father said.

"It is not widely known yet," Natasha said. "It is known in Earth's future, but the first camps were in Africa, run by the British empire, years before your time."

"John, we can't go home" his wife said. "We will never be left alone by the government."

"I agree, Kathy. The people will never leave us alone," John agreed. "We will stay with these kind folks."

On Earth, the time witches were trying to rescue their ship. The storm was already upon them. They needed all their combined powers to get to the ship and fly away quickly. Shimick appeared frantic looking outside through the monitor. Shanice proved once again just how powerful she could be by redirecting the storm with the assistance from Crystal. Their team effort helped to move the tornado to one side, and watched as it tore up barns and buildings, like they were nothing; tearing to shred properties and military armaments. Nothing was safe from this storm, not even livestock.

Foster had put the shields up to protect them, and let them down when they knew Crystal and Shanice were coming. Crystal told Foster to navigate the ship towards the enormous alien space craft which was being monitored by the government. Aircrafts were watching at what they considered a safe distance, ready to attack if necessary. All were eager to make contact with the aliens. However, the aliens were reluctant to do so, due to the hostility of the humans, judging from past experience. The aliens opened up the hatch to accommodate the time vessel, allowing them to dock in their hanger. Crystal led the crew out and were greeted by their alien friends. They looked oddly at Shimick and Foster, but smiled and greeted them like old friends.

Natalie and Elaina explained the circumstances of the human guests and their eagerness to remain with their new alien friends, and the aliens promise to love and protect them on their own planet. Crystal agreed approving of the idea as long as they could see this world for themselves. Shanice simply nodded with approval, and collapsed on a seat, exhausted after using her powers to steer away the tornado.

The aliens sent a farewell message to Earth before their departure, explaining why they refused to acknowledge their signals, and offer of friendship. It was very direct and explained a great deal why the aliens would never be part of Earth in its present state. The message came with advice on cleaning up the Earth. The whole message was broadcasted to the world, but possibly ignored.

"But then, who are we to say?" Natalie said.

"We are the ultimate girl power," Shanice said.

"That's right. We are girl power," Eliana said proudly.

THE RETURN OF MEREK

The universe could be described as a wonderful place; full of beauty, colourful, and a place of mystery. There are a lot of unexplored areas in the vast place, planets that have yet to be discovered, mysteries to be explained. To add to this is the air of magic that seems to sparkle like the stars, but not all magic is good. In one area of space is a vortex which is like a prison in a mass energy form. This holds the criminals in space, so that they can do no harm. But one of the prisoners causes a fracture to occur in a wall allowing access into the time portals. The prisoner who is contained in a blue fire is none other than Merek, the evil wizard.

Due to his condition of agoraphobia (a fear of open spaces), he will not enter the time portals. Instead, he brings what he needs to the vortex within this whirlwind of energy like a tornado, which was witnessed in Kansas.

Merek was vengeful and wanted to find the time witches. His plan was to not only destroy them, but erase any memory of them from time. This would mean to take away any trace of them and their ancestry away, starting with Annabella, and working through time. The easiest subject would be Shanice, a strong powerful witch, but easily fooled, rash, and irresponsible.

The time witches had left the planet Dulera, where the humans were readapting to a new life, helped and assisted by the aliens. It was the time witches' plan to revisit in six months, so that they could check their progress, but everything appeared fine. They were living in an oxygenated home, eating healthily.

The time witches were discussing where they would spend Christmas. Naturally, they preferred to be with their families. The beauty of time travel meant that they could actually visit each one for Christmas as it didn't matter. Flitting forward and back in time gave them flexibility, freedom to choose more than one time, if they so desired. Each one said something different which was quite interesting. They could spend a week travelling to each destination in turn.

Crystal wanted to see her father. Natasha and Elaina with their families, and Shanice wanted to see her family and friends.

"I would like to go back in history, and see Christmas how it used to be," Shanice said.

"What, like a Dickensian Christmas?" Natasha asked.

"Exactly; with snow on the ground in old London town where I was born," Shanice explained.

"I thought you were born in Manchester?" Natasha said, surprised.

"No, we moved there later," Shanice continued. "That's why I am posh or well spoken."

"That makes sense," Chrystal said. "One posh lady with girl power," she laughed.

"So, can we go back in time, please?" Shanice said politely.

"Yes, let's have a white Christmas in London with posh Shan," Natasha said.

"Charming. Thanks, Nat," Shanice said.

Crystal set course for London England in 1844, during the reign of Queen Victoria, who was twenty-five at the time. Foster went through the history of the time, although Shanice was knowledgeable about this point in time. She was very bright as well as well spoken, confident about her history, although beauty therapy was her favourite subject and nail design, better known as a nail technician in the trade. Foster mentioned in his explanation that Queen Victoria came on the throne in 1837 at the age of eighteen, succeeding William the Fourth of England.

Charles Dickens was a writer of the time and wrote fictious stories of people of that age based on real characters. He spoke about the class system and the how they lived, rich and poor people, some starving on the streets of London. Some less fortunate lived in work houses, and worked very hard in order to exist. His story Oliver Twist explains this in detail. Christmas may be colourful and looks nice on historical picture, but in reality, the real story can also be quite grim.

"Now, I am depressed," Natasha said.

"Oh, Foster, give them the grim details, why don't you?" Shanice said. "Why don't you just tell them to shoot themselves?"

"Sorry, Shanice," Foster said. "I am just highlighting the facts."

"It was the best of times and the worst of times according to Dickens," Shanice explained.

"Well said, Shan," Natasha said. "Let's have the best of times."

"I suppose they haven't got cats here, have they?" Shimick asked.

"Only Ginger ones," Elaina said, transforming into a Ginger cat with long ears.

"Oh, god! Not you too," he said annoyed.

The rest of them laughed.

The craft did its usual flight through the time portal. The crew sat in their seats and waited for their arrival into the 19th century. The journey went without any problems, and they arrived on schedule and safely just outside London, after which they all got changed wearing the appropriate attire for the age. Shimick looked odd in his costume, being a green goblin, and Foster looked slightly odd too as an android. Although, Foster's beard suited him, the witches tried to make him look human with that magic touch. They all left the ship and headed for the streets of London, discussing things to do and a place to stay.

London was not disappointing with the snow on the ground and period buildings. It was as if they had entered a book of Dickens or a pictorial book of Victorian England. It had lots of chimneys with smoke rising up into the sky, people in period costumes milling about, selling newspapers, flowers, and various other items. Carol singers in the street singing to a wide audience, dressed very much alike. The whole atmosphere was like the movie 'Oliver' without the singing, of course.

The crew found an inn to rest overnight, which was in a convenient spot, with a window in each room looking out onto the street. Natasha shared with Elaina, Shanice shared with Crystal, and Foster shared with Shimick. Each room looked nice and the beds were comfortable, although Foster merely settled in a chair and switched off. Shimick snored like a traction engine, and the girls slept like angels.

The next day, the crew set out to look around and take in the atmosphere. All seemed to go well at the time. Each one seemed to enjoy this classical Christmas morning that they even shared Christmas dinner with a hospitable family. The witches managed to use their magic discretely and produce food and refreshments in their kitchen. The cooks had no idea where all the food came from, but they all tucked in and sampled everything.

"Now, that's what you call a magical Christmas," Natasha said, smiling.

"How wonderful!" Crystal said.

"Now, this is what I call Christmas," Shanice said. "Who wants to pull my cracker?" she asked holding up her cracker.

"How splendid," Foster said.

"Doesn't he eat?" a lady commented about Foster.

"He has an eating phobia," Crystal said. "He won't eat in public."

"What about the man in green," she asked, "in that disguise dressed like a goblin?"

"He eats," Natalie said.

"He is very fussy," Shanice said, "unlike me."

The crew settled down for the night after a long day of festive activities, each one of them were tired, and Foster needed to reserve his energy supply.

On boxing day, fresh snow was on the ground, and Shanice was eager to make the first footprints in the ground. She told the others about wanting to do this. She did get a few odd looks, but she proceeded to do it anyway. It was her plan to just walk down the street and back, but she was still supplied with a bracelet containing a locator, just in case she went astray as Shanice was prone to do. Foster was able to track her every move which covered a vast area. It made Shanice feel like a prisoner and she was a little annoyed about it. She was not used to being observe and not free to venture out, but the others considered her reckless and unpredictable, with the tendency to do things without thinking of the consequences. It is bad enough in her own time zone, but in another time and place, it can be dangerous and fool hardy.

Shanice walked down the street, occasionally looking back at her freshly trodden foot prints in the snow. She enjoyed being on her own and found the experience exciting, even if it was just a walk. She looked at the building with great fascination and liked the idea that there were few people about, just a few people walking their dogs. She had been walking for a while when she decided to turn round and walk back. She suddenly heard a scream. It appeared to be coming from between two buildings. She walked towards the sound. As she got closer, the screaming was heard again. She hurried towards the one building and peeped down the alleyway. It was then that she noticed a man pulling a woman's arm. She chased after them concerned for the woman's safety. After all, he could have been anyone, even a vampire, she thought to herself. As she got closer, they seemed to vanish. Without a thought, she continued forward into a time portal, travelling helplessly in a whirl. Once again Shanice never thought about the consequences of her actions, so she never notified the others telepathically. Fortunately, Natasha was close enough to Shanice to know when she was in trouble, reading her thoughts.

"Shanice has done it again," Natasha said to the others. "I sense that she is in danger. We must find her."

"I wonder what has happened," Crystal said.

"I don't know, but she seemed to look for trouble," Natasha replied. "She will be the death of me."

"I hope she is okay," Foster said. "There, there."

"She could be captured or worse…" Shimick said, "dead!"

"There, there, Mr. Green man," Foster said with affection, or at least attempting this human behaviour.

"Why don't you just switch yourself off again, you bunch of

worthless bolts," Shimick said angrily.

"My, oh, my, Shimick! There is no need for that," Foster replied. "As a matter of fact, I did locate her steps."

"Is she far away, Foster?" Crystal asked.

"A few streets away," Foster replied.

"We need to find her quickly," Elaina said, hurrying on with her coat.

"Okay, stick close together," Natasha said. "We don't want to lose anyone else."

Shanice was rendered unconscious from the journey through the time portal. She woke up in a glass cubicle which looked out in to a strange blue fire. Her nose was bleeding badly. She found a handkerchief in a small bag that she had with her. Her dress was torn and she was disorientated; nothing seemed real. She thought that she was dreaming. But just then, she noticed a figure of a woman in another cubicle. It was the woman that she tried to rescue. The woman looked injured with cuts and bruises on her face and arms. She also had a torn dress, but she looked poor, like someone from the workhouse. The cubicles seemed to be floating mid-air. There were a number of them, each with people inside. Shanice began to cry uncontrollably. Her body was shaking. It was at this time that she noticed her bracelet, and could at least feel a glimmer of hope within this nightmare. But the worst was yet to come as she saw images of the dark witches directly in front of her, staring at her present state and laughing.

"I thought that you would be behind this madness," she shouted.

They were flying around the cubicles looking into each of them, and tormenting the captives. The prisoners were all helpless, while the witches thrashed at the cubicles like wild animals. They spent a short time flying around, and then they disappeared. The next thing Shanice saw was the witches in Manchester attacking Kayleigh and Jessica. She tried to intervene by knocking on the glass, but to no avail. She searched frantically for her wand, but it was nowhere to be seen; she was helpless. The witches had killed them, followed by her mother Rosa, who died in her home. She died mercilessly killed by one of the dark witches. Shanice placed her hands on the glass and slowly slid down, making marks on the glass. Her forehead was pressed against the glass. She cried and cried in frustration, feeling completely alone for the first time, alone with her own thoughts thinking about the friends and family she had lost. She was left feeling guilty for leaving them, and angry at herself for putting herself in this predicament. There was no one to console her, not even the other captives. She was feeling hungry, but probably couldn't eat due to her present loses. Suddenly, the light changed outside the cubicle, from blue flames to an array of different colours, ranging from blue to purple and red. Spectacle of white glowed a little like stars in bundled formations. It was like a visual light display, like the type that you would see in a sensory room with calming music. This seemed to go on for a while, as did her tears. Her face was wet and her nose had stopped bleeding.

"Please, God," she said in a weak voice. "Bring them back, I beg you."

Suddenly there was silence, followed by each cubicle descending slowly until they arrived on solid ground within two metres of each other. The cubicles opened on one side and a platform appeared. Androids were waiting to take the prisoners away from the glass prisons. Shanice recognised them as belonging to one of the space bases owned by the federation. She never spoke to them, just walked along the platform. Eventually, they reached a room where they would be staying, in providing refreshments, a bedroom and shower facilities. The room was tastefully decorated with white walls and a carpet on the floor. It had soft lighting in blues and reds, like the larger room with the cubes in them.

"This is your room, time witch," one of the androids said.

"How did you know that I am a time witch?" she asked. But

the android refused to answer. He just gave a gentle shove into the room.

Shanice knew she would have to eat something, and started to eat and drink. She had to keep her strength up. She also exercised, doing yoga and other means of keeping fit. She even did kick boxing and other martial art movements, hoping to be rescued by her friends in the near future. She slept quite well in her bed, and dreamt of her time captured by the wicked wizard Merek. She fought him in her sleep and woke up with superficial cuts on her body.

Meanwhile, Crystal was instructing Foster to find the time portal after they had found the area where Shanice had gone missing. They had all returned to the ship and located Shanice's last whereabouts. It was a matter of time before they could rescue her. A man proved useful at the scene of the abduction, stating that the people including Shanice had vanished into a wall. He stated that, he thought his eyes were deceiving him. It was like an optical illusion, like a magic act; everyone just disappeared. The only explanation could have been a time portal of some description, but who was behind the abduction and why?

Shanice could hear music coming from speakers in the room next door, so she went to investigate. She noticed on the bed was clothing for her to wear. It was a tank top and jogging bottom. Next to this was a pair of trainers. So, she tried them on before leaving the room. Amazingly, they all fit as if they were made for her, even the trainers. As she left the bedroom and entered the lounge, she noticed a television screen and sensed someone watching her. Two cameras were in a corner of the room.

The television came on and she saw herself on it. She performed for the unknown audience, doing something to keep fit, and then began kick boxing. Her image vanished and was replaced by that of the android that spoke to her. He began to speak to her and the other prisoners.

"Good morning. I address you as our guests," he began. "You are staying here for the foreseeable future. I expect you to conform to our rules. In a moment after you have washed and are tidy, you will be partaking in breakfast when you can meet each other for a while, and then return to your cubicles for reconditioning."

It was in fact an hour before the androids came to collect each prisoner from their room. Each one seemed refreshed and ready to eat. Shanice was trying to come to terms with the death of her family and friend, knowing that this was futile. When they reached the dining room, Shanice kept pinching herself in order to see if it was all real. Each time she did that, she cried out, "Ouch!"

One of the ladies had long black hair and a hooded black shroud. She seemed out of place with the others as if she had stepped out of time.

"Hello, who are you? Shanice asked.

"My name is Annabella," she replied.

"What a lovely name," Shanice said. "Where are you from?"

"Scotland," Annabella answered. "Where are you from?"

"England, originally from London, but now I live in Manchester."

"Do I know you?" she asked. "You look familiar."

"No, I don't think so, but I suppose you know my grandmother," Shanice said.

"What was her name?" she asked.

"Annabella or her dark witch's name was Lamia," Shanice explained. "But she died centuries ago."

Annabella looked shocked and nearly choked on her food. Shanice tried patting her back.

"God, are you alright," Shanice said, concerned.

"I am Annabella," she said. "But, I have no children, only a friend called Eric."

"My grandfather," Shanice said excitedly.

"This is impossible," Annabella said. "It can't be. I don't understand."

"Someone must have snatched you from your time zone," Shanice said. "It's the only explanation. All these people must be from different times and places, both in the past and in the future. Look at them, I have seen many of them before. It's like they are all out of my memories, placed here for some reason."

"So, what time zone are you from?" Annabella asked.

"I am Shanice from the twenty first century," Shanice replied. "But I am a time witch."

"Hello, Shanice," she replied. "What is a time witch?"

"Basically, we time witches travel through time and space. We help others as white witches, and teach people how to respect their own planet," Shanice said proudly.

"So, the white witches did survive," Annabella said with relief.

"Yes, very much so," Shanice said.

"So, if you are my granddaughter, who has not been born until the twenty first century, who is my daughter?"

"She is Rosa, my mother," Shanice explained. "It is a long story, but she came from the seventeenth century. She was said to have died in a cave and came back to life in the twentieth century."

"So, the resurrection does work. People can come back from the dead," Annabella said. "Your mother, my daughter, is proof of that."

"Yes, and the number eight is significant," Shanice tried to explain it to her as part of the secret of the universe. She also explained that she used her magic to resurrect Doran.

"I would love to meet Rosa," Annabella said.

"She is dead, killed by the dark witches," Shanice said sadly with tears filling her eyes.

"Oh, I am so sorry, Shanice" Annabella said, hugging her. "It must be so hard for you."

The time witches were still trying to get an exact location to find Shanice. It was rather unusual not to get an immediate response. Something was blocking the signals, but they continued trying, picking up faint signals and unusual music. They were already travelling through the time portal relying on the last coordinates to get them there, but not giving up on their search. Suddenly, a storm occurred across the time portal making it even harder to get a clear location; they were in danger.

In the meantime, the prisoners returned to their cubicles, and ascended back into the air. The colours and music returned, and they were left to face whatever came next. Time seemed to pass quite slowly until the next frightening event. This began with a thunderstorm, both lightening bright and almost blinding, followed by loud claps of thunder, and then came the rain. Some of the rain began to enter the cubicles and started to fill them up. The weight caused them to descend. Shanice saw a vision of the time vessel coming to her rescue, but the storm was holding them back. Desperately, they tried to combat the storm, but it was too fierce and the ship eventually crashed into heavy boulders like meteors. Shanice let out a yell, forcing her arms forward. Her fingers were spread out and her chamber began to glow. The energy omitted from her body was so strong it shattered the reinforced glass case and the water seeped out making her float. She had also affected the other cubicles and they did the same. She could see Annabella who responded with a wave. She had used her powers without her wand. This proved that the wand served as a conductor and a useful tool to do acts of magic. She was at the point of despair again crying and rolling herself into a ball, resting her head on her knees; she wept silently.

The cubicles dropped slowly once more, and the androids took the prisoners to the dining hall. Shanice looked for Annabella for comfort. Annabella was waiting for her to console her. She was also upset and squeezed Shanice so tightly.

"I can see you have lost your friends," she said.

"Yes, they were supposed to rescue me," Shanice said.

"You are a powerful witch, Shanice," Annabelle said, stroking her head.

"It doesn't help in here," Shanice replied. "I don't feel powerful."

"You must try to control your powers and concentrate on escaping," Annabella advised her.

"I have no wand," Shanice said. "How can I use my powers effectively?"

"Concentrate on the energy within. Use your arms as conductors, like you did in the cube. You can do it. You have the ability and the mental strength," Annabella said, encouraging her.

"What happened to you in the cube?" Shanice asked, concerned.

"It was Eric. He was killed by the Major. Mallet killed him in a forest," Annabella said sadly.

At that moment, a woman stood in front of them. She seemed surprised to see Shanice, and she was staring right at her with disbelief. Shanice recognised her and smiled, but for some reason the woman started crying, so Shanice hugged her.

"Tristana, whatever's wrong?" Shanice asked.

"You were killed and it was my fault," Tristana said. "The dark witches including my mother, Ramona, found you and killed you."

"As you see, Tristana, I am very much alive," Shanice reassured her.

"You are a dark witch?" Annabella asked her.

"I was until I met the time witches," Tristana explained. "Now, I am a white witch with a dark witch family."

"Just like me," Annabella said. "My mother was Albelenda."

"This is beginning to make sense now," Shanice said, thinking more positive. "Of course, we are being tormented by someone who wants us to think these people are dead. Eric is alive. He marries you, Annabella… sorry grandmother. I am alive and we are supposed to think otherwise. It is all part of a sick game. Someone is getting high on our misery. Perhaps it gives them power.

It was time to rest again in their rooms. They only had short periods in their cubicles. The idea of cubicle was not explained to them, neither was the illusions of death and despair. Although Shanice had guessed what it was all about, in the form of power and control, a narcissist way of having fun at their expense. They can manipulate and control people and have some kind of personality disorder. Shanice could only think of one person who would fit such a personality, this could only be Merek, the wicked wizard from Zena. But he was held prisoner by the Federation, in the hands of androids and he had lost his powers.

The next day consisted of the same routine: washed, dressed, and breakfast, followed by the time in the floating cubicles. But this time, they floated up and blue flames emerged. The cubicles were getting warm and uncomfortable. Then suddenly, a large head appeared. At first, it was blurred; the image was unclear. Gradually, the head became clear. It was a man with a dark beard and shaven head. It was the evil Wizard Merek.

"Shanice, my child, how are you?" Merek asked her, not really looking for an answer.

"Merek, I knew it," Shanice said. "Up to your usual tricks, I see."

"Why, of course, my dear girl," Merek said cunningly. "What more can you expect from a powerful wizard?"

"You are nothing more than an old, pitiful narcissist," Shanice said angrily. "You have major issues such as a personality disorder. I am not afraid of you," she continued.

"Silence, child!" he replied furiously. "You dare to speak to me in this tone?"

"So, what are you going to do?" she said, challenging him. "All mouth and nothing else."

"You forget I have killed your family and friends," he said trying to weaken her will.

"Have you?" she said. "Or is this some kind of mind game? A powerful illusion made to weaken me and suppress my powers."

"So, child, you are clever, but no match for me," he said challenging her. "Let us see who is the most powerful."
"What do you truly want, Merek?" Shanice asked him.

"To rule the universe, of course. Kill all witches, including time witches, and learn about the power of the resurrection," Merek explained.

"So, you want to be the only one with powers and live forever?" she asked.

"That is my plan," Merek said smirking. "I will rule like a god and show no mercy; rich beyond comparison with limitless powers."

The time witches were very much alive after their ordeal. The ship was in need of repair, but Foster had got an exact fix on Shanice's location.

"She is safe at present," Foster announced. "Her vital signs are coming through clear."

"Can we communicate with her?" Crystal asked.

"Try telepathy, Crystal," Natasha said. "Wait, I am picking her up."

"She is with Merek," Natasha said. "He has her prisoner."

"We need to get there fast," Shimick said, "He will kill her."

"There, there, Shimick, my dear friend," Foster said, trying to comfort him.

"Will you stop calling me green?" Shimick replied angrily.

"But you are green," Foster replied.

"Foster, switch off," Crystal said, trying to be diplomatic.

"Green, indeed," Shimick mumbled.

"Well, you are green; just as I am ginger," Elaina said.

In the vortex, Merek was busy trying to locate witches within each time zone. This was in order to erase everyone from time. It was like casting a net over each time period and reeling each one into the vortex. Many people were involved from time and space. All his energy was being used to get each one. Even Shanice's mother, Rosa, was taken from her time zone and dropped into one of the cubes. Shanice saw her arrived and sighed with relief. This not only meant that she was alive, but also her friends.

Shanice seized her chance to break free, while the wizard was preoccupied taking witches from time zones. She summoned up the energy and held out her arms, concentrating on her inner strength and inherited powers. With one mighty surge of energy, she concentrated all her powers on the cube. All of a sudden, the cube shattered outwards bursting like a balloon filled with water. Fragments of glass flew in every direction, and she dropped to the ground on her feet. Looking up, she was aware that she had to help the others, including her mother, who looked down at her daughter proudly. The wizard didn't expect her to escape and continued with his plan to capture all the witches from time. Doran was one person trapped in the time portal, trying to break free, a victim of his own brother Merek.

"Obliterate," Shanice said, casting a spell.

She had aimed her arms at the guards, and each android exploded. She had managed to float up by levitation and free everyone from their cubicles. They all descended as if they had been floating on a cloud, using their own powers to guide them. Shanice was reunited with her mother Rosa and Rosa met her mother, Annabella. It was a pleasant moment that was short lived as more androids appeared and attacked them.

"Cumhachd do na buidsichear," Shanice shouted, flexing her muscles which meant in Scottish Gaelic 'power to all witches'.

Just then, a voice come in her head that excited her.

"Fada a beo an uine buidssichean, (long live the time witches)," it came from Natasha, letting her know that they were on the way.

Those words encouraged Shanice to fight on along with Rosa and Annabella. Tristana had joined some of the others who had been formerly captured. The androids were falling at their mercy in a large heap.

By the time, Merek had returned. The area was a mess with broken glass and twisted metal. Merek flew into a rage and sent a lightning bolt towards Shanice. She was taken by surprise and fell to the ground. A battle broke out, including Merek, who had summoned up vampires and Lamians from time in order to stop the witches. Rosa helped Shanice up just in time for the time witches to appear. They immediately transformed Shanice's clothes into her time witch protective costume.

"Right timing, witches. Let's show Merek who is boss, with girl power," Elaina said proudly.

Elaina moved swiftly with Natasha fighting the androids, while Crystal fought off the vampires with Doran. Shanice, Rosa, and Annabella planned their attack on the wizard by being as cunning as him.

"So, this is my daughter," Annabella said, looking at Rosa.

"Yes, this is Rosa," Shanice replied. "But this occurs later in your life."

"This is strange; meeting you long before you had me," Rosa said awkwardly.

"Well, let's take care of Merek and discuss this later," Annabella said. They had discussed strategies, and the wizards' weaknesses.

Now, it was time for action. Merek started hurling the androids that were out of action at the girls using his powers. He was getting weaker after becoming exhausted earlier using his powers on transferring witches and vampires across space. The difficulty was not being able to move from the vortex due to agoraphobia (fear of open spaces) this was limiting for him and required a lot of his energy to do this. His androids and an occasional vampire or Lamians could assist by travelling through time portals, but it was very risky. Merek even used a few pirates in order to increase his numbers, and speed up his mission to capture witches. But he really also needed the Book of Shadows, the ancient records of magic, and the number eight, representing the resurrection and the sanctity of life. Rosa had the Book of Shadows, and Shanice had copies of the ancient parchments. All together with other documents and spells, they had the secret to the resurrection. But all the link to their ancestry lay in places on Earth and in space; the question was where? One theory was that the energies that the two planets had fused when the planets collided, and then broke off as meteors are headed for Earth. One question that remained for centuries was, where both the energies came from and how did these contain a magical power that was transferred to the ancient cave dwellers. These cave dwellers later became known as sorcerers or witches, fighting each other for power and becoming white and dark witches.

Merek began attacking the witches with lightning bolts and wind storm. The witches used counter attacks in the same manner. He was jumping on and off the platforms, levitating from one place to another, balancing on what was left of the cubicles.

Shanice suddenly had an idea. Merek, like most witches and wizards, had a familiar. In his case, it was a black cat. She transformed herself into a cat, looking very much like his cat. Annabella had locked his in a cupboard, and so Shanice was able to fool Merek with her version of his cat, climbing up one of the cubes. Merek tried to rescue it and fell into the cube. As he was about to get out, he stumbled over the cat and fell flat on his back. Quickly, Rosa created a storm, and Natasha cause lightning to flash just as Merek had done before. Shanice, as the cat, climbed out of the box and transformed back again, leaving Merek bewildered. Natasha passed her a wand and Shanice conjured up a vast waste land all around his box, making him think it was outside. Merek went rigid and froze on the spot, feeling his anxieties of open spaces. His agoraphobia had taken over him. He was a prisoner of his own fear, and he remained trapped once again with his powers sapped.

After a short while, all the androids were out of action. Some were salvageable, others completely destroyed. The ones that were salvageable were reprogrammed.

It was now time to return each person to their own time zone and planet. Some journeys were easier than others. Crystal gathered her crew of time witches and took Annabella and Tristana with them, along with the girl from the Victorian age. Doran returned to his own ship, and also took passengers, dropping them off at various locations across the galaxy. Shanice was the last to leave with Rosa in the time ship because they wanted to reseal the vortex and divert the time portal.

"Are you going to leave Merek in the cube?" Elaina asked.

"Let me just say that some spells don't last forever," Shanice said. "So, maybe not."

It was easier to take Annabella home first as she lived in the seventeenth century. She had an interesting conversation with her daughter to be and granddaughter before returning to Eric, and discovering that she was pregnant. The young girl from the Victorian period called Molly had been talking to Natalie and Elaina. She left the ship and returned by the street that she vanished in. Moments before she vanished, and bumped into the young man who witnessed her vanish, she later married him. Tristana was talking to Crystal who she was fond of. They spoke like old friend and then, she wanted dropping off in the twentieth century in the sixties. Rosa wanted to get back home, and Shanice promised to return for Christmas, which was a few weeks ago, after they spent Christmas with Crystal's father. The time crew made a big fuss over Shanice after chastising her about rushing off to rescue Molly back in the Victorian age. Shanice cried once more but was it because of what she had done, or was it tears of joy being reunited with her friends.

THE GOBLIN'S CURSE

In a galaxy far away from our universe, there exists inhabitable planets much like are own. But as with Earth, some planets have inhabitants that are hostile to each other, such beings battle for supremacy and survival. The planet of Grancarna is no exception better known as the green planet, due to its atmosphere of mixed gasses that make the entire planet look green. The pigment of the inhabitants is green due to these gases. This sustains them in their world. The Grammarians are a world of Goblins; each slightly different identified by various sized pointed ears, large noses, and some have sharp teeth like sharks.

Shimick came from this planet and lived on Zena working for the wizards of Zena, before Merek disposed of his brothers and became the sole wizard. The one portion of the planet was occupied by the Goblins which was split into four provinces: Lompas which was North, Apacula was West, Mellindus was East, and Roamus was South. Each province had its own ruler and each was at war with each other. Dragons lived in the mountains and giants lived miles away from them all.

In the land of Lompas, the leader, Omlius, signalled the time witches to come to their aid. They were sick of fighting and needed to find someone neutral to negotiate a peace treaty. Farick, leader of his people in the land of Apacula, agreed, and also contacted the time witches for the same reason. Statria, female leader from Mellindus, did not trust the witches, and Portula, female leader from Roamus, was opposed to everyone and had her own green witches to consult with.

Mellindus brought an army to fight Portula. There army was many and they fought hard to try to defeat Mellindus. However, Portula used her witch's magic powers to over throw the army. Many were wounded; some died, and others fled. Portula was ruthless and spared no mercy as she ploughed the enemy down crops in a field, much blood was spilt on that fateful day. If there was to be a truce, it was clearly not on this day. It was evident that neither side wanted to be at peace in the near future.

The time witches had travelled to each destination enjoying the delights of at least three Christmases, and they were exhausted from being so sociable and spending time in party fashion. Shanice had recovered from her ordeal with the evil wizard Merek, and spent time with her friends, Kayleigh and Jessica. She was relieved that they were well and missing her as much as she did them. Natasha was keeping a close eye on Shanice since the Vortex experience, not wanting to make it too obvious, but she was afraid of losing her again. Crystal insisted that she wore the bracelet with the tracker, so that she could locate her if ever she wandered off. Shimick just worried about her as usual, being very protective, while Elaina related to her need to be independence, and free to roam. Elaina had grown fond of Shanice, seeing much of her personality in her, especially the wild reckless side that she considered was more fun. The other time witches hadn't seen the wild side of Elaina, the rebel in her, even though Natasha was related to her. They were about to travel to the Federation base when they received contact from the plant Grancarna, Omlius the goblin, leader was sending a message to the time witches inviting them to visit their planet. They had heard about the fine work they did around the galaxy in restoring peace and helping other planets with there environment. Evidently, their reputation preceded them. Their work was to be commended, which made feel worthy and wanted, in many places.

They headed for the planet where Foster described the atmosphere and history. although Shimick was familiar with it all, having been born and grew up on the planet. Foster described the atmosphere of green gas that surrounded and gave it the nickname, The Green Planet. The name was known throughout the universe. According to Foster, the gasses were not harmful, but it was the reason for the goblins and other life having green pigment in their skin.

Crystal set course for the green plane after alerting the federation that they had been diverted at the present time to visit the goblins on Grancarna. Shimick was not very happy about returning for some reason. Although he refused to say why, he wouldn't even confide with Shanice about it. But clearly, something was troubling him, because for the rest of the journey, he was quiet and withdrawn. This was most out of character for the talkative goblin that made such a noise at time. In fact, often they wished he would remain silent. Shanice tried to converse with him, but to no avail. It was like he had suddenly had a vow of silence.

The time witches arrived on the planet, in the neutral zone between each of the four provinces, closest to the northern region. Lompas and his army of goblins went to meet the crew. They offered to escort them to their purple castle through the forest of purple trees, along the road past the lake and local river to the village; it was an awesome sight. They ventured on up to the hills and stood for a moment to observe the mighty purple castle that stood on top of the hill. Each of the time witches were wearing their costumes and displaying the time witch logo. They were so proud to wear them. A display of green outfits easily identified, reminding people that they existed and were willing to help others. The villagers came out of their homes to greet the time witches. It was as if they were royalty or nobility.

A fanfare greeted them as they entered the castle. People cheered and waved at the ladies, making them feel good and special. Once they had settled into the castle, they were orientated to place, being shown around and given accommodation with on-suit facilities. It all looked nice and cosy like four- or five-star hotel. They felt highly privileged like ladies of the manor or even princesses. When they had settled in, they were offered food and refreshments, being provided with freshly picked fruit and vegetables. The course of conversation surrounded the need for peace and harmony throughout the provinces. They told the witches about the history of the planet and how they had tried a peaceful settlement on previous occasions, but to no avail. Portula was usually the instigator of wars. This was due to the dark witch element in the southern province. Much like many dark witches, they seek to destroy the weak and needy. Their objective is to dominate the land and take what they wanted from the other provinces.

They eventually settled down in their rooms and slept soundly until the next morning. They had a few days off and then they could discuss a treaty. In the meantime, they wished to be orientated themselves to the village and get to know the people further. Elaina and Shanice wanted to go for a walk by the lake. They took their bracelets knowing that Crystal would have wanted it that way. Especially after Shanice's experience with the wizard and that nightmare vortex, with all kinds of phobias and nightmares. The goblins knew that the time witches had their interest at hand. They were safe within the northern zone, the east zone, and neutral area. However, the west and southern zones were a little different, and as previously mentioned, they were hostile areas and they knew that entering these places could be dangerous.

Elaina and Shanice went for a walk as planned, so they entered the neutral zone, where they had seen on the way to the northern zone. When they reached the lake which was covered in a fine mist, they decided to remove their clothes and jump into the water. It was warm and inviting. They swam for a while and basked in the sun. It was very quiet and peaceful, and no one appeared to disturb them. They had been in the lake for half an hour before stepping out and drying themselves off with towels that they had magically conjured up.

"You see, magic can be good and useful at times," Shanice said.

"I totally agree, Shan," Elaina replied.

"Who taught you to use your magic?" Shanice asked.

"The School of Magic," Elaina said. "Oh, and my parents, of course."

"My mother taught me, and Natasha," Shanice said. "Some things just came to me."

"I made many mistakes trying to use magic. I was rubbish with a wand," she admitted. "So, I learned to use my hands for most spells."

"I mastered the ability to control my powers with the guidance of Natasha. She said to stay focused and control my anger. She said that my powers were affected by my emotions. Anger is the key, but controlled anger. She said to project that anger and channel it in order to use it effectively," Shanice explained.

They were so busy talking that they strayed off track and headed down south to the land of Portula. When they arrived by the orange river, they saw a figure running across a wooden bridge.

He appeared to be being chased by two goblins. He looked scared to death and almost tripped up. Elaina encouraged Shanice to follow them wanting to rescue the other man. He too was a goblin, but appeared slightly different. Shanice was reluctant in case she got into trouble with Natasha. It was normally Shanice that was reckless, but this time Elaina was the one to take risks.

"Where did they go?" Elaina asked.

"I don't know, but we should go back," Shanice said, concerned.

"Shan, he could be hurt," Elaina explained. "We can't just leave him."

"Okay, you're right. Lead on," Shanice said. But as they entered the forest of purple trees, they found the man lying down in a bed of leaves. He appeared injured. Shanice rushed forward, and Elaina had already reached him when an army of goblins suddenly surrounded them. One jumped on Elaina and pulled her to the ground; another caught Shanice by the throat, and began strangling her.

"My damn throat!" Shanice said, booting him in the groin. "Always the bloody throat. Why is that? Do they like it?"

Shanice pulled out her wand and aimed it at the other goblins while her attacker rolled about the ground in agony. The wand glowed and faded straight away. Shanice stood there astonished, and then tried again, but it just omitted tiny sparks.

"My wand," she said. "What is happening?"

Elaina tried to use her powers, but nothing happened. They were both powerless and were captured by the army. They were taken to the black castle, where they met the green witches of the south province. The goblin leader, Portula, was present. Bermina was the leader of the witches, looking like Melinda, only green and just as mean with very long black finger nails. She was very thin and kept twitching as she spoke. It appeared like an affliction; the more she got worked up the worst it got.

"You are time witches?" she asked them.

"Yes, that's right," Shanice said. "We are the girl."

"Girl power," Elaina said.

"Don't you have girl power on your planet?" Shanice asked.

"You clearly have no powers," the witch said laughing.

"What has happened to us?" Elaina asked.

"Your swim in the lake has taken them away," Bermina said, continuing to cackle.

"Very funny," Shanice said. "What do you do for an encore?"

"Boil young girls in the cauldron," Bermina replied. "Make you into a nice stew."

"Have you got a brother called Merek?" Shanice asked.

Bermina put her hands around Shanice's throat and dug her nails into her neck. She managed to make her bleed.

"You have far too much to say, girl," she said, releasing her grip.

"Not my throat again," she rubbed her neck and noticed the blood.

"Everybody does this. Honestly, cuts and bruises."

"Take them away to the dungeons," Bermina ordered. The girls were taken down a stone spiral stairway into the dungeon area. Shanice noticed camera on stone walls high above them. They were told to enter a large cage with a door that led off into other rooms. One of the green witches drew a big circle outside the cave with a drawing in it. She used her wand to bring the drawing to life. It was a magic circle designed to prevent anyone finding them.

"There. Now, nobody will find you," she said.

"Is that supposed to stop them?" Shanice said. "Children's magic."

"Yes," Elaina agreed. "Our magic is much stronger and more powerful than this circle."

"We will see," she replied. "Enjoy your stay."

"Well, here we are in the best hotel we could afford," Elaina said.

"My neck hurts," Shanice said, holding it. "I bet it looks bad."

"Not as bad as your hair," Elaina explained.

"What's wrong with it? Is it untidy or something?" Shanice asked, touching it.

"It's green," Elaina explained.

"Green?!" Shanice said, horrified. "What do you mean green?"

"Seriously, it's really green," Elaina repeated. "You have green hair."

"Curses! Find me a mirror, quick!" Shanice said, flapping.

They searched the rooms for a mirror and finally found one in the bathroom. It was a full-sized mirror that Shanice was staring into.

"Holy crap! You're right. It's green," Shanice said. "I wonder how this happened."

"Swimming in the river, it could only be that," Elaina said.

"Well, how come your hair has remained ginger?" Shanice asked.

"I don't know," Elaina replied. "Wait, look at my ears," she said, looking into the mirror. "Do they look pointed and bigger?"

"Yes, to both questions," Shanice replied. "Big and pointed."

The green witches had been watching them in the cage and could hear them in the bathroom, due to the fact that they didn't have cameras in the other rooms, respecting the prisoner's privacy. The all looked at each other smiling and some were even laughing at the girl's dilemma: one with green hair and the other with large pointed ears.

"So, the goblin's curse is true," Bermina said. "They are turning into goblins."

"Is that so?" Portula replied. "And I do believe they have lost their powers."

"How sad," Bermina said. "So much for time witches. So weak and pitiful, not a challenge for us. We can still rule this planet and even the galaxy."

"My dear, Bermina, how I have yearned to hear those words," Portula said, smiling and revealing her sharp pointed teeth.

The time witches, Crystal and Natasha, were enjoying the hospitality of Lompas, but they couldn't help wondering what was happening to Elaina and Shanice. They returned to the ship temporarily in order to try to find them, searching through their instruments for a location.

"Foster, can you pick them up on the radar?" Crystal asked.

"Yes, Crystal," Foster said. "Right away."

After a short while, Foster announced that they were undetectable. No trace of them anywhere. This was very disturbing. The last location was in the neutral zone which showed the lake on the monitor and the orange river.

They took a walk to the lake area where they found a bag belonging to Shanice. Walking further, they arrived by the bridge where the girls were abducted. Foster used his machinery to detect traces of blood and life signs. Shanice's blood showed up on the machine with evidence of a struggle. This confirmed that they had been abducted, and that they were injured and in trouble. Crystal advised that they go back to Lompas and discuss the situation further. They needed extra support from his army of goblins.

Meanwhile, Elaina and Shanice were discussing their dilemma. How to stop their transformation, if it was that, or prevent any more changes.

"Shanice, your hair is turning brown, and your face is turning green," Elaina said.

"You are turning green, and your ears are sticking out," Shanice commented.

They both ran into the bathroom and checked that this was true, almost stumbling as they entered the room. Sure enough, they had changed again and were becoming goblins. Each day that they were there, they changed a little bit more. Shanice had darker hair and the pigment of her skin had gone completely green from head to toe. She tried showering it off but it was in her skin and there to stay. The same with Elaina, but she maintains her own hair colour, a lovely ginger tone that she was known for with everyone.

A few more days went by, and Shanice's ears had become pointed and her nose altered. She was beginning to resemble Strania, an attractive goblin girl from the northern province. The days had gone by just like in the vortex, but not as bad. Despite the transformation, in a sense it looked quite appealing, and to goblins they looked attractive, even trendy if you like that sort of thing.

"What was the vortex like?" Elaina asked.

"It was horrid," Shanice replied.

"How so?" Elaina asked inquisitively. "Did he harm you?"\

"The wizard Merek used to enjoy tormenting us, by putting anything we feared in the cubicle. It could be a snake, spider, bats, or maybe rats," Shanice explained.

"Such a horrid man. He could conjure up elusions and make situations seem real, such as the death of family and friends." She thought for a moment, and then continued, "He made dark witches fly around the cubicles, and Lamians climb up them like monkeys. They were demon creatures."

"It must have been frightening. How did you escape?" Elaina asked eagerly.

"I don't know. Somehow, I summoned up my powers and smashed open the cubicle. I started falling, but then I ascended or levitated and broke open the other cubicles.”

“Wow, that’s incredible,” Elaina said, gasping.

“I really can’t explain where the power come from, but all the cubicles shattered and fell to the ground, leaving all the prisoners levitating,” Shanice demonstrated with her arms stretched out.

“I bet you can do that now,” Elaina said. “We could escape.”

“But our powers have gone,” Shanice said sharply.

“Didn’t they go then in the vortex?” Elaina said, trying to encourage Shanice. “You are powerful. You can do it again.”

“I will try,” Shanice said.

“Think of what you were like then. You were angry and upset. You thought that everyone was dead and no one was coming for you,” Elaina said urging her on.

Shanice thought back to the situation and concentrated hard on that moment.

Meanwhile, Crystal and Natasha were talking to Lompas, trying to sort out some sort of rescue plan that would prove effective. They were also transforming into goblins.

“Fear not, ladies. Your friend will be fine. The southern goblins may be war mongers, but they are not murderers,” he explained.

“So, you are saying they won’t harm Elaina or Shanice?” Crystal asked.

“I don’t trust them,” Natasha said. “How do you know this?”

“Because that’s the way they are. They want to negotiate with you,” he said reassuringly. “I told you days ago; trust me.”

“We do,” Crystal said.

Shimick was listening to the conversation, but had his own

issues to deal with. He thought back to when he lived on the planet and what led to his departure. He was actually in love with Strania. He was going to get married, but something went wrong. Strania was very much like Shanice. She resembled her in many ways, and now that Shanice had almost fully transformed, she was like a twin. This is why Shimick is so fond of Shanice and helped her get away from the wizard in the past.

Shimick had stolen a silver bracelet belonging to a queen of the north to give to Strania as a present and a token of his love for her. The queen had never worn the bracelet and it was in her jewellery box. He was a servant at the time, and Strania was the queen's lady in waiting. She loved Shimick and wanted him to marry her, making her very happy, and never wanting anything in life but him. Shimick was desperate and thought that the bracelet would show how much he loved her. He was so excited when he gave it to her. But, when the queen noticed it on her wrist, she questioned her. Strania explained about Shimick and how he had given it to her. The queen flew into a rage and sent for him. When he arrived, she banished him from the north province and sent him to the southern province with a letter to Portula explaining what he had done. Portula did not trust him and sent him to the planet Zena to work for the wizard Merek, never to return to the green planet of Grancarna. Now, the queen had passed away from some kind of disease and left the province with no monarch. As for Strania, she remained single and working for Lompas as a servant.

Shanice was still attempting to summon up her powers, but found it hard and exhausting. She tried to rest for a while.

"Shanice, don't worry; it will come," Elaina said. "Besides, we are not treated badly."

"Do you remember The Wizard of Oz film?" Shanice asked.

"Yes, green witches and such," Elaina reflected back.

"I was thinking how much this place is like it," Shanice said.

"Really?" Elaina said with surprise.

"Yes, the green witches, Foster as the tin man, goblins as the munchkins," Shanice continued. "Crystal as Glenda, the good witch."

"You really have a strong imagination," Elaina said laughing.

"Seriously," Shanice said.

"So, who is the dog Toto?" Elaina asked.

"That's easy," Shanice said. "It's my Shimick. He is cuddly."

"Perhaps you could marry him now that you are a goblin," Elaina teased her.

"Ew, gross! Thanks for that thought, Elaina," Shanice said, trying to kick Elaina.

Instead, she managed to kick the metal bars on the cage that was imprisoning them.

"Ouch!" she said as she felt a sharp pain and danced about in agony.

"Shanice, are you alright?" Elaina asked.

"Of course not, you, idiot. I am in pain," she rubbed her foot. "I have probably broken it," she said cursing. "How am I going to do my exercises now."

"You are obsessed with exercise; doing it every hour of everyday," Elaina said critically.

"You should try it. Get rid of your flab," Shanice said sharply.

"What damn cheek. How dare you call me flabby?" Elaina said angrily, "Goblin lover!"

"How dare you say that?" Shanice was also angry.

"You're a green creepy goblin, and I hate you," Elaina said, fighting her.

"You're a racist," she said fighting back. "Racist against green people."

The girl's fight was being watched by the green witches and the goblins of the south province. They were getting excited by what they saw. Two girls throwing each other around the cage, punching and kicking each other. They were so mad, and were crying at the same time. No one wanted to stop it, but Portula thought that any injuries may be blamed on his people and not from the girls. So, he sent the guards in to stop them. They were soon in the cage and splitting them up. The girls both found a pocket on the guards and hid the bracelets inside them. Shanice was moved next door in another cage and left to calm down. When the guards had gone, she put her thumb up to Elaina indicating that they were alright with each other.

"Did it work?" Elaina said in a whisper.

"Absolutely," Shanice replied in the same way.

"Are you okay?" Elaina said, putting her thumb up as gesture.

"Yes, that was fun," Shanice said, holding her thumb up again.

Foster picked up the signal from the bracelet. He immediately told Crystal and Natasha, who were delighted knowing they were safe. It also indicated that they could have escaped. Shimick was pleased too that his friend was alive and well. The one he had grown so fond of over the last few years. Foster printed out the girl's vital signs over the last four days each reading was good, they also wondered how the atmosphere had affected them.

By now, both Crystal and Natasha were appearing very green and were determined to discover an antidote for this condition, which was known as the Goblin Curse. Natasha was relaxing on her bed when she suddenly heard a voice. She was convinced it was Shanice. She listened carefully and heard it again. This time, she replied, sending a telepathic message asking if she was well. *Yes* came as a reply but not liking her green complexion or ears. She managed to wake Crystal up who's lying next to her by fidgeting. Crystal could also hear the voice, and asked her about how she thought she contracted the goblin curse; Shanice replied, *from the lake.*

Natalie asked her if she was still in captivity. She answered *yes for now*, but the bracelets are with the guards in their pockets. After these word, Shanice went silent.

Natalie and Crystal went to sleep happy that they had heard from Shanice. The next day, Elaina got out of bed and went into the shower. She noticed that she hadn't altered much looking in the mirror at her green body and her hair remained ginger. Shanice did exactly the same, but she was completely different and had become a green goblin, only her teeth and eyes were her own. She got dressed and said to herself, 'I am beginning to hate green.' She left the rooms to enter the cage once more, but this time there was a man on her left side.

"Hello," she said politely. "I am Shanice. Who are you?"

"I am Omlius," he replied. "Are you a prisoner?"

"Yes, me and my friend next door," Shanice replied.

"You look familiar," he said.

"Is that all you have as a chat up line?" Shanice said, laughing.

"No, honestly," he said, not quite understanding her humour.

"I am not from here. I don't usually look like this," she added.

"Oh, you can't be her then," he said, disappointed.

"Who did you think I was?" she said inquisitively.

"Strania," he said "She is a lady I like, but she was in love with my friend Shimick."

"I do know Shimick," she said.

"Is he your lover?" he asked.

"No, just a friend," Shanice quickly replied.

"Where is he now?" he asked curiously.

"He is in the northern province," she said. "Helping to create peace on this planet."

"He is a good friend and so kind," he said. "It's a pity he did what he did."

"What did he do?" she asked.

Omlius explained about the bracelet and wanting to marry Strania. He explained about the queen and how she banished him for good. Shanice understood and showed concern for Shimick and his foolishness. She could also understand why he liked her. She obviously reminded him of his girlfriend, Strania. She actually felt sorry for him and his situation.

Just then, Elaina came into her cage. She had caught the end of the conversation.

"I love a good love story," she said.

"This is Elaina," she said, introducing her friend.

"Hello," he said, waving at Elaina.

"Did you send a message to Natasha?" Elaina asked Shanice.

"A telepathic message?" Shanice asked.

"Yes, did you hear it?"

"Yes, loud and clear," Elaina said excitedly.

"Wait, isn't telepathy a kind of magic?" Omlius asked. "But only witches can do magic?"

"That's right" they both said.

"We are time witches," Shanice said. "I did say we don't usually look like this."

"Do you want to see some magic?" Elaina asked.

"Why, yes of course," he said. "But not dangerous things."

"Not at all," Shanice said producing her wand.

"Watch out goblin," Elaina said in a joking manner.

Shanice destroyed all the cameras waving her wand in each direction. The witches noticed them go down from the main control area.

"How has that happened?" Bermina asked.

"We are trying to locate the fault, Bermina," one of the technicians said.

"Well, hurry!" Bermina said impatiently. "I want to know what they are saying."

Elaina had asked Shanice about boyfriends, hoping to hear something pleasant.

"Boys or men, in general, I find a bit tiresome, to be perfectly honest; a waste of breathable air. How about you?"

"To be honest, I prefer women to men," Elaina said. "Does that surprise you?"

"Yes, a little," Shanice replied "But, that's okay."

"I did have someone special at school," Shanice explained. "His name was Alan."

"What was he like?" Elaina asked curiously.

"Handsome, of course," Shanice said laughing. "Kind with a great sense of humour. He needed it being with me. We got on really well until we went to Scotland to find answers to the mysterious number eight, which is mentioned a lot throughout history. You notice the figure eight all over my skirt. It is said to be part of the resurrection and the secret of the universe in conjunction with time and relativity, life being sacred and precious. The balance of cosmic order throughout the universe and beyond, we studied it to detail before the book of shadows went missing from the library. Dr. Stokes guided us. He is my grandfather. He has an amazing mind; he is at Manchester University. But getting back to Alan, he was my boyfriend for a few years, until we went to Scotland to find your ancestor's cave, unfortunately, he became possessed by Major Mallets spirit and used Alan to try to get me. It was an ordeal, and once we resolved the problem, I found I could not trust Alan after that. So, we parted and Alan's memory was erased. He only remembered that we had gone out together, but nothing else."

"Wow, what a story," Elaina said, yawning. "So, what are we

doing now?"

"We have to wait for Natasha to get in touch," Shanice said.

Natasha was back at the ship with the others. Foster and Crystal were working on the formula for the antidote. The solution seemed to be atrophase– a chemical component in the green gas which was in the atmosphere that Foster termed as harmless. It was certainly harmless to the goblins, but not to humans, as the transformation indicated. The side effects were headaches, fever, agitation, and aggression, but so far, no one had suffered from the side effects. Natasha had the first dose of atrophase in order to see if it was affective. This was followed by observing for side effects within the twenty-four-hour period. After which, if all went well, Crystal would try it. This would mean that when they find Elaina and Shanice, they could be cured. As for the orange water which sapped the powers of the girls after swimming, could prove useful in the battle with the green witches.

Shanice was encouraging Elaina to exercise by demonstrating moves. She was very fit and nimble. She was so adaptable and a good fitness instructor, even Omlius joined in. They were disturbed by the engineers who had come to check the cameras. They were discussing the damage to each one.

"What have you done to these cameras?" one of them asked.

"How can we do anything in here?" Shanice said.

"Yes, our powers are sapped," Elaina said in agreement with Shanice.

"It's true. The orange lake did it. They went swimming there," Omlius said.

"They just exploded," Shanice said, lifting her arms. "Boom!"

"We will have to take them away," the other engineer said.

Both the girls smiled and watched as they dismantled the cameras. They could rest knowing that they were not being watched. The cables leading to the rooms were broken which meant they could not be seen or heard. They could now plan their escape. All they needed to do was wait for Natasha to contact them and give them the go ahead, which hopefully would not take long. In the meantime, they continued occupying themselves with exercises and relaxation lessons.

The green witches decided to pay the girls a visit as they were unable to see them. As the witches arrived in the dungeon area, they noticed them exercising and made comment.

"What, are we doing ladies? Keeping fit, are we?" Bermina asked.

"Yes, we are," Shanice said. "We need to do this each day in order to stay healthy."

"Your friends will be here soon to negotiate a deal that suits us all," Bermina said. "But we have other plans; peace treaties never work."

"Peace and harmony take effort and understanding of human needs," Elaina said.

"Rubbish, child! Life is about conquest and power," she said sternly.

"You sound like the dark witches working against mankind," Shanice said.

"You are all weak and the goblins are weak," she said. "We shall survive in this world. We are the powerful ones and we shall rule the galaxy, with or without the dark witches. As for you time witches, your days are numbered," she said laughing, and the other witches laughed too.

"Do you aim to kill us, Bermina?" Elaina asked.

"Of course, I do. All in good time," she said, leading her witches up the stairs.

"What does that mean, Shan?" Elaina said.

"When she is ready to kill us," Shanice replied. "We need to escape."

Crystal had been observing Natasha for any side affects from the antidote, but to Crystal's surprise Natasha's green skin pigment was returning back to her own colour and she was looking better. Crystal asked Natasha to inject her with the antidote so that she could return to normal. During the day, Crystal seemed fine too. So, they decided to work on their next plan which was to take water from the orange lake. They needed a lot of water, and so they filled the cargo bay with containers full of water.

Elaina and Shanice used their restored powers to get them out of the cages. They decided to take their new goblin friend Omlius. They skirted around the magic circle and travelled up the stairway, and then making themselves invisible, they headed towards the door. Omlius was hiding under one of the girl's cloaks, trying not to be seen. Finally, they were outside having been undetected.

"God, Omlius, you stink," Elaina said, holding her nose.

"I can't help it. I get nervous and break wind," he said.

"The smell is going to give you away," Shanice said, also holding her nose.

They went out of the gate and didn't look back until they reached the bridge. Natasha had been in touch with Shanice telepathically, in order to find out where she was with her escape plan. But everything seemed too easy with the escaped, they reappeared in time to cross the bridge. At that moment, they looked back and noticed a dozen green witches flying on broomsticks in the sky.

"I thought our escape seemed too easy," Shanice said. "That's what Bermina meant by all in good time. She planned this."

"Dive for cover, Shan!" Elaina shouted. "They are going to try and kill us."

Bermina sent lightning bolts at them and this was swiftly followed by the others doing the same. Shanice was knocked to the ground but soon recovered, and returned the fire, hitting one of the other witches and knocking her off her broomstick. Elaina used her hand to do the same and made a few more fall. The battle continued for a while. In the meantime, Crystal flew her ship overhead with the others aboard. Shanice held her arms up and concentrated. She gathered up strength and with one powerful thrust of her hand, caused a gush of wind so powerful it sent the witches flying backwards. Elaina joined in and their combined efforts held the green witches back for long enough for the time witches craft to hover above them. Shimick was the hero of the moment as he risked life and limb, opening the cargo hatch and releasing sprays of orange water over the green witches. They dropped like swotted flies to the ground, falling down with a thud one after another until they were all helpless and powerless. The ship returned to where Shanice and Elaina were, and landed at a convenient spot. The goblins of the northern province met them there. Shimick noticed Shanice was injured and ran to her, but he didn't think that she was Shanice but his lost love Strania. He knelt down to comfort her with tears in his eyes, reaching out to her and holding her in his arms.

"Strania, my dear, are you hurt?" he asked.

"I will be if you call me Strania again," she said, pushing him away.

"My word! It's you, Shanice," he said, recognising her stroppy attitude.

"Of course, it's me," she said irritably. "What an idiot."

"I do apologise," Shimick said, embarrassed by his behaviour. "I really thought you were Strania."

"Just because I am green?" she said, wincing in pain.

"No, you do actually look like her," Shimick said disappointedly. "The hair, the ears, and your cute nose."

"He could be right, you know, Shan," Elaina said.

"I will believe it when I see it. Thank you," Shanice replied, disgruntled.

"Then, believe it," came a voice from the crowd.

Everybody looked round with surprise as a girl walked forward looking just like Shanice, with green skin, pointed ears, black hair and a cute nose. Her eyes sparkled as she smiled looking directly at Shimick. Shimick looked back at her and their eyes met. It was a wonderful moment for them both as they just looked at each other both smiling and looking as if they were both in a trance.

"Is that what its like to fall in love?" Elaina asked.

"Yes, I suppose it is," Shanice replied. "And I do agree she looks like me, or I look like her... Whatever."

During all the excitement, everybody had forgotten about Omlius. Elaina searched for him in the immediate area but he was not to be seen. Others searched too and he was discovered down a bank, lying lifeless on the ground in a bed of leaves. They discovered on examination of his body that he had been badly burnt by the green witches as they shot at him with lightning bolts. He was suffering from third degree burns on his arms and chest. He was in a very poor way, probably dying. Shanice looked at Elaina. She was clearly upset and felt her eyes welling up with tears. She tried to hold them back but still they came rolling down her face.

"What can we do for him?" she asked.

"Well, you're the powerful one," Elaina said. "Do something."

Shimick raced down to join them followed by Strania. They

got close to him and touched him gently.

"Omlius, old pal. Come on. Please, don't die," he said sadly. "It's your friend, Shimick."

Omlius opened his eyes and focused on Shimick. He was blurred but visible. After a while, he could see his features. He recognised his podgy nose and his pointed ears, and then those friendly eyes, the ones that said you can trust me I am your friend.

"Shimick," he said in a weak voice.

Strania spoke next hoping that he would respond to her. She smiled sweetly and whispered in his ear. No one heard what she said but he smiled and then passed away. His wounds were too severe to survive, but he died smiling. Both Shimick and Strania wept in each other's arms, without discussing what she had whispered about. Shanice and Elaina went onto the ship to be treated for wounds. They also had their vaccines to turn them back to how they used to be.

"Shanice came out with these words to reverse her hair colour. Something like 'root restorous'. Is that even a spell?" Elaina asked.

"Not exactly," Natasha said. "I think she must have been so mad that her hair had turned green. She went into one of her strops."

"I don't have strops," Shanice insisted. "I am not a teenager."

"You were. Last week, you're only just twenty," Natasha said.

"Well, people wind me up," she replied.

"How long does this take to work?" Elaina asked.

"A few days," Crystal said. "It has to work into your system and you were exposed to the water and the gasses."

"Three days of this? My god! That's torture; injustice, a travesty in fact," Shanice went on.

"You were reckless as usual going in that lake," Natasha said.

"It wasn't my fault," she snapped.

"Then, who's fault was it you jumped in?" Natasha was becoming inpatient with her. "You have to be responsible for your actions. Dragging Elaina in there? You can't go blaming others."

Shanice did not reply for fear of getting Elaina into trouble. Although it was Elaina's idea to swim in the lake.

"It was me," Elaina finally said. "I encouraged Shanice to jump in naked in the lake."

"Elaina, I am surprised at you, but at least you're honest about it," Crystal said.

"Did I hear an apology?" Shanice said sarcastically. "Anyway, Foster said it was safe like the atmosphere. What do you say, tin man?"

"It never read as dangerous. It would not kill you," Foster said.

"Look at my face! Green, and these marks on my throat from the goblins," she continued moaning. "Why, do they always go for my throat? Have I got a sign there saying: strangle me please?"

"Shanice, that will do," Natasha said, finally snapping.

"I was just saying," she said, trying to get in the last word.

"Well, you just said it," Natasha said. "Now, shut up before I strangle you."

Shanice continued to mutter away and sat in one of the seats sulking. Everyone ignored her and continued doing what they had to do. Crystal had attended to Shanice's wound and noticed that Elaina needed attention too, but she never complained about her injuries.

Lompas, the leader of the northern province, came aboard the ship and addressed Crystal and Natasha. He had concerns about the peace treaty.

"Mellindus is here from the western province," he said. "He wants to know about the peace treaty."

"We have just disarmed the green witches, Lompas," Natasha said. "Making it easier to enter the land without any fuss."

"I appreciate that, of course, but –," he was interrupted by Natasha.

"No buts," she said, wagging her finger. "Do you forget why we are here?"

Lompas stood like a little boy being told off by his teacher. It amused the others because someone else was on the receiving end. At that moment, Mellindus entered the ship and demanded answers. At this point, Shanice put fingers in both ears and said to herself *here we go*. Elaina also knew what Natasha was capable of, even without her powers. She was a force to be reckoned with. She banged her fist on the table and marched over to Mellindus. Crystal looked shocked but continued to observe.

"What in thunder do you want from us?" she said angrily. "You call from space and ask us here to be a witness to your peace treaty. We arrive to see some of your provinces at war. We also see green witches like the dark witches out for their own gain. So, do you want peace or not?"

"Yes, of course," he said nervously. "We do want you at the peace treaty."

"So be it. We will be there, won't we Crystal?" Natasha said, calming down.

"Yes, we will," Crystal said, smirking.

They all prepared to set off to the black castle for the treaty. On the way, they met the leader of the East, Apacula. She was reluctant to meet Portula after they had been fighting each other, but she felt it was worth trying to negotiate a settlement. Besides, she had heard of the defeat of the green witches, and this was an incentive to meet and talk.

With all four provinces in one castle, things were crowded. Only a percentage of goblins could attend the great hall at the assembly table. Food and beverages were laid on. The tables dressed finely and with great effort, demonstrating the good hospitality of the hosts. At the head of the table sat Lompas and two of his men. Next sat Mellindus and two of his men. At the opposite end sat Apacula and three of her men, and near them was Portula and three of her men. The time witches Crystal, Natasha, Shanice, and Elaina sat in the middle with Shanice and Elaina on opposite sides of the table. The meeting began with the host talking. She addressed the members with her strong booming voice that travelled around the room, like a clap of thunder.

"My friend," came the hypocritical words from a war mongering leader, intent on destruction. "We are gathered here today in order to negotiate peace among us," she looked across the table at the reaction of her audience and continued. "We have been at war for many years, bickering over land and wealth without let up. It is now time to settle such issues and get on with each other, without feeling the need to argue and fall out over trivial matters.

"I agree," said Apacula. "We need to find common ground to sort out our differences."

"We have done this before and where did it get us?" Lompas said, disgruntled.

"Yes, you speak of peace and at the same time, raise an army to defeat us," Mellindus said.

"And you use your witch's power to defeat us," Lompas said.

"So, now, the time witches have to intervene to prevent further bloodshed," Mellindus remarked.

"And look what happened to them; they got stricken by the goblin curse and turned green. Look at these girls – Shanice and Elaina," Lompas said.

"And, why were they arrested and thrown into your dungeons?" Melindus asked.

"Because they trespassed on our land," Portula said. "They did not ask permission to enter."

"They were lost," Lompas said. "They had wandered out of the neutral zone."

"They never said that," Portula said.

"We didn't get chance to. You just got us carted off and thrown in the dungeon," Shanice said.

Natasha gave Shanice a look that told her to be quiet. Shanice responded with a grunt and said under her breath *sorry, I am sure*' Elaina looked at her but said nothing in case it made matters worse.

The meeting continued for an hour, and then they rested. The time witches returned to the ship, while everyone else put-up tents outside the castle walls. The meeting went on for days. Meanwhile, the green witches were hidden away in the dungeons. They were hoping that their powers would be restored and they could continue with their evil ways. The time witches wished it was all over, and they could leave the planet with peace restored across the provinces. The problem was being able to trust Portula. She obviously must have known the witches plan to create war and rule supremely.

As for Shanice and Elaina, they were beginning to look human again. Their skin pigment was back to normal and their features were altering back to themselves. Strania and Shimick were getting on well, and had Lompas permission to date each other, or whatever it was called on Grancarna the green planet. Shimick proposed again to Strania. This time, he did nothing foolish like stealing bracelets. Instead, Lompas gave him a precious emerald ring for the good work that he had done for the province.

The peace negotiations had entered the second week and things were improving. People settled on ownership of land, more freedom to roam without being arrested. Trade negotiations, bargaining with goods and exchanging crops, dividing wealth so that each province was equal, with no more poverty.

Taking care of other life like the Metapians, a lion like creature in human form, living mainly in the northern province, but once slaves of the eastern province, or the Yamasalins, giants of the northern mountains, who were hunted by the witches for sport and killed. Only a few remain. Other creatures were included regarded as special creature that needed protection for the rest of their days. But, what of the green witches, what must be done with them, as they were a potential threat to all creatures of the planet and who would certainly fuel another war and cause desolation throughout the land, this was still a subject to address in the negotiations.

Meanwhile in the dungeons, the witches were talking amongst each other. Some getting very excited and shouting. Bermina asked them to keep their voices low in case someone was listening in to their conversation.

"Farwick, what have you to say?" Bermina asked.

"We have to dispose of the time witches. They are our biggest threat," Farwick said.

"And, Statria what have you to say?" Bermina asked her.

"Kill the time witches, and then we can start a war," Statria said.

"Then, so be it. We will do this," Bermina said. "Kill the time witches."

That night, Natasha and Shanice stayed in the castle. They wanted to see if they could find out what happened to the witches. They were told that they had headed south beyond the southern province. Little knowing that the cunning witches had planned to kill them all as soon as they got their powers back.

The night seemed to drag on for the time witches. They were very restless wondering whether peace would be restored to the land, and allow people to live in harmony. Natasha and Shanice explored the castle looking for secret rooms or hidden corridor. Natasha was staying with Shanice because she didn't want Elaina and her working together in case they got into trouble again. Shanice was reluctant to complain as she had already upset

Natasha, and she wanted to keep the peace, being fond of Natasha. They managed to find a hidden door which was part of the panel of a wall. It slid open at the touch of a tiny button, which was hidden away from view. They entered a dark corridor and the light switched on that was attached to their head bands automatically detecting the darkness. They were able to see quite a distance. The beam was powerful and increased the darker the area was. The girls proceeded along the corridor, wiping cob webs from their faces. The corridor was narrow with a low ceiling. Natasha was cussing at the state of the place as they seemed to be treading in soft wet matter like slime.

"Someone should clean this mess," she said. "It's hardly the Hilton Hotel."

"It not just the mess; it's the smell," Shanice said. "It's hanging."

"I won't invite anyone to this dump," Natasha said. "It's a hotel inspectors' nightmare."

"It's gross; I feel sick," Shanice remarked.

"Now, Shanice, don't do this by throwing up," Natasha said. "I saw what you ate for supper, and that was nasty the first time. Regurgitated would be awful."

"It was noodle with something added," Shanice described the food in detail.

"Oh my god! I can't even imagine that the second time," Natasha remarked pulling a face.

They managed to find some stairs that took them down to the next level. As they descended down the stairs, they could hear voices. As they walked further, the voices became louder. So, they decided to stop walking and listened carefully.

"Bermina, wait. We need to act now," came the voice.

"Farwick, you don't understand," Bermina said. "Without our powers, they can defeat us."

"Do you know a better idea to kill them?" Farwick said.

"I do," Statria said. "We can get Natasha and Shanice in their sleep."

"Two gone and two to go," Farwick replied.

"Let's get prepared," Bermina said.

Natasha whispered to Shanice, "Let's go back."

Shanice nodded and they walked back up the stairs and down the corridor. They returned to the bedroom and discussed a plan on how they could survive an attack from the green witches. A few hours later, the witches travelled along the secret passage towards the bedroom that the time witches were staying in. They crept in and one by one they entered the room, and across the room to the bed.

"Look, they are asleep," Statria said, pointing to two lumps on the bed.

"Take out your daggers," Bermina commanded.

They all took out their daggers and plunged them into the lumps. They repeated these actions three or four times, hoping the time witches were dead. They were about to pull the sheets back when they heard a noise from behind them.

"Nice try, Bermina," Shanice said, holding her wand to her neck.

"How do you know that we haven't regained our powers?" Bermina asked.

"Just in case, we brought some orange water," Natasha said, spraying them with it, but being careful not to get any over Shanice or herself.

"Curses!" Bermina shouted.

At that point, Crystal and Elaina entered the room with some of the guards. They all laughed seeing very wet witches cussing and swearing. They were taken down to the dungeons and this time locked up, awaiting their fate. All the time witches stayed in the room to rest and be refreshed for the next meeting.

The next day, the meeting took place and it was a successful result. The witches were to be banished immediately and never to return. If they did, they would be soaked in orange water and would be executed forthwith. They left for the far south region taking all their belongings. All parties from each province returned home, and the time witches travelled to the neutral zone and awaited their departure. Before leaving the planet, the time witches said farewell to the goblins of the northern province. They also said goodbye to their friend Shimick.

"Shimick, we are sorry you're going," Crystal said. "You have travelled with us all this time."

"Shimick, we will miss you," Natasha said. "Who can I play up now?"

"Goodbye, Shimick. Be good," Elaina said.

"Shimick, my good old faithful friend," Shanice said with tears in her eyes. "Be happy, won't you?"

Shimick was going to miss them all especially Shanice, who he had grown fond of, but he had Strania to think about and was determined to marry her.

"Goodbye, Shanice, my friend" he said, kissing her and giving her a hug.

"Don't forget to invite me on your wedding," Shanice said, wiping the tears away.

"Yes, of course. All of you, even Foster," he said, looking at his tin man friend.

Foster looked at Shimick, and noticed the tears in his eyes and had to comment.

"There, there, little green goblin friend."

With that, the time witches left for another adventure, but what they didn't realise was they had a stowaway aboard called Laptus, another male goblin.

GURU OF GUDESH

Centuries ago in India, a man known to be a Guru from Gudesh, went missing. Bakul Patel was a wise and clever teacher brought up as a Hindu by faith. He had a loyal following and wanted people understand about love and understanding, and of peace and trust in others. Many stories were told of his disappearance. Rumours of abduction or even murder. Much of this was idol gossip, bearing no truth or evidence of foul play. For centuries, stories came about, passed on from each decade up until the twenty third century, when the time witches were in search of a missing book that was passed down through the generations. This book was last located in Scotland, in the seventeenth century during the reign of King Charles the First of England. The time witches were all familiar with that period, as it was the time of the English civil war. It was also the time when witch hunting was well known and many people were accused of witchcraft. They made a visit to Scotland during King James the First's reign, and Natasha was imprisoned in a dungeon.

The time witches were now reflecting on their experiences, discussing where they think the book of shadows may be. They knew that mayor Mallet had it at one stage, having taken it from the dark witches after hunting them down. He obviously didn't hunt them down personally, but arranged for his soldiers who were witch hunters to do his dirty work. He would then take the credit for their capture and execution, although they were executed beforehand and their skulls brought back to the town of Teversham. Eight witches were killed and eight skulls were collected after they had been decapitated, these were the eight skulls of Teversham.

The time witches picked up the trail on the planet Gudesh. The name is not a coincidence, as the time witches discovered when they explored the planet. They came across an unusual sight. There in amongst a cluster of palm trees was a building. This building resembled a mosque, with its characteristic dome shapes and Indian style construction, a very colourful sight to behold. The planet's atmosphere was agreeable for them to breath without wearing any apparatus. This planet definitely didn't contain any harmful gasses, unlike the previous planet, but still the time witches were cautious and taking no chances.

"Where is this again?" Shanice asked. "Gudesh," Crystal replied.

"And, we won't turn green or red, or anything like that?" Shanice said with apprehension.

"It is perfectly safe," Foster stated. "Nothing will harm you here."

"That's what you said about the last planet, and we all turned green," Shanice said disagreeably. "Forgive me if I don't trust you,

Foster."

"The building ahead of us is known to be a sanctuary. People come here to seek refuge in God's house, as they call it," Foster explained.

"So, why are we here again? Obviously, not to seek sanctuary," Shanice asked.

"Why, to seek the book of shadows, if you remember?" Natasha replied.

"It was thought to have been taken from the dark witches and in the possession of Mayor Mallet. From there, we think it got in the hand of the dark witches again." Crystal explained. "We have reason to think the dark witches travelled through a time portal and found themselves here. They may have hidden it here somewhere."

"Well, I was on their planet, and didn't see any book," Shanice said.

"Exactly. It would be safer here," Natasha said.

"What is in this Book of Shadows, and who is its owner?" Elaina asked. "Obviously, I know what a Book of Shadows is, but what is in this one?"

"We don't exactly know the owner, but we do know it has spells, potions, and unlocks the mysteries of the universe," Crystal said.

"So, shall we investigate?" Natasha asked.

As they were about to get ready to leave, they heard a noise coming from the sleeping quarters; so, they all went to investigate. Each of them searched every room in turn. Nobody found anything until Shanice entered the last room. Somebody had been in there according to the state of the bed. So, they continued to search the ship until they reached the cargo bay. They all split up and searched the entire area. All was very quiet until Shanice let out a scream. The others came rushing to her aid and found her standing in front of a green goblin.

"Where have you come from?" Natasha asked.

"We seem to have a stowaway," Crystal said.

"He must have come aboard when we were on the green planet," Elaina commented.

"Well, what do we do with him?" Natasha asked.

"Keep him," Shanice proposed.

"He isn't a pet," Natasha said sharply.

"Let us take him with us and decide later," Crystal said, eager to explore the building and find the Book of Shadows.

They started their journey and travelled a rough path which led to the building. Everything was quiet on the way to their destination. They knocked on the door even though it was open. When nobody came, they decided to enter cautiously. It was that quiet. They could hear their own footsteps on the stone floor. Every sound echoed, but nobody was about. It was quite eerie. It felt as if they were being watched. In fact, they were by a dark shrouded figure lurking around the corner behind them. His face was hidden by his hood. Eventually, a man appeared. He looked Asian dressed in a cream shroud. He greeted them and then led them down a corridor.

"I am Bakul Patel, the Great Guru from India," he said.

"We are the time witches," Crystal said. "Nature is our religion and the Earth is our church."

"I have heard great things about you all," he replied. "You are a legend in your own life time," he continued.

"That's nice to know," Crystal said with surprise.

"I hope you will find peace while you are here," Bakul said. "This place is a sanctuary for those people who wanted to be safe, and find peace with God. No one is allowed to pester another guest or know of their reason to be here. It is a safe Avon for you to rest and collect your thoughts."

"We do need to know one thing," Natasha said.

"Please ask me," he replied.

"Have you heard about the Book of Shadows?" Natasha asked.

"Yes, we have kept it safe. It was left here by another guest," he said. "It is an old tatty book, containing old spells, potions, and a history of the author. The book is large, with a brown hard back cover with hundreds of pages."

"Can we see it?" Crystal asked.

"Of course," he said, leading them into a room.

They all entered and walked up to a table. The book was displayed on a dark green table cloth opened on a page about magic potions. The girls gazed upon it as if it was a treasured copy of the Bible or Koran, a holy book of significance. Each one of them were concerned about touching it in case it fell apart. It was stained with various things and slightly torn, but the hand writing was legible and easy to understand for the time witches. It was written in Gaelic like the one that Rosa had, but contained much more.

The author wrote neatly and took time in adding every detail. The author was called Rodicka Dineham from a place in Scotland. She was a white witch and lived around the fourteenth century. She lived in a stone cottage and grew herbs, and made potions. She was known to the town folk and was one of the victims who was accused of witchcraft and was hung. The book was discovered and passed down through the generations. It survived being burnt and at one stage, buried underground in a wooden box. Her ancestors were the cave dwellers who survived the attacks of the dark witches. As a white witch, she was always in fear of her life, in case the dark witches discovered her or her book of shadows. But most importantly, she had written about the resurrection theory in the book along with the meaning of the figure eight. The whole thing began to make sense and this is why this book is sort after. Many people wanted this book. Some had it and then it was stolen. The magic that binds it is very powerful and only allows certain people to understand it fully, because this book is shrouded in mystery. The time witches left the room, but they were apprehensive about leaving the book behind. Bakul reassured them that it was safe in the room and that cameras would be watching the room. But this has been said many times, and the book has gone missing. Nobody felt confident about the book being safe.

The crew had got together in one room, which was fairly large with enough space to accommodate all of them. They had sufficient individual beds and seated area by the large window. This was the largest room to stay in reserved for groups who were travelling this way. There was much to discuss about the Book of Shadows, and about the other guests and their activity. They are most concerned about other people who were seeking the book of shadow like themselves.

That night, the time witches took it in turns to patrol the corridors. Natasha and Shanice went first until two o'clock in the morning, Crystal and Elaina chose the second watch from two until five. It was a long night and uneventful until three o'clock when Crystal and Elaina were resting on a couch near the dormitories. They heard noises, and having fallen asleep, woke up with a stark. Crystal leapt to her feet jumping like she does when she plays tennis.

"Elaina, wake up," Crystal whispered, nudging her.

"I am awake what was that noise?" Elaina asked inquisitively.

"I don't know," Crystal replied. "It came from that room," she said pointing to a room close by.

"Let's go and investigate," Elaina said eagerly.

They entered the room cautiously gazing into the darkness.

The torches on their heads lit up and they saw a body on the floor. In fact, Elaina nearly stumbled over it, as it was lying crumpled on the floor covered in blood.

"Is he dead?" Elaina asked.

Crystal crouched down and checked the body. She nodded at Elaina. "Definitely dead," she replied.

"What do we do?" Elaina asked anxiously.

But before Crystal could reply, a number of guards came in the room and arrested them, and then took them to a holding cell. The pair of them were bewildered thinking it was part of a setup.

They feared that they might be blamed for the murder of this woman. Natasha and Shanice were told about the incident, but not until the morning when they were worried about the whereabouts of their friends. It was 7 o'clock by the time they were told. They were about to search for them. Laptus, the green stowaway goblin, went with them to see Bakul. The guards had informed them. They were relieved that they were not going to be arrested thinking it may have been a time witch conspiracy. Bakul had notified the space federation and he was waiting for a visit from them, but in the meantime, carried out his own investigation. He welcomed the time witches to his office. He looked serious, but reassured them that he was on their side, and felt that the time witches were blameless judging from their reputation. But he had to investigate and eliminate them from the inquiries, after all they merely found the body.

As for the Book of Shadows, it had gone missing. It would seem that more than one person was searching for the book. In fact, quite a few people knew of its whereabouts. All rooms had to be searched in case it was in any of them. The dormitories were emptied; all the guests were asked to go to the main hall. Everyone was accounted for, all but Bula Seraph, a mysterious man who wore a shroud like a monk, disguising his scarred face and grey complexion. He was related to Merek and known for his evil ways. He was obviously here for the Book of Shadows, and murdered the woman who turned out to be a dark witch. She was called Foraker, and she was sent to retrieve the book by the dark witches of Alba Two (Sabina), as instructed by Ramona. Some of the other guests were a bit more discreet about their desire to get the book or even ask to see it, but they knew it was there.

The Book of Shadows was well sort after by the many planets of the universe for its content. People were fascinated with its reputation of holding many secrets. When the federation arrived, they held a staff meeting and set up an inquiry room. They went through a camera footage and discovered that thehooded figure of Bula Seraph entered the room before the time witches. Foraker fired at him with her wand hitting him in the shoulder. Evidence of this was scorch marks on the wall in the opposite side of the room where she slept. Bula fired back with his wand and then stabbed her. He was more accurate despite being wounded. The sounds that Crystal and Elaina heard confirmed this. Cries from both of them as they battled for the book of shadows, Foraker stole the book and Bula took it from her and then vanished. It was almost as if he was never there, but the video footage proved otherwise. Word was sent back to commander John Shepherd, and he insisted on speaking to the time witches. Once the two had been released from the holding cell, he appeared on the monitor looking at the time witches standing next to each other looking distraught.

"My friends," he began, "sorry that you got caught up in this. So, there are four of you now," he said, noticing Elaina.

"Yes, we rescued Elaina from that doctor, Edward Douglas."

"Oh, yes!" he said. "I remember that he is being monitored. Things are different now."

"He is a nut job, creating freaks," Shanice said, disgruntled.

"Now, Shanice, he is eccentric not insane," the commander said, defending him.

"He nearly turned me into a freak," Elaina said. "These friends rescued me."

"Yes, I read your report," the commander replied. "But you are all safe now."

"Yes, we are," Crystal said. "But we need to find the book of shadows."

"Good luck with that. Some say it is very powerful," the commander said. "I will speak to you soon. Take care," he said and disappeared.

The time witches left the building after saying goodbye to

Bakul. He said that he was sorry about the confusion, and said that they were welcome any time, and wished them luck on their quest for the book of shadows. They arrived back at the ship disappointed about the book. But they were determined to find it. They were so concerned about the book that they had forgotten that they had a stowaway called Laptus; so they decided to let him join them on their quest.

SRS BOOKS

- EIGHT SKULLS OF TEVERSHAM
- THE ADVENTURES OF THE TIME WITCHES
- THE CURSED
- NOTHING IS REAL
- UNDERSTANDING JODIE
- BLOOD TRAIL ACROSS TIME
- CRACKED PORCELAIN ACTS OF ABUSE
- MY COLOURFUL WORLD OF POETRY

KAYLEIGH || SHANICE || JESSICA

CHARACTERS

Shanice

Natasha

Crystal

Legend of time witches in space:

ABOUT THE AUTHOR

Stephen Robert Sutton author and poet has written many books. Some in his own name, others under other names such as Sarah Ruth Scott and Simon Robert Sinclair. The reason for more than one name was to write from a more feminine perspective, drawing from his working colleagues and good female friends. The other was to write in various subjects providing knowledge from past experiences and studies of people. Some stories have been altered and include his real name for credibility.

Stephen is also an artist and photographer who likes to work on most of his own book covers. When he wrote Cracked Porcelain, it was based on factual events on psychiatric wards and experiences of nurses both on the wards and in the community. It is Stephen's hope that one day, he will see his work on Netflix and other movie companies that will portray his work as it is in his books.

Stephen is dyslexic and dyspraxia, and self-educated. He believes in self-motivation and the encouragement of others to enable him to keep writing.
To date, he has written thirty books all published.

HOW IT ALL BEGAN